THE PINK LOTUS

Garrett Hutson

Warfleigh Publishing first edition January 2023

Cover design by Steven Novak

For more information, or to book an event, please contact the author at www.garretthutson.com

ISBN 978-1-953846-03-7 (paperback)
ISBN 978-1-953846-15-0 (eBook)
ISBN 978-1-953846-13-6 (audio)

For Paige, who inspired me to do better

1

Monday, March 28, 1938

Subic Bay Naval Base, Philippine Islands

The whir of the helicopter's rotors accelerated into a steady 'chuff chuff chuff,' and a moment later the contraption lifted off the ground, its blades creating wind sufficient to lay the tall grass flat.

Commander Douglas Bainbridge clasped his hand on his hat and looked down, blinking his eyes rapidly while moisture streamed from them, driven across his cheeks by the force of air.

"Seventy-five horsepower engine!" shouted Commander Morris Whitburn, the visiting Research and Development officer.

At twenty feet off the ground, the experimental craft shifted gears and moved forward.

Doug and the three men beside him—Intelligence Officers assigned to the U.S. Asiatic Fleet—watched the strange metal craft circle the giant clearing in the jungle in less than a minute. Its nose was shaped like a bullet, and the pilot sat in an open cockpit like a single seat airplane, just four feet below a giant rotating blade that resembled a horizontal fan. The craft's tail was a tapered open frame, with a smaller vertical blade spinning at the rear.

"As you can see, unlike the autogyro the Spanish Navy uses, this Sikorski prototype utilizes powered transverse twin rotors for both lift and propulsion," Whitburn shouted. "Like the Spanish autogyro, it will be able to take off from and land on the deck of a ship. And those pontoons will enable amphibious takeoff and landing."

The pilot brought the experimental craft down in the center of the clearing some fifty yards from the observers, and powered down the engine.

Whitburn continued. "Besides the obvious search and rescue possibilities at sea, we believe the Sikorski prototype will enable long-distance scouting for cruisers outside of carrier groups."

"But how will it defend itself?" Doug asked, pointing toward the sleek silver shell encompassing the front and sides of the craft. "There's no gun turret, and no room to mount one in front of the pilot."

"It's not like the Japs will let us watch their fleet from above without firing on the damn thing," one of Doug's companions agreed.

"That's one of the issues we've asked the engineers to solve," Whitburn said. "We expect significant design changes before this prototype becomes operational."

"How soon do you think that's gonna be?" one of Doug's other companions asked.

"We're optimistic that the Sikorski can be operational in one to two years."

The four intelligence officers exchanged a doubtful look. One let out a low whistle. Doug shook his head.

Whitburn's lips tightened, but he gave no other visible reaction. "The latest cruiser design already incorporates space for one of these babies. Every cruiser coming out of dry dock starting next January will have a launch pad right on deck, at the stern. The Spanish autgyro's been taking off from their ships since '34, and the Secretary's determined for us to catch up."

"How soon do you expect the design changes?" Doug asked.

Whitburn's lips turned down in thought. "I can't pin that down too precisely, you understand—but I would expect modifications to be approved this summer."

"And you'll get copies of the new designs to us then?"

"That'll be my top priority," Whitburn said.

Doug highly doubted it but kept that thought to himself.

"Any other questions?" Whitburn's gray-blue eyes held Doug's in a way that might have been meant to convey confidence, or it might have been meant to intimidate.

"Let's see it go again," Doug said.

**

Port of Manila, Philippine Islands

Doug stepped off the wharf at one PM, raising his hand to the front bill of his cap to shield his eyes from the blazing sun, and looked up at the five-story gleaming white Art Moderne building before them. The Marsman Building, the fleet's HQ. The intelligence officers had a lunch appointment with Admiral Yarnell at his office on the fifth floor.

Doug had been here before, though this would only be the third time he'd met Admiral Yarnell. The anticipation still gave him butterflies in his stomach.

A lieutenant on the fifth floor showed the four intelligence officers into a spacious dining room with giant windows looking over the port. Doug could tell the others were nervous, as well; everyone walked around, fidgety. He went to the window and looked across the bay at Cavite Naval Station, where the *Valparaiso* was docked.

A side door opened, and Admiral Yarnell entered from his office. All of them snapped to attention and saluted, but the admiral waved them off. "As you were." He looked toward a Filipino waiter in a white jacket. "Bring lunch in now, Angelo."

The waiter nodded without a word, and stepped outside.

"Have a seat," the admiral said, taking the chair at the head of the table. "We'll begin lunch, and once everything's set you can brief me on this morning's demonstration." A moment later, the waiter Angelo returned pushing a cart with five silver trays, plus a silver pitcher covered in condensation. He set one tray in front of each of them, and poured a glass of ice water from the pitcher.

3

Once Angelo had departed, closing the door behind him, Admiral Yarnell said, "Alright, let's hear about this prototype demonstration."

**

"Bainbridge, I'd like you to remain a moment," Admiral Yarnell said after the lunch, when they stood near the door. He turned to the other three intelligence officers and thanked them for the briefing.

Doug's heart leapt into his throat while he watched the others leave. Once the door was closed, Yarnell told him to take a seat.

"With spring here, we expect the Japanese to resume their offensive in China any time now."

Doug nodded. "I agree, sir." Where was the admiral going with this?

"A few years ago, ONI had a man in Shanghai who ran Chinese agents in and out of Japanese ports posing as fishermen, observing their movements. His identity is still secret, but we know he's no longer in Shanghai. I don't know what became of his network of agents." Yarnell leaned back, tenting his fingers in front of his chin. "Bainbridge, we'd like you to rebuild that network. Chinese laborers digging ditches, fishermen trawling the rivers—whoever would be innocuous to the Japanese. If we piece together enough tiny pieces, we can get some idea what those bastards have planned."

"So the aim is to fill the gaps in our intelligence—where and when the Japanese are going to attack next?"

"Exactly. And with what forces. Can you do that, Bainbridge?"

It was exciting, the thought of building a network of Chinese agents to spy on the Japanese navy and marines. But it would also test his abilities in ways he wasn't entirely confident.

"Yes, sir."

**

Cavite Naval Station
Manila Bay, Philippine Islands

Doug stepped off the gunboat at three PM, after a brief run from the Port of Manila. He stifled a yawn as he took off on foot through "Cavite City" toward the building where he had temporary quarters. It was only mid-afternoon, but it had already been a long day.

He'd risen before dawn to take a gun boat from Cavite station to Subic Bay, a forty-two nautical mile trip that took two hours. Half of the Asiatic Fleet's ships were docked at Cavite, which jutted into the southern part of Manila Bay and guarded the entrance to the capital city and its port; and the other half were stationed at the much larger Subic Bay base up the coast. He'd met the other three Intelligence Officers there at eight o'clock, and they'd ridden in a truck seventeen miles into the forest on a dirt road that made a giant loop through the massive naval base. A guard shack manned by three Marines stood at the entrance to a trail through the jungle, and the Intelligence Officers had proceeded alone on foot, to the top-secret demonstration in the secret clearing.

After the demonstration they'd done all of that in reverse, except the gunboat took them to Manila for the meeting with the admiral. Although the briefing went well, Doug was keyed up and exhausted by the time lunch ended.

And now his mind was preoccupied with the task the admiral had given him.

At least the two-hour boat trip from Subic to Manila had afforded him time to draft the report about the Sikorski prototype that he'd give to Captain Jansen upon his return to Shanghai. His work was done for the day, so when he walked past the USS *Valparaiso*—the cruiser to which he was assigned—he didn't board and instead walked toward "home" in one of the concrete block buildings that housed officers.

The breeze coming off the bay billowed the sheer white curtain on either end of the giant window and alleviated much of the heat and humidity. Two items lay on the cool tile floor of the airy room overlooking Bacoor inlet. Doug picked up an envelope addressed to him in Lucy's handwriting, postmarked Shanghai, plus a smaller unmarked envelope.

He sat on the end of the bed and opened Lucy's letter first.

March 23, 1938

Dear Doug,

Not much news since my letter last week, except that I got confirmation that Mother arrives on the 15th of April, and will be staying with us for two months.

I can already hear your groan over all this distance. I know it's going to be a challenge, for <u>both</u> of us, but I can't tell her to leave sooner. She's my mother, after all, and I haven't seen her in almost two years. And you know as well as I do we can use her help once the baby comes. Of course we can rely on Bao, that's not a question, but it's going to be a new experience for him as well. I think having the benefit of Mother's experience will be a god-send.

And before you say anything, Abbie has already promised me that she and Kenny will drag us out of the house at least once a week to be with our friends. You know Mother won't want to come along on those nights. She might insist on joining us for dinner, but she won't want to go to any nightclubs. Yes, I know she might make comments, but we can ignore that, can't we?

I miss you terribly. I know I said this in my earlier letters, but I've gotten to be as big as a house, and it's tiring trying to do anything outside of the house. Bao has been a tremendous help, so don't worry about me. Just get home on time. In ten days I'll be back in your arms and all will be right.

Your loving wife,

Lucy

The letter brought a broad grin to Doug's lips. He held the paper to his nose, and thought he could detect a whiff of her perfume. Chanel Number 5.

He'd been gone from Shanghai almost three months—the longest absence since he was posted to the *Valparaiso* last May. Following the fall of Nanking in December, their ship had been sent after the first of the year to patrol the Chinese coast to guard American ships in the sea lanes, from Tianjin on the Yellow Sea in the north, down along the East China Sea all the way to Guangdong—Canton—on the South China Sea. After two months on patrol, the *Valparaiso* put into Manila Bay for their semi-annual visit to fleet HQ. They'd been docked at Cavite for the last month.

But he would see her soon. He refolded her letter and put it back in the envelope. Then he turned his attention to the smaller unmarked envelope and removed the slip of paper inside.

A bunch of us have gone to Long Beach for the afternoon. Come join us when you get back.

Scott

Doug looked at his watch—it was almost three-thirty. By the time he caught a rickshaw down there, it would be four o'clock. And it would be so nice to take a nap instead...

He took his swim trunks from a drawer, grabbed a towel, stuffed them both in his shoulder bag, and headed out the door.

**

Long Beach

Cavite City, Philippine Islands

Doug spotted dozens of crewmembers from the USS *Valparaiso* when the rickshaw stopped in front of a bathhouse on the edge of the beach, four miles south of the base. At least a couple hundred other American men frolicked in short swim trunks on the sand or in the waves, representing the crews of several ships in the fleet. A group to his right played a vigorous game of touch football, their torsos glistening with sweat.

He waved to several men who called his name, and walked into the bathhouse. He closed the door of one of the changing rooms and got out of his white uniform and into the pair of dark blue light woolen swim trunks he'd bought a few months after arriving in Shanghai. That first beach outing with Kenny and Abbie and their friends—now his friends as well—in September 1935 had been an exercise in letting go of inhibitions.

The swim trunks in style in 1935 were a bit shorter on the thigh than the swimsuits he'd grown up with in the '20s—a four-inch inseam instead of six-inch—and the A-top had a deeper neckline; plus, the top was now separate and detachable. Doug had left it buttoned on, and

Pete, George, Fred, and Stuart had laughed at him. Kenny had been nicer about it and whispered "I know that's part of the suit, but no one under forty wears it." So Doug had reluctantly braved a bare torso in front of Abbie, Julia, and Betty, and it took most of that first day to get comfortable with that.

He wasn't sure why he'd thought of that, but nowadays he would have felt far more awkward with a top on walking out onto the beach full of bare-chested men in trunks. *How things can change in just two and a half years.*

"Doug, over here!" Scott Farnsworth waved at him from a beach towel, grinning, propped up on an elbow. Doug smiled back and spread his towel next to Scott's.

And then averted his eyes from his friend's new trunks—super short, and awfully form-fitting—but not before he saw Scott's grin widen. Then Scott rolled onto his left side, facing Doug, bent his right knee and pulled his right foot up behind his left knee.

Showing off.

"You like my new swimsuit? I found it in Manila a couple weeks ago. The latest style."

Doug only glanced at him before looking back toward the waves. "I see a bunch of our men out in the water." He concentrated on counting the familiar faces. He was definitely not thinking about the curve of Scott's thigh, golden from the sun. How short were those damned trunks? Did they even have a one-inch inseam?

Scott chuckled and looked toward the water. But he didn't shift back onto his back, Doug couldn't help but notice. "I went out there a little while ago. Played in the surf. Today's our last chance." He leaned his head back and closed his eyes. "It's nice here in the sun."

"I'll be glad to get home," Doug said, furtively glancing at Scott's upturned face from the corner of his eye.

Scott looked back at him. "Of course you are. You've got that baby coming soon."

Doug nodded. "In about four weeks."

"I bet you're excited for that."

A flutter swept through Doug's belly. He couldn't help but smile. "Yeah, I am."

Scott was quiet for a moment, looking down at the strip of sand between them. "What do you think it'll be like when we get back there?"

"With the Japanese occupation, you mean?"

"Yeah. With the Japs in control of the whole area now, the international concessions are surrounded. What's that gonna be like? I mean, we haven't really spent much time in Shanghai since the city fell. Is it gonna feel like being under siege?"

Good question. "I don't think so." Lucy's letters hadn't said much about it, so Doug could only assume things in the International Settlement and French Concession were the same as before. He couldn't rely on his own observations, since they'd been called away a couple of weeks after the Japanese took the final Chinese strongholds in Shanghai and rushed to Nanjing to help protect the American embassy during the Japanese assault on the Chinese capital.

What they'd seen there would haunt Doug's nightmares for the rest of his life.

Doug closed his eyes and shook his head to clear the grisly memories. They'd returned to Shanghai in time for Christmas but had to leave a couple of weeks later for coastal patrol. And they'd been gone almost three months. Any number of things could have changed in that time.

A dark-haired young man with a deep suntan ran into the space on the other side of Scott, stretching to catch a football. His foot sprayed sand onto Scott's torso. Scott squinted his eyes and turned away.

"Careful!" Doug shouted. He wasn't sure why the football would have been thrown this direction; they were a good twenty-five yards from where that group was playing.

The catcher looked down at Scott with a touch of a smirk. "Sorry about that, *Ensign* Farnsworth." The way the young man stressed Scott's rank, and the way his mouth curved into a wicked half-smile told Doug the encounter wasn't accidental.

"Out of bounds!" one of the other players shouted, hands cupped around his mouth.

The young man waved his hand at them dismissively. "Yeah, yeah." He stayed rooted in place.

"How are you, David?" Scott said, shielding his eyes from the sun and looking up at the young man. His tone sounded flat, emotionless.

"Fantastic!" the young man said with a grin. Then he looked at Doug, stepped around Scott and extended his hand. "Lieutenant David Saunders."

Doug stood and shook his hand. He and Saunders were about the same height, but the younger man had at least twenty extra pounds of muscle. "Commander Douglas Bainbridge." He hoped his rank put him at advantage, though Saunders had mentioned his first. That was obviously connected to the way he'd stressed Scott's lower rank a moment ago.

"Farnsworth report to you, Commander? My condolences." He laughed.

"Not directly."

"Farnsworth and I go way back, you see. We came through the Academy together."

The way he said "the Academy" made the back of Doug's neck prickle. It was true what they said—how do you know if an officer graduated from Annapolis? He'll tell you.

"Come on, Saunders! Quit hoggin' the damn ball!" one of the other players shouted.

David Saunders grinned again and pointed his thumb toward the game. "I'd better get back. Pleasure meeting you, Commander. Maybe see you at the Officers' Club one night." He jogged off through the sand.

"What was that all about?" Doug asked when he'd sat back down on his blanket.

"He was my roommate at Annapolis," Scott said. "We were pretty good friends there. He got assigned to the *Marblehead*, based out of San Francisco. I was on the *Richmond*, same home port; at least until I got reassigned to the *Valparaiso* last April."

All three ships were Omaha-class cruisers, nearly identical.

Scott nodded toward where David Saunders intercepted a man running with the football, touching him with both hands to 'tackle' him. "They got reassigned here in January. The *Marblehead*, I mean."

He didn't sound thrilled, and Doug watched his friend's face. Scott was quiet for a moment, looking at his hands and picking at his thumbnail. "He got promoted to lieutenant about that time. A whole bunch of our classmates got their promotions last year." He exhaled hard through the nose.

"When did you graduate?"

"Almost three years ago."

Two years as an ensign before promotion to Lieutenant Junior Grade was typical. And Scott Farnsworth was more than a capable officer. Doug wondered if Commander Rose had somehow sabotaged Scott's promotion opportunities last summer. It wouldn't surprise him. Even though Rose was out of the picture now, anything he'd reported might still hinder Scott's advancement.

"I'm sorry, buddy." Doug started to pat Scott's shoulder but stopped short and let his hand fall awkwardly to the sand. He'd speak to Captain Jansen about it when they got back to Shanghai.

"I'm fine." Then Scott scrambled up from his beach towel, grabbed Doug under both arms, and hauled him upright. He put his hands on Doug's waist and slapped his belly. "C'mon, let's go jump in!" He jogged off toward the water.

Doug smiled ruefully, absolutely not noticing the way the muscle rippled along the backs of Scott's thighs, and followed his tall friend into the waves.

**

Cavite Naval Station

Doug met several officers from his ship for drinks that evening at the Officers' Club. After ten months attached to the *Valparaiso*, he was finally starting to feel socially integrated with the ship's officers. Mostly.

Commander McHugh—Montgomery Rose's replacement at the helm of the *Valparaiso*—wasn't a drinker, and he never joined the others at the Officers' club. Lt. Commander DeVries, the XO, was on the ship, so the Valpo's contingent that evening were all junior officers, Doug's age or younger.

Doug was finishing his third gin and tonic and was about to slow down and order a beer when Lieutenant David Saunders appeared at the bar next to him.

"So you're Scott Farnsworth's buddy, eh?" Saunders signaled the bartender and held up his empty beer glass.

"Yeah, we're friends," Doug said, ignoring that Saunders had cut in front of him to order a refill.

"He's a good guy. I've known him for years, and would never say anything bad about him." Saunders leaned in and continued just above a whisper. "But be careful. Rumor is he hasn't gotten promoted because he's, well, a bit light on his feet."

Doug kept his expression neutral. "Oh?"

Saunders nodded. "I know you can't tell by lookin' at him. He's a big strappin' fella. But I'm sure it's true. I was his roommate for four years. Never once saw him canoodling with any of the townie girls. *Everybody* did. But not ol' Scott. Sure, he had a girlfriend back in Connecticut—I met her a couple of times when we visited his folks—but he never married her, now did he?"

I never married my first sweetheart, either. But Doug decided to avoid comparisons. "That's interesting. Where'd you hear that rumor? If you don't mind me asking."

"Course not. I've heard it around. A few people whispering about it. Someone said his commander was onto him—guess that wasn't you, huh?"

Doug shook his head. "No, that wasn't me." He wished he was surprised that Montgomery Rose had started a whisper campaign against Scott.

Saunders put his arm around Doug, clapped him on the shoulder; it stung Doug's sunburned skin, and he flinched. "You seem like the solid sort. If you're Scott's pal, give him some advice, for his own good—tell him to find a nice girl and marry her. The rumors will go away, and he'll get promoted."

The bartender brought the beer, and Saunders straightened, took a step away. Doug pointed to the glass. "I'll have one of those."

"Right away, Commander," the bartender said, and began filling a glass from the tap.

"Nice talking with you, Commander," Saunders said, and walked off.

Doug returned to where his group stood a moment later, beer in hand. Scott Farnsworth watched him while everyone else talked, and then circled around the group to stand next to Doug.

"You getting to know David Saunders?" he asked, innocently enough, but with a hint of tension in his tone.

Doug forced a smile. "He said you were a good guy. Couldn't say anything bad about you."

Scott looked conflicted. He stared off toward where Saunders laughed with some of the officers from the *Marblehead*.

"Everything alright?" Doug asked.

Scott looked back and grinned. "Yeah, sure. Hey, out of curiosity, how long were you an ensign before you got promoted to lieutenant?"

"I came into the navy as a lieutenant. I was never an ensign." At Scott's questioning look, Doug explained, "ONI doesn't have ensigns, that's why I started as a lieutenant."

"That explains how you made commander before thirty." He downed the rest of his Old Fashioned. "I'm gonna get another drink."

**

Their group left the Officers' Club together an hour later and walked toward the complex where they had temporary quarters, a quarter mile from the club. The moon hadn't risen yet, and the night sky was awash with stars. You never saw skies like that in Shanghai.

Doug was a touch tipsy after three cocktails and a beer, but hardly drunk. Most of the others were in a similar condition, laughing and talking a bit louder than necessary, but walking normally.

Scott Farnsworth, on the other hand, had crossed that invisible line into drunkenness. His gait was off, and a touch crooked in its direction. He threw an arm around Doug's shoulders when they reached the front of the building where they both had a room.

They waved goodnight to the others, and then Scott whispered in Doug's ear, "We should go down to Long Beach. Nobody'll be there. And it's real dark tonight. We can go skinny-dipping."

Doug laughed. "That's a four-mile walk."

"You ever go skinny-dipping at night? It's fun."

"I'll take your word for it. Let's turn in. Need help with the stairs?"

"No, I'm alright."

Doug turned off on the next floor and walked down the hall. Scott followed. "Aren't you forgetting you're one more flight up?" Doug said with a chuckle as he unlocked his door.

"I didn't forget." Scott stepped into the open doorway after Doug walked through. He put his arm around Doug's shoulders again in the moonlit room, and his face came close. His lips were inches from Doug's, his breath warm on Doug's face...

Doug put his hand flat on his friend's chest and held him back. "Scott." His voice sounded sharper than he'd intended, and he cringed.

Scott straightened, and for a couple of seconds the startled look on his face was as if he'd been slapped. Then he cleared his throat and looked away. "I'm sorry if I misread the situation," he said, and cleared his throat a second time.

Doug's gut tightened, as if someone had poked him in the stomach. *Misread the situation?* "I don't understand. I'm married. You know that. Why did you think...?" His voice trailed off, leaving the question half asked.

"I mean, it's just that you..." Scott seemed to search for words. "You've always been understanding; after you found out, I mean. And, well...you know about those places in Shanghai."

He means the places where the nán jì *work.* Doug almost groaned when he realized how that must have looked. "No, you don't understand, that's because—"

"And when that Chinese boy—Bao—when he moved in with you, I assumed...I mean, he's rubbing you down on the regular, isn't he?"

Doug's face flushed, and he stiffened. "No. It's not like that at all. He needed a place to live, and we need an *amah*." He wasn't sure why he felt the need to explain that.

It was hard to tell in the faint light coming through the open window, but Doug was pretty sure Scott Farnsworth had gone pale.

"Shit!" Scott ran a hand through his wavy hair, took a few jerky steps toward the open window looking out toward the bay. Then he spun back to face Doug. "You won't say anything, will you? Keep this to yourself, OK?"

"Of course." No one needed that kind of scrutiny, Doug included. Given the rumors Saunders had told him about, it was best not to even have any hints of association with Scott's preferences.

"I'm sorry," Scott muttered again, and bolted from the room.

2

Friday, April 1
Shanghai

Doug was mildly disappointed that Lucy hadn't come to the Bund to meet him after the sampan delivered him to the downtown docks from the USS *Valparaiso*, anchored in the middle of the Huang Po River. She always had before.

There was bound to be a first time. And from the tone of her letters, it seemed that getting around now wasn't as easy as it had been.

He caught a motor cab uptown. Their new apartment, a big two-bedroom affair on Guling Road, was in a nice middle-class neighborhood of clean brick buildings a block west of Thibet Road, and four blocks south of Soochow Creek. It was a short walk south from there to the racetrack and recreation grounds, and when they moved in last fall Doug and Lucy found themselves enjoying Shanghai's largest green space on a regular basis.

The narrow cobblestone street was awash with sunlight when the cab dropped Doug off in front of the building. Back in December and January, the long shadow of the twenty-two story Park Hotel two blocks to the southwest had blocked the afternoon sun, but it didn't reach this far now. He paid the cab fare and bounded up the stairs to their third-floor apartment.

Lucy stepped out from the kitchen after he opened the door, and she beamed. His eyes involuntarily dropped to her belly, which was

17

easily twice the size it had been when he left; but he looked back at her smiling blue eyes, opened his arms and hurried to her.

"God, I missed you!" he said, holding her tight as best he could, and kissed her on the lips.

"Likewise, sailor," she said, and swept his hat off, tossing it onto the table. "I was beginning to forget what you look like." She grinned and kissed him again. "And no comment about how I look—I know I'm huge."

"You look beautiful."

"Good answer. But you're supposed to say that." She took a step back toward the kitchen. "I was just making myself a cold duck sandwich. Want one?"

"Where's Bao?" Doug asked.

"At the market, stocking up for your return. Do you want a sandwich or not?"

"Yes, please."

She cut another slice of meat off the half-eaten duck in the ice box, and then cut a couple of pieces from the end of the bread loaf on the counter. "Everyone's been very attentive in your absence," she said, putting the rest of the loaf in the breadbox in the back corner of the counter. "I never got lonely. And of course, Bao's been a dear."

"I'm not surprised," Doug said, and accepted the plate with his sandwich. He set it on the table, then held her chair for her.

"Thank you, darling," she said after she'd sat. "These days I can pretty much set my plate on my belly, and it's a lot easier than trying to reach the table. Until Mother gets here." She squeezed his hand before he stepped away, and smiled at him as he sat next to her. "And don't you dare tell her I do this."

She proceeded to set her plate on top of her belly and ate her sandwich like that. He laughed. "My lips are sealed."

She sighed. "I'm looking forward to her visit, and yet dreading it at the same time. Does that make me sound crazy?"

He laughed again. "Not at all. I'd be shocked if you *weren't* conflicted."

"You understand me so well."

He took a bite of his sandwich. It was hardly fancy, but it was a step up from the food he ate onboard the *Valparaiso*. Canned or powdered everything. "Tell me everything I've missed."

"I hope you got my last letter, about Mother coming on the 15th and staying for two months. I knew it would be close, but I just had to write you."

He nodded. "Yes, it arrived the day before we left."

"Oh, good." She sounded relieved. "Then you should have gotten everything I sent. There's not much more to tell, really."

"Your letters were nice and newsy," Doug agreed, squeezing her hand. "Anything new since the last one?"

She leaned back. "Let's see, when did I write that?"

"On the 23rd."

"And what day was that? My brain works slower these days. George says it's because the baby is growing and taking so much of my energy, that's why I tire easily and can't think as well."

"It was last Wednesday," he said. "Nine days."

"Nine days," she said, looking up in thought. "I had an appointment with George last Friday, and he said everything is good. We should still expect this little one sometime around the 25th. The bassinet was delivered on Tuesday, and it's all set up in our bedroom. Abbie, Betty, and Julia took me out for tea on Wednesday afternoon. Everyone's missed you. By the way, Pete's insisting on taking all of us out for dinner on your birthday, the whole group."

Doug groaned. "I don't need a big celebration. I'd rather have a quiet evening with you. We need to take advantage of the quiet before the baby comes."

"You can say that again," she said with a rueful smile, and then sighed. "But they want to, and I think we should."

"Hmmm," he said, frowning. "It's not like it's a big one, like Pete's thirtieth in December."

"Or George's thirtieth in February," Lucy reminded him. "You were away for that one, too."

The *Valparaiso* had been anchored in the Yangtze by Nanjing on Pete's birthday; its heavy guns aimed directly at the Japanese vessels in the river after the "accidental" sinking of the USS *Panay*. Doug had already been disappointed that the U.S. government hadn't taken a stronger stand against Japanese aggression during the Battle of Shanghai that summer and fall; but after a Japanese plane strafed the *Panay* on December 12th and sank the gunboat—fortunately, none of the crew were killed—he'd expected war. They all had. The navy had been preparing for war against Japan for almost twenty years. This was the moment they'd been preparing for.

But nothing happened. The American government accepted Japan's tepid apology for the "accidental" attack—the *Panay*'s American flag was clearly displayed—and the navy was ordered only to protect the American embassy while the Japanese ravaged Nanjing.

And they watched helplessly while Japanese troops massacred civilians and summarily executed surrendered soldiers, shooting them in the back of the head, one after another, after another...

Doug shook his head to clear the terrible images from his mind.

"What is it?" Lucy asked, concerned.

"Nothing," Doug said, and his cheeks heated.

"You weren't even listening to me just then," she said, still eyeing him in curiosity.

"I'm sorry, dear. What were you saying?"

"I was telling you about George's birthday dinner. It was at this fancy restaurant in the French Concession. Pete was kind enough to buy my dinner in your absence. They all went to Ciro's after, but I was tired and came home."

Bao came through the door, a large paper bag under each arm, and he grinned from ear to ear when he saw Doug at the table.

"Mista Doug, you home!" He went into the kitchen with the bags. "I got special treat for dinner—beef, hairy crab, *and* shrimp."

Doug looked at Lucy. "Can we afford all that? I mean, with the baby coming so soon."

Before they got married in September, Doug had lived well on his navy salary; plus he got a small monthly stipend from a trust fund his maternal grandparents had left him, and a modestly bigger one from the trust fund his paternal grandparents had left. But inflation in Shanghai had grown steep since the Japanese invasion, their new apartment was more than double the cost of his old one, and after the loss of Lucy's income in December their budget didn't have much wiggle room.

"Relax, I've been saving all month for this." Lucy patted his arm. "You've been gone for a while, and I felt like celebrating your return. *And* that you'll be here for the birth of our child. That's worth a celebration."

He couldn't help but grin. "You win."

**

Saturday, April 2

Doug joined his friends for a baseball game the next day at the Recreation Grounds. The U.S. Marine Corps 4th Battalion fielded a team every year, and today was the opening game.

"Who are these 'Friends of Riley'?" Doug asked. "They seem a pretty scruffy bunch. And they dress like hoods."

Kenny Traywick laughed beside him. "They sure don't look like your typical baseball team, eh?"

Pete Tolbert looked around George and Kenny, and motioned downward with his hands. "It's because they *are* hoods, you dummies!" he said quietly with a crooked grin. "See that man standing over there by first base? That's the team manager, 'Lucky Jack' Riley. You know, the Slots King of Shanghai."

Doug had indeed heard of 'Lucky Jack' Riley. Everyone in Shanghai had. Rumor had it he was wanted for a laundry list of crimes back in the States, but in Shanghai he was known for dive bars featuring slot machines. It was said he bribed the police in the French Concession to look the other way, and so his Manhattan Bar on Rue Chu Pao San operated illegal gambling right out in the open.

It was a rough area, just off the French Bund. Popular with sailors, Rue Chu Pao San was popularly known as 'Blood Alley' because of the frequent fights there. *No wonder the players all look like street toughs.*

"He's not the king everywhere," Fred Perry said from the other side of Pete.

George barked a laugh. "You're gonna argue with a gangster, Fred?" His deep, resonant baritone voice sounded as amused as it did doubtful.

"No, but it's true!" Fred insisted. "At Del Monte's, out in the Western Roads. He's tried a whole bunch of times to get his slots out there, and Al Israel keeps telling him 'no thanks.'"

George scoffed. "He's looking for a cover to launder his dirty money."

Fred shrugged. "How should I know? And who cares, anyway? Del Monte's is aces!"

"Del Monte's is pretty swell," Pete said, nodding. "You been there yet, Doug?"

Doug shook his head. "It's pretty far out there."

"It's worth the trip, let me tell you," Pete said. "The orchestra's the best in town. They got a great singer, too. And they're doing so much construction out that way, it's no trouble getting a cab anymore."

The Hixi district—what most European and American Shanghailanders called 'The Western Roads'—was a fairly rural section of the Chinese municipality to the west of the International Settlement and French Concession. The Columbia Country Club catered to wealthy Americans, while around it the wealthiest Shanghailanders had great mansions on sprawling estates. The upscale Del Monte nightclub was the only nightlife to be had out there—and it was considered way out of town by most.

Doug shrugged. "Maybe we'll try it sometime."

"How about tonight?" Pete asked.

Doug shook his head. "Thanks, but I'm spending the evening at home with Lucy. I've been gone a while, and I'd like to spend some time alone with my wife before the baby comes."

"'*Alone.*'" Pete waggled his thick eyebrows, and the rest of them snickered.

Doug had to laugh. "You know what I mean, wise guys." He didn't mention that he'd asked Bao to take the night off.

"Then next weekend. For your birthday," Pete insisted.

"Twist my arm, why don't ya?" Doug grumbled, but he wasn't mad.

**

After the game—the marines won, seven to three—they walked the short distance to the racetrack and entered the neo-classical Shanghai Racing Club Building beneath the iconic 10-story clock tower, then passed through the grand atrium to the grandstand beyond. The stands were decorated with flags and banners for spring opening day, and the seats were filling up fast.

Pete's eagle eyes managed to find them an open space big enough for four of them on one row, with two open spots right below. He and Stuart each had a copy of the morning Herald and flipped to the page with the odds for the day's races.

"Looks like good odds on Foley's Folly," Pete said, perusing the first race. "Seven to two on winning, two to one on win place show."

Stuart turned around from the row below, shaking his head. "Don't do it. See the jockey? Mark Chapman didn't have a good showing in any race last fall. And he rode some pretty damn good horses, too. Lost his edge. He got too cautious for some reason, waited too late to make his move, so when he surged from the back of the pack, he never got higher than fourth place."

"Who are you going with, Stu?" George asked.

Of all their friends, Stuart Vandermeer was a true horse racing enthusiast. The rest of them put a fair amount of weight on his predictions, and he was usually right. Doug never placed a bet—it wasn't that he was *against* betting per se, though his Presbyterian upbringing made him uncomfortable with the thought—but he enjoyed the races themselves, and Stuart could read the most subtle cues during the race like tea leaves.

"This race, I'm putting five bucks on Shepherd's Hook to win."

George let out a whistle. Doug looked over Pete's shoulder at the newspaper, and his eyes widened at the odds. Pete grinned and slapped Stuart on the shoulder. "Look at the big spender, fellas! I'm not betting more than a buck, and I'll stick to Foley's Folly, win place or show."

"That's the safe bet," Kenny agreed. "I think I'll do the same."

Stuart shook his head. "You can kiss that buck goodbye, Pete."

"Look who's talking!" George said. "You're out of your mind risking five whole bucks on twenty-to-one odds, Stu."

"Shepherd's Hook is young and untested, but he's got fantastic lineage," Stuart said. "And his jockey's one of the best."

Doug looked over Pete's shoulder again to check the jockey's name. Jimmy Lockhart. That name did sound familiar, and Doug was far from an enthusiast.

"Time to put your money where your mouth is," Pete said, slapping Stuart on the shoulder again. "Let's go place our bets. Kenny, I got you for a buck on Foley's Folly, win place show. George, what are taking?"

"Put me down for a buck on Molly's Pride, to win." He handed a dollar to Pete.

"Three to one on Molly's Pride to win for Dr. Howerton, got it," Pete said with a grin, accepting dollars from George and Kenny. Stuart had taken Fred's bet, and Pete followed him toward the club.

Gambling was illegal in the International Settlement, with the conspicuous exception of onsite betting on horse races. The rich British men who had run the Shanghai Racing Club for the last seventy-five years had assured that profitable loophole.

"It's good to see life's back to normal here," Doug said to Kenny. "After the Japanese victory, that is."

"It didn't take long. Most everyone who left last August came back a few months later, once the fighting moved on from Shanghai. Things got back to normal pretty fast after that."

"Where else was everyone gonna go?" George said. "It's not like there are jobs to be found back in the States. In fact, things have gotten worse again."

George was right, unfortunately. After four years of painfully slow recovery from the Depression, the American economy had taken a sudden downturn in the second half of 1937. Unemployment back home had risen almost to 1935 levels again—nineteen percent, after having fallen to fourteen percent last summer.

The easy availability of jobs in Shanghai had drawn thousands of Americans and Europeans in recent years—including all of Doug's friends here. Pete and Julia had arrived in 1931, and the following year had brought George and Betty. Kenny and Abbie had come here in '34; Fred and Stuart had both come straight out of college that year. And he was pretty sure Jonesy had arrived in '31.

Not that Jonesy was really his friend, though. No matter what Lucy said. Doug wasn't sure why he'd included him in that mental list.

"The main thing that's changed is the Japs have checkpoints now at all the crossings out of the Settlement," Fred said. "Except, of course, from here into Frenchtown; that's still the same."

"You've been out of the Settlement recently?" Doug asked.

Fred nodded. "Yeah, I've been out to Del Monte's a bunch of times. The checkpoints aren't a big deal, you just have to show your ID, and the Japs shine a bright light in your face for a second. They're careful not to harass westerners, so it's pretty easy."

"He's going to Del Monte's all the time now because his new girlfriend lives out there," George said with a grin, poking an elbow playfully into Fred's back.

"Oh, you have a steady girl?" Doug asked, eyes widening in surprise. Fred and Stuart were notorious for picking up Chinese girls at nightclubs and taking them home for the night. And rarely more than once.

Fred's cheeks colored a little. "Yeah, her name's Liling. Yang Liling. Her family's got a big house out there."

So still Chinese. "Congratulations, buddy. How long have you been seeing her?"

"Since December. We met at the Paramount. Her father's a client of Pete's, so he put in a good word for me. Her folks have had me out to the house for dinner recently, so that's a good sign."

"We were all with him the night he met her," Kenny said. "She's a lovely girl."

Pete's thirtieth, of course. "I'm sorry I haven't met her yet."

Pete and Stuart returned a few minutes later and passed out claim tickets for everyone's wagers.

"We were just telling Doug about Fred's new girlfriend," Kenny said.

"Quite a catch, that one," Pete said. "She's gorgeous, for starters, and her family's well-off."

"I heard her father is a client of yours," Doug said.

"That's right. Lucky break for ol' Fred here," Pete said, laughing and giving Fred's back a slap. "Mr. Yang seems to like him, for some reason. We might be hearing wedding bells soon."

Fred colored again. A hint of frown crossed Stuart's face for the barest of seconds.

Doug wondered what that was about. Losing his roommate of four years?

"You'll have to stay in China forever if you marry her," George said. "No going home. You can't bring a Chinese wife back to the States, you know."

Fred shrugged. "We could always go to Honolulu."

"He's right," Doug said. "The Hawaiian Islands are exempt from the Chinese Exclusion Act. The sugar planters there made sure that was part of the annexation treaty."

Fred shrugged again. "Besides, why would I want to leave China?"

Ten horses and riders came onto the track, and lined up in the stalls at the starting gate. The crowd grew quiet. Then the starter's gun went off with a bang and a puff of smoke, and the crowd roared as the horses surged forward.

Doug and his friends shifted to the front of their seats while the pack of horses stretched out going around the first turn. Molly's Pride was leading, and George pumped his fist.

Then midway down the back stretch, Shepherd's Hook suddenly surged forward with an incredible burst of speed, moving from ninth position to fourth when the pack reached the third turn.

"There he goes!" Stuart shouted as the crowd rose to its feet as one. "He's got 'em! He's got 'em for sure!"

Shepherd's Hook was creeping up on Foley's Folly in third place— but then midway down the short shoot he stopped moving up, seeming to hold position right at Foley's Folly's right rear.

"What's he doing?" Stuart shouted. "You've got it. Go! Go!"

Coming out of the fourth turn, the jockey riding Foley's Folly suddenly made his move, slipping his horse through a dangerously narrow opening between another horse and the rail, and the crowd gasped. Then he slipped past the startled jockey frantically urging

Molly's Pride forward. When they crossed the finish line, Foley's Folly won by half a length over Molly's Pride.

Pete and Kenny jumped up and down, cheering as if they'd won the race themselves. George shook his head.

Shepherd's Hook lumbered across the line in fourth place, and Stuart put his forehead in his hand. "Damn it!"

"That's five bucks down the drain, buddy!" Pete said, slapping Stuart's back. "And that happens to be the exact amount I just won, as a matter of fact."

"Rub it in, why don't ya?" Stuart groused.

"That was an exciting race," Doug said, grinning. Even without any money on the line, his heart raced with the thrill of the sudden shift in fortunes.

**

Stuart had better luck in the next few races, and by the time the fifth race had been run he was ahead. That's when Doug got up to leave.

"There's still three races to go," Pete said.

"I know, but I've been out all day," Doug explained. "I'm going home to Lucy. See you fellas next weekend."

Pete waggled his eyebrows again, and then roared with laughter when Doug whacked him on the shoulder.

3

Saturday, April 9

It's great to be all together again, Doug thought, looking around the table at the Chateau de Vert in the French Concession, where his friends had gathered for his birthday dinner—Pete and Julia, George and Betty, Kenny and Abbie, Fred, and Stuart. *It's been too long.*

"Tommy's started lifting his head this week," Betty gushed. "While he's in his play pen, so he can see what we're doing."

"He's *trying* to lift his head," George said. "It's still pretty wobbly. But he's not quite three months old yet, so we can't expect much."

"But you said just yesterday that he's advanced for his age, doing that already," Betty protested.

George's cheeks colored. "And I meant it, he is advanced—I just don't want to exaggerate to our friends, that's all."

Betty's expression looked only partly mollified. She turned toward Lucy. "I'm so excited for you. I can't wait for our kids to become great friends."

"If you and Lucy have a girl, Betty's gonna have them betrothed before the end of the month," George muttered out of the side of his mouth, leaning toward Doug. Doug chuckled.

"What did you say, dear?" Betty asked, the slight arch of one eyebrow indicating she assumed it wasn't nice.

"I was just asking this young man what he wants to do tonight for his last weekend of freedom," George said without missing a beat.

"We're taking you to Del Monte's," Pete said before Doug could respond. "You said you've never been, so I arranged some entertainment out there."

Doug laughed. "Should I be concerned?"

"Of course," Pete deadpanned.

Doug groaned.

"I'd expect nothing less, Pete," Kenny said.

"You can count me out, fellas," Lucy said, rubbing her belly. "I'm afraid I can't handle a night out on the town in my present condition. I'll never make it to six AM. I'm fighting to stay awake as it is now—and I promise that has nothing to do with the company."

"He can count all of us ladies out," Julia said to Lucy. "Peter informed me in no uncertain terms that we're not included this time. It's a 'boys night,' isn't that what you called it, dear?"

"That's right," Pete said with a boastful tone and big grin, ignoring his wife's subtle reproach. "Like George said, this is Doug's last weekend of freedom. His mother-in-law will be here next weekend, and soon after that he's going to have a kid at home. This is his last chance, poor fella."

Doug wasn't sure of the logic, given that Kenny and George both had 'a kid at home,' as Pete put it. But he went along. "Now I *am* concerned!" he said, laughing.

"I'm not concerned in the least, Pete," Lucy said, fitting a cigarette into the end of a holder. Doug struck a match. "I'll bolt him down soon enough. Take him while you can. You boys go do your worst." She glanced at Doug and gave him a sly half-smile before taking a long drag on her cigarette.

"You really are something, Mrs. Bainbridge." He grinned, taking her left hand in both of his.

"If you want breakfast when you get home, you just wake up Bao and let me sleep," Lucy said, and blew a puff of smoke in his face. "If you wake me up at six AM, you'll be sleeping on the couch for a week."

"What's this about six AM?" Doug teased. "How long has it been since we stayed out *that* late?"

"I probably never mentioned it in my letters, but the ten o'clock curfew is still in place," she said.

"That's right," Pete said with a grin. "And so all the clubs lock their doors at ten, and won't let you out until six. They don't want the cops picking anyone up on the street and asking too many questions about where they've been."

Doug groaned. *Of course.* He should have known Shanghailanders would never let anything as trifling as a police curfew put an end to the party.

"Why don't the ladies come back to our place for cocktails?" Julia said. Betty and Abbie agreed, but Lucy declined.

"I'm afraid I'm worn out. But I'll take a raincheck."

Julia gave her one of those trademark enigmatic smiles she was so good at. "Of *course*, dear. You go rest while you still can."

Doug looked at Pete. "I'll take Lucy home now, and then I'll meet you fellas at Del Monte's in thirty minutes."

**

The venue surprised Doug when the cab pulled up in front. It was a giant three-story mansion with a covered entrance framed by tall palm trees, but with neon signage added over the door identifying it as Del Monte Café. It stood at the end of a tree-lined drive leading off Avenue Haig south of the Great Western Road. He'd been expecting something flashier, like the Paramount. Pete hadn't said anything about a dress code, like at Ciro's, but Doug was still glad he hadn't changed out of his dinner jacket when he dropped Lucy at home.

The cab door was opened by a waiting attendant in a black tuxedo. Doug hurried to tip the driver, and then when he got out, he also tipped the attendant. "Welcome to the Del Monte, sir," the attendant said in a faintly Germanic accent. "Right this way." He motioned down a short concrete walk leading from the drive to the front porch.

The inside of the club still resembled a mansion, except that there was a long bar in what he supposed used to be the dining room. The place wasn't packed, but a good number of people milled around with drinks in hand, as if this were an ordinary cocktail party. The swanky jazz drifting down from somewhere upstairs was the only indication that this was a nightclub.

"You made it!"

Doug looked away from the grand staircase he'd been gazing up, and spotted Kenny coming in from a portico out back, with Pete, George, Fred, and Stuart trailing.

"Swell place," Doug said, nodding appreciatively as he looked around.

Pete put his arm around Doug's shoulders. "Hottest digs in Shanghai. First, let's get you a drink. Next, let's go back out to the portico—Kenny's arranged surprise number one for the night."

Intrigued, Doug went with Pete to the bar. Gin and tonic in hand a moment later, he let Pete lead him back into the central hall, and then steer him toward the open French doors leading to a grand colonnaded portico. Kenny stood at the open door with a big goofy grin on his face.

Off to the side of the portico, between a pair of columns, stood all of his friends from the ship.

"Happy birthday!" they shouted. Scott Farnsworth stood at the end of a line of five young men in off-the-rack suits that included Ben Trebinski, Patrick Callahan, John Franklin, and Seth Hahn. Lt. Ross Stephenson stood behind the others, and raised a glass of dark liquid above his head in silent toast.

"Surprise," Kenny said with a laugh.

"You arranged this?" Doug said.

"Not all by myself," Kenny said, shrugging with false modesty. "Ensign Farnsworth gave me a hand with the invitations."

Doug turned to Scott. "Thank you for helping him with that." He felt a little awkward; he and Scott had barely spoken since that last night in Manila. He suspected Scott had avoided him on the ship.

"I was glad to," Scott said, hesitated a second, and then shook Doug's hand. "Is today the big day?"

"Monday."

"How old you gonna be, Commander?" Ben asked with a broad grin, the kind that always dimpled his cheeks.

"Twenty-eight."

Ben thought about that for a moment, looking upward. "That's not so old."

Kenny laughed. "And how old are you, young man?"

"Twenty-one," Ben said, innocently. He seemed unaware of the deeper meaning of the inquiry.

"Young'uns," George said, shaking his head. He looked at Doug and put a hand on his shoulder, serious-like. "Is this what you do on that ship, Doug? Hang out with young'uns all day to try and stay hep?"

"I'll be twenty-two in June," Ben grumbled, looking a little put out.

"I meant no offense," George said. "We were all your age not so long ago."

"Enough chit chat," Pete said, taking his usual role of the gregarious ringleader. "Everyone's got a drink? OK, let's go up and see the show."

A large ballroom took up half of the next floor, and couples whirled around to the music of a eight-piece orchestra. Doug nodded, impressed. The bands at the Paramount, the Majestic, the Cathay, and other Shanghai nightclubs were usually five- or six-piece orchestras.

Pete spoke to a middle-aged white man in a white dinner jacket, and a moment later they were shown to one of the largest round tables in the room. "Courtesy of Al Israel," Pete said to Doug in an understated way as they all sat. Meant to impress, without sounding like he meant to impress.

"Excuse me a moment, fellas," Fred said a moment later, got up and hurried across the room toward a crowd of people, mixed Chinese and white, on the far side.

"His girlfriend just arrived with her parents," Pete said, nudging Doug with his elbow.

Doug craned his neck to get a good look at Miss Yang Liling and her apparently important father. Fred was ingratiating himself to a middle-aged Chinese man in a white dinner jacket and black bowtie, talking to him animatedly.

It was some time later that Fred walked back their way, trailed by a small entourage.

On Fred's arm walked an elegantly-dressed young Chinese woman in a silk evening gown. She closely resembled the older man Fred had been talking to a few moments before, but with flawless skin like porcelain, her cheeks delicately rouged.

Behind her trailed a pair of young Chinese women in western-style cocktail dresses, one of them made up modestly, and the other more elaborately made up, with a black feather standing tall from her hair. This one pursed her lips when she passed Stuart, and then gave him a haughty sneer and a sniff, looking away with raised nose.

What's that about? Doug wondered. A brief scowl flitted across Stuart's face.

Fred led them to Doug. "Liling, this is my good friend Douglas Bainbridge. He's recently returned from Manila. You know everyone else, of course. Doug, this is my girlfriend, Yang Liling."

"I've been looking forward to meeting you," Doug said in Shanghainese, taking her offered fingers lightly.

"The pleasure is all mine, Mr. Bainbridge," she replied in bell-like Mandarin. "Fred has told me you speak our language, and I looked forward to speaking with you. You sound like a most interesting man."

"That is very kind of you, Miss Yang," Doug said, switching from Shanghainese to Mandarin.

"Allow me to introduce my cousin, Yang Yajun." She indicated the modest young woman behind her, who nodded and murmured a greeting in Mandarin.

Then Liling conspicuously switched to Shanghainese to introduce the girl with the black feather, heavily rouged cheeks, and bright red lipstick. "And this is my dear friend Pan Yintao."

"I am Liling's fashion advisor," Pan Yintao said with an enigmatic smile—reminiscent of a look Julia might give him—and held out her hand wrist up for Doug to kiss it.

From his seat below Doug, Pete nearly snorted while choking back a laugh.

Doug kissed the top of Pan Yintao's hand—and then noticed the slight bob of an Adam's apple at her powdered throat.

Doug stiffened, but he forced a pleasant smile and quickly looked back to Fred and Liling. It was none of his concern, after all.

"I didn't understand a word of that," Fred said with an apologetic half smile. "I've been trying to learn some Chinese, but it's not coming too easily."

"It is not his fault," Liling said, switching to English and patting Fred's hand. "He doesn't yet understand the difference between Shanghainese and Mandarin, so it is all confusing." She looked at him adoringly. "I have been teaching him polite phrases in Mandarin, and he has used them with my parents to great advantage."

A blonde woman in a shimmering silver evening gown slit midway up one thigh sauntered toward their table, a very short and slender man in a pinstriped charcoal suit holding her arm. She was taller than him by half a head at least. Pete stood and stepped forward to meet them, kissing the woman on the cheek.

"Dolores! Thank you for coming." He looked at the short man beside her, and his smile seemed a bit more forced. "And you brought a friend with you."

"That's Jimmy Lockhart," Stuart said before Dolores had a chance to make the introductions. He'd stood, and now took a few steps toward them.

"That's right," Lockhart said, giving Stuart a tight smile. "Are you a fan?"

Doug couldn't read Stuart's expression.

"Sure," Stuart said, *sounding* normal at least. "You did cost me a few bucks at the track yesterday. And last week, too."

Now Doug recognized the name. Jimmy Lockhart was a jockey at the horse track. He'd looked like he was going to win that first race on opening day last week, but his horse's surge had fizzled out in fourth place.

Lockhart shrugged. Now that Stuart stood next to him, it looked comical; he was so short, his head didn't even come to Stuart's shoulder. "I'm in a tough streak this spring, but the luck will change soon enough. Always does."

"I ran into Jimmy downstairs," Dolores explained to Pete, almost apologetic. Her dark eyebrows contrasted sharply with her blonde hair, which was piled into fashionable curls atop her head.

"We go way back," Lockhart said, putting a second hand on Dolores' arm.

"We met at a party a couple of years ago," Dolores murmured, slipping her arm from Lockhart's grip and sauntering over between Pete and Doug. She extended her hand. "And you must be the birthday boy. I'd recognize you from Pete's description any day."

"Dolores Moody, this is Doug Bainbridge," Pete said, and Doug took Dolores' fingers for a brief shake. "Dolores is a singer. She even performed on Broadway before she came to Shanghai a few years ago."

"Joe Farren recruited me for the Paramount," Dolores explained. "He was managing the chorus then. Much easier schedule than a Broadway show. And better pay, too." She added that last with a sly smile. "After he left last year, I didn't stick around too long. The owners prefer Chinese headliners."

"What do you do now?" Doug asked.

"Private events," Dolores said, vague. She slipped her arm through Doug's.

"I'll go fetch us some drinks," Lockhart said, his jaw tight. "You want a martini, doll?"

"That would be lovely, thanks," Dolores said, airly, barely glancing at Lockhart.

Lockhart gave Doug a scrutinizing look, then smirked and stalked off toward the bar.

Doug took a drink of his gin and tonic.

"Oh! You have a wedding ring!" Dolores said, sounding almost delighted by this detail.

"Yes, I'm married," Doug said. "We're expecting our first child soon."

"Congratulations!" she tightened her grip on his arm, shifted closer to him. Her warmth radiated through the glimmering fabric of her dress. "I'm always impressed when I see a man wearing a wedding ring, willing to announce to the world that he's taken." She half-turned toward Doug, beaming. "It's very progressive of you, Mr. Bainbridge. Quite modern. And why should women be the only ones to advertise when they're taken?"

"I quite agree," Doug said. He wasn't sure how to take Dolores' attitude, since she kept sidling closer to him.

Scott Farnsworth appeared at Doug's shoulder with Kenny.

"We never got to throw you a stag party, old chum," Kenny said. "Things were pretty chaotic last fall. But now with your birthday coming right before your baby, Pete thought tonight would be our chance to make it up to you."

"Still a last weekend of freedom," Pete said.

Dolores' gray eyes lit up when she looked at Scott Farnsworth. She slipped her arm from Doug's and extended her hand to Scott. "And who is this tall drink of water?"

Scott's cheeks colored, and his smile looked embarrassed as he took Dolores' fingers. "Scott Farnswoth."

"No ring on your finger, handsome. Is that because you're not taken? Or are you just hiding it?"

Scott looked taken aback. "Not taken." He glanced at Doug awkwardly.

"Well then! Aren't I a lucky girl? I'll dance with your friend first, since it's his birthday, but then I'll find you and we can spin around the floor. What do you say?"

Jimmy Lockhart returned then, a tumbler of whiskey in one hand, and a martini in the other. He thrust the martini at Dolores. "I got your drink, doll." He flashed a look at Doug and Scott.

Doug excused himself, walked around the table, and took a seat between Stuart and George.

**

"You ok, Stu?" His friend was staring at Fred and his three young Chinese companions.

"During the day, his name is Liu Fan," Stuart said, nodding toward Pan Yintao. "Dresses like a man and everything. He lives in some hole-in-the-wall place off Foochow Road downtown. But at night 'Pan Yintao' sings at a seedy joint out here in the Western Roads—one of those new bamboo barns they slapped up in a few days. The Pink Lotus. The show is all female impersonators. Seems this has become his regular nighttime persona now. Kind of a split personality thing, I guess."

"I take it you've seen the show?" Doug asked.

Stuart snorted. "Yeah, Liling brought Fred and me out there one night about a month ago. One of those evenings her cousin promised Liling's parents she'd chaperone us, but then she went off to meet some fella. Fred and I, we didn't realize what kind of show it was. They're real convincing. Anyway, he was performing that night—*she*, I mean." He shrugged one shoulder. "Liling says we have to treat her like a woman when she's in her Pan Yintao get-up. 'He' when it's Liu Fan, and 'she' when it's Pan Yintao."

Doug suspected there was more to Stuart's dislike of Pan Yintao. "You didn't know at first, did you?"

Stuart turned bright red. He looked away. "Not until we'd been going at it pretty hard for a bit." He looked at Doug and rushed to explain. "After her act was done, she came to our table, you see. Sat next to me. After a couple of drinks, she sat on my lap. Fred and Liling were necking, so Pan suggested we do the same." He snorted again, shook his head. "I thought she was pretty. We went at it, pretty hard, too—necking, and some over-the-clothes stuff. And then I felt *it*."

A sour expression washed over him, and he looked down. "Fred said to let it go, forget about it. He's just saying that because Liling thinks the world of Pan Yintao. But Liu Fan is a big lousy liar."

Pan Yintao sat on Ben Trebinski's lap. Ben looked delighted, putting an arm around her shoulder. Doug thought about going over to Ben and whispering in his ear; but he decided not to. It might create a scene. And for all he knew, Ben wouldn't mind—he did let men suck him off, after all, so maybe this wasn't all that different.

Pan Yintao flashed a look at Stuart, and whispered something in Ben's ear.

"What did you do?" Doug asked. "When you realized, I mean."

"Well, I took my hand off his dick real fast!" Stuart said, almost spitting the words. His face turned red again. "I pushed him off my lap, told him to get his hands off me."

A tiny young man entered the ballroom with two taller men in tow, and several people near the entrance started clapping. The small one acknowledged their applause with a raised hand and went to the bar. He passed Jimmy Lockhart on the way, and the two exchanged a cool nod.

"That's Mark Chapman," Stuart said. He sounded in awe, and his face had lit up. "The jockey who did that crazy move at last week's races and won the first race."

"He seems to have a lot of admirers." Doug nodded toward the bar where a middle-aged white man in a black tuxedo jacket was ordering a drink for young Mr. Chapman.

**

Doug stood at the bar with Pete and George, ordering another round of drinks. Jimmy Lockhart came up a moment later, shouldered his way between Doug and Pete, called out to the bartender. "Another whiskey, and another martini, pronto."

"One moment please, sir," the Chinese bartender said in careful English. "Right after these gentlemen."

Ben came up to the bar then, Pan Yintao holding his arm with both hands. "Good party, Commander!"

Jimmy Lockhart's eyes narrowed when he saw Pan Yintao. "Hey! What's that freak doin' here?"

Ben looked confused. "Freak?"

Lockhart puffed out his chest and barged toward Pan Yintao. "This ain't your kind of place," he snarled.

Pan Yintao glared down at him, then looked away with a sneer. "We go downstairs bar," she said to Ben in a thick Chinese accent. "Better crowd downstairs bar." She glanced back at Lockhart with an audible sniff and led Ben away.

Lockhart smirked. "That fella's gonna be in for a hell of a shock later, when he finds out his 'dame' has got a little somethin' extra in the drawers."

Doug scowled. "I take it you know this from experience?"

Lockhart's face flushed, and his hands fisted at his sides. "I don't go for faggots in disguise as dames, mister."

Pete moved in between Doug and Lockhart. "My friend meant no offense. He only wondered how you knew about that person. Let me buy your drink for you, as an apology for the misunderstanding." He put his hands on both of Lockhart's shoulders and steered him toward the bar.

"Yeah, thanks fella," Lockhart said to Pete, not looking back at Doug.

Doug looked down, ashamed that he'd let himself get caught up. Pete was better at this than he was. He'd been offended for Ben, and his temper had snapped.

**

Doug found Stuart at the end of the bar, talking animatedly with Mark Chapman.

"...and then the way you slipped through that gap along the rail! I couldn't believe it! I've never seen a move like that."

"Thanks, mate," Chapman said in an English accent. He was young, probably early to mid-twenties, and his brown hair was unoiled. "I needed the win, so I took the only opening I had."

"It was amazing!" Stuart gushed.

"You must be talking about last week's opening race," Doug said.

"That's right," Stuart said. "But he won his race today, too."

"Oh, congratulations."

"Thank you." The tiny young man extended his hand to Doug. "Mark Chapman."

"Douglas Bainbridge. I saw your race last week, and I agree with Stuart—it was amazing what you did. I didn't see today's races, though."

"Thank you, sir. I appreciate your enthusiasm." He turned back to Stuart. "You're quite knowledgeable, have you worked with horses?"

Stuart grinned. "No, but I've gone to the races since I was young. My parents are aficionados."

Chapman's blue eyes widened and lit up. "Ah, brilliant! I can probably get you a pass for the stables next Saturday before the races. You can have a look around at the horses, meet the other jockeys."

"That would be aces, thanks!" Stuart beamed.

"My pleasure, mate."

"Let me get you my address," Stuart said. He reached into his jacket and pulled out a card and a pencil. He turned the card over and scribbled on the back. "This is my business card. And this is the address where you can send that pass."

Mark Chapman took the card, read the address, and then flipped it over. "HSBC, eh? Wouldn't have taken you for a banker."

"Investments," Stuart explained.

"And horses are good investments, is that it?"

"No, I just like the races. I mean, yes—they are good investments, but they're not my specialty professionally. I look for companies the bank can back, or commercial real estate construction."

"That sounds riskier than horses," Mark Chapman said with a sardonic half smile that tugged up one corner of his mouth.

"I don't know about that!" Stuart said with a laugh.

Doug excused himself and went looking for Kenny.

**

He found Kenny standing with Scott Farnsworth in a corner. He was talking quite animatedly, and continuously touching Scott's arm.

Like he had at Doug's wedding.

Doug wasn't prepared for the pang of jealousy that ripped through him again, just as it had then. He tried to ignore it. "Hey there, fellas."

"Oh! Hi there, Doug." Kenny's cheeks flushed, and he glanced back at Scott, embarrassed. Like a kid caught with his hand in the cookie jar. He cleared his throat. "Pete and George went upstairs to the roulette tables. What do you say we join them?"

"I'm game," Scott said.

"Why not?" Doug followed his friends out of the ballroom to the staircase leading up to the third floor.

Dolores Moody emerged from the lady's room about the time they reached the bottom of the stairs. She beamed at them. "What fortunate timing! And where are you handsome gents off to?"

"Roulette," Doug said.

"My favorite game. Much better than cards or slots. Mind if I join you?" She slipped one arm through Doug's, and the other through Scott's.

"Not at all," Kenny said, and led the way up the stairs.

Dolores glanced over her shoulder as they started up, expression serious, perhaps even concerned; then she smiled at Doug and Scott in turn, hugged their arms to her side, and sashayed up the stairs.

**

Muffled, angry words. Doug hesitated before he pushed open the door to the men's room, not wanting to interrupt something private. But his three-and-a-half gin and tonics demanded that he interrupt whoever the hell expected to hog the men's room for some private disagreement.

"...and keep your damned mouth sh—"

Mark Chapman and Jimmy Lockhart stepped away from each other, faces flushed crimson. Chapman's jacket and tie were askew. It was Lockhart's voice Doug had heard in that second after opening the door.

And yet the first thought that popped into his head was how funny it was that these two shorties stood eye-to-eye.

"Apologies, gents," Doug said, and hurried toward an empty stall.

"This is a private conversation, mister," Lockhart huffed, pointing his finger at Doug when he passed.

"I'll only be a moment," Doug said. "Let me finish my business, and I'll be out of your hair."

Doug felt incredibly self-conscious standing at the toilet while two men stood in silence outside the stall, waiting for him. But those gin and tonics demanded attention and wouldn't let his self-consciousness derail their intentions.

On his way to the sink, he smiled awkwardly at Mark Chapman, who stood between the sink and the closed window. "Awfully stuffy in here, isn't it?"

"Yeah." Chapman mumbled, and reached for the crank at the base of the window.

Lockhart's hand dropped onto the crank first, and stayed there, unmoving. Keeping the window shut.

Doug avoided eye contact with either, barely took time to dry his hands, and hurried out. He almost collided with Stuart outside the door.

"Sorry, Doug," Stuart said, and slipped around him.

Doug opened his mouth to warn Stu about the duo of jockeys arguing in the men's room, but Lockhart's voice rose loud and threatening. "Private conversation, so scram!"

Pete, George, Kenny, and Scott Farnsworth were leaving the gambling hall and heading down the stairs, and Doug joined them.

"We're going to get some air," George said, fanning himself with his hand. "It's a bit warm upstairs."

"Good idea. I'll come along."

They gathered on the portico a moment later. Fred and Liling were already there, standing in the partial privacy of a potted palm, holding hands. Some ten yards away, Ben Trebinski was talking nonstop to Pan Yintao, whose wide-eyed enthusiasm while she listened had to be put-on. *She is a performer, after all.*

"Anyone seen Stuart?" Pete asked, but directing his question at Fred.

Fred shrugged. "Not for a while. Last I saw him, he was at the Roulette table with you fellas."

"I passed him a few minutes ago," Doug said. "I'm surprised you fellas didn't see him at the top of the stairs. He couldn't have gone by there ten seconds before you."

Kenny laughed. "Near miss, eh? He'll probably come down when he realizes none of us are up there anymore."

"I haven't seen the others in a while," Scott Farnsworth said to Doug, nodding toward Ben.

"Me neither. I wonder if they snuck out early, went back into town." Doug nodded toward the woods on either side of the club.

Scott frowned. "Surely they would have said goodbye."

He sounded more than just irritated. Doug wondered if there was more to it, since Scott and Patrick Callahan had a history.

"Did you hear that?" George asked, a touch loudly.

"Hear what?" Pete asked, looking around.

"I heard a 'thud,' like someone dropped a big bag of dry concrete," George said.

"I heard it, too," Fred said, looking around.

Pete shrugged. "I didn't hear a thing." He shook his empty glass, and the remnants of ice rattled around the bottom. "Who wants another? I'll get this round."

Doug raised his hand—he'd left his half-full glass at the roulette table with his friends, damn it—and the others hurried to down the last of their drinks so they could raise an empty glass at Pete.

Pete's finger moved through the air, counting. "Got it," he said, and went through the open French doors. Doug had no doubt that every drink would be correct; Pete had a knack for that.

The sound of a woman's scream, shrill and sharp, filled the air a moment later.

All conversation on the portico stopped.

"That way!" George said, pointing beyond the hedge with his empty glass still in his right hand. He took off that direction.

Doug and the others ran after George, cutting through a gap in the hedge and around the corner of the house to the east side, where a garden stretched toward the woods.

Dolores Moody stood in the moonlight at the edge of the garden, hand clasped over her mouth.

In the grassy center entrance to the garden, between rows of rose bushes near the house, Stuart knelt next to the sprawled form of a man lying face down. The light from a nearby open door reflected in his glasses.

It was a very small man. In a pinstriped silk suit. One leg and both arms were bent at unnatural angles.

George rushed forward, reaching for the man.

"Don't touch him!" Kenny warned. "Don't disturb anything until the police get here."

"I'm checking his pulse, damn it!" George barked, scowling back at Kenny, who seemed to shrink in on himself.

"Of course," Kenny muttered. Then he straightened again, resumed his composure. "Just be careful not to move him."

"If he's alive, I'm gonna treat him," George grumbled, fingers moving down the side of the figure's neck and slipping under the collar.

Everyone was still for several seconds, and then George shook his head and stood.

"He's dead."

4

Sunday, April 10

"Where were you when Mr. Lockhart fell out the window, Mr. Bainbridge?" the club's in-house detective asked Doug an hour later, in a private office on the ground floor of Del Monte's. A white man with a deep southern drawl—probably Georgia or South Carolina, but not the refined kind of drawl that one heard in the movies—he was dressed in a crisp silk suit, navy blue with a red pocket square to match his necktie; but the outfit contrasted with a scruff of beard and shaggy hair. Not at all what Doug would have expected.

"I was on the portico with my friends. My friend George said he heard a thud."

"That would be Dr. George Howerton?"

"That's right."

"Did you hear the thud, Mr. Bainbridge?"

Doug thought for a second, then shook his head. "I don't think so."

"You don't think so?" Detective Russell said, arching one eyebrow. "I need you to tell me truthfully, sir—did you hear it, or didn't you?"

Doug squared his shoulders. "If I did, I didn't recognize it. There was a lot of conversation around me, you see."

The house detective scrutinized him for several seconds before glancing back at his notebook. "You said you were with your friends— tell me their names."

Doug listed off Kenny, Scott, Pete, and Fred, while Russell's pencil moved down a list in his notebook. "And also Dr. Howerton, as I said."

"Hmmm," Russell said, making a note, and looked up. "I assume Stuart Vandermeer wasn't with you?"

A chill ran through Doug's midsection. "No."

"And I assume you're not aware of Mr. Vandermeer's whereabouts at that time?"

Doug swallowed, and shook his head. "Not until a few minutes later…" He stopped.

"When you saw Mr. Vandermeer crouched beside the body."

Doug narrowed his eyes and held the house detective's gaze. "That's right." Russell's declarative tone was disconcerting.

"How long was it after Dr. Howerton heard the thud that you gentlemen found Mr. Vandermeer beside the body?"

Doug tensed. He didn't like the direction the detective was taking this. "Probably two minutes."

"What prompted you gentlemen to go to the scene of the crime?"

Doug took a deep breath. "Because we heard a woman scream. I'm sure you've already been told this several times by the others."

"We want everyone's recollections of the event while they're still fresh, sir," Russell said, voice flat, staring at Doug unblinking.

"Of course." Russell must fancy himself a real detective in a gritty crime novel. This was probably way more exciting than their usual pickpockets and card cheaters. Hell, Doug wouldn't be surprised if *he* had more experience solving murders than 'Detective' Russell.

"How long would you say it took you gentlemen to reach the scene after you heard the scream?"

Doug shrugged, looked up in thought. "Maybe fifteen seconds? We had to run around a hedge, you see, we didn't have a direct path."

"When was the last time you saw Mr. Vandermeer prior to that?"

Doug thought about that for several seconds. How long had it been exactly? He tried to figure how long it took to get downstairs, and out the French doors to the portico. And then how long had they been talking out there?

"I think about five minutes before."

"And where was that, exactly?"

Doug swallowed hard. He could tell where this was going. "Upstairs, on the third floor, going into the men's room."

"You were coming out of the men's room, I presume?"

Doug nodded. "Yes."

"And was anyone else there at the time?" His expression was blank, his tone flat, but the gleam in Russell's eyes said he already knew the answer.

"Jimmy Lockhart was in the men's room when I left. But so was Mark Chapman."

Genuine surprise registered in Russell's eyes at that second remark, and Doug suppressed the urge to smile in victory. Russell scribbled in his note pad for several seconds, his brows knit.

"That was quite an active place, then, wasn't it?" Russell leaned forward, suddenly interested. No more routine questions, corroborating what others had said. "Did Mr. Chapman and Mr. Lockhart speak to each other while you were there?"

Doug described what he'd overheard when he opened the door. Russell scribbled furiously.

"Did Stuart Vandermeer speak with either of them when he entered the room?"

"I don't know."

Russell pursed his lips. "What was the state of Mr. Vandermeer's clothes tonight?"

"Excuse me?" Doug asked, confused.

"His suit, what was its state this evening?"

"It was clean, if that's what you mean."

"No rips or tears?"

"No." Doug's mind raced. It had certainly been intact earlier, but it was dark when they'd found Stuart kneeling beside the body—had his suit been torn then? He wished there had been more light, but the moon had been behind them. Had he just said something that might incriminate his friend? "Where is Stuart?"

Detective Russell stared at Doug in silence for several seconds. "He's with other detectives. We haven't finished talking with him."

And yet you've finished pretty quickly with everyone else. "How long do you think this is going to take?"

Russell looked at his note pad, ran his pencil down the page. "I think we're done, sir. You can leave. The police'll contact you at the address you gave me if they have any questions for you."

That wasn't exactly what Doug had meant. "How much longer will you keep Stuart?"

Russell's eyes narrowed. "I can't really say, sir." He stood. "Now if you'll excuse me, I have other witnesses to talk to."

Doug nodded, standing, and hurried from the room.

He found most of his friends standing around the portico—except for Stuart, Fred, and Ben Trebinski. Pete and George wore shell-shocked expressions, but Kenny's brow was knit in a look of determination. He motioned Doug to the side.

"I already asked the others, Doug, and now I'm going to ask you to tell me what you discussed with the 'detective.' Every detail."

Doug forced a grin. "Are you acting as my lawyer?"

The show of joviality was lost on Kenny, who crossed his arms. "I'm always your lawyer, Doug. And I'm going to represent Stuart as well, if the length of his questioning means what I think it might."

Doug nodded, grave. He had the same fear. He told Kenny everything, keeping his voice low.

Kenny nodded. "That's very interesting about Mark Chapman arguing with Jimmy Lockhart in the third-floor men's room. Especially since that's the window Jimmy Lockhart probably fell from a few minutes later."

"You think Mark Chapman killed Lockhart?"

Kenny made a tiny shrug with one shoulder. "Too soon to say. But it might help cast reasonable doubt that Stuart did. *If* we need to cast reasonable doubt, that is."

"So you think the house detectives are going to hand Stu off to the police in the morning?"

"I hope not. But yes."

"Do you think the police will look into that angle? Mark Chapman, I mean."

Kenny frowned. "I have no idea. I would hope so, but sometimes the police focus in on one main suspect and forget the rest. That happens all too often."

"Like bulldogs," Doug muttered.

The corner of Kenny's mouth twerked in amusement. "Exactly like bulldogs." He put his hand on Doug's shoulder and pulled him farther away from the others. When he spoke again, his voice was almost a whisper. "Doug, you've had some experience with murder investigations. If the police try to pin the blame on Stuart, can I count on you to help me prove his innocence?"

"Of course." Doug nodded resolutely. "Stuart's our friend, we owe it to him to do everything we can to help clear his name. I'll help however I can, Kenny."

Ben Trebinski emerged from the club just as Kenny and Doug were starting to return to their friends. Ben spotted them in the shadow, and hurried over.

"Have either of you seen Yintao?" he asked, his deep blue eyes heavy with worry.

"Pan Yintao?" Doug asked. "The last time I saw her, she was with you. Here on the portico."

"I haven't seen her since that woman screamed and they found a body," Ben said, sounding concerned. "She let go of my arm about the time you fellas ran off, and she disappeared."

Doug supposed Pan Yintao wanted no part of the police, and had probably high-tailed out of the club the second it became clear the police would be called, curfew be damned. No doubt his identification papers identified him as Liu Fan, and the police would hardly take kindly to a female impersonator out on the town.

"I'm sure she's fine," Doug said, opting to reassure his friend instead of identifying the reason Pan Yintao might not want to stick around. "I think others left when they heard screaming. Can't really blame them, can you?"

"I s'pose not. It must be especially scary for the ladies when something like that happens."

It was all Doug could do not to correct Ben's misperception.

Kenny motioned for both of them to follow him into a shadowy corner. "Ben, would you mind telling me what the detective asked you, and what you told him?"

"Mr. Traywick's a lawyer," Doug reminded Ben.

"Sure thing, Mr. Traywick," Ben said, and recounted his brief conversation with a house detective. It had been quite short indeed, since Ben could only really say what he'd heard from the portico. No, he hadn't interacted with Jimmy Lockhart that evening.

"What about Mark Chapman?" Doug asked.

"Who?" Ben asked.

"The other little man," Kenny said. "Same size as Lockhart. Another jockey."

"Oh, yeah, I know who you're talkin' about. Saw him around. I didn't meet him, though."

"Did you see him talking with Jimmy Lockhart?" Doug asked.

Ben looked up in thought. "Yeah, I think so."

"Were they arguing?" Kenny asked.

Ben shrugged. "I dunno. Couldn't hear 'em. But they didn't look like they liked each other much."

Fred came through the French doors then, and Kenny thanked Ben and hurried to intercept him.

"Liling's going home with her parents," Fred said, seeming a bit distracted. "Their escort's coming." Doug wanted to ask who their escort was, given the curfew, but Kenny pulled Fred aside and talked with him in a hushed voice that Doug couldn't overhear.

Scott Farnsworth appeared at Doug's side. "That was a little more than we bargained for tonight."

Doug chuckled without humor. "I was having a great time until then, so thank you all for that." He put a hand on Scott's and Ben's arms, and turned them toward the central hall. "Let's go find the other boys from the ship."

The hallway was packed with people, all now chattering about the 'excitement' of the evening. But Doug stopped in his tracks at one sight; at the open front doors stood a trio of *Kenpeitai* officers—Japanese military police, easily identifiable by the white armbands on their left arms with two red characters in Kanji script—and they were conversing with Liling's parents, Mr. and Mrs. Yang. Liling and her cousin, Yang Yajun, were nowhere to be seen.

"What's that all about?" Scott whispered, nodding his head toward the front.

"I'm not sure," Doug muttered out the side of his mouth. The conversation appeared to be cordial. That contrasted sharply with the confrontational way the *Kenpeitai* usually treated Chinese nationals. Then Mr. Yang laughed at something the *Kenpei* major said.

That didn't sit well. Doug made a mental note to look into Mr. Yang's financial dealings, and search for any Japanese connections.

**

"Has anyone seen Kenny?" Doug asked when the club's bouncers threw open the front doors at the stroke of six.

"Closing time!" they shouted on repeat, hustling stumbling and bleary-eyed revelers out the door and toward the line of waiting motor cabs.

"Not in hours," Pete slurred, and threw an arm around Doug's shoulders. He leaned against Doug, heavy. "He's prob'ly been with Stu. Poor Stuey. Kenny'll help him, though. He's a good lawyer. And he can get his own cab home. C'mon." He tugged Doug out the door.

George was right behind them. "He'll be ok, Douggie." George stumbled on a step but caught himself with his hands in the middle of Pete's and Doug's backs. He righted himself as if it hadn't happened. "It's not like he can get lost. The bouncers will make sure he leaves."

They joined a disorganized line of people shuffling toward cabs. Doug looked around in the glare of the marquee lights and spotted a group of perhaps a dozen policemen in the uniform of the Shanghai city police—Chinese Municipality—standing off to the side. Waiting.

He pointed them out to his companions.

"The bouncers won't let 'em inside," Pete said. "The gangs pay good money to keep the cops out of their clubs."

Something else Doug might need to look into.

5

The apartment was silent when Doug arrived home around six-thirty. The first gray light of dawn was inching around the window blinds. He found Lucy in bed asleep, so he undressed as silently as he could and slipped carefully beneath the sheet beside her.

She stirred at the creaking of the bed springs and propped herself up on an elbow.

"Did you have a nice time?" she asked sleepily, and leaned in to give him a quick kiss.

"For the most part."

"Oh?" She moved her hand to cover a yawn.

"The fellas did a great job," he hurried to explain. "Kenny even arranged for some of my buddies from the ship to be there. We all had a nice time. But then around midnight a man fell out of a third-floor window and died. The police suspect he was murdered."

"Oh no!" She sounded fully awake now.

"A horse jockey, no one you've probably heard of."

"I'm not gonna lie, Doug—I worried a little bit about you boys leaving the Settlement. Everyone says crime is worse out in the Chinese city."

"Why didn't you say anything?"

"Because I don't want to be that kind of wife, nagging her husband about going out with his friends. You're free to spend time with your friends any way you like. You know that, don't you?"

He stroked her cheek. "Yes, I know that. It's just one of the reasons I love you so much." He kissed her. "Now go back to sleep. We'll talk about it more at breakfast."

**

Doug was roused from sleep at nine-thirty by the ringing of the telephone. From the other room, he could hear Bao answer.

"Mista Doug! It's Mista Kenny on phone for you!".

Doug slipped out of bed, conscious that the bedroom door was ajar, and crept along the wall to where his bathrobe hung on a hook on the back of the door.

Tying his robe tight, he trudged out to the living room and took the phone receiver from Bao. Putting his hand over the mouthpiece, he asked Bao, "Where's Lucy?"

"Missy Lucy went to bathroom," Bao said, as matter-of-fact as he could be, as if that weren't at all a sensitive subject, and went back into the kitchen to finish breakfast.

No matter how many times they told him to call them Doug and Lucy, he still insisted on the title. But at least he no longer called them Mr. and Mrs. Bainbridge.

"Good morning, Kenny."

"Morning, Doug. I'm sorry to wake you. I waited until after nine."

"It's fine. What's going on?"

"They took Stuart to the station in Nantao last night," Kenny said. His voice was scratchy, and he sounded exhausted. "I'm still waiting for formal arrest paperwork, but I know he hasn't been released."

Doug found none of that surprising. "Have you been to bed, Kenny?"

"For about an hour. The police in the Chinese municipality have a reputation for being slower with foreigners they arrest, to make a point, so I'm trying to stay on top of it."

"Have you spoken with Stuart yet?"

"Briefly. I had to threaten them that the American Court would throw out the charges if they interrogate Mr. Vandermeer without his counsel present, and they reluctantly let me see him."

"How is he?"

"Scared, as you might imagine. Oh, of course you understand, you remember what it's like."

"I'm afraid I do." Doug had been arrested once, in September 1936 for the attempted murder of a Japanese agent name Kawakami Takahiro, and he'd spent a painful night in the municipal jail. "How soon do you think you'll be able to get him out?"

"That depends on whether or not they decide to formally charge him with the murder. I reminded them of American law's twenty-four-hour requirement for charges, or the person has to be released. If they file charges, he'll have a hearing on Monday morning."

Doug closed his eyes. Poor Stuart. He said a little prayer that they wouldn't charge him. Surely they didn't have enough evidence.

"His suit was torn, and that seems to be the main piece of evidence they're basing their suspicions on," Kenny continued, as if he'd read Doug's mind.

"That explains those questions last night. So they're saying he got in a fight with Jimmy Lockhart, and pushed him out a window?"

"Presumably. They aren't saying much yet."

That figures. "I saw something before we left Del Monte's that might be significant." He told Kenny about the *Kenpeitai* and the Yangs.

"That is interesting," Kenny said. "I'm not sure if it's significant or not, but it bears looking into."

"I think I have someone who could dig into that for us," Doug said, thinking of Jonesy. The reporter knew someone everywhere, it seemed.

"If we need to," Kenny said, vague.

"It sounds like we agree that we should probably focus on Mark Chapman," Doug said, reading between the lines.

"Yes, that's the most likely angle. What were they arguing about, and why? But we should also find out why Dolores Moody was alone in that area shortly after Jimmy Lockhart fell from the window."

That was an excellent point, and Doug was ashamed he hadn't thought of it. His cheeks flushed in embarrassment even though no one was there to see. "She never seemed too thrilled at Lockhart's company. Though I never got the feeling there was more to it than that."

But there was something about that dynamic that seemed a little too close to Nick Bonadio's behavior toward Lola Cunningham last year. Doug couldn't just ignore that.

"She's as good a suspect as anyone," Kenny said. "Women are as capable of murder as men."

But would she have been strong enough to push Lockhart out a window? Maybe, given how short and slight the jockey was.

"Pete knew her, didn't he?" Doug said, thinking back to her introduction in the ballroom.

"I don't know if he really *knows* her. But he did arrange for her to join our little party last night. He can probably give us her address. He knows how to get ahold of her somehow."

Doug wondered what Kenny meant about Pete not really 'knowing' Dolores Moody, but he left that for another time.

Lucy entered the apartment then, so Doug told Kenny he'd call him later.

"It smells like Bao has breakfast ready," Lucy said, sniffing the aroma of bacon and eggs in the air.

They sat down to eat, and Doug filled her in on his conversation with Kenny.

"Poor Stuart!" she said. "It sounds to me like they mean to charge him for the murder. Which is just ridiculous. Stuart wouldn't kill anyone. Of course the police don't know that, I understand. But it doesn't make any sense. How would he have had time to push that Jimmy Lockhart out a window, and then get downstairs and outside in time to be there with the body when that woman saw them and screamed?"

Doug cringed. "Technically, it's possible. It was at least two minutes after George heard the thud that Dolores started screaming. Theoretically, someone who pushed him out the window might rush down to make sure he died."

"Oh Doug, really!" Lucy crossed her arms and scowled at him. "It's a stretch, to say the least. And Stuart would never, you know that."

He put his hand on her forearm and smiled reassuringly. "Of course I know that. I was only trying to explain it from the perspective of the police—that it's physically possible, that's all."

She looked barely mollified, but uncrossed her arms and resumed eating.

"And you yourself just said that the police wouldn't know that Stuart would never kill anyone. Their job is to suspect anyone."

The look she gave him said loud and clear that he should *not* have used her own words in argument against her. He looked away and ate his breakfast in silence.

"I think I might go out to the Western Roads and look around a little bit," Doug said when they'd finished eating. He looked at Lucy and asked, "Would you like to come along, dear?"

She hesitated a few seconds. "Not this time, darling. You know I love these little adventures together, but I don't think I have the stamina for it right now." She rubbed her belly. "Besides, if you really need to look around, you shouldn't take a cab. Why don't you ride a bike? You could borrow Bao's. Couldn't he, Bao?"

Bao paused from clearing the dishes off the table, and bobbed his head. "Of course, Mista Doug. You borrow my bicycle."

It had been years since Doug had ridden a bicycle. *They say you never forget how.* "Thank you, Bao. I'll have it back this afternoon."

**

It was a six-mile ride from home, and it took Doug almost an hour to pedal out there. He was definitely out of practice. He navigated Avenue Edward VII—the crowded downtown boundary street between the International Settlement and the French Concession—with his heart in his throat until it merged into Avenue Foch further uptown, and then became the Great Western Road a mile and a half later when it crossed into Chinese territory.

Doug encountered the Japanese check point immediately beyond the boundary, and he fished his identification papers and passport out of his coat pocket while he coasted to a stop. A Rolls Royce limousine passed him on the left, and instead of stopping at the check point the chauffer held his arm out the window with some sort of card in his hand. The Japanese sentry waved him on.

Doug put his foot down to stop the bike and handed over his papers. The sentry took a quick look at them, glanced at his face, and thrust them back. It was as quick and routine as it had been last night—though he'd noticed both of his Chinese cab drivers had gone stiff and silent while going through the check point.

The Japanese were on tricky legal ground with the check point here, thanks to quirks in the international treaties. While the waterways all belonged to China, even where they passed through the foreign concessions, the western extension roads all belonged to the International Settlement, though they passed through Chinese territory. Doug wasn't about to argue, of course; and besides, it made sense that the Japanese would check everyone coming into their occupied territory, even if the road itself technically wasn't occupied.

Doug's thighs already burned from the long bike ride, and he still had a long way to go. It was about one and a quarter mile from here to the Columbia Country Club—Doug had been there a couple of times in 1935 and '36, as a guest of Pete and Julia—and Del Monte's Club was in a villa well beyond the country club.

In the daylight, the changes to the area were obvious. One short year ago, everything west of the Settlement's boundary was fairly open country, dotted with scattered mansions and a handful of other buildings, including the German church and school just outside the boundary, and the small "Country Hospital" that the rich preferred. But where there had recently been open space was now packed with small buildings of cheap bamboo, lining both sides of the Great Western Road. Doug glanced to his right, and that new view continued to the north.

One of those buildings was the Pink Lotus, where Pan Yintao performed. With other female impersonators, according to what Stuart had said last night. Doug wondered how long it would be before the police shut it down.

Or perhaps the better question was how much did the owners pay the police to look the other way?

The air rang with the sound of hammers and saws. Construction everywhere, even on a Sunday. The new construction got gradually thinner as he pedaled, and by the time he neared the Columbia Country Club there was little to be seen. Here, the scattered villas of the wealthy still had their green breathing space.

He wondered which of these mansions belonged to Yang Liling's parents.

Stopping his bike at the entrance to Del Monte's front drive, he pulled off in the tall grass along the side of the road. He had a good view of the front of the house—of the *club*, that is. The trees that lined the drive were young, only about eight to ten feet tall, none of them big enough to obstruct the view.

Which meant anyone inside could see him as well as he could see the front of the club.

Doug got off and crouched beside the front wheel, pretending to inspect the tire.

There was a construction site on the next lot, to the east. It was only a frame still, so no real cover, but he walked the bicycle there as if he were taking a look at what they were building. Just a downtowner curious about what they were putting up all the way out here.

Doug scrutinized the square frame. No walls yet, but it was possible the metal beams could have hidden a murderer in the dark. Anyone could have fled here unseen under cover of night.

From here he could see the side of the club where Jimmy Lockhart's body had landed in the middle of a rose garden. Glancing that way frequently—but always briefly—he identified the third-floor window directly above the spot. Exactly in the middle of the wall, it was in the right spot to be the third-floor men's room.

Unlike the first two floors, the third floor was gabled. Lockhart's body would have slid down the roof several feet before reaching a gutter at the top of the second-floor veranda. That gutter was wide, extending from the roof at least a couple of feet.

Jimmy Lockhart must have been heaved pretty hard out that window to have not gotten caught in the gutter.

A thick hedge hid the rose garden from the road. Doug wasn't brazen enough to just trudge over into the rose garden and look around. Sure, he might be able to pull off the hapless tourist bit, pretend he didn't realize he was trespassing... But he cringed at the thought of acting so stupid. They wouldn't buy it. *Of course* it was trespassing, any idiot would know that.

And given that it was only twelve hours since a man had been killed there, it wouldn't seem innocent, no matter how dumb he acted.

I could pretend I read about the murder in the morning paper, and came to take a gander at the spot. But no, he still might get himself beaten up for snooping. And he might deserve it.

Still, he'd biked all the way out here, he could hardly let it be for nothing...

He debated with himself for a couple of minutes. Then he realized he could always say he'd left something valuable at the club last night, and had come back to retrieve it.

Doug unfastened the leather band of his wristwatch and slipped it into his pants pocket, where the tail of his jacket hid the small lump. He walked the bicycle across the grass, parallel with the curved drive, toward the rose garden. He carefully moderated his pace, acting casual.

He managed to reach the edge of the rose garden without detection and leaned the bicycle against the hedge. Walking into the garden proper, heading toward the spot where Jimmy Lockhart's body had lain, he accidently startled an old Chinese man with a small garden shear in his right hand, several withered branches in his gloved left hand.

"What wantchee?" the man asked, breathless. He was about sixty, judging from the lines on his face and the gray sprinkled through his black hair, the little bit that was visible below the wide-brimmed black gardener's hat he wore. He held the dry and withered cuttings aloft, and Doug realized the thorns would leave deep scratches if wielded against an intruder.

"Deepest apologies, Grandfather," Doug said in Shanghainese, bowing a little more deeply than he would ordinarily for a worker. "I was here last night, and I lost my watch. I came to this garden after the man fell out of the window, and I thought perhaps the watch fell off here. It was so chaotic I didn't notice until after I got home that it was not on my wrist." Doug held out his arm and pulled up the jacket and shirt sleeves to show his bare wrist.

The gardener got over his initial surprise at a white man speaking Shanghainese, and grunted understanding. "The business is closed, the bosses gone or asleep. Come back this evening and ask."

Doug bowed again, the normal depth this time, to show thanks. "May I please look around the garden before I leave? If it fell off here, I might find it in the grass."

The man's eye narrowed in suspicion. After a couple of seconds' hesitation, he nodded slowly, without a word, and went back to trimming away any dying branches.

The rose bushes were full of tiny green buds. Doug walked around the area where Jimmy Lockhart had landed, slower than necessary, conscious to appear he was looking for a small item in the grass.

French doors opened to his left, and he glanced over to see a bleary-eyed man on the ground floor veranda in pinstriped gray slacks, barefoot, with suspenders slung over his shirtless torso. His black hair was flattened on one side and stood straight up on top. "Who the hell are you?" he demanded in an American accent.

"I'm sorry to disturb you. I was here last night, and I think I lost my watch somewhere in this garden. I was looking for it."

"The joint's closed," the man said, and waved his arm toward the road. "Come back later."

"I won't disturb anything. I just need to see if my watch is here in the grass."

"Scram!" the man ordered, louder.

Another French door opened to the right, and house detective Russell came through, also barefoot, in black slacks and a white A-shirt, staring down the veranda at the first man. "Keep it down, wouldja? You wake Al, you're in for it." His southern drawl sounded even more pronounced than it had last night.

"We got us a trespasser," the first man said, pointing at Doug.

Russell squinted at Doug. "I know you. You was here last night. You're Mr. Bainbridge, right?"

Doug nodded. "I seem to have lost my watch during all the commotion last night, and I came back to look around the garden and see if I can find where it fell."

Russell took a couple of steps toward the rail and glared down at Doug. "You had your watch on when I was interviewin' you after."

Shit. Doug remembered glancing at his watch during the interview, wondering how much longer it would take. He faked a sheepish look and shrugged.

"It must have come off inside, then. Sometime after that. Could I look around?"

Russell's eyes narrowed, and he shook his head. "The place is closed. If you wake Mr. Israel, there'll be hell to pay. I'll look around later, and if I find your watch, I'll give you a call. We got your number. Now beat it."

"Yeah, scram!" the first one added, for no apparent reason other than to not let Russell take over.

Doug nodded and trudged back toward his bike propped against the hedge. He glanced back to see Russell and the other man watching him, so he waved and hurried back to the road.

He got on the bike and pedaled toward the city. He wished now he'd taken the time to find out the Yangs' address before he came out here. The Rolls Royce limousine that had passed him at the check point was now pulling out of the Columbia Country Club, heading back into town, the driver no doubt having dropped off his employer for a round of Sunday golf.

Before he got back to the Japanese check point, Doug turned off the road on a whim and pedaled down one of the new alleys between the flimsy-looking new buildings. *The summer monsoons might blow all of this down.* He stopped beside a pair of middle-aged men working— one sweeping dust out of a doorway, the other hauling out garbage— and asked in Shanghainese if they knew where to find the Pink Lotus.

They eyed him suspiciously for a moment, and then the one with the broom nodded to the north without a word.

The alley curved around the end of an irrigation canal—the rice fields it had watered just last year now long gone—and a short distance beyond that bend he found a narrow two-story bamboo building with a small, easy-to-miss sign out front announcing it was the Pink Lotus Club.

He stopped his bike in front of the plain wooden door with a tiny peep hole. Two small windows flanked the door, but set high so that almost anyone standing on the street wouldn't be able to see inside. Doug was taller than the average man, so he stood on his toes and stretched, and he got a glimpse of the interior.

It was dark inside, but he could make out plain wooden tables and chairs sitting on a bare wood floor. An unadorned stage stood at the far end of the long and narrow room, and a small bar stretched along the wall to his right. He didn't see a soul inside the place.

He'd hoped to find someone to answer some questions. He took a chance and knocked on the door, in case someone was working in an office out of sight. He waited a moment before knocking again, harder.

Disappointed, he got back on his bike. It was a half-block to the corner of a main road, and when he got there it was marked Yu Yuen Road. He knew where he was now.

A Japanese military check point stood immediately to his right, a block this side of the International Settlement's western boundary. In contrast to the check point on the Great Western Road, this one was gated with barbed wire. No such hassle for the wealthy westerners on their way to and from the Columbia Country Club.

A Japanese corporal barked questions in Pidgin to a trio of young Chinese men in working clothes coming from the International Settlement. A sergeant asked Doug for his papers, almost sounding bored, and only glanced at them before handing them back and waving him through.

Yu Yuen Road curved to the right, and then he passed between the gates of the International Settlement. A half-block later, he pedaled past the four-story façade of the Paramount, Shanghai's largest nightclub, and a favorite among his friends. Its neon lights were dark, and the sidewalk in front was littered with last night's cigarette butts. From here it was just a block to Bubbling Well Road, the main east-west drag through uptown. Two more miles, and he'd be home.

**

"Stuart's been charged with murder," Kenny said on the phone line when Doug called him after noon.

"Damn," Doug muttered. Then he told Kenny about his visit to the Del Monte this morning, and what he'd seen in the daylight.

"I need to go talk to Stuart again, now that he's been formally charged—but would you call Pete and find out where to find Dolores Moody? We need to have a chat with her, and find out what she knew about Jimmy Lockhart."

6

Doug found Dolores Moody's apartment building in a crowded neighborhood off East Canton Road downtown, on one of those half-dozen narrow little streets that crisscrossed the block between Canton Road, Fokien Road, Shantung Road, and Avenue Edward VII. The three-story brick buildings all had Chinese-style tiled roofs and gables, and the signage on all of the ground floor stores was exclusively in Chinese.

A lot of people lived in this building, judging by the volume of conversations and unique voices clearly audible through the thin walls. Most were in Shanghainese, but a couple of conversations were in Russian.

Two flights up, Dolores answered Doug's knock, and her widened eyes and sudden smile registered both surprise and pleasure. She held a rag in her hand, and was wearing a tight pair of black slacks, off-white short sleeved blouse, and her blonde hair was pulled back in a ponytail. That last detail made her look surprisingly youthful, though she was probably a few years older than Doug; early thirties, judging by the fine lines starting to form around her eyes.

"Oh, Mr. Bainbridge, wasn't it? From last night. This is a surprise. What brings you by my place, handsome?"

"I wonder if I might come in and have a word with you about last night?"

"Of course, honey, come right in." She stepped aside, and closed the door after him. Then she hurried to take a stack of glossy magazines off a chair, revealing the faded and fraying fabric of its seat. "Sorry about the mess, I'm just in the middle of my weekend cleaning. As you can see." She motioned down her side with both hands, indicating her outfit.

"Quite alright." The one room apartment had a Murphy bed that was folded up in the wall. Two windows allowed in light, and the warm spring breeze. One overlooked the narrow lane below through a gable, and the other faced the brick wall and a window in the neighboring building, barely three feet away. From that window, a man and woman were arguing unashamedly in Shanghainese; the wife blamed their lack of meat on her husband's stinginess, but he accused her of being a shrill nag.

"Well, ain't this a lucky break. A girl could only get luckier if your tall friend came here with you—I mean the single one, that blond hunk of man, not the skinny one."

She means Scott and not Kenny. "I'm not here for a social call, unfortunately. I'd like to talk with you about Jimmy Lockhart."

Her gray eyes clouded. "Yes, that's a shame about him. Tough break, going the way he did. The way the police were asking questions, they must think he was pushed."

"It would seem so. How did you know Mr. Lockhart?"

Dolores rolled her eyes. "He was a former client. He hired me a couple of times when he needed a date someplace. The Race Club ball last spring, before the war. Then some dinner party with some people he wanted to impress."

That surprised Doug, but he wasn't really sure why. She had hinted at something like that last night, but he hadn't put two and two together about what kind of business she ran. His cheeks flushed. "I didn't realize."

The look in her eyes was a mix of amusement and weariness. "No, honey, I'm not a hooker. Men pay me twenty bucks plus dinner to be their date for an evening. That's all, just company, someone to go with them somewhere. I don't sleep with clients." Then she shrugged and added, "Well, not unless I *want* to. But then *that's* on the house."

Doug ignored that detail. "You said Mr. Lockhart was a 'former client'—so, then, he wasn't with you last night?"

She rolled her eyes again and shook her head. "No, I was hired by your friend, Mr. Tolbert, for your party. He wanted you fellas to have some female company. As soon as I walk into the club, who should I run into but little Jimmy Lockhart. And he latches right onto me like I'm there to see *him*. I told him I had a job that evening, but he insisted on 'escorting' me up there." She frowned. "I really didn't expect him to stick around once I was with you fellas."

Not so different from Nick Bonadio after all. Just as he'd suspected.

"When was the last time you saw him?" Doug asked.

"Gosh, it was probably last summer sometime."

"No—when was the last time you saw him *last night*."

She shrugged. "Like I told that house detective, I don't really remember. Maybe twenty or thirty minutes before I saw him dead on the ground?"

"What was he doing then?"

Her eyes narrowed. "Why do you want to know?"

"I'm trying to find out what happened last night."

She waved a hand in the air and grinned at him. "Oh honey, let the police handle all that."

"The police have arrested my friend, the one who found him on the ground."

Her eyes widened. "The sweet one with the glasses? Aww, that *is* a shame. I never would have pegged him for the type."

Doug shook his head emphatically. "He isn't. And he doesn't have a motive, anyway. The police are focusing on him because he was seen with Mr. Lockhart five minutes before he was found dead. His suit got torn, and so they've speculated that he and Mr. Lockhart were fighting."

"They were fighting, and then Jimmy got thrown out the window," Dolores finished for him.

"That's the angle the police are taking," Doug said. "But I think there was more going on. That's why I'm asking what Mr. Lockhart was doing the last time you saw him."

She pursed her lips, looked up in thought. "He was talking with that other jockey, the little British one."

Doug's pulse quickened. "Where was that?"

"At the upstairs bar, in the ballroom."

Doug didn't hide his surprise. "Not the third-floor roulette tables?"

She shook her head. "No, but I'd seen Jimmy up there earlier."

"When you saw him with Mr. Chapman—the other jockey--did they look like they were arguing?"

She shrugged. "I don't know. I mean, I didn't hear them shouting or anything."

"Did they seem tense?"

She shrugged again. "I'm not sure. I didn't really pay them much mind."

Doug nodded. That made perfect sense. He took a deep breath and considered how best to address his real question.

"When was the last time you saw my friend Stuart?" he asked, hoping that would lead them to the subject of the rose garden.

"Was he the one with the glasses?" she asked.

"Yes, the one who was crouched beside the body when we all came running toward your screams."

"So you mean the last time I saw him before that? It was a minute or two before, outside the front door of the club. He went running past me. He was in a big hurry, for some reason. Ran around the corner of the house."

Doug's breath stopped. He swallowed hard, and it resumed short and fast. *What in the hell were you running from, Stu?* "This was outside the front door, you say?"

"That's right."

He gave her a dubious look. "Were you leaving?"

"No, not that early." She waved a dismissive hand in the air. "No cabs after curfew even if I wanted to leave. It was getting stuffy inside, so I went out for some air. I know the bouncers, they let me go outside when it's warm like that."

"When you saw my friend running, did you follow him? Is that how you found him with Mr. Lockhart's body?"

She smiled and shook her head. "Not exactly. I mean, I *was* curious what he was running for, but Del Monte's rose gardens are some of the best in Shanghai, so I wanted to see them in the moonlight. It just happened to be the same place he'd run to."

Something about that still seemed off, but Doug wasn't quite sure what. He let it go for now.

"Thank you, Miss Moody. I appreciate your help. Good day."

She hurried to the door after him. "Tell your tall handsome friend— Mr. Farnsworth, was it?—I wouldn't mind a visit from him sometime. A nice, good-lookin' fella like that, and with prospects, too? A girl's gotta keep that one around." She handed Doug a business card. "I have a telephone, tell him to call me sometime. Strictly personal, no charge." She winked and closed the door.

**

"Learn anything interesting?" Lucy asked when he walked through the door. She was sitting on the couch, a book open on her belly; she put a bookmark in it and set it on the end table, and gave him her full attention.

He took off his hat and shook the rain drops from it. "Yes, but it's not good."

He leaned down to kiss her, then removed his suit jacket, damp at the shoulders. It had been such a beautiful sunny day this morning, when he biked to Del Monte's and back; but in Shanghai, spring rains are possible at any time, and the odds caught up with him while he rode home in a rickshaw from Dolores Moody's place.

"How bad is it?" she asked, concerned.

73

He explained about Dolores seeing Stuart run from the club, and hurry around the corner toward the rose garden.

"Did she tell that to the police?"

"I'm not sure," Doug said. Damn it, he should have asked that. "Kenny can find that out, though. The police have to give him all of their evidence."

"Do you believe her?"

Doug thought about that for a second. "I think so, yes."

"You don't sound too certain."

He frowned. "I got the feeling there was more to the story than that. There's something off about her following Stuart to the rose garden, but I can't put my finger on what it is."

"Oh Doug, really!" Lucy shook her head in a tsk-tsk sort of way. "A woman does not go walking by herself in the dark to look at a rose garden, no matter how spectacular they're supposed to be. And how well would she see them at night anyway? Besides, it's too early for roses."

Doug's cheeks warmed. "Roses bloom in May, don't they?"

She nodded. "But the most important part of what I just told you is that a woman would *never* go walking in the dark by herself. *Ever.*"

Doug frowned at that. "She must have had a reason, because that's exactly what she did."

She arched an eyebrow at him. "Such as checking to see if the man she just threw out the window was dead or not? And if she saw Stuart running toward where the body landed, then she *had* to get there so she could scream and throw everyone off her trail."

Doug realized his mouth was hanging open. He closed it and looked away, embarrassed. He should have thought of all that. "I told you something about it felt off," he muttered.

She folded her arms. "You never considered that a woman might have done it, did you? Women aren't strong enough, huh? If Jimmy

Lockhart was as little as I understand horse jockeys to be, then *I* could have thrown him out the window even in my condition."

The phone rang just then, saving him from an awkward follow-up. He answered on the second ring. "Hello?" first in English, then in Shanghainese.

"Doug, it's Kenny."

"How's Stuart holding up?"

"He's better now. I reassured him we'll get him out of there in the morning, when we have his bail hearing."

Doug's heart went out to Stuart; two nights in jail was twice as long as he'd spent there, and that had been torture. "I located Dolores Moody, but I don't think she helped us any. Probably the opposite, in fact." He recounted the conversation.

"Damn," Kenny muttered.

"Did Stuart tell you why he was there, why he was alone when he found Jimmy Lockhart?"

The line was silent a few seconds. "I'm afraid I can't tell you what Stuart told me, Doug. It's a privileged conversation. I haven't told him yet that you're helping us out—but once I get him out on bail tomorrow we can all sit down together and hash everything out. Do you have any free time in your work schedule?"

Doug suppressed his irritation. "I can make time. When is the bail hearing?"

"Eight-thirty. I'm not sure how many other defendants will be on the docket, so it's hard to say how long it will take. I'll call your office when we're finished." The line clicked off.

Attorney Kenny was not as effusively friendly as regular Kenny.

Lucy was looking at him in expectation, so he told her what Kenny said.

"Why wouldn't he have told Stuart right away that you're helping?" she asked, brows knit in confusion. "I would think that would reassure him everything's going to be fine."

Doug shook his head and shrugged. "I thought the same. Maybe he forgot because he's exhausted. I don't think he got much sleep."

She sighed. "No, probably not. Poor Kenny. Maybe he'll get some rest now, sleep away the afternoon. Speaking of which, it's my nap time."

She pushed herself up from the chair with effort, arching her back to push her belly forward as she did. Then she took his hand. "Bao's out for the afternoon. You could join me." The look in her eye said sleep could wait. "I've been told it's good for me, and might even prompt labor."

Doug grinned. "No need to ask me twice."

7

Monday, April 11

"Doug's helping us figure out who really killed Mr. Lockhart, Stu," Kenny said when they had all gathered in his office late in the morning.

"I have a little experience," Doug explained in response to Stuart's questioning look. He was sitting on the corner of Kenny's desk. This was his first look at Stuart since they found Lockhart's body; his suit jacket was indeed torn, and a corner of his front pocket hung loose. He sat in a wooden chair, wiping his glasses on his pants.

"Oh, I suppose you do." Stuart pushed his glasses up his nose. "You figured out who killed that sailor from your ship."

"Seaman Bonadio."

Kenny continued, all business. "Doug already talked with Dolores Moody—the woman who screamed when she saw you beside Mr. Lockhart's body—and she told him she saw you running that direction a couple of minutes before then. Why don't you tell Doug what happened that night, and why you were there?"

Stuart swallowed and nodded, wiping his palms on the thighs of his pants. "I'd been sitting at the roulette table for a while, and I'd had a couple of drinks while I was there, so by the time I gave up my seat I really had to go." He looked up at Doug. "You saw me, Doug. We passed each other at the bathroom door."

Doug nodded. "I heard Jimmy Lockhart tell you to scram."

Stuart flushed. "Yeah, he was real angry. I guess he and Mark Chapman were arguing about something. You must have heard them?"

77

Doug shook his head. "Not really. They stopped when I entered. But it was easy to tell they were having a disagreement."

Stuart nodded.

"Go on," Kenny prodded. "Tell him the rest."

"I would've just left, but I really had to go, you see. So I told him I'd only be a minute, and I started toward the stall. He grabbed me by the lapel and told me I had to leave, now." Stuart stopped, swallowed hard, his eyes looking far away. "I told him I'd be quick, I just really had to go bad, but he started shaking me. He said, 'You got potatoes in your ears? I said scram!' So I did. I hurried down to the next floor, where the ballroom was, but there was a line for the men's room.

"Ordinarily, I'd just wait, but I *really* had to go. So I hurried down to the ground floor. There was one fella in line there, which wouldn't be so bad, except I was starting to get scared I'd pee my pants. That's why I ran out the front door. I figured I'd find a bush somewhere, no one would see. I ran around the side of the house to get some privacy. It was dark, and I didn't see anybody around, so I found a bush by the wall and did my business."

Doug nodded. He'd have likely done the same thing in his shoes. "Is that when Lockhart came flying out the window?"

Stuart nodded, his eyes wide at the memory. "I kind of saw it out of the corner of my eye. And I heard the thud right behind me, maybe ten feet away."

"And that's when you knelt beside him?"

Stuart shook his head. "Not right away."

Doug frowned. "Why would you wait?"

Stuart flushed again. "I wasn't finished."

Doug's mouth opened, but it took him a second to form the words. "You weren't *finished*? Stu, a man fell out of the window, and you *waited* to go see if he was alive? If he needed help?"

Bright red splotches appeared at the tops of Stuart's cheeks, his brow knit tight, and his eyes narrowed. His hands fisted and pounded against his knees.

"Damn it, I was in mid-stream, Douggie! What the hell was I supposed to do, pee on the body?"

Doug's throat tightened, suppressing a laugh. He looked away from Stuart toward Kenny, hoping that would help. Kenny's serious demeanor remained, mostly, but his lips had tightened into a thin line, and the corners twitched.

Doug lost it, laughing out loud. Kenny lost it a second later, and they both howled with laughter.

"Assholes!" Stuart said, crossing his arms. But then he began to laugh as well.

A minute later, wiping the tears from the corner of his eyes, still chuckling, Doug cleared his throat. "How long did it take you to, um, finish?" he managed. Then he burst into laughter again. Kenny laughed again, too.

Stuart told them what they could go do to themselves.

"I'm sorry, buddy," Doug said when the laughter subsided again. "But in seriousness, how long did it take before you went over to look at the body?"

Stuart shrugged. "I don't know, twenty or thirty seconds?"

"What did you do?"

Stuart was quiet for a few seconds. "I kind of stood there for a minute, staring at him. It's like at first I couldn't really understand what I was looking at. Like it took a bit to sink in. Once I realized it was a man, I got down beside him, and put my fingers on his neck. You know, to see if he had a pulse."

"Was there one?" Doug asked.

Stuart shook his head.

"How long was it before Dolores Moody found you?"

"I looked up then, right after I checked the pulse, and I saw her standing there. She hadn't been there a few seconds before, I'm sure of that. It was dark, but it wasn't *that* dark. There was some moonlight."

"What was she doing?"

"She had her mouth open. She looked from the body to me, like she wanted to say something, but then she looked back at the body and started screaming."

*

"The biggest piece of evidence the police have tying Stuart to the murder is that his handkerchief was stuffed in Jimmy Lockhart's mouth," Kenny said. "That was the prosecutor's main argument for high bail. He hit our blind side with that. The police hadn't told me." His words carried a bitter bite.

Doug exhaled hard. Now he understood why Stuart had been arrested—his presence beside the body had seemed pretty flimsy grounds on its own, given that the crime hadn't occurred there. And even the torn suit was a pretty weak link. But his handkerchief in the victim's mouth? That was more damning.

"That's bad," he said, wiping a hand across his face and sighing. He kept his hand on his chin, elbow on his other arm crossed over his chest, and looked at Stuart. "Do you have any explanation for how your handkerchief got in his mouth?"

"I keep it in this pocket," Stuart said, poking a finger at the flap hanging loose from his jacket. "It must have fallen out when he shook me."

Of course! Doug's pulse quickened, and he looked at Kenny. "And Mark Chapman was there to pick it up."

Kenny nodded. "We need to find Mr. Chapman and have a chat with him."

Doug looked at Stuart. "Did he give you his address or telephone number? I know you gave him yours."

Stuart looked pained. "No, he was going to call me when he had the stable pass." His voice trailed off, and he looked down.

"What is it?" Doug asked.

Stuart's face screwed up, and then he shook his head. "I can't believe he'd do that to me. He was such a nice fella. He didn't have to offer me a stable pass, you know. That's pretty damned extraordinary. So why would he want to frame me for killing Jimmy Lockhart? It just doesn't seem right."

"Maybe he wasn't trying to frame you, necessarily," Kenny suggested. "It might have been a means to an end. He saw your handkerchief and stuffed it in Mr. Lockhart's mouth so no one would hear him scream. The provenance of that handkerchief might have been unimportant at the time."

Doug nodded in agreement. "That seems likely to me. If it was a crime of passion, as it seems, then he wouldn't have been thinking ahead. No time for that. His only thought for getting away with it was probably just to keep anyone from hearing."

Stuart looked relieved, and his posture relaxed.

Doug found that a little strange. But Stuart was a fan of the horse races, after all, and he'd been excited to talk with Mark Chapman, even before Chapman offered the stable pass. His new star hadn't betrayed him. And that was important to him.

Kenny looked at Doug. "Any idea how we can find Mr. Chapman?"

Doug took a breath, nodded. Jonesy would know how. Doug still hated asking him for favors, but he had to admit that reporter could find just about anyone.

"Let me talk to Jonesy. And if he can't help us, maybe we can talk our way into the stables. It might be good to talk to the other jockeys, anyway. We'll want to hear what they have to say about Mark Chapman's and Jimmy Lockhart's relationship off the track."

Kenny nodded vigorously. "Excellent idea! I'm sure they've seen and heard things that we could use."

*

Doug used Kenny's office phone, and asked the Chinese operator to connect him with the residence of Arthur Jones uptown.

After ten rings, she told him there was no answer, and so he asked her to call the Associated Press office downtown.

A woman's voice answered. "Associated Press Shanghai."

"Hello, is this Mrs. Thompson? This is Doug Bainbridge, calling for Jonesy."

"Oh, hello, Mr. Bainbridge. Yes, this is Gladys Thompson. Jonesy's out, but he did check in this morning for a little while. I expect he's lunching at the Cathay as usual."

Doug looked at his watch. Ten minutes past noon. But he could be at the Cathay in ten minutes.

"Would you like to leave a message?"

"No, thank you. I'll see if I can find him at the Cathay. I'll call back if I can't."

He hung up, and turned to Kenny. "I'm off to the Cathay. Want to join me?"

"Yes, I'll come." Kenny said that so quickly, Doug had barely finished the question.

Stuart stood. "I need to go home and clean up so I can get to the bank. Pete's going to need me at work this afternoon."

"I'm sure he'll understand if you take the day off, after what you've been through," Doug said, putting a hand on Stuart's shoulder.

"I've already missed the morning," Stuart said. "Beside, I'd like to get back to normal."

Doug nodded. "I understand. Take care of yourself, buddy."

**

Doug and Kenny found Jonesy sitting at his usual place at the bar on the ground floor of the Cathay. The big luxury hotel was one of the few places in Shanghai with air conditioning, and it was already turned on this early in the season. The sudden chill made Doug shiver after passing through the revolving door.

"Douglas! What an unexpected pleasure. I don't think I've seen you since you got back from Nanking in December."

"I've been away most of that time."

Jonesy chuckled. "I already know that. I see Lucy around town from time to time, and she always gives me the skinny on what you're doing."

Jonesy always had a way of knowing. That's why Doug relied on him sometimes. But it was also occasionally disconcerting.

"Now Kenneth here I just saw a few days ago, at the men's pool."

Kenny's cheeks flushed, and he laughed a touch too hard. "That's right."

An amused twinkle lit Jonesy's green eyes, and a wry half-smile turned up a corner of his mouth.

The swimming pools inside the Administrative Building at the Recreation Grounds were old-fashioned affairs that were segregated by sex, bathing suits not permitted. The kind of thing they'd all grown up with twenty years ago, but which was rare these days. Kenny's embarrassment was probably that he and Jonesy had encountered each other naked.

Jonesy looked from Kenny to Doug. "What brings you two gents here to see me?"

Doug took a seat on the stool next to Jonesy, and Kenny took the one on Jonesy's opposite side. "We need to find someone, and I figure you're the best person to help us do that."

Jonesy chuckled. "You're a smart one. And you know I can never say no to you, Douglas."

He winked, and Doug sighed. Jonesy was always saying and doing things like that to him.

"But at least tell me the reason my services are needed. Will I get a story out of it? Or is it just a personal favor?"

Doug looked around Jonesy to Kenny, who nodded. Doug turned back to Jonesy. "Both. Our friend Stuart has been arrested for killing a man out in the Western Roads district. He didn't do it, and we have someone who we think might have done it."

"Out in the Badlands, huh?"

Doug gave him a questioning look.

"That's what folks are starting to call it out there," Jonesy said. "Probably for a couple of reasons—the Jap occupation forces are harsh with the Chinese, so it's a bad place to go if you're a Chinese resident of the Settlement; and second, there's a crime wave out there, now that the gangsters have set up shop."

Doug didn't hide his surprise at that.

Jonesy chuckled again. "That's right, you haven't read the papers for three months." He drank the last dregs of his martini, and raised the empty glass toward the young Chinese bartender, who bobbed his head and started mixing another. Doug ordered tea, and Kenny did the same.

Jonesy popped the last olive in his mouth. "Since the Japs took over the whole area, the Green Gang's lost their hold on power in the underworld. They always had rivals, of course—Shanghai's a pretty big oyster—but they had official protection, with Big-eared Du's connections to Chiang Kai-shek and all that. Well *that* all went up in smoke as soon as the Japs surrounded the Settlement and French Concession. We're kind of an island now, you know.

"Anyway, Du himself lit out before the Japs could surround us. Word has it he's down in Hong Kong, but keeping in contact with Dai Li."

Doug suppressed the automatic revulsion he felt at the mention of Dai Li, the infamous head of China's secret police. A brutal man, and a brutal organization. He'd had a run-in with some of Dai's henchmen a couple of years before.

Jonesy paused while the bartender set his new martini in front of him, and then continued. "With Du gone, and the *Juntong* gone, the rival gangs and gambling operations have elbowed their way in. And the Badlands are where they're doing it."

A few puzzle pieces seemed to fall into place—the roulette tables and craps game upstairs at Del Monte's, the white 'house detective' in the Chinese municipality. "I take it the police have been recruiting pretty hard out there as a result."

Jonesy snorted. "In the Chinese part of the city? Not a chance. They're just trying to keep the Japs happy, and as long as the victim isn't Japanese, the crime gets shoved to the side. That's why the bigshots along the Western Roads have hired their own protection. It's all extralegal, of course, and they've hired some nasty characters to be their enforcers."

That explained 'Detective' Russell's scruffy appearance. He was a mercenary, it seemed.

"Did you know that?" Doug asked Kenny.

Kenny looked embarrassed and shook his head. He looked away and sipped his tea.

"That gets you up to speed, Douglas. Now tell me who you want me to find."

"A horse jockey named Mark Chapman."

"That should be easy enough," Jonesy said. "Spring season's going, and my press pass gets me into the stables on race days. The winning owners and trainers are always eager to talk to a reporter. Mind if I ask why you want to find this Mark Chapman?"

That was a fair question. Doug glanced around to make sure no one was eavesdropping on them, leaned close and said quietly, "We think there's a good chance he's the killer."

Jonesy's eyebrows shot up, and he nodded appreciatively. "You don't say? Far be it from me to doubt your deductive powers, Doug, given all your experience with solving murders."

Doug ignored the subtle jab.

"Better fill me in on why you two think he's the killer."

Doug recounted the interactions he witnessed between Mark Chapman and Jimmy Lockhart.

"It's a decent theory," Jonesy said, though his tone told Doug he wasn't entirely convinced.

"What are you thinking?" He watched Jonesy closely and scrutinized every detail of his expression, to no avail. The man had the world's best poker face.

Jonesy exhaled hard through his nose. "Sounds to me like both men were caught up in something. Fixing races, maybe? That would be a first. But if so, any number of nasty characters might have wanted Jimmy Lockhart dead."

8

The bartender set their bills on the bar in front of each of them, but Kenny jumped up and grabbed Doug's. "My treat. For your birthday." Then he grinned. "You thought I forgot, didn't you?"

Doug didn't admit that he'd thought exactly that.

"It's your birthday today?" Jonesy said, face lighting up. "And you didn't say nothing?"

Doug shrugged. "I don't make a big deal out of it."

"Well, happy birthday anyway," Jonesy said, and raised his martini glass in a salute before finishing the last little bit of it. "How old are you now?"

"Twenty-eight."

"Twenty-eight, huh?" Jonesy wore a strange sort of smile. Then he put his fingers around Doug's chin and shook it gently. "Just a young'un still. I remember being twenty-eight...fifteen years ago."

It was a remarkably frank statement from Jonesy. Doug wasn't sure if he'd ever known the stocky reporter's exact age, though forty-three was about what he would have guessed.

Jonesy turned toward Kenny. "And how old are you? Older than twenty-eight, I hope." The two martinis had obviously loosened his lips.

"Twenty-nine," Kenny said, with a sheepish sort of smile creeping across his mouth.

Jonesy chuckled, looking down at his empty lunch plate and shaking his head. "Young'uns."

Doug wasn't really sure what to make of Jonesy's reaction. He didn't sound mocking, though the words might be interpreted that way.

87

And the little bit of evidence he'd seen told him that Jonesy's interests lay with men in their twenties…

He put that thought out of his mind right away.

Jonesy stood, picked up his bowler hat. "Well, gents, I'd best be going. I've got a lead on a story I'm working on, so I'm headed out to Yangtzepoo this afternoon. But I might have some time later to stop by the stables on my way home and see who's around. Which one of you should I call if I learn anything useful?"

"Kenny's in charge," Doug said, happy to pawn Jonesy off on his friend.

Jonesy nodded to Kenny. "I'll be in touch." And he marched off toward the lobby.

Doug grabbed his hat. "I've got to change back into my uniform, and get back to the office. I've been gone more than two hours." Not that anyone in the Navy's Yangtze Patrol office would pay that much mind. He was the only Intelligence Officer based there, and none of the staff had much idea what his work entailed.

"I've got work waiting for me as well," Kenny said, accompanying Doug through the cavernous lobby toward the brass friezes framing the revolving door out to Nanking Road. "I'm working several cases already for the British Court, and I haven't touched them all morning. I'm afraid it's going to be a long day for me."

Outside the door, they bid each other good afternoon, and parted ways—Doug heading for the Bund, Kenny hailing an empty rickshaw heading uptown.

From the corner of the Bund, Doug looked back to make sure Kenny got far away before he turned north instead of south. He wasn't going to the office.

**

Multitudes of Japanese seamen and marines wandered up and down the riverfront in the Hongkou district, in the northern part of the International Settlement. The wharfs here were occupied by Japanese naval vessels, ostensibly there to protect the Japanese civilian population, Japantown lying only a few blocks inland from here. In effect, Hongkou was the only part of the Settlement under Japanese occupation, though unofficial.

Several groups of Japanese marines eyed Doug suspiciously as he walked east down Broadway, though none bothered him. The American consulate was here, for one thing, between the Soviet and Japanese consulates; and since the invasion last August, American marines stood guard in front of the consulate, and on its roof. He would be inconspicuous at least as far as the bridge over Hongkou Creek.

The teahouse grew silent the moment Doug walked through the door. Dozens of Chinese faces stared openly at him for several seconds before resuming their conversations in several languages.

"What wantchee?" asked a rail-thin woman of about forty in a blue tunic, with long hair woven into a single braid down her back.

"Oolong tea, please," Doug said in English. He wasn't about to let on that he spoke Shanghainese, let alone Mandarin and Cantonese.

He sat at a table with his copy of this morning's Shanghai Times—the English-language paper—and listened to the Chinese conversations around him. Maybe today he'd hear something useful.

And maybe today someone would accept his offer to work for him.

**

Back at his office, Doug stared at the little brass clock on his desk. Only quarter to four. He sighed in boredom, all of his necessary tasks long finished.

It had been quiet in the Navy's Yang Pat office since he returned from Manila. The staff there said it had been this way since the start of the year. With the Japanese in control of the lower Yangtze valley, international trade along the river had slowed, leaving the American gunboats with little to do on their patrols. And with the main fighting having moved hundreds of miles inland, the army's Military Attaché from the American Embassy—now in Hankow with the Chinese government after it fled Nanjing—was the main source of observations on Japanese maneuvers.

In a switch, Doug now preferred his work onboard ship while they were away. At least he wasn't bored then. But everyone else in the Navy office was often bored as well, so at least he wasn't alone in that. Though everyone was magically busy whenever Captain Jansen was around.

Doug got a piece of paper and drew a chart, similar to the one he'd made for his investigation of Nick Bonadio's murder last summer, and started filling in the squares with suspects.

First on the list was Mark Chapman. His motive was still hazy, but it was clear that *something* was there. And he was the last one known to have seen Jimmy Lockhart alive, in the very spot where someone threw him from the window. Both of those combined to make him the prime suspect; but Doug left blank space for what Jonesy learned.

And he found himself wondering if Jonesy were at the stables now.

But what if it wasn't Mark Chapman? That niggling thought urged him to think of other possibilities. *Don't put all of your eggs in one basket.* He sat there for several minutes, thinking over who else might have had a motive for killing Jimmy Lockhart. Jonesy had hinted at underworld operatives fixing the horse races. He put that down at the bottom of the chart. Too much speculation to take seriously just yet, but he wouldn't ignore it.

He put Dolores Moody down below Mark Chapman. He didn't think she'd done it, but it was too soon to rule her out. There was something she wasn't saying, that much was certain. But motive? He put a great big question mark there.

But then he thought of Nick Bonadio's behavior toward Lola Cunningham last summer. He'd gotten a vaguely similar feeling from Jimmy Lockhart—but something about that felt off. Lockhart didn't seem as single-minded in his pursuit. Or at least, Doug hadn't seen any evidence that he was. But he hardly knew Jimmy Lockhart at all, in contrast to Nick. He jotted down a note to find out more about that.

After another moment's thought, he put down Mr. Yang. He didn't have any concrete reason, but something about the way the rich out there had hired their own "protection," combined with the fact that Mr. Yang had seemed chummy with the Japanese military police, told him not to overlook Mr. Yang.

He stared at the chart, at all of the blank squares remaining. But maybe he didn't need to fill those. Maybe the four suspects he'd written down—three names and one unknown underworld operator—maybe that was it. Most likely the killer's name was already staring him in the face.

He looked at the desk clock. Three minutes after four. That whole exercise hadn't even taken twenty minutes.

It was his birthday, damn it, and he would just leave work early.

He folded the chart and stuffed it in his jacket pocket, grabbed his hat, and glanced down the hall toward Captain Jansen's office. The lieutenant who served as the captain's adjutant was sitting at the desk, looking bored. The door behind him was open, and the captain's desk was unoccupied, the office dark. Doug nodded to himself, locked his door, and strode from the Navy office. He told the lieutenant at the front desk as he passed, "If anyone calls for me, I'll be back in the morning."

9

Tuesday, April 12

The intercom buzzed on Doug's desk shortly after nine o'clock, and the front desk lieutenant said, "A Mr. Art Jones to see you, Commander."

"I'll be right out." Doug grabbed his hat, intending to talk with Jonesy outside of the Navy office.

"Good morning, *Commander*." The twinkle in Jonesy's green eyes said that he never tired of stressing that word. The few times he'd encountered Doug in uniform, anyway.

"Morning, Jonesy. Let's take a walk." Out in the corridor, he walked toward the stairs, but Jonesy pushed the call button for the elevator. With a sigh, Doug stepped back to wait with him.

After the elderly Chinese elevator operator deposited them on the ground floor, Doug asked, "What did you learn at the stables?"

"That everyone there was Jimmy Lockhart's best friend, of course," Jonesy said with a huff, and pushed open the door, stepping through to the sidewalk on the Bund. They started walking. "Funny how when a man dies, everyone remembers him fondly, and conveniently forgets how much they hated his guts when he was still breathing."

"'Don't speak ill of the dead.' It's ingrained in us."

"Whatever you say," Jonesy muttered. "But *I've* known some fellas I wasn't sorry to see end up in a coffin. And that's all I'll say on that."

Doug let that go. "Did you learn anything helpful?"

"I think so. Most of the men at the stables didn't think there was anything special about Lockhart's relationship with Mark Chapman.

Described them as competitors, cordial if not friendly. But then I talked to this trainer named Justin McCormack—a young fella, maybe thirty-five years old tops, not my age or older like most horse trainers—and he overheard some pretty interesting things recently, when Lockhart and Chapman didn't know anyone was around."

Doug's pulse quickened. "What did he hear?"

"Something about there being a lot of money in it if you kept your damn mouth shut." Jonesy gave Doug an 'I told you so' kind of look, nodding. "What did I say about race fixing? This would fit, huh? McCormack didn't have a whole lot of specifics, unfortunately; the conversation was almost over, and they left shortly after that."

"Which one of them was it that said there was a lot of money in something?" Doug asked.

"Lockhart."

Interesting. But Lockhart was the one that had lost a few sure-things recently, not Chapman. Something seemed off. "How recent was that?"

"He couldn't remember exactly how long ago, but thought maybe a few days before opening day. I'm tellin' ya, they were fixing races, and taking a cut of someone's winnings."

Doug thought about that for a moment. "But we don't know why they were arguing about it on Saturday night at Del Monte's."

Jonesy shrugged. "Maybe Chapman changed his mind, wasn't going to throw any more races."

Doug frowned. "But Chapman won his last two races."

"Maybe he wasn't supposed to win them," Jonesy suggested.

"Hmmm," Doug murmured, doubtful. "Don't those gangster types break someone's legs for not following the program? If Mark Chapman was supposed to throw a race, but he won it instead, wouldn't it make more sense for *him* to have been the one tossed out the window, and not Lockhart?"

Jonesy was silent for a moment. Doug quietly enjoyed having stumped the great Art Jones.

"What if Lockhart was sent to warn Chapman to get back in the game, or else?" Jonesy suggested. "And what if Chapman wasn't having it, and things got rough. Next thing you know, Lockhart's flying out the window."

Doug took a breath, considering that. "If so, then Mark Chapman is in serious danger."

Jonesy stopped in his tracks. "He wasn't at the track today. I never found him."

**

"Now let me get this straight, Mr. Bainbridge—you don't *know* if a man is missing or not, you just want us to check if he is? Did I get that right, sir?"

The voice on the other end of the line, somewhere between an English and a Scottish accent, belonged to Detective Inspector Wallace of the Gordon Street police station uptown. Doug had worked with DI Wallace on a couple of previous occasions, and Wallace was an honest cop.

Doug cringed as much at the awkward truth implied as at Wallace's mocking tone. "Yes, that's correct—but we have good reason to suspect that something might have happened to Mr. Chapman. Doesn't what I've told you give you probable cause to at least check on him?"

"It's pretty flimsy, I'm afraid, sir."

Doug couldn't really argue with that. "Can you at least put an alert out for his neighborhood patrol to watch for him?"

"But you don't know his address, or what neighborhood he lives in."

Doug sighed. "No, we don't. I'd hoped you would have access to those records."

"I could, if I knew a crime had been committed," Wallace said. "It's a bit awkward to call up the municipal records department asking for the address of someone who may or may not have been a victim of a crime that may or may not have happened."

Doug nodded in silence, resigned. "Thank you, Detective Inspector. We'll find another way."

He hung up the receiver and leaned back in his office chair. He steepled his fingers under his chin and sat in thought for a moment. Jonesy probably had someone at the municipal records office who owed him a favor. He seemed to have those contacts all over the city.

He picked up the receiver, and asked the front desk lieutenant for an outside operator. He asked the operator for the residence of Arthur Jones uptown.

Jonesy picked up on the third ring. "Hello?"

"Jonesy, it's Doug. Is there any chance you know someone at the Municipal Records Office who could find the address where Mark Chapman lives?"

Jonesy exhaled hard. "Yeah, I know someone down at the Municipal Records Office who's helped me out a few times—but I owe him a favor, and not the other way around. I'll have to see if I can sweet-talk someone into giving me the address."

Doug looked at the desk clock—it was already after four-thirty. "When do you think that might be?"

"I can try to do it tomorrow, but it might have to be Thursday."

That would have to do. *Don't look a gift horse in the mouth.* He hated how often his father's pet sayings sprang to mind these days. The perils of getting older. "That would be swell. Thanks, Jonesy."

**

Stuart and Fred walked out the front of the HSBC building on the Bund a couple of minutes past five o'clock. Doug was waiting for them on the sidewalk, and they looked surprised to see him.

"Are you waiting for one of us? Or for Pete?" Fred asked.

"For Stuart, actually," Doug said. "I need to ask if you've heard from Mark Chapman at all since Saturday night."

Stuart shook his head. "No. Not yet." That second part sounded hopeful. "Why do you ask?"

"I wondered if he'd arranged for that stable pass he offered you." The looks on their faces told Doug they didn't buy that as the only reason he asked, so after a couple of seconds he added, "Kenny and I really need to speak with him, but we don't have any idea where to find him. We had someone look for him at the stables today, but he wasn't there."

Stuart shrugged. "Maybe he didn't have any reason to be there. I don't think they go every day. I'm sure he'll show up there soon, in the next day or two anyway."

Doug put on a reassuring smile. "I'm sure he will." No need to worry Stuart with their concerns for Chapman's safety. They'd deal with that later, if they had to. "What are you fellas up to this evening?"

"I'm meeting Liling and her friends for a couple of drinks before dinner," Fred said. "Both of you can join us if you'd like."

"Yeah, I'll go," Stuart said.

Doug would normally decline, and go home to dinner with Lucy and Bao; but it might be good to have a chat with Yang Liling, and any friends she had with her who had also been at Del Monte's on Saturday night.

"Where, and at what time?"

"The Majestic, at seven," Fred said.

That gave Doug a couple of hours to go home. "Mind if I ask Lucy if she'd like to come along? She might not, but I'd like to offer."

"Sure, that would be swell!" Fred said, lighting up. "We love spending time with Lucy, and she hasn't met Liling yet."

Doug chuckled. "I will offer that as an incentive. See you boys at seven."

**

The look that crossed Lucy's face at first seemed doubtful—it would be tiring for her, he was sure—but then she smiled and said,

97

"Sure, why not? It would be good to get out of the house for a bit. Are we coming home for dinner after? I'll have to tell Bao if we're not."

He nodded. "Yes, it's just before-dinner drinks. I'll tell Bao we can be home by eight."

**

There was a moderate sized crowd at the Majestic Café Ballroom that evening, and Doug and Lucy had no trouble finding Fred and Stuart at the bar.

One of several popular upscale nightclubs on Bubbling Well Road uptown, the Majestic was unique in that it catered to a mostly, though not exclusively, Chinese crowd. It was famous across the city for its dance hostesses—popularly known as "dollar girls"—and as such it was also popular with visiting seamen of multiple navies. They contrasted with the well-dressed Chinese patrons, but it was still early in the evening for the seamen to have arrived.

Which was just as well, in Doug's opinion. The atmosphere at the Majestic was much more relaxed before the not-so-friendly competition for dance hostesses began. The competition was known to sometimes devolve into scuffles, usually quickly handled by the Majestic's big bouncers; but Doug had been here last July when its most notorious brawl had broken out between American and Italian seamen. People across the city still talked about that one.

"Doug, Lucy, you made it!" Fred exclaimed, beaming. He seemed to already be a drink in, and that always relaxed his usual reserve. "Doug, you remember Liling. Lucy, I'd like to introduce you to my girlfriend, Yang Liling. Liling, this is Lucy Bainbridge, Doug's wife."

"How do you do?" Lucy asked.

"Very well, thank you," Liling said in perfect English. "It is a pleasure to make your acquaintance, Mrs. Bainbridge. I have heard much about all of you."

"Please call me Lucy."

"Thank you. And you may call me Liling." Liling bowed her head, a hint of smile gracing her red-painted lips. "Please allow me to introduce my friends, Yang Yajun, and Pan Yintao."

Yang Yajun made a slight bow, expression demure, but kept her mouth closed. Pan Yintao, on the other hand, stepped forward boldly and held her hand out to Lucy, wrist up. Lucy took Pan Yintao's fingers in hers and gave them a light shake.

"You are very forward thinking, madam," Pan Yintao said in heavily accented English. "Not many women are brave enough to come out in public in your condition." She gave Lucy a broad smile, but there was a devilish gleam in her dark eyes that suggested it was intended as a back-handed compliment.

Lucy, however, was always pleased to be called forward thinking, regardless of the intent. She smiled back, pretending to be unaware. "Why, thank you! That's kind of you to say. I am grateful that we have more freedoms than our mothers, aren't you?"

Doug suppressed a laugh. His wife was good at this. Julia had once learned that the hard way, when they first met.

A frosty look crossed Pan Yintao's eyes, and though her smile never wavered it now seemed stiff. "You will find no one more modern than me."

In a manner of speaking, Doug thought, suppressing the urge to snort at Pan Yintao's statement.

She turned away then, and cast a withering look at Doug's gray suit before strutting back to the bar with Yang Yajun, where a handsome young Chinese man in a black tuxedo stood with three beverages.

Stuart rolled his eyes with an ever so slight shake of his head. Fred and Liling were too wrapped up in talking with each other to have noticed the exchange.

Lucy leaned toward Doug. "Is she actually...?"

"Yes, I believe so."

Lucy nodded appreciatively, which caught Doug by surprise. "She's a very good one, I'll say that. I almost didn't realize at first."

"It doesn't shock you?" Doug asked, though he really shouldn't have been surprised by that.

"Not at all!" Lucy said it as if it were the most obvious thing in the world. "You know I've spent a lot of weekends in New York, whenever my friends and I could get away from Vassar for a couple of days."

"Of course I know that. Can I infer from the reference that you've encountered female impersonators in New York?"

"You may so infer." She leaned in again, a gleam in her eyes and a devilish smile on her lips, like a woman about to dish the juiciest gossip, though gossip wasn't really Lucy's style. "They have these big events called 'Drag Balls' in the East Village, where hundreds of homosexuals would dress in women's evening wear and dance with men in tuxedos. My friends and I often saw a parade of them leaving those venues late at night and strutting *en masse* toward the dive bars in Greenwich Village. You know we loved the cafés and dive bars in the Village. Such freedom! That's where I learned to smoke cigarettes."

She slipped one into her cigarette holder, and Doug struck a match. "I've talked to plenty of those 'drag queens,' as they call themselves; and let me tell you, Douglas Bainbridge, the things they know about fashion and make-up would rival any grand dame on Fifth Avenue."

He had to smile. "You are truly something, you know that?"

"Of course I know that. I'm just happy to have found a man who appreciates that."

Doug nodded toward Pan Yintao, careful to keep the movement subtle enough to not be noticed by any but Lucy. "That one was at Del Monte's with Yang Liling on Saturday night."

One of Lucy's eyebrows raised a little. "Interesting."

Doug cocked his head. "What do you mean?"

"Oh, just that it's awfully brave to go to a regular nightclub in full drag. Like I said, she's an awfully good one, but it's not impossible to tell. She risks getting beaten up. Or worse."

Doug agreed, but was still a little confused why Lucy found it interesting that Pan Yintao went to Del Monte's in full drag, but didn't have the same reaction to Pan Yintao's presence tonight. "But isn't it just as interesting to be here in that attire?"

Lucy shrugged. "I suppose it is. One shouldn't make assumptions, of course, but I had assumed that because this is a mostly Chinese crowd here, perhaps their attitudes are different. I don't have any experience with the Chinese perspective on such things."

Neither did Doug, if he were honest; but *his* assumption was that it wasn't much different.

"I can think of reasons I made that assumption," Lucy continued, as if she needed to defend herself to him. "At the Chinese theaters, most of the female roles are played by men, and no one in the audience bats an eye at that."

Doug did know something about that. "Women weren't allowed to perform in public until after the revolution. It's still frowned upon, so that's why there aren't many women in the theater. Things change slowly."

Lucy nodded. "Things weren't so different in the west once. In Shakespeare's time there were no actresses. Juliet was played by a teenage boy, you know."

"No, I didn't know that," Doug said, quietly.

She grinned triumphantly. "Now you do. Obviously that all changed quite some time ago in the west. But you see why I thought that men playing women's roles on stage might mean Chinese attitudes toward cross-dressing could be different than western ones?"

Doug was tiring of the subject, but he nodded in agreement. "Yes, I can see that." Then a memory sprang to mind. "Now that I think about it, Jimmy Lockhart had a nasty reaction when Ben brought Pan Yintao to the bar. He asked who brought the 'freak,' and then he told Pan 'This isn't your kind of place.'"

Lucy's eyes widened. "Then I think we need to talk with her about that encounter, and find out if there were others later that night."

"You mean '*him*,'" Doug said.

Lucy gave him one of those looks that she used whenever she thought he didn't know what he was talking about. "It's good manners to call a female impersonator 'she' or 'her' when she's in female attire, and 'he' or 'him' only when he's out of drag."

Doug frowned. "Stuart said something similar the other night. Liling told him and Fred to do that."

"You see? I'm not making it up. There is a protocol to these things. It's a fantasy, but we're supposed to play along." She took his arm. "Now be a good boy and play along, and don't embarrass me. Come on."

They approached the trio at the bar—Pan Yintao, Yang Yajun, and the unknown Chinese young man in the black tuxedo and brilliantined hair who was clearly a *mopu*, a 'modern boy' who favored western ways. Doug bowed his head to them. "Good evening ladies," he addressed them in English, for Lucy's benefit. "I haven't been introduced to your gentleman friend."

The young man stuck out his hand, western style. "Good evening, sir. I am Tong Jian. Yang Yajun is my fiancée." His English was crisp and precise, with only a touch of Chinese accent.

Doug shook his hand and introduced himself and Lucy.

"Jian is medical student," Yang Yajun said, her English more careful and halting.

"St. John's University medical school," Tong Jian said.

St. John's University was out on Jessfield Road, west of the International Settlement; in the Western Roads district. But Doug had a hard time imagining the so-called "Badlands" encroaching on that venerable Anglican institution. Students at St. Anne's Academy, the

Episcopal school in the Settlement where Lucy formerly taught English and American literature, were prepared for enrollment at St. John's. They were all good Christian kids, whether white or Chinese.

Pan Yintao slipped her arm through Tong's, leaning close to him. "Jian is at the top of his class." Yang Yajun made no obvious reaction to the female impersonator leaning against her fiancé.

"Congratulations," Doug said. "One of my best friends is a physician. Dr. George Howerton. He's in private practice, but he also does shifts at St. Luke's Hospital. Perhaps you'll work with him when you do rounds."

Tong Jian's faint smile looked embarrassed. "I am only second year. When we start rounds next year, I will be at Lester Hospital."

Doug could have smacked his forehead. Lester Hospital downtown was for the Chinese community, while St. Luke's treated the foreign communities—though last year during the Battle of Shanghai they had taken in Chinese and Japanese wounded. It still surprised him sometimes the number of Shanghai institutions that segregated Chinese from western citizens.

Doug turned toward Pan Yintao, still leaning on Tong's arm. "How do you know Tong Jian, uh, Miss Pan?"

The words felt unnatural, but he was proud of himself for using the feminine salutation. He glanced at Lucy, who seemed as amused as anything.

"From Dr. Yang, of course," Pan Yintao said, swatting a hand at Doug's arm and barely missing.

Doug wasn't sure what Pan meant, let alone why he—no *she*—felt it was so obvious.

Tong Jian provided the explanation. "Dr. Yang is Yajun's father. I took his course on endocrinology last semester."

Endocrinology, that would be 'within' something. Doug's etymology knowledge was a bit fuzzy. "That would be internal medicine?"

A hint of smile tugged the corners of Tong Jian's mouth. "Specifically, the study of glands and hormones."

It took Doug a second to grasp the implication.

"I wonder if I might have a word with you in private, Miss Pan?"

Pan Yintao cast a haughty glance at Doug's suit. "You are dressed atrociously," she said in Shanghainese, and put her nose in the air. "But if you'd like to buy me another drink, I can offer a moment of my time. But if you don't hold my interest, I will return to Jian and Yajun."

Doug looked at Lucy, excused himself to the group, and took Pan Yintao's elbow to guide her toward an empty space near the end of the bar. "I wanted to ask you about something I saw at Del Monte's on Saturday night," he said in Shanghainese.

"I don't need a lecture from anyone," Pan Yintao said, steeply arching one plucked eyebrow.

Doug's cheeks flushed. "No, that's not it at all. I only want to ask you a few questions."

The bartender approached, and Doug ordered in Shanghainese. "A gin and tonic for me, and for the lady..." he waited for Pan Yintao to answer.

She rolled her eyes. "Nothing so boring as a gin and tonic. I'll have a Tom Collins, if you please. With a cherry." She looked back at Doug as the bartender hurried off to mix the drinks. "You are losing my interest, Mr. Bainbridge. You can't skate by on your looks with me. Say something interesting or I'm going back to my friends the moment my drink arrives."

"Did Jimmy Lockhart try to hurt you on Saturday night?" Doug hated jumping right to that without warming her up first, but he was in danger of losing the opportunity.

A flash of anger clouded her dark eyes. "I will not discuss such things with a stranger." She started to walk away, but Doug grabbed her elbow.

"I heard him call you a freak, and tell you that you didn't belong there. Did he come find you later, and try to hurt you?"

"You are impudent!" Pan Yintao practically spat the words. The bartender set their drinks on the bar in front of Doug just then, and Pan Yintao reached around Doug to snatch her glass off the bar and storm off with it.

Doug returned to where Lucy stood, and watched helplessly as Pan Yintao put one arm through Tong Jian's, the other arm through Yang Yajun's, and spun them away from Lucy in one swift move. She marched them across the room, muttering angry Shanghainese words that Doug couldn't hear.

Lucy looked at him, bewildered. "What happened? I take it your conversation didn't go well?"

"She refused to talk about Jimmy Lockhart. If it weren't for the fact that she was on the portico with Ben at the time we heard the thud of Lockhart falling out the window, I would add her to the top of our suspect list."

"Were you tactful, Doug? How did you ask?"

He scowled. "She didn't give me time to ease into it. I had to ask her directly, or she was going to leave because I wasn't 'interesting enough.'" He said that last part in a mocking tone, and Lucy's expression cracked into laughter. "It's not funny," he said, crossing his arms.

"It's hilariously funny!"

He was plenty interesting, damn it. "Well, now what?"

Lucy finished laughing. "Just because Pan Yintao was somewhere else at the time, that doesn't mean someone wouldn't have attacked Jimmy Lockhart on her behalf if he'd tried to hurt her. Don't discount it yet."

Doug nodded, embarrassed that he hadn't considered that. "I saw, um, her, with a few different people that night."

"We should talk to Liling about Saturday night. Maybe she saw something that might help explain what happened to Jimmy Lockhart—

whether it's to do with Pan Yintao or not. And since Stuart is Fred's friend, she's probably inclined to help."

Doug looked over to where Fred and Liling stood close, talking intimately, hardly aware that all of their friends had gone elsewhere. Stuart was on the dance floor with a Chinese dance hostess, and Liling's Chinese friends were ensconced on the far side of the room.

"Let's go see what she remembers."

**

"No, that Mr. Lockhart never threatened Pan Yintao," Yang Liling said in careful, deliberate English. "He spent too much time trying to get attention from the woman who was with your friends, Miss Moody." She cast a quick sideways glance at Lucy, as if unsure how much to say in front of her.

"You're certain?" Doug asked, recalling how Fred and Liling often seemed oblivious to anything but each other.

"Of course."

Ben had probably spent more time with Pan Yintao that night than Liling had. He'd have to ask Ben if Lockhart had tried to make any trouble.

"You didn't happen to see him argue with anyone else, did you?"

Liling's eyes widened ever so slightly, as if she'd just remembered something. "I think he argued with the other horse man."

"Chapman," Fred said. "His name was Chapman."

"Where was that?"

She pursed her lips, thinking. "We were at the roulette table," she said, looking at Fred. "Mr. Chapman sat across from us, on the other side of the wheel. Mr. Lockhart took his arm, like this"—she played grabbing at Fred's arm. "I didn't hear them, but they both look angry."

"Yeah, they left right after that," Fred said.

"Together?"

"Yeah, I think so. I wasn't really watching them, though."

"We should go," Doug said to Lucy after glancing at his watch. It was a couple of minutes past eight, and they'd promised Bao they'd be home for dinner by now.

At the door, they encountered a group of American seamen getting ready to enter, including several from the *Valparaiso*. Ben Trebinski waved.

"Hey, there Commander! How are you, Mrs. Bainbridge?"

While Doug greeted several of them by name, Lucy beamed at Ben. "Hello, Ben! It's been a while. I heard you came to Doug's party on Saturday night. That was awfully nice of you."

"It was a swell time, ma'am," Ben said, his grin bringing out the dimples in his cheeks.

Inside the door, Pan Yintao made a beeline for Ben. Doug briefly wondered if Ben were still ignorant of her secret, but the way he grinned when he saw her said he probably was.

"We'd love to stay and chat, but we have somewhere we need to be," Doug said. "Have fun, fellas." He put Pan Yintao's deception out of his mind and hailed a cab.

10

Wednesday, April 13

"I found him for you," Jonesy said on the phone line shortly before eleven. "He's alive, and he looks unharmed to me."

"Mark Chapman?" Doug asked. "Where is he?"

"He's got a place downtown; but not far from you, actually, just on the other side of Thibet Road. Easy walk to the Race Club stables from there, even for a shorty like him. I watched him head that way a little bit ago."

"Did you call Kenny?"

"The operator said his line was busy, so I called you."

"Do you have time to go talk to Chapman with me?" Doug asked, standing to grab his cap from the hat rack next to his desk. "I can be there in ten minutes."

"I'm at a phone booth on Bubbling Well Road, I can be there in less than half that time. I'll meet you there."

Doug put down the receiver and hurried out of the office and down the stairs to the Bund. The street car had just arrived at the corner of Nanking Road, between the Cathay Hotel and the Palace Hotel—the latter now restored from last year's accidental bomb damage—and Doug ran toward it. He jumped on as it started back west.

It was a five-minute ride uptown, and Doug jumped off at the Recreation Grounds near the Race Club.

Jonesy was waiting for him at the gate leading toward the stables. That was a switch, and Doug was amused to have the stocky reporter be the one left waiting for him.

"Here's my friend I was telling you about," Jonesy said to the bearded guard manning the gate.

"Thank you for showing me your pass," the man said to Doug in a Russian accent, though Doug had shown him nothing. He opened the gate and waved them through.

"I gave him a half-dollar," Jonesy muttered out the side of his mouth when they'd taken a few steps toward the stable building. "You owe me a drink later."

"That's fair," Doug said, though not relishing having to sit at a bar with Jonesy. There were worse things, but none came to mind at the moment.

They found Mark Chapman brushing a horse near the end of the row.

He cocked his head in curiosity at the sight of Doug's uniform. "I remember you," the little man said to Doug when he entered the stall ahead of Jonesy. "I saw you this weekend. At Del Monte's wasn't it?"

Doug didn't buy the hazy memory bit. Not even if his navy whites threw Chapman off a little. "Yes, at Del Monte's. The place where Jimmy Lockhart was thrown from a window."

A look of sadness fell over Chapman's face, which Doug would have identified as fake at twenty paces. "Yes, terrible business, that. Such a loss."

"A friend of his was accused of murdering him," Jonesy said, nodding toward Doug. "Do you know Stuart Vandermeer?"

Chapman's expression went blank, but a look of wariness settled in his eyes. "I wouldn't say I *know* him, no. We talked for a while at Del Monte's, though; he's very knowledgeable about horse racing. I was impressed. I'm used to talking to fans who don't know more than the basics. It was refreshing, actually. Nice, chap, too."

"He is a nice fellow," Doug said. "And he's not a killer. No one I've talked to saw him interact with Mr. Lockhart until he found the body in the rose garden. Tell me, did you ever see him with Mr. Lockhart?"

Chapman shook his head. "No, I don't believe so."

That was a lie, of course. Doug would have guessed that from the rapid shifts in Chapman's eyes, even if he didn't already know about the disagreement in the men's room.

"Stuart said he left the third floor men's room without using it because Jimmy Lockhart told him to, in no uncertain terms. He said you were there as well—can you confirm that Stuart left?"

Doug held his breath. He'd been careful not to sound like he was implying guilt when bringing up Chapman's presence there, and treating him only as a witness. He hoped Chapman wouldn't clam up.

"Oh, right, I guess I wasn't thinking of that when you asked if I saw them interact," Chapman said with a sheepish expression. "Yes, he did leave. That's correct."

Doug and Jonesy exchanged a look. "That's good to know," the stocky reporter said. "Goes a long way toward clearing him of the crime."

"Thank you for confirming that, Mr. Chapman," Doug said. "My friend will be grateful to have a witness corroborate that he wasn't at the scene of the crime when it was committed. I know he admires you, so it will mean a lot."

"Glad to be of help," Chapman said with a nervous half-smile, his tone a bit breathless.

He's anxious about something. But what? If Chapman had killed Jimmy Lockhart, it wouldn't be in his interest to remove Stuart from the scene, not since Stuart was charged with the crime. Did that mean there was an unknown third party involved? Was Chapman afraid of them?

"The main reason the police arrested Stuart for killing Jimmy Lockhart was because his handkerchief was found in Lockhart's mouth," Doug said, and watched Chapman's reaction carefully. A hint of something crossed his eyes—was that fear? Doug continued, "Stuart says it must have fallen out when Lockhart grabbed his lapels and shook him. Would you by any chance have noticed if his handkerchief fell out? Maybe you saw it on the floor?"

Chapman's eyes widened a tiny bit, for only a fraction of a second. Then he exhaled a puff of air, as if out of breath, a nervous half-smile opening his mouth. "Yeah, now that you mention it, I believe I did notice his handkerchief on the ground when he left. Where he'd been standing. I would have picked it up and returned it to him, but Jimmy told me to get out, too. Seeing how he'd treated your friend when he hesitated, I didn't make the same mistake. I left in a bit of a hurry."

That was a lie, too, but Doug wasn't sure how to prove it. "So it was still on the ground when you left?"

"Yeah, sorry about that. I should have grabbed it and given it back to your friend." He shrugged, the movement a little too fast and jerky.

Doug wasn't sure where to go next, but thankfully Jonesy jumped in. "Was anyone waiting to come in when you left?"

Now Chapman's eyes really widened, and for at least a full second before he forced an unnatural chuckle. "No, I didn't see anyone." His tone was nervous, and his chest rose and fell rapidly with short, fast, shallow breaths.

"That's not what Dolores Moody said."

Doug turned his head sharply from Chapman to Jonesy. The reporter had delivered the brusque statement in a completely believable straight-forward tone, and now stared hard at Mark Chapman, like a father who had just trapped his young son in a lie.

Doug looked back at Chapman, whose mouth hung open, eyes wide as saucers and staying that way.

"But—but—where was Dolores? I didn't see her when I left."

So Mark Chapman knew Dolores Moody. That was interesting.

Jonesy shook his head with a tsk-tsk expression, looking every bit the disappointed father. "She didn't know who it was, but she saw them go in there plain as day."

Jonesy's performance was so believable, Doug found himself wondering if the reporter had actually talked with Dolores Moody, and somehow got her to say more than she'd told Doug. But that didn't make any sense; there was no reason for her to divulge more to a reporter than she had to Doug. She clearly liked Doug, and wanted him to deliver her invitation to Scott Farnsworth. Jonesy would have been at a disadvantage on both counts.

Chapman shifted his feet, and started fidgeting with his hands. There was a tremble in his voice when he answered, "I—I don't know."

"That's a lie, Mr. Chapman. We all know it," Jonesy said, stern. "Why don't you come clean and tell us who was there?"

Now Mark Chapman was visibly shaking. He kept shifting his feet, but clasped his hands in a vain attempt to steady them.

Jonesy took a step closer, puffing out his chest in a menacing manner that had to be intimidating to the diminutive jockey. "Well?"

Chapman took a step back, bumping up against the wall of the horse stall. "I can't. You don't want to tangle with those people, trust me. I can't say anything more. Now please leave."

Doug and Jonesy exchanged a look. Now Doug took a step forward. "Mr. Chapman, please. A man's life could be in jeopardy, if he's convicted of a capital crime that he didn't commit. Won't you please help us?"

Chapman pressed himself harder against the back of the stall. "Please, just leave."

Jonesy took a couple of steps back, exhaling hard through the nose. Doug touched the rim of his cap and nodded at Mark Chapman before walking out.

**

Outside the stables, Jonesy motioned Doug to come close.

"He's right to be scared. The Shanghai Race Club has a solid reputation for being completely legit, no hanky-panky with the horses, *ever.*"

He motioned Doug closer, and said even quieter, "Now when it comes to the dog races down in the French Concession, that's another matter altogether. It's an open secret that Jack Riley fixes those races all the time, dopes rival dogs so his dog can win. He's connected with Carlos Garcia, who owns the Canidrome, so they all look the other way. And woe to anyone who publicly suggests tampering—the 'Friends of Riley,' or Riley himself, will take a knife to 'em in no time."

Jack Riley—the 'Slots King of Shanghai'—Doug had briefly seen him at Del Monte's that night.

Jonesy pulled a cigar from inside his jacket, and jabbed it in the air toward Doug's face. "I see those wheels turning in your head. You'd better stop 'em real fast. I mean it, Douglas. Give those fellas a wide berth."

Doug looked Jonesy in the eye, squared his shoulders. "I have to do everything I can to keep my friend out of prison." *Or the hangman's noose*, but he left that unsaid.

Jonesy struck a match, but jabbed his unlit cigar at Doug one more time before lighting it. "You've got a baby coming in a couple of weeks, and you want to be alive to meet it, dontcha? I'm serious. Leave those fellas the hell alone."

11

It was almost noon when Doug left Jonesy at the stables. He needed to tell Kenny what he'd learned—though maybe he'd leave out the part about Jack Riley. Given how busy Kenny said he was this week, the odds were better than even that Kenny wasn't rushing out to lunch right at noon. Still, there was no time to waste.

He hurried to Bubbling Well Road, and tried to flag down a motor cab. It was just over a mile to Kenny's office on West Peking Road downtown, and if he wanted to catch him he'd never make it on foot. The cabs were busy at lunchtime, but the fourth one that came by pulled over.

He gave the Chinese driver the address, and tried to relax in the back seat. But everything Mark Chapman and Jonesy had said kept tumbling around in his brain, recombining in random combinations.

The cab dropped him off in front of the building where Kenny had an office—and where Doug had once had his pretend office, while he was on his classified immersion in Shanghai. Doug paid the fare, plus an extra quarter for hurrying, and rushed out the door.

He took the steps two at a time, arriving at Kenny's office at four minutes past twelve o'clock. Sounds of movement came from behind the closed door, and he smiled to himself that his guess had been correct; Kenny hadn't left yet. He took a breath and was about to knock, when he detected the muffled sound of a voice, almost like someone trying to shout with a hand clamped over their mouth.

His heart jumped. He knocked hard. The sounds of movement stopped, but so did the muffled voice.

After several seconds with no response, Doug knocked again. His heart raced, imagining thugs holding Kenny hostage at knifepoint while they looked through his file on the Jimmy Lockhart murder. Still no response, so Doug put his mouth near the door jam. "Kenny? It's me, Doug."

Silence. He knocked one more time, though he hardly expected a different result at this point. "Kenny? Are you there?"

Still nothing, so he backed away from the door. He turned toward the stairs, but looked over his shoulder at Kenny's door, listening hard for any sound, and hearing none.

He went down the stairs slowly, mind racing. It was a stretch to think that gangsters would have gotten to Kenny, though he couldn't get that image out of his head. *This isn't some hard-boiled detective movie*, he chastised himself.

Still, it could be thieves. Kenny might well be in danger, even if it wasn't the fanciful image of gangsters trying to cover up Jimmy Lockhart's murder. Stepping onto the sidewalk, Doug looked up and down Peking Road, looking for a police constable on patrol.

Not a single one in sight. *Damn it!*

Another thought struck him, and he hurried to the alley in the middle of the block, then ran behind the buildings until he reached the fire escape long the back wall of Kenny's office building. He paused to catch his breath—but only for a few seconds—and then crept as stealthily as he could up the stairs. Slowly, slowly, not making a single creak on the metal.

The painfully slow climb gave him time to consider what he would do if he peeked through the window and saw thieves holding Kenny hostage. He remembered he was armed almost as an afterthought, and took his service weapon from the holster at his hip.

By the time he crept to Kenny's open office window, almost five minutes had passed.

Muffled cries came from inside Kenny's office, and Doug's fist tightened around the handle of his Colt .45. His heart pounded, his pulse roaring in his ears.

He moved his face close to the windowsill, so he'd be minimally visible when he peeked around the edge, and then slipped forward until his eyes crossed the threshold and looked over Kenny's desk.

He froze.

Once it sank in, he pulled his head back in a hurry. His cheeks burned hot.

Kenny wasn't in imminent danger. Not unless his wife found out he was having an affair.

**

Doug watched from the corner until Kenny emerged from his building twenty minutes later with his companion. They were both smiling, and Doug's stomach muscles tightened in annoyance. They talked for a minute, and then parted—Kenny going east toward Honan Road and the tavern there where he liked to lunch, the other coming west, toward where Doug hid at the entrance to the alley.

The second that figure reached him, Doug stepped out beside him and grabbed his arm.

"Damn it, Scott! He's married."

Scott Farnsworth's eyes almost bulged out of his skull. There was nearly as much white visible as blue.

"Doug! I—I—I didn't see you."

"He's *married*, Scott."

At six-foot-three—nearly as tall as Kenny—Scott towered three inches over Doug, but now the tall young man seemed to deflate before his eyes. "How did you find out?" his voice sounded small and breathless.

"That's not important," Doug said, trying to force the image from his head; both of them naked as the day they were born, Kenny on his back on the desk, legs reaching toward the ceiling...

"Please, Doug! Keep this to yourself, OK?" Sweat had broken out on Scott's forehead and upper lip, as if it were already June and not April.

Doug glared at him. "He's my best friend, damn it! And *his wife* is my friend, too."

Scott swallowed hard and looked at the ground, but kept silent.

Doug glanced around at the midday crowd on the sidewalk, conscious for the first time that what they said was clearly audible. Fortunately, theirs were the only white faces on this block, and few of the Chinese surrounding them could understand what they were saying, let alone put two and two together.

Still, Doug kept his voice quieter when he continued. "This isn't like you and Callahan, or any of the other fellas on the ship. It's adultery, Scott. He's married."

"They're *all* married, damn it!" Scott's voice was little more than a whisper, but the frustration was clearly audible. "Don't you understand? Eventually they all get married."

Something about the intensity in Scott's blue eyes as they stared at him held the impression of an unspoken '*You did*.' Doug looked away.

Then he thought of Lieutenant David Saunders' words at the Officers' Club at Cavite Naval Station. Scott would help himself and his career if he found himself a wife.

He reached into his jacket, and fished out Dolores Moody's calling card. "Here," he said, thrusting it at Scott. "You remember Miss Moody from Saturday night. She'd like for you to call her."

Scott stared at the card in his hands for several long seconds. Then he swallowed hard, made an almost imperceptible nod, and slipped the card into his pocket.

**

Doug found Kenny sitting at the bar in the Liberty Tavern on the corner of Honan Road and Peking Road, reading the newspaper and finishing a sandwich. A pint glass stood next to the plate, a small measure of beer left at the bottom.

"Oh, hi Doug," he said with a grin, and patted the empty bar stool next to him. "Have a seat."

Doug sat at the bar, not making eye contact with his friend. "I have an update for you, about Stuart's case. I talked with Mark Chapman earlier."

Kenny glanced around at the tavern's full crowd. Then he leaned closer to Doug. "Anything confidential? We should wait until we get back to my office to discuss it."

That image of Kenny lying naked across his desk flooded back, and Doug tried hard to banish it.

"Something wrong?" Kenny asked.

"No."

"Are you sure? You have a strange look on your face."

"I'm fine," Doug said, a little too quickly. "We can talk here. The main thing is that Mark Chapman confirmed Stuart left the third-floor men's room after Jimmy Lockhart shook him and told him for the second time to leave."

A big smile spread across Kenny's mouth, but it didn't extend to his eyes. "That's fantastic news! I'll have him give that testimony under oath. I can schedule a deposition within a few days."

He sounded happy, but there was something wary in his eyes that Doug couldn't mistake.

"Are you getting lunch?" Kenny asked, obviously trying to sound friendly and nonchalant.

Doug shook his head. "I have to get back to my office. I'll grab something from a street vendor on the way."

Kenny paused for a second, and then nodded. "I should get back, myself. Busy, busy these days." He laid a dollar on the bar and told the bartender to keep the change.

Doug exited with him. The five seconds it took to walk from the barstool to the door, he debated whether or not to say anything; then once they were on the sidewalk he motioned Kenny toward the corner of the building, a few extra feet from passing pedestrians.

"I know about you and Scott Farnsworth," Doug said, not bothering to mask the anger and disgust in his voice.

Kenny went pale.

"How can you do that to Abbie?"

Kenny swallowed hard, and his shoulders slumped. He glanced around. "Can we please go back to my office and talk in private? I'd like to explain."

That was the last place Doug wanted to go. "I don't have time, Kenny."

Kenny grabbed Doug's forearm, and his eyes held Doug's, pleading. "Please, Doug. I need to explain."

Doug hesitated, took a breath, and then nodded.

They walked in silence the entire block to Kenny's building, and silently climbed the stairs. Neither spoke until after Kenny had closed his office door.

"Listen, Douggie, I can explain," Kenny began, but Doug jumped in and wouldn't let him finish.

"Are you going to explain to *your wife*?"

Kenny cringed and looked away. He seemed to wrestle with something, and Doug just crossed his arms and waited.

"I love Abbie," Kenny said, his voice quiet and small. "I love her with all my heart, I always have. But you have to understand, there are certain things she can't give me, and—"

"Oh yes, I understand *exactly* what Scott Farnsworth can 'give' you, Kenny." Doug nearly spat the words. His anger had risen so fast he couldn't stop it. And he wasn't sorry.

Kenny cringed again, and fell silent. Doug waited, but he didn't continue. They stood as if rooted in place, neither speaking, for a long moment.

Finally, Doug broke the uncomfortable silence. "Last summer, when Lucy and I came to stay with you, you told me that you and Abbie weren't..." he let his voice trail off, leaving the words unspoken. "Is she still not...?" he waved his hand in a circular motion to complete the unfinished question.

Red blotches appeared in Kenny's cheeks, which were otherwise still paler than usual. "That's much better now. When she came back from Hong Kong in November, she'd missed me, and the intimacy returned. It's still not like it was before Margaret—maybe only once or twice a week now—but it's good. I'm not unhappy."

Doug flushed in embarrassment. He hated talking about this. But he also couldn't leave it alone. "Then, why?"

Kenny sighed, hard. His shoulders slumped even more than they had outside the tavern. "I've tried, Doug. I've really tried." He looked up from the floor and stared into Doug's eyes. He squared his shoulders. "You know how it was before Abbie left, all those months without—and then imagine those lonely weeks without her, while she and Margaret were in Hong Kong and I was alone. It was hard, Doug. Really hard. I met Scott at your wedding, you remember. I could tell right away, you know. About him, I mean."

"I know what you mean," Doug muttered, jaw set.

Kenny flushed. "Right. Well, we got together for a drink a few days later." A hint of smile curled up the corners of his mouth, and his eyes looked far away, lost in memory. "It was nice to have that kind of attention from someone again. It had been so long."

Kenny's voice cracked, and Doug's heart broke in spite of himself. "I understand why you gave into temptation, Kenny," he said, quietly. "But it's still wrong. You should have ended it."

"Don't you think I tried?" Kenny shouted, taking Doug aback with the intensity of his words. "While Abbie was gone, I let myself get caught up in it for a while. I *needed* it, Doug. And I wasn't getting it anywhere else. But after she and Margaret returned, I tried to be faithful. I really did."

A lone tear broke free from his eye, and Kenny swiped a hand at it.

Doug looked away, embarrassed. He sighed and looked down. "I don't know what to say to that, Kenny. I wish you'd talked to me before it got this far. We love you both, you know that."

Now tears flowed from both of Kenny's eyes, and he let them be. He stared out the window and nodded. "Yes, I know that. I never—" his voice cracked, and he swallowed hard. "I never wanted you to think less of me."

A sharp pain jabbed through Doug's chest. He didn't have any answers, no matter how hard he sought them.

"What are you going to do now?"

Kenny shrugged, but didn't answer.

"It's not good for either of you." Doug hesitated, considering how much he should say, but decided it might help if Kenny knew the whole truth. "Scott's navy career has been held back because of rumors about him, and he's been urged to find a wife."

Kenny looked up, and his face had gone pale again. "Oh! I didn't realize that..." his voice trailed off.

Doug reached out awkwardly, and patted his friend's shoulder. "You have to let him go, Kenny. For both of your sakes."

Kenny nodded, tears streaming again. He didn't say a word, just walked to his window and stared out at the grimy brick wall of the building opposite the alley, his back to Doug.

Doug let himself out.

12

Thursday, April 14

"Mr. Bainbridge! What brings you by?" Pete's surprise looked more pleased than not as he came out from his office.

Doug was standing next to the desk where a middle-aged British secretary sat, and he had to smile at the way Pete pretended he was a client. The secretary's brown hair was streaked with gray and pulled back into a knot at the back of her head that gave her a severe look. The old-fashioned tweed suit she wore only added to the severity. That, and the purse of her thin lips from the moment Doug had asked to speak with Mr. Tolbert.

"I have an inquiry that requires your expertise," Doug said, maintaining the charade.

"Then come right in." Pete put his hand on Doug's shoulder and guided him into the office. "Hold my calls, Miss Peabody."

"She's a jolly one," Doug said with a laugh after Pete shut the door.

"I believe 'efficient' is the word you're looking for, Douggie," Pete said. But his wry half-grin said he shared Doug's assessment. "She's my boss's sister-in-law. His wife's spinster sister, and he brought her over a few years ago, after her parents passed away."

"And they hoisted her off on you, you lucky devil."

Pete chuckled and sat in the black leather chair behind his big mahogany desk. "Take a seat and tell me what really brings you by."

"I hope you'll tell me what you know about Mr. Yang, other than that his daughter has her heart set on our Freddie. Specifically, does he have business with the Japanese? Anything that would make the Kenpeitai uncharacteristically friendly?"

A veil fell across Pete's eyes. "Mr. Yang's business with the bank is confidential, Doug. You know I can't discuss a client's business without his permission."

"If the police were asking, you'd cooperate, wouldn't you?"

Pete frowned. "Of course—but you aren't the police."

"No, and the police aren't doing any investigating into Jimmy Lockhart's murder now that they've pinned it on Stuart."

Pete was silent for several long seconds, his expression unreadable. "Listen, Doug..." he began, and then hesitated. "I know Kenny's got you helping him with some kind of investigation to clear Stu's name, and you know I'd do anything I could to help. But I can't break a client's confidence. And you can't possibly think Mr. Yang had anything to do with that jockey's murder. What motive would he have?"

He had a point. Doug wasn't going to tell Pete that his interest in Yang's relationship with the Kenpeitai was mostly professional curiosity as an Intelligence Officer. But something kept telling him there was a connection with the shadowy events at the Del Monte.

"I don't want to say too much, you understand," he said, hoping he was implying he knew more about Yang's connection than he could reveal. "It's not Yang himself, you see, but one of his possible connections."

Pete's arched eyebrows said he wasn't buying it. "Listen, if Kenny thinks something's connected to Stu's case, he can ask the Judge to issue a subpoena. Then I'll be happy to hand over everything I have, if it'll help."

Doug sighed. "But nothing without a subpoena, is that it?"

"Not a word. Sorry, buddy."

It had been a long shot, but worth the try. And not without benefit—the look in Pete's eyes when Doug asked was confirmation that there was something there.

"I'll tell Kenny. Thanks, Pete." Doug stood and turned toward the door, but Pete stopped him.

"Don't rush out, or Miss Peabody will know this wasn't business."

Doug chuckled. "Afraid she'll go right to your boss?"

"She's got 'spy' written all over her face."

"Ha! You're probably right. At least if she checks, I do have an account here."

"Oh, I remember," Pete said. "I can cover my tracks."

Living with Julia, Pete had probably learned long ago to dot every I and cross every T. "Since I'm here, did Julia tell you about dinner on Saturday? Lucy wants everyone to meet her mother."

"She did, and we'll be there. Looking forward to it. The question is, are you?"

Doug laughed out loud. "Lucy is, and that's all I'll say about that."

"Your secret's safe with me. Alright now, run along and let me get back to work."

"Thanks, Pete. While I'm here, would it be alright if I stopped in to see Stuart?" Another long shot, but it might save him a lot of trouble.

"Be my guest. Junior Account Managers are down the hall on the left."

**

Stuart's was one of a row of smaller offices along the side of the typing pool. A couple of dozen pretty young white women tapped away in the open space surrounded by paneled wood walls; not a Chinese face to be seen anywhere.

Stuart's door was open, and Doug rapped his knuckles to get his friend's attention.

"Doug! What brings you by?" Stuart closed the folder he'd been studying and shoved it aside.

"I came to meet with Pete, and on my way out I thought I'd check on you. How are you holding up?"

"Oh, I'm fine. No need to worry about me. Kenny and you will get me off the hook soon enough."

His forced smile and breathless tone said he was more anxious than he'd let on, but Doug let that go. He stepped close to Stuart's desk and asked him quietly, "Just between us, do you by any chance work with Pete on the Yang account?"

Stuart shook his head. "No, Fred helps him with that one. Why?"

"Just a thread I'm following. Thought I'd ask. But listen—keep this between you and me, ok? No telling Pete or Fred."

"Cross my heart," Start said, and mimed turning a key in front of his lips.

**

Leaving the HSBC building and turning toward his office, Doug filed all that away for another time. Whenever he succeeded in building a network of Chinese agents, he'd send one to spy on Mr. Yang and his Japanese connections. But until then, he had bigger fish to fry.

13

Friday, April 15

The giant ocean liner in the Huang Po River slowed to a crawl as it approached the wharf in front of the Customs House on the Bund. Then the engines rumbled into reverse, churning the filthy water and scattering flotsam. Chinese stevedores on the wharf caught thick ropes tossed down by crewmembers, and swiftly tied them to giant steel cleats.

Lucy clenched her white gloves in her fists. "I'm so nervous and excited all at the same time."

Doug rubbed the middle of her back. "You'll see her any moment now."

The Dollar Line gangway was lowered, and Chinese porters hauled heavy steamer trunks from the first-class deck, arranging them on the shore. It was several minutes before well-dressed passengers started coming down the gang-walk, and Lucy stood on her toes, craning her neck to look.

A few minutes later, a plump middle-aged woman in a long navy blue dress came ashore. Lucy rushed to her and threw her arms around her.

"Oh, Mother! It's wonderful to see you at last!"

"It's wonderful to see you, dear," Mrs. Kinzler said. "You look radiant."

When they broke the embrace, Doug smiled at his mother-in-law and leaned down to kiss her cheek. "We're very happy to have you with us, Mother Kinzler. Welcome back to Shanghai."

"Thank you, Mr. Bainbridge. May I call you Douglas now? We are family."

"Call me Doug."

"Doug," she said, as if testing the feel of the name on her tongue. "I'll stick to Douglas. You're not a little boy, now are you?"

Lucy gave him a knowing look, and he just shook his head. "No, I'm not at that."

"Let's find your luggage, and get you through Customs so we can take you home," Lucy said, taking her mother's luggage ticket and handing it to Doug.

The two women followed Doug toward the collection of first class luggage at the end of the wharf, arm in arm. Doug gave the ticket to a young Chinese porter, who hurried off and returned carrying a large steamer trunk, which he hauled to the Customs officer in the stand along the edge of the Bund, joining a line of passengers and porters waiting to be checked through.

The imposing limestone edifice of the seven-story Shanghai Customs House dominated the view ahead of them, its iconic clock tower doubling the building's height. Lucy pointed to the much longer six-story limestone building directly to the left of the Customs House.

"See that big building with the gold dome, Mother? That's the Hong Kong and Shanghai Bank—the HSBC. That's where three of our friends work—Peter Tolbert, Fred Perry, and Stuart Vandermeer. I've written about all of them."

"Yes, I know the names."

"You'll get to meet them this weekend," Doug said. "We're having dinner tonight with our best friends, Kenneth and Abigail Traywick, so you can get to know them first. Then tomorrow night all of us are going out to dinner, to give you a proper Shanghai welcome." He gave his mother-in-law a broad smile, hoping to convey some excitement.

"I look forward to it," she said, not sounding much like it at the moment.

She's just tired from traveling, Doug thought.

"Your father sends his love, of course," Mrs. Kinzler said to Lucy, patting her hand. "He told me to cable him as soon as I arrive, and let him know if you look well. I'll be happy to tell him that you do. Oh, Douglas, I almost forgot to tell you; I left Chicago a few days early so that I could stay a couple of nights in San Francisco before my ship departed. I had dinner with your parents while I was there. They have a lovely home. We were all eager to meet one another, and they were only disappointed that Herbert didn't come with me. I explained that he can't leave Chicago for such an extended time, with business and all."

Doug's heart plummeted into his stomach so fast he thought it might explode.

"We had a very nice time getting to know each other. I found them very pleasant and agreeable, which made me quite happy. After all, we're going to share grandchildren."

"That's wonderful, mother," Lucy said, and cast a sideways glance at Doug.

Doug forced a smile with tremendous difficulty and hoped it didn't look stiff. "I'm so glad you enjoyed your time with them."

Please God let them have not asked her why she was coming to Shanghai now, instead of in June.

When he'd written to his parents about their wedding in September, he hadn't mentioned the baby; and when he wrote them again a month later to tell them that Lucy was expecting, he let the implication be that it was a honeymoon baby. He'd never said anything *specifically* about when the baby was due, he let them assume it would be June.

They might be six thousand miles away, but he still dreaded getting a lecture on morals.

**

It took several minutes to get through the line to the pink-cheeked Swedish Customs officer in the stand. Once he'd stamped Mrs. Kinzler's

129

declaration and welcomed her to Shanghai, they went to the edge of the Bund to hail a cab, the porter in tow with Mrs. Kinzler's trunk.

Dozens of rickshaws loitered near the wharfs, but a rickshaw wouldn't fit all three of them, even without luggage, so Doug stepped a foot into the street to hail a motor cab. When one stopped, Doug opened the back door and helped Lucy inside, and then followed her mother in. He gave the driver their address.

"No, I need to stop at the American Express office first," Mrs. Kinzler said. "I promised Herbert I'd cable him just as soon as I saw Lucy, and let him know that she's well."

Doug had heard that on the wharf, but had assumed she hadn't meant it so literally. "I'll see if he can wait for us." He gave the new instructions to the driver in Shanghainese.

He dropped them off five minutes later at the American Express office on Kiukiang Road downtown, and Doug told him in Shanghainese not to wait.

As the driver removed her trunk, Mrs. Kinzler looked at it in irritation, then turned to Doug and asked, "Did you tell him to wait?"

Doug shook his head. "This might take a while, and it could be expensive to leave the meter running. Cabs cost six dollars an hour these days."

Mrs. Kinzler's lips tightened into a thin line, but she remained silent and marched into the American Express office. Doug stayed outside to guard the trunk. Lucy gave Doug a sympathetic look as she waddled past him, following her mother inside where she could sit.

**

When they departed American Express twenty minutes later, Mrs. Kinzler grumbled about how expensive it was to send a trans-Pacific cablegram. "Almost twenty-five dollars! I could stay two nights in a suite at the Astor House Hotel for that amount."

Doug kept to himself that he knew for a fact she'd spent that much on a cable home three years ago, or that she'd spent almost fifteen times that amount on first class passage from San Francisco. He just nodded in implicit agreement.

He told the ladies to stay there, and went to the corner to hail another cab. A couple of minutes later, a cab pulled around to where Lucy and her mother waited, and the driver got out to load the trunk in the back.

Church bells began to peel from the nearby Anglican Cathedral, and were soon joined by others across the city. Doug glanced at his watch; noon on Good Friday, the crucifixion observance had begun.

"I know you young people don't go to church regularly," Mrs. Kinzler said as Doug gave Lucy a hand into the back seat of the cab. "But we do plan to go to Easter services, don't we?"

"Yes, of course," Doug assured her. Once she'd gotten into the cab he followed her in, and gave the driver their address. They were soon back on their way uptown.

"Doug and I went to the Presbyterian Church last Easter," Lucy told her mother. "And for Christmas Eve, as well. The minister there was the one who married us."

"Yes, your parents told me your family is Presbyterian," Mrs. Kinzler said to Doug. "I think it distresses her that you two don't attend services more regularly, but I told her that's just how young people are these days; they only go on Christmas and Easter."

Doug could think of many older people who were the same, but he kept that to himself.

"We're Lutheran, of course," Mrs. Kinzler continued. "I tried going to the Lutheran Church here when Lucy and I visited three years ago, but they don't have any services in English. They alternate services in German, Swedish, Norwegian, and Danish. Can you imagine? You'd have to keep track of which Sunday it is each month, and if you show up on the wrong one you won't understand what's being said."

Doug assured her that the Presbyterian Church on Tianjian Road had English services.

**

Arriving at their building five minutes later, Doug paid the driver and tipped him an extra quarter, then lugged his mother-in-law's trunk up the stairs to their apartment door. The ladies waited while he unlocked the door, and hauled the trunk inside.

"Welcome to Chez Bainbridge," Doug said with a smile when his mother-in-law entered the apartment.

Mrs. Kinzler looked around, lips pursed slightly. "Well! It's not much bigger than a hotel suite at the Astor House, is it?"

Lucy sighed. "It's a little bigger than that, Mother."

Mrs. Kinzler patted her daughter's cheek. "If you say so, dear."

"Besides, how much more room do Doug and I need? There's plenty of space for us and the baby, plus a spare bedroom. Our *amah* is going to sleep on the couch while you're here, so you can take his bed."

As if on cue, Bao came out of the kitchen. He was dressed in his cleanest pair of trousers and shirt—per Doug's instructions this morning—but he was barefoot as usual. He looked at Mrs. Kinzler and bowed more deeply than he usually would.

"Mother, this is Li Baosheng. Bao is going to be our *amah*."

"How do you do?" Mrs. Kinzler said to Bao, her tone stiff and commanding.

"I am pleased to meet you, Mrs. Kinzler," Bao said. "You like some tea?"

"Yes, a cup of tea would be lovely." Mrs. Kinzler sat in one of the armchairs in the living room to wait.

"We'd all take some tea, Bao," Lucy said. "The jasmine one would be perfect. Thank you."

Then Lucy eased herself onto the couch near her mother—not an easy feat at almost nine months pregnant, but she'd worked out a pretty good system, holding onto the arm of the couch with her left hand and reaching for the back of the couch with her right.

After his first day home, Doug had learned not to offer to help her.

"You look exhausted, dear," Mrs. Kinzler said.

"I'm fine, Mother," Lucy replied, though Doug couldn't help noticing the tired look in her eyes.

He was about to explain to her mother that the activity had been a bit much for Lucy, but thought better of it. *She wouldn't be so tired if we hadn't had to stop at American Express.* He definitely kept that thought to himself.

"I'm still not sure I understand why you hired a young *man* as your amah, and not an experienced woman," Mrs. Kinzler said, in an exaggerated stage whisper, as if she were afraid that Bao might overhear her from the next room.

Doug's abdomen tightened in irritation, but he let Lucy deal with her mother's quibbles.

"Bao is a dear friend, Mother. He's like family, really. It was only natural to engage him for the role. We couldn't trust anyone more to help us take care of the baby."

"*Family* is like family, dear."

"Since we don't have any actual family in Shanghai, our friends have become like family to us, Mother Kinzler," Doug said, careful to keep his tone friendly and not challenging. He even managed to put on a smile while he said it. "That's why we're so eager for you to meet all of them."

A strange sort of look crossed her gray eyes, and Doug couldn't tell what her reaction was. "Yes, I can see how that might be," she said.

Bao emerged from the kitchen with a tea pot and four cups on a tray. He set it on the side table, and handed them each a steaming cup, finally taking a seat at the dining table and sipping from the last cup.

Mrs. Kinzler cast a glance at Bao sitting at the table. "You may take your tea in the kitchen, Bao."

"Mother!" Lucy scolded, cheeks flushing.

"Servants don't eat and drink with their masters, dear," Mrs. Kinzler said in the sort of tone that suggested she would accept no argument to the contrary. Then she looked back to Bao. "To the kitchen with you, Bao. Leave us with our tea."

Crestfallen, Bao took his tea cup and trudged to the kitchen.

Doug's pulse pounded at his temples. His face burned hot, and he held his tongue with great difficulty. As much as he wanted to jump to Bao's defense, he had to let Lucy handle this.

And he desperately hoped Lucy would handle it, and not just let it go.

He shouldn't have worried. Lucy crossed her arms. "Mother, that's not how we do things. I already told you, Bao is like family. We don't treat him like a servant."

"It sets a bad precedent, Lucy," Mrs. Kinzler said, as if scolding a child. "It's undignified. And don't take an impudent tone with me."

Lucy scowled. "I'm not a child, Mother. I'm twenty-four years old, married, and about to be a mother myself. This is our house, and we'll go by our rules. Your opinion is respected, but it is not accepted. Now that you've spoken your mind on the subject, kindly keep it to yourself for the rest of your visit."

Mrs. Kinzler sniffed and looked away. She sipped her tea in silence.

Doug couldn't help the smile he gave his wife. Then he sipped his tea—the jasmine variety she favored more than he did, but he wasn't about to complain.

**

"Where are we going?" Mrs. Kinzler asked when they left for dinner that night.

"Our favorite restaurant," Lucy said, starting carefully down the stairs, holding onto the rail with one hand and Doug's arm with the other. "It's called Velardi's, and it's not far from here, on Honan Road downtown."

"That sounds I-talian," Mrs. Kinzler said.

"That's because it's an Italian restaurant."

"But we're not I-talian, dear."

"Everything there is wonderful, Mother," Lucy said, slightly out of breath from going down the stairs. "We'll find something you'll like. Try the lasagna Bolognese, it's delicious."

"Do they have anything that's not spicy?" Mrs. Kinzler asked. "I hear those I-talians like to put a lot of garlic and spices in their food."

"It's not spicy, Mother," Lucy said, letting her exasperation show. "At least, most of it isn't. I'll warn you if something is."

"I'm sure you'll enjoy it, Mother Kinzler," Doug said.

"Hmmm," Mrs. Kinzler replied. "I'll keep an open mind, of course."

"Of course," Doug said, and he and Lucy exchanged a small smile behind her mother's back.

Kenny and Abbie were waiting for them at the front door when the cab dropped them off. Lucy made the introductions while Doug paid the driver.

"I see you've all met," Doug said when he approached them, clustered outside the front door.

"Yes, we were just telling your mother-in-law how often the four of us come here," Kenny said.

"At least a couple of times a month, I'd say," Doug said, trying to sound cheerful.

This was the first time Doug had seen Kenny since their discussion in his office two days before, about Scott Farnsworth. He hoped his discomfort didn't show to anyone. He hadn't told Lucy about the situation. It felt strange keeping something from her, but he would have felt worse divulging such a secret about Kenny.

"You'll love it," Abbie said to Mrs. Kinzler, briefly touching her sleeve. "I've never had anything here that wasn't delicious."

"Shall we then?" Kenny said, opening the door.

Doug had made a reservation, but Giancarlo Velardi recognized them, greeting them all by name, and escorted them to their table.

"And who is this lovely lady with you this evening?" Giancarlo asked, his Italian accent thick and languid, holding Mrs. Kinzler's chair while Doug held Lucy's.

"This is my mother, Mrs. Kinzler," Lucy said. "She's visiting from Chicago. She'll be staying with us for a while after the baby's born."

"Wonderful! The little *bambino* will have lots of family to greet him." Giancarlo took Mrs. Kinzler's hand, seeming oblivious to the shocked look on her face, and kissed it. "Welcome to Shanghai, *Signora*."

Mrs. Kinzler's cheeks colored, and she scowled at his back when he left. "Well! They certainly are *friendly*, aren't they?" The way she stressed the word didn't make it sound like a good thing.

Lucy started going over the menu with her mother, and Abbie leaned across toward Doug. "I'm so glad you're helping Kenny with Stuart's case. He's got so much research to do, on the intricacies of American law. Some things are a little different, you know. I'm afraid it might overwhelm him if he had to also find evidence to support the case all on his own."

"I'm happy to help."

"I've been to Canada," Mrs. Kinzler announced. "When the children were young, Herbert and I took them on a train trip to Quebec City, and then to Montreal. What year was that dear?"

"It was in '22, Mother. I was eight, and Marty was ten."

"That's right. You were just learning some French." She turned back to Kenny and Abbie. "Quebec City was lovely, like old Europe. It felt like stepping off a steamship in Le Havre, but not so far away."

"I've never been to Quebec," Kenny said.

"Me, neither," Abbie added, shaking her head.

"The farthest east I've ever been was Ottawa," Kenny said.

"Same," Abbie said.

"Oh, that's a shame," Mrs. Kinzler said. "It felt just like provincial France. Not that Lucy and her brother had any frame of reference at that time. We didn't take them to Europe for a few more years."

"When Marty graduated from high school," Lucy said. "That summer before he went to Columbia, we all did a tour of Europe."

"Yes, that's right—1930. The Depression hadn't ruined things yet, it was just a little dip still. Although I will say I was amazed at how much *different* everything was from my own European tour when I was nineteen. And I don't just mean the automobiles."

Kenny grinned. "You can't stop progress, not even in Europe."

"Yes," Mrs. Kinzler said, drawing out the word a little, an odd sort of look in her eyes that said she agreed, but hated to.

"What did you see the last time you were here, Mrs. Kinzler?" Abbie asked.

"I remember the Yangtze Gorges were quite beautiful," Mrs. Kinzler said. "That was when we left Shanghai the first time."

"You won't be able to get there this visit, I'm afraid," Kenny said. "The Japanese and Chinese armies are battling between here and there. It wouldn't be safe to go upriver past Nanking."

"That is a shame," Mrs. Kinzler said. She turned to Lucy. "What else did we see here, dear? I remember some pagodas, and lots of dragons carved into the eaves somewhere that you insisted on going."

"That was in the old city, Mother."

"That's right," Mrs. Kinzler said, with one firm nod. "We were in the French Concession—not as much like France as I would have hoped; even Quebec was more French—and you said we were close to some old Chinese temple you wanted to get a look at."

She looked at Abbie and added almost conspiratorially, "I wasn't comfortable going inside a pagan temple, you understand; but we do these things for our children, don't we?" She looked back at Lucy. "You'll understand soon enough, dear."

The waiter came by and explained—unnecessarily for most of them—that they had no veal, so the Marsala, Piccata, and parmesagna dishes were only available in chicken. There had been no veal in Shanghai since August, thanks to the war, but that was still news to Mrs. Kinzler.

"That is a shame," she murmured, looking back at the menu.

"But you already decided on the chicken parmesagna, didn't you, Mother?" Lucy said, pointing at something on the menu. "See? That's what you decided on, right there."

"Yes, I'll have that," Mrs. Kinzler said, and snapped the menu shut.

"It's one of my favorites," Abbie said, then looked up at the waiter. "I'll have the same."

**

They were finishing their antipasto a short time later, when Doug saw Scott Farnsworth—his head of wavy blond hair easily visible above the crowd—at the host's stand. A moment later, he was taken to a table near the window, a bottle blonde woman in a black dress on his arm.

Doug waited a moment before excusing himself. "I just saw someone I know. I'll be back in a moment."

Scott's smile when Doug approached seemed a touch strained. He stood a touch too quickly and shook Doug's hand a touch too hard.

"And how are you this evening, Miss Moody?" Doug asked the woman seated across from Scott.

She gave Doug her hand, palm down, without rising. "Very well, thank you. And you can call me Dolores, I won't mind."

"I didn't expect to see you two," Doug said, purposely cheerful. In truth, he was glad to know that Scott had followed through and called Dolores.

"My first time here," Scott said. "It came highly recommended, so I thought Dolores might enjoy it."

I bet it did, Doug thought, and knew exactly who had recommended it. "You won't be disappointed."

"I've been here once or twice," Dolores said, but didn't elaborate. Paid dates, no doubt.

Doug nodded to both of them. "Enjoy your dinners."

"I return to the ship tomorrow," Scott hastened to add before Doug left. "My leave ends in the morning."

Doug wasn't sure why Scott was so eager to inform him of that. "I hope you two have a lovely evening, then. Good night."

"Good night, Doug." The look in Scott's blue eyes seemed sad, but Doug forced himself to turn away, feeling a bit awkward, and returned to his table.

"Who was that over there?" Lucy asked.

"Someone from the ship," Doug said. "You remember meeting Scott Farnsworth."

Lucy nodded. "Oh yes, I didn't get a clear look. He's a very nice fellow."

"I agree," Kenny said, a little too quickly, with a smile that seemed forced. "He is a nice fellow. Doug has good taste in friends."

Lucy craned her neck around her mother, toward the front windows. "Is that a young lady I see with him?" she asked. Doug detected more than one question in her tone.

"Yes, her name is Dolores Moody. He met her last Saturday at Del Monte's." He held Lucy's gaze for a couple of extra seconds, hoping his look conveyed that he'd tell her the rest later.

The tiny nod and look in her eyes told him she'd understood.

The waiter arrived with a giant tray filled with steaming plates, saving Doug from any further uncomfortable subjects.

**

Saturday, April 16

Doug found the collection of seamen, NCOs, and officers from the *Valparaiso* clustered near the Peking Road pier, waiting for an available sampan to take them back to the ship, which was moored in the middle

139

of the river. He scanned the faces for Lt. Stephenson, but didn't see him there yet.

"Hey, Commander! What's with the civvies?" Seaman Chet Heiselmann called to him from a short distance away, where he stood with several buddies, including Ben Trebinski and Roger Aikins.

Doug strode over to them. "I'm not going aboard, fellas. I need to speak with Lt. Stephenson before he leaves, though. Have any of you seen him?"

Several shook their heads. "Not yet," Ben said.

Roger Aikins slapped Ben on the arm. "Trebinski here's been tellin' us about his new Chinese girlfriend. Nobody's met her, so we think he's makin' her up."

"I'm tellin' you fellas, she's real!" Ben said, cheeks flushing.

Aikins and Heiselmann both shook their heads, while their companions snickered.

"He said you've met her, though, Commander. Bet he didn't expect you to show up here, though."

Doug hesitated, not sure if he could confirm that Pan Yintao was a 'girlfriend' given what he knew; but that second's hesitation brought a satisfied know-it-all sort of look to Aikins's face, so Doug looked at him and nodded. "I saw them together."

"See?" Ben said.

"If you don't score, it don't count," Heiselmann said. "Chinese dames, they're for fucking, they ain't for marrying. So did you score, or didn't ya?"

"Yeah, did you hump her brains out with your Trebinski meat?" Aikins asked, and the group guffawed.

Ben's face turned scarlet, all the way to his ears. "I mean, it was her time of the month, so…"

Doug almost laughed at the excuse Pan Yintao had given. The seamen, though, guffawed even harder. Aikins whacked Ben up the back of the head. "Trebinski, only you would pick up some Chinese dame who was on the rag."

The red crept all the way down Ben's neck and under his white lapels. "So she let me go in the back door instead, if you know what I mean."

The laughter morphed into wide-eyed appreciation. "Damn!" someone said. Another whistled.

Aikins crossed his arms. "Hold on—you mean to tell me she took that thing *back there*?" he said those last two words in almost a whisper. "No way!"

A certain swagger came to Ben's bearing, and he raised his chin in obvious pride. "Yeah, that's right. She had a hole in the back of her panties, see, and I ripped it bigger."

"I bet you did!" Heiselmann said, and the group guffawed again.

Doug spotted Lt. Stephenson emerging from the back of a cab, so he slipped away from the group of seamen quietly and met Stephenson at the entrance to the pier.

"Commander Bainbridge, I didn't expect to see you," Stephenson said, eyeing Doug's gray suit.

"I haven't had a chance to talk with you since last Saturday night, at Del Monte's," Doug said.

"I had a swell time," Stephenson said. "Your friends are a great crew."

"I'm glad to hear that. I was worried the incident with the man getting killed falling out the window, with the police involvement and all, that would ruin the evening."

Stephenson shrugged. "Sure, that was a bad break. But it wasn't that much trouble, really. I only had to talk to the detective a couple of minutes, and that was it. Otherwise, I just talked with the fellas and drank my whiskey."

"If you don't mind me asking, what did the Detective ask you?"

"He asked me if I'd seen that little fella, the one who died, and I told him I'd seen him around. Never talked to him, though. I didn't even know his name until the Detective asked about him."

"Anything else?"

Stephenson shrugged. "I mean, he asked if I'd seen anything suspicious—anyone arguing with him, or maybe some shoving. I told him I hadn't seen anything like that."

Doug nodded. "And that was it?"

"Yeah, that was it. There wasn't anything else to tell. I didn't know the fella."

Doug considered that a few seconds. "So he didn't ask you anything about my friend Stuart?"

Stephenson cocked his head. "No, not at all. Why?"

Doug sighed. "They arrested Stuart, and charged him with murder. It's all circumstantial, and pretty flimsy at that. I wondered if they were already focusing on him when they talked with others."

Stephenson shook his head. "No. At least, not when they talked to me."

That was good. At the very least, it meant that they hadn't been looking for a scapegoat from the beginning.

"You remember the lady who joined us on Saturday night—Miss Moody—did you ever see her talking to Jimmy Lockhart?"

Something seemed to dawn in Stephenson's eyes, and they widened a tiny bit. "Yes, now that you mention it, I did see her with him once. It was late in the evening, up on the third floor. Joe and I, we had just come out of the casino—black jack, nothing more—and I remember seeing her down the corridor, with that Jimmy Lockhart."

A tingle ran up Doug's neck. "Were they alone?"

Stephenson nodded. "Yes, I believe they were."

Doug's pulse quickened. "Did they look like they were arguing, perchance?"

Stephenson thought for a second. "I don't know for sure, but possibly. She didn't look happy, that much I'm certain of."

"How do you mean exactly?" Doug asked.

Stephenson shrugged. "The look on her face, I suppose. She didn't look *angry* exactly, but sort of...pained I guess is the best word for it. Her face looked pained."

Doug could feel his excitement building, and his breathing came fast. "What was Lockhart doing at the time?"

"Well, he had his hand on her elbow—" Stephenson stopped, his eyes widened, and he snapped his fingers. "I saw her pull it away from him. From the corner of my eye, when Joe and I were going down the stairs. She pulled her elbow out of his hand. Sort of forcefully, actually, now that I think about it. Like she tugged it from his grip."

Doug's breath really came short and fast now. "Could you hear what they were saying?"

Stephenson shook his head. "Sorry, Commander. If they were talking loudly enough for us to hear, I wasn't paying enough attention to them to notice."

Angry words are often spoken very quietly.

Doug grinned, and patted Stephenson on the arm. "Thanks, Ross. That was more helpful than you realize."

**

Something was wrong. Doug could tell the moment he stepped through the apartment door.

Bao was standing in the middle of the living room, shoulders slumped, looking morose. Lucy stood near him, leaning one arm against the back of the couch for support; her eyes looked heavy, almost droopy. He guessed that was from exasperation as much as physical exhaustion.

He couldn't see his mother-in-law, but he could hear her footfalls in the spare bedroom, and they sounded agitated.

He slipped up beside Lucy, who looked relieved to see him, and kissed her cheek. "What's going on?" he asked, just above a whisper.

She placed both hands flat against his chest. "Why don't you take Bao to visit the tailor's?"

He cocked his head in curiosity. "Alright. Mind if I ask why?"

Lucy closed her eyes, took a deep breath through her nose. "According to Mother, he doesn't have a single thing suitable to wear at dinner time. I tried explaining that we don't expect that, but she's worked up about it for some reason. Says he has to have a jacket and tie, or what will people think?" She rolled her eyes and shook her head.

Doug glanced over at Bao, who stared at a distant spot on the floor somewhere behind them. He could only imagine the tone Mrs. Kinzler had taken with him on the subject.

Doug took a deep breath, and put his hands on her shoulders, looking her in the eyes. "It'll be fine. I'll take care of it."

"Thank you, Doug," she said, and then mouthed the words 'I'm sorry.'

He gave her a faint smile, touched her cheek, and gave her a quick peck on the mouth before turning toward the young Chinese man behind her. "C'mon Bao, let's go get you fitted for a suit."

**

It was a fifteen minute walk to the nearest Chinese tailor shop on Lloyd Road downtown, but Doug enjoyed the fresh air. It was a beautiful warm spring day, with just the right amount of breeze counteracting the first hints of summer humidity.

Mr. Zeng, the tailor, got up from a sewing machine in the back room, visible from the show room in the front, and greeting them in Shanghainese. Doug and Bao both bowed to him and returned the greeting.

"We need a full suit for my friend here," Doug said, and Zeng jumped right to work, taking Bao's measurements and then rushing to a rack in the back, from which he returned with an armload of suits.

"These are all your size. First we will pick the style, and then you will put it on so I can mark the alterations," Zeng explained to Bao, correctly guessing that he'd never been through the process before.

As Zeng held up various options, Doug was careful not to direct the conversation, and allow Bao to choose the suit he liked best. But Bao often looked bewildered, overwhelmed by the choices, so Doug found himself chiming in on each one.

They got it narrowed down to three choices. "Let us see how they look on you," Zeng said to Bao, and directed him behind a folded screen that shielded him from view on the street, but not from the entire room. Doug was a little startled to find that Bao didn't wear anything under his trousers, and he averted his eyes until the young man came out in the first suit.

"Do you also sell undergarments, Mr. Zeng?" The absence was unfortunately more obvious in tight suit pants than in the looser trousers that Bao usually wore.

The tailor bowed, and regretfully said, "Go to department store for undergarments."

Doug returned the bow. "Thank you, Mr. Zeng." A visit to Sincere Department store was in order. His mother-in-law was probably too prudish to look at the front of a man's pants, but he couldn't guarantee she wouldn't notice, and her need to share a strong opinion might outweigh any prudishness about the subject.

After trying on all three suits, Bao made a choice—the heather gray checkered one with a light blue shirt. Mr. Zeng had him step toward the front window, where the light was brightest, so he could mark the alterations in chalk.

A young Chinese man passing by in Western attire—a stylish *mopu* with a scarlet red handkerchief folded in the pocket of a tan suit, and a red hat band on his tan fedora, tipped at a jaunty angle—glanced in, and then did a double-take at Doug and held his gaze. A look of surprise widened his dark eyes, and he stopped abruptly and backtracked to the front door.

"Hello again, Mr. Bainbridge," the young man said in Shanghainese, and Doug cocked his head in curiosity at how he knew his name. Or that he spoke Shanghainese. The young man glanced over at Bao with an amused half-smile. "I didn't realize you had a young 'friend.' And you're buying him a new suit. Aren't you a man of secrets?"

Mr. Zeng cleared his throat, but otherwise appeared to concentrate quite hard on marking the cuffs of the pants.

The young man's voice was *very* familiar, but Doug couldn't quite place it—then it dawned on him. It was the same voice as Pan Yintao, only a note lower. The pitch difference was subtle, but it had nearly thrown him off.

Liu Fan's eyes tracked down unashamedly to the front of Bao's suit pants, and his smile widened. He glanced back at Doug with a look of appreciation. "So many surprises. You have good taste."

Doug hoped Liu Fan meant the suit.

"Li Baosheng is our *amah*," he hurried to specify.

Amusement twinkled from Liu Fan's eyes. "A young man engaged as an amah—how interesting."

Doug chose to ignore the implication. But Scott Farnsworth had jumped to the same conclusion. He forced that from his mind.

"You are a man of secrets and surprises yourself, Liu Fan."

Liu's amused smile turned frosty.

"You should have told my friend Ben the truth," Doug continued, lowering his voice.

"How I find love is none of your business," Liu hissed. He cast a sideways glance at Bao, and added with a vicious sneer, "Nor is it my business how you find yours, Mr. Bainbridge."

"It's my business when it's my friend who is deceived."

The sneer on Liu's face was almost grotesque in its exaggeration. "Men like him do not want to know the truth. Believe me."

Mr. Zeng stood without looking at either Liu Fan or Doug, and told Bao to go change, and bring the suit back to him. He turned to Doug, but didn't meet his eye. "The cost will be twenty dollars for the suit, plus three dollars for the shirt, and seventy-five cents for the neck tie, please."

Doug removed his wallet and counted out exact change, while Liu Fan's eyes glowed in triumph.

Liu peered around the screen to catch a glimpse of Bao's backside, and then gave Doug a haughty grin before grabbing a cerulean blue silk tie and matching handkerchief. He handed a dollar bill to Mr. Zeng, who wrapped the items in brown paper.

"Enjoy your purchase, Mr. Bainbridge," Liu Fan said over his shoulder as he headed toward the door. "I always enjoy mine."

Bao came out from behind the screen in his regular clothes and handed the suit jacket and pants to Mr. Zeng.

"I will complete alterations by day after tomorrow," Zeng said. Then he wrapped up the shirt and tie, tied the package with twine, and handed it to Bao.

"I have seen that person before," Bao said to Doug in English when they left Mr. Zeng's tailor shop. "The one who came in, who was teasing you about me. No one likes him."

"I'm not surprised, Bao."

"He always say nasty things about everyone," Bao continued. "I don't listen to things he say. Like Charlie always tell me, don't worry what people say about you. They can't change the truth."

"Those are wise words." Doug wished he felt it. "We should all remember that more often. Now let's get you some socks and underpants." They continued walking toward Sincere Department Store on Nanking Road.

**

The dining room at the Astor House Hotel rang with lively conversation and laughter, but Doug still worried that their table's boisterous banter might be too much for his mother-in-law. He kept glancing at her face, and her expression remained one of stony endurance more than enjoyment. But Lucy seemed not to be paying the least attention to that, so he tried not to worry about it over much.

Stuart sat on her right, and he told her all about his legal trouble. "Doug's helping Kenny prove my innocence."

"Perhaps if you didn't go to such dangerous places, you wouldn't need help proving innocence."

"Del Monte isn't a dangerous place," Fred said from the other side of Stuart. "It's a real swanky joint."

At her mother's bemused look, Lucy said, "He means that it's an upscale establishment."

"I see. Have you been there often, dear?"

"I haven't, but Doug has. Once. It's way out in the country, probably six or seven miles from here."

"How was your steak, Mother Kinzler?" Doug asked to change the subject.

"Quite satisfactory, thank you, Douglas," she said with a nod, pushing her almost-empty plate an inch farther away from her.

Pete raised his hand, and the waiter hurried over. "Another two bottles of wine, please." Pete's gregarious smile warmed the whole table. "Something to go with dessert this time. On my tab, if you please."

They had the largest round table under the giant round stained glass window in the center of the intricately carved ceiling, its many colors twinkling in the light of several glittering chandeliers hanging all around the cavernous room. They were eleven total: Pete and Julia, George and Betty, Kenny and Abbie, Doug and Lucy, plus Fred and Stuart. Fred was alone tonight—no Yang Liling—so Mrs. Kinzler made an odd number.

"What do you say after this we have a nightcap over at Ciro's?" Pete asked the table.

"I'm game," George said. "We told the *amah* we'd be out late tonight."

"Count us in," Kenny said with a grin.

Doug glanced at his mother-in-law, who had stiffened a little. "Lucy? What do you think?"

Mrs. Kinzler touched her daughter's arm. "You need your rest, dear. We mustn't over tire you in your condition."

"I'm fine, Mother," Lucy said, brightly. "But you can go home, if you're tired. Doug can have the cab drop you off on the way."

Mrs. Kinzler frowned. "I shouldn't be alone with that young man in your apartment. It's simply not done, dear."

Doug couldn't help the smile that crept across his mouth at the thought of her reaction if she knew she had absolutely nothing to fear from Bao because his interests lay entirely elsewhere. Or that her daughter had spent countless days and nights alone in the apartment with Bao. She'd be scandalized. He hid it with his hand.

"It's Bao's night off, Mother," Lucy said, as breezily as if she were talking about tomorrow's weather. "He won't be home until morning."

"Well, then, I think I shall like to retire early," Mrs. Kinzler said. She cast a sideways glance at Doug before looking back at Lucy. "If you two want to go out cavorting, it's no business of mine. You're adults, as you've pointed out to me, and you can make your own decisions. Just remember, we have Easter services in the morning."

The back-handed way she delivered that was worthy of his own mother. Doug almost shook his head in wonder at how similar they could be on occasion.

"Just a nightcap," Pete said. "We can all be home before ten. Gotta beat curfew."

Doug suppressed a laugh. No one could deliver a deadpan like Pete.

"I think that sounds like an excellent idea," Lucy said, and put her hand on top of her mother's on the table, not seeming the least bit perturbed at her mother's tone. "We'll be careful not to wake you."

Doug almost laughed out loud this time, and deliberately turned away so his mother-in-law wouldn't see the mirth on his face.

"We all have an older relative like that," Abbie whispered to him. "For me, it's my Aunt Maude. She's an old spinster, and I adore her, mostly. But she does hold onto certain old-fashioned maiden lady attitudes, and isn't shy about sharing them. With anyone and everyone."

Doug smiled, and leaned closer to her to whisper. "I can't complain. My mother's worse that Lucy's. I can't imagine what she'd say if she were here."

But she'd never be here, not in a million years. He was suddenly reminded that Mrs. Kinzler had dined with his parents in San Francisco, and a rush of dread poured through his midsection as he imagined the topics of conversation.

He'd find out soon enough, the next time he received a letter from his mother.

14

Monday, April 18

The unmistakable roar of the seaplane through Doug's open office window rattled his desk seconds before the audible splashdown in the Huang Po River. A tingle of nerves swept down his back and settled into his stomach with a flutter. Was it the seaplane from Hong Kong? Or the one from Manila?

He knew in his gut it was the one from Manila; it had been a couple of weeks since they'd received mail from the United States.

He'd find out soon enough.

**

Lucy smiled at him from the couch when he walked through the door that evening. "Good day at work?" she asked, before he leaned down and kissed her.

"Quiet."

"There are a couple of letters for you on the table. From San Francisco."

Dear God, let them be from Ellie or Franny. Or hell, even from Will. But he knew in his gut before he looked at the handwriting that they wouldn't be from his sisters or his brother. The look in Lucy's eyes seemed to confirm his suspicions.

He almost ignored them until after he'd changed out of his navy uniform, but that would only prolong the agony, so he strode to the table and picked up the two thin envelopes, with colorful Air Mail stamps.

He chose to open the one from his father first. It was predictably brief.

April 1, 1938

Dear Doug,

We had the pleasure of dining with your mother-in-law at the house last night. She told us she's on her way to Shanghai now because your wife is expected to deliver your baby in less than a month. You can imagine the shock this caused to your mother, and to me. We are educated people, son, and we know how long it takes to produce a baby. We can also do math.

I don't know what we're going to say to people at the club.

At least you married her. We couldn't have a bastard in the family.

Dad

Doug sighed. He almost could have written that letter in his father's voice himself. He took a deep fortifying breath before opening the envelope addressed to him in his mother's handwriting, his fingers already trembling.

Friday, April 1, 1938

Dear Douglas,

Mrs. Kinzler was kind enough to call on us when she came to San Francisco before her passage to Shanghai to visit her daughter and you. She is a most respectable lady, which is more than I can say for the two of you at this moment. You can imagine our shock when she told us your baby is expected at the end of this month. Babies should not arrive a mere seven months after their parents' marriage.

We raised you with better principles than that, Douglas Preston Bainbridge. You cannot imagine the disappointment and perplexity we feel toward your behavior. We expect you to behave better than the wickedness of your generation. I don't know how we'll explain your lapse of judgement to people at church once they find out, as I'm certain they will.

On the subject of church, second only to our disappointment in your licentiousness was word from Mrs. Kinzler that you and Lucy have only attended church three times since Lucy's arrival in Shanghai. That's been nearly two years, may I remind you.

I have suspected for some time that you have not been diligent in your church attendance since you've been in Shanghai these past three years, based on things Reverend Allen has written to me. But I was not aware of just how negligent you've been in that regard. Only three times in almost two years! It's clear to see the cause of your moral failing.

It is small solace that you and Lucy chose to marry once the fruit of your sin manifested. I can take small comfort in that, hoping that you are not completely lost. I pray that the arrival of your child will anchor you, and that you will seek God's blessing on your new family through the gift of baptism.

With heavy heart, I am sincerely,

Mother

The audacity of telling a twenty-eight-year-old adult how to live his life! Doug dropped the letter onto the table and stormed out of the room.

**

Tuesday, April 19

Dr. Yang's office sat at the corner of Love Lane, a narrow street not much more than an alley that diagonally cut the corner from Bubbling Well Road to Yates Street uptown, west of the British Country Club; the latter hadn't actually been in the country for twenty years.

Love Lane was a notorious "den of sin," in sharp contrast to the upscale restaurants and nightclubs just a block away on Bubbling Well Road, and Doug wasn't entirely comfortable coming here. He tugged the rim of his hat lower. The daytime crowd was sparse enough, and exclusively Chinese—but what if someone he knew happened to see him turn off Bubbling Well Road onto the infamous Love Lane?

He shuddered to think what that might do to his reputation, but he forced that thought from his mind. He had a purpose, damn it. This was for Stuart. Still, he walked faster.

He passed the darkened entrance to the St. Anna Ballroom, the one respectable establishment on the two-block lane, and home to XQHA Radio's nightly broadcasts. It was an exclusively Chinese nightclub, but with an American swing band.

A pair of middle-aged Chinese men in western business suits entered the building next door, and Doug avoided eye contact. The "Medical Massage Clinic" was rumored to finish every therapy session with a massage of the genitals. And one of the unmarked buildings near it was the infamous brothel of Madam Kennedy, an American woman who only employed European girls, charging high fees to wealthy Shanghailanders. The joke around Shanghai was that Madam Kennedy was closed on Sundays to honor the Lord's Sabbath.

He spotted the sign for Dr. Yang's office on the corner at Yates. He hurried through the door, all too eager to be off the street.

The young Chinese nurse at the desk looked at Doug with unmasked curiosity. "You wantchee talkee pidgin with doctor?" she asked in Pidgin.

"Yes, I'd like to see Dr. Yang, about a problem I have," Doug said in Shanghainese. At the nurse's arched eyebrow, he added, "It's a delicate matter."

The nurse didn't react to that, only pulled a form from a drawer and took a pen. "Your name please, sir?" she said in Shanghainese.

"John Smith," Doug said, hoping the nurse wouldn't recognize the obvious pseudonym.

She didn't react, only wrote it down and told him to have a seat.

**

Dr. Yang reacted with obvious surprise when he saw a white man sitting in the waiting room. He pulled a chart from the nurse's desk, looked at it, then back at Doug. "Mr. Smith?"

Doug stood. "I have a sort of delicate hormonal problem, Doctor," he said in Mandarin, gambling that the doctor understood but the nurse wouldn't. "I heard about you from someone named Pan Yintao, who I assume is a patient of yours."

Dr. Yang ushered Doug into his office and closed the door. "I cannot discuss other patients, you understand," he said in Mandarin.

"I understand," Doug said, and hopped onto the edge of the exam table.

"What is the young man's name with the 'problem,' Mr. Smith?" Dr. Yang asked, picking up a notepad.

"It's my problem."

Dr. Yang smiled indulgently, and switched to English. "Perhaps you misunderstood my question. We are discreet, but I still need the name of your young man who is in need of the hormone therapy, for my records. Ethically, I must know his real name before I can treat him for you. You may remain anonymous, though, Mr. Smith."

Dr. Yang's English was impeccable. And the way he said 'Mr. Smith' that time gave no doubt that he understood perfectly well that it was a pseudonym.

"His name is Li Baosheng." The only young Chinese man Doug knew.

Dr. Yang scribbled on his notepad. "How old is Mr. Li?"

"He's twenty-two."

"And how extensive is the therapy for young Mr. Li?"

"Pardon?" Doug asked.

Dr. Yang looked up from his notepad. "How much estrogen do you want for him? And should we assume his testicles will remain intact? We can have them removed, if they bother you, Mr. Smith; but most clients do not mind them. Or even enjoy them in private, so long as no one outside can tell they exist."

Doug's mouth hung open for several seconds, and he was at a total loss for words. He wasn't sure what he had expected exactly, but he would have never imagined this conversation.

"I—I don't know," he managed to say. "What do you recommend, Doctor?"

Dr. Yang set his notepad on the desk, crossed his legs in a most western fashion, and folded his hands over his knee. "More than a decade ago, physicians in Germany pioneered the use of high doses of estrogen on transvestites who want to physically become women, and the patients lost their beards and grew full breasts. With a high enough dose, this could be obtained either with or without an orchiectomy." Scrutinizing Doug's face, he added, "Surgical removal of the testicles. But most of my clients do not wish for their beloved to become a woman, only to hide his masculinity in public. In my experiments, I have discovered that much lower doses of estrogen will bring the desired beard loss, with only minimal increase in breast tissue in young patients."

Doug had no doubt his expression looked completely dumbfounded, judging by the way Dr. Yang looked at him.

"If you wish for your beloved's body to remain masculine in the bedroom, but not appear so in public, then I recommend one milligram daily."

Doug wanted to keep Dr. Yang talking, so he nodded and said, "Whatever you think is best, Doctor."

A faint smile stretched Dr. Yang's lips. "You are nervous, Mr. Smith. There is no need to be. No one here will judge you; not for your preferences, and not for your decisions."

A nervous laugh escaped Doug's mouth before he could stop it. Sweat had soaked the pits of his shirt, and he only hoped it wouldn't soak through his suit jacket and be obvious. He wiped his mouth, removing the sweat off his upper lip. "I'm not used to that level of frankness, that's all."

Yang pursed his lips. "I assume that is why you sought a Chinese doctor. Westerners are judgmental, but in China we value discretion. Attitudes have shifted some since westerners arrived, but not that much."

That piqued Doug's curiosity. "What do you mean?"

Yang took a deep breath through the nose. "For centuries, it was traditional in China for wealthy men to maintain concubines, in addition to their wives. Sometimes, the concubine was a young man instead of a young woman, and he is called *Jiǎn xiù*, a 'Cut Sleeve.' This was accepted in China across centuries and dynasties, and not questioned until westerners came here and imposed their values.

"Now, wealthy men who keep a beloved Cut Sleeve want him to appear to be a woman in public, so to not bring scorn; but they do not want them to *become* women. That is how I came to experiment with low estrogen doses." Yang paused for a second before adding, "It is also useful for professional female impersonators, who do not wish to have the shadow of a beard to mar the fantasy image. You said that Pan Yintao referred you to me, so that is why I mention that."

But you won't discuss other patients, but Doug left that unspoken. "I understand now, thank you."

"I will need to examine your young Mr. Li before I can prescribe the therapy," Dr. Yang continued. "Will you be able to bring him soon?"

Doug was stumped as to how to proceed.

Dr. Yang seemed to read his thoughts. "There is much to consider. Please take your time. When you are ready, you may bring him to me and I will prescribe the appropriate dose after examination." The doctor got up, and extended his hand.

Doug shook it, mumbling "Thank you, Doctor," before hurrying from the exam room and out the office door. He tugged his fedora low over his face and hurried up Yates Road, away from Love Lane as fast as he could, toward the street car on Bubbling Well Road.

Sitting on the street car headed downtown, he questioned the purpose of the outing. Had he learned anything of value? Or was he just satisfying his own morbid curiosity about Pan Yintao?

Just because she was on the portico with Ben at the time Jimmy Lockhart plummeted from that window, didn't mean she wasn't involved. Instinct kept bringing him back to that. There had been bad blood between Pan Yintao and Jimmy Lockhart, and even if she wasn't personally the one to shove him through the window, she might be the key to finding out who did.

He needed to talk to Jonesy.

**

He found Jonesy exiting the Cathay Hotel after lunching there, as usual.

"Hi there, Douglas. To what do I owe this pleasure?"

"You know anything about *Ji ǎn xiù*?" Doug asked.

"Don't use big Chinese words with me, wise guy. What is that in English?"

"Something called a 'Cut Sleeve.'"

"Oh, sure," Jonesy said, and a devilish twinkle came to his eye. "That's an old story, about one of the Han Dynasty emperors who didn't want to wake his boyfriend, who was sleeping on his sleeve, so he cut it and went back to court with half his sleeve gone." He pointed his cigar at Doug. "The Chinese used to be pretty open about that, until American and British missionaries came along and told them it was wrong."

Doug took the point. He was pretty sure he'd told Jonesy at one time or another that his mother's parents had been Presbyterian missionaries in Guangdong province.

"Why do you ask?" Then the devilish twinkle returned to Jonesy's eyes. "You looking to get one for yourself?"

Doug scowled. "Of course not. This is for Stuart's case."

"Of course," Jonesy said, but he still had that annoying twinkle in his eyes. "What's the angle?"

"There was a female impersonator at Del Monte's that Saturday night when Jimmy Lockhart was thrown from the window, and I noticed there was some friction between the two of them. It might have been incidental, but I suspect there's more to it than that."

"Tell me more."

"This female impersonator—the professional name is Pan Yintao, and she performs at a club in the Western Roads called The Pink Lotus— she has a personal alibi for the time of the murder."

"How solid is the alibi?"

"Pretty solid," Doug said. "I saw her. She was outside on the back portico with a friend of mine when the victim flew out of a window on the other side of the house."

"That's pretty solid," Jonesy said with a chuckle. "So you must think she's connected in some way to the real killer."

"That's right. And she's got some interesting connections. She seems to travel around the nightclub scene with Yang Liling, Fred's girlfriend, along with Liling's cousin, Yang Yajun. Yajun's fiancé is a medical student at St. John's, and he studied under her father, who's an endocrinologist. That's a hormone and gland doctor."

"I know what it is," Jonesy interrupted, gruff.

"Sorry, just making sure," Doug said, holding up his hands in a conciliatory gesture. He leaned close, and lowered his voice. "Dr. Yang's practice seems to focus on prescribing low doses of estrogen to these Cut Sleeve boys, just enough to lose their beards and raise their voices enough to pass in public, without changing their masculine appearance in private."

"Interesting," Jonesy said, nodding.

"And Dr. Yang also prescribes low doses of estrogen to female impersonators—including our Pan Yintao—to help them create the illusion."

Jonesy was silent a few seconds, looking up in thought. "Alright—I'll grant those are interesting connections. But unless you've got reasons to suspect any of the Yangs in Jimmy Lockhart's murder, I don't see where you're going with this."

Neither did Doug, really. That's what he was hoping Jonesy would help him with. He held his hands out palm-up. "That's what I don't know. But I suspect there's something there."

"Sounds like a pretty big fishing expedition to me."

"Don't tell me you haven't gone out on some pretty big fishing expeditions when you thought there was a big story hiding somewhere."

Jonesy chuckled. "Yep, you got me there. But on any fishing expedition, you have to know where to start, where to cast your first line."

"I'm all ears," Doug said.

A wicked grin creased Jonesy's heretofore serious demeanor. "Sounds like you and I are going to pay a visit to The Pink Lotus one night this week."

15

Wednesday, April 20

"Commander, Mrs. Bainbridge is on the line," the voice of the front desk lieutenant crackled over the intercom.

Doug's heart did a double beat. Lucy didn't call him at the office—especially not barely an hour after he arrived. There was only one reason that she'd be calling. *But the baby's not due for another five days.* And everyone said first babies were almost always late.

"Put her through." He answered before the first ring was barely started. "Lucy? Are you alright, dear?"

"It's coming today, Doug," she said, sounding breathless.

His heart jumped again. "Are you sure? It's early."

"Yes, I'm sure. Mother agrees. The pains started right after you left this morning. Not five minutes after you walked out the door, doesn't *that* just figure? It's like the baby knew this was the least convenient part of the day."

"Other than the middle of the night," Doug said, more boisterous than he'd intended, and now suddenly conscious that his grin was so big the corners of his mouth ached.

He was glad to hear a laugh from her. "That's true. At least our baby won't be a complete brat from the beginning."

He loved her sense of humor. He God damn loved it.

"But you're really sure? Have you called George?"

"We're sure. This isn't like those random ones I've had the last few days. They're regular, and they're strong. Mother's helped me time them—they were eight minutes apart, but it's down to about six minutes now. And no, I haven't called George—I wanted to call you first, silly."

"I'll be there in ten minutes!" He dropped the receiver into the cradle a little too hard, and cringed at how loud it would sound on Lucy's end of the line. Too late now. He grabbed his cap and sprinted out the door.

"My wife's having a baby!" he said to the front office staff. He might have been embarrassed at how loudly he said it, almost shouting it, but he was too damned excited to care.

The announcement was greeted with a chorus of congratulations that he barely acknowledged in his rush toward the stairs.

**

Lucy was sitting on the couch when he hurried in, her mother next to her and holding her hand. Lucy's face was flushed, and her forehead sweaty. Her suitcase stood beside the couch. Bao was on his hands and knees in the middle of the room, scrubbing a large spot on the floor with a sponge.

"No doubt at all now," Lucy said with a faint smile.

"Your timing is perfect, Douglas," Mrs. Kinzler said, rising from the couch. "It's time to take Lucy to the hospital."

"I've got a cab waiting," Doug said, breathless from his sprint up the stairs.

"Go change," Lucy said, an amused half-smile gracing her lips.

Doug looked down and realized with a start that he was still in his navy uniform. He sprinted to their bedroom, practically tore the uniform off without even bothering to close the door and dressed in his light wool suit as quickly as he could.

Mrs. Kinzler helped Lucy up from the couch while Doug grabbed the suitcase and held the front door. "I'll call you in a little while, Bao, and let you know how it's going."

He enjoyed the slight scowl that flitted across his mother-in-law's face.

It was only a five minute cab ride from their apartment building to St. Elizabeth's Hospital, the women's hospital of the American Episcopal Church. Doug paid the driver, and tipped him a half-dollar before helping his wife out of the backseat.

A young nurse immediately took Lucy's hand and helped her into a wheelchair. "We'll take her from here, sir," she said in an American accent with a patient smile. "Check in at the front desk, and the doctor will come and talk to you soon."

"I'm her mother," Mrs. Kinzler announced.

"Then you may come back with her briefly, while we get her prepared," the nurse said. "Follow me, please."

Doug stood immobile for a few seconds, staring after the two women taking his wife through a double door into a long white corridor. "How are you feeling, Mrs. Bainbridge?" the nurse asked before the doors closed behind them.

"Sir?"

Doug looked over, startled, at the young Chinese orderly standing just inside the hospital entrance, looking at him expectantly. "I'm sorry. Where do I go? I need to check my wife in. She's having a baby."

The orderly's knowing smile said he'd had to direct nervous fathers countless times. "This way, please." His accent in English was good, and Doug didn't think to switch languages. He mumbled thanks in English, and followed him to the front desk, where a middle-aged white nurse with dark hair looked up and seemed to appraise him in one second.

"Yes, sir?" she asked in a crisp British accent.

"I'm checking in my wife, Lucy Bainbridge. To the maternity ward."

"Fill out this form please," the nurse said. She handed him a clipboard with two pieces of paper. "And then sign this consent form, so that we'll be able to put her under ether in a little while."

He handed the completed forms back to her a couple of minutes later. She smiled at him, warm and kindly, and told him to have a seat in the waiting room. "These things take a while, Mr. Bainbridge, but the doctor will be out to talk with you in a little while. Just try to relax and stay patient."

Easy for you to say. But Doug just nodded and took a seat.

**

An hour passed. He tried to remain calm, but sitting alone with no news wouldn't let him, and he got up a few times to pace a lap around the waiting room.

Mrs. Kinzler came to the waiting room a little over an hour after they arrived. Her lips were pursed, her face stony, but Doug thought he saw worry in her gray-blue eyes.

"The doctor has arrived, and so they won't let me stay with her any longer," she announced, not sounding at all pleased with that development.

She took the empty seat next to Doug, crossed her ankles, and folded her hands atop her knees. "When I had both of my children, my mother was able to stay with me the entire time. My mother *and* her sister." Then she sighed. "But those were different times; we had babies at home in those days. The doctor and his nurse came to us. We didn't go to a hospital, and they didn't put us under ether."

Something in her tone told Doug she didn't think that was progress.

"I'm glad to hear the doctor is seeing her." *At last.* "I've wanted to call our friends, but I didn't have anything to tell them yet."

"Hmm. When I had my children, Doctor Ewald gave Herbert regular updates. That was easy to do at home—I was upstairs in the bedroom, and Herbert was downstairs in the drawing room, or in his study."

Again that tone that said the old way was better. Doug just nodded in implicit agreement.

**

It was another half-hour before the doctor came out to talk to him. He was about forty, balding, with a spate of thick brown hair around the back and side, and wispy strands on the top.

"Mr. Bainbridge, I'm Doctor Rodgers, your wife's obstetrician." He had the sort of posh mid-Atlantic lockjaw accent that came from schools such as *Hah-vahd*.

"How do you do, Doctor?" Doug said, shaking hands. "This is my mother-in-law, Mrs. Kinzler."

"How do you do, ma'am?" The doctor nodded to Mrs. Kinzler, and then addressed himself to Doug. "Your wife is progressing quite well. I would expect you'll have a son or daughter by late afternoon or early evening, Mr. Bainbridge."

That could be another six hours. Doug suppressed a groan. "Then we can go have lunch, and not miss anything?"

"Absolutely. There's nothing to miss at this point. I'll come out again in a few hours and give you an update."

**

Doug found a pay telephone in front of the hospital. He deposited a nickel, and asked the operator to dial Dr. George Howerton's office. His Chinese nurse answered, and Doug asked for Dr. Howerton.

"One moment."

It was a couple of minutes before George came on the line. "George, it's Doug. Lucy's in labor at St. Elizabeth's. Dr. Rodgers told me it'll probably come in the late afternoon or early evening."

"I know, he called me about twenty minutes ago."

It irked Doug that Dr. Rodgers had called George before coming out to speak to him in the waiting room. "What did he say?"

George launched into an explanation of centimeters in dilation, and something called 'effacement,' whatever that meant.

"And all that means?"

"That things are moving along well. Don't worry, Douggie. That baby will be here soon enough. And that's when the real fun begins." He laughed, deep and hearty, and hung up.

Doug called Kenny next, and Pete after that. By the time Pete answered his office phone at the HSBC, Mrs. Kinzler was beginning to look cross at the wait, so Doug kept it brief, and asked Pete to pass on the news to Fred and Stuart.

He took his mother-in-law to the Park Hotel, less than two blocks away. He knew the restaurant there served club sandwiches, and knowing how picky Mrs. Kinzler was with 'strange' food, he thought it best to keep it familiar.

They mostly ate in silence, both of them alone with their thoughts.

"Is she suffering right now?" Doug asked, finally giving voice the worry that had been nagging him for a couple of hours.

A sad sort of smile creased Mrs. Kinzler's lips, and her gray-blue eyes looked kindly at him, more so than he could ever remember. "There's always suffering in this, dear." She sighed. "But nowadays, they'll give the mothers ether when it gets close, and she'll sleep through the worst of it. When she wakes up she'll have a baby to care for."

**

Six-fifteen PM

Doug shot up from his chair the second Dr. Rodgers entered the waiting room. The last time he'd been there—almost two hours ago, damn it—he'd said they were getting close.

"Congratulations, Mr. Bainbridge; you have a son."

Doug's stomach flew away. Were his feet still touching the ground? The grin that stretched his mouth to its maximum let out an excited burst of air, almost a laugh. No longer 'the baby'—some faceless, nameless thing—but a *son*, a person, someone with a name.

Or at least, a name soon enough.

"A healthy one too, good size," Dr. Rodgers continued. "Seven pounds, four ounces; twenty and a half inches. Born at six-oh-one PM."

"Oh, that *is* a big baby," Mrs. Kinzler said, beaming. When had she appeared beside him?

"Ten fingers, ten toes, everything where it's supposed to be. Congratulations, sir."

"And how is Lucy?" He was so out of breath he barely got the question out.

"She's fine. She should wake up in about thirty or forty minutes. Once the nurse can get her to answer a few questions, you can go back and see her." The doctor started to step away, but then turned back. "Oh, and another nurse will be out in a few minutes so you can put the name on the birth certificate."

"But my wife and I never came to an agreement on a boy's name," Doug said. Wouldn't it figure, they had settled on a girl's name—Amelia, or Amy for short—but they disagreed on boys' names.

"Put down the one you want," Dr. Rodgers said, chuckling. "Legally, it's your decision. You're the father. Congratulations, again."

A smiling middle-aged Chinese nurse came out almost as soon as Dr. Rodgers had disappeared behind the ward doors. "Need baby name for birth certificate," she said, handing Doug a clipboard.

Doug hesitated, the pen hovering over the blank line on the form. He'd wanted to go with Miles, but Lucy didn't like that one for some reason. She wanted Daniel. It wasn't that Doug didn't like that name—it was perfectly fine—but it didn't have the pizazz of Miles. And it called to mind silly Bible stories about a lion's den.

The pen hovered another second, and then he wrote:

Daniel Timothy Bainbridge

The first name she wanted, and the middle name he did. And they sounded good together. Handing the clipboard back to the nurse, who beamed at him while she bowed and backed away, he felt a rush of exhilaration.

'The Baby' was now a real person—Danny.

16

The young American nurse who had escorted Lucy in that morning now led Doug upstairs to the Newborns Ward. A giant plate glass window along one side of the corridor showed dozens of swaddled babies in wooden cradles, arranged in neat rows.

He searched the signs taped to the ends of the cradles, until he found the one that read "Bainbridge, Daniel." It was in the middle of the second row, and the blanket swaddling the tiny infant was baby blue. The little head, slightly elongated at the crown, was covered with a dusting of pale yellow hairs, almost white. He was asleep, but his little face was bright red, as if he'd been crying a moment ago. Perhaps he had been.

"Hi there, Danny," Doug whispered, touching his fingers to the window. His throat grew tight, and he blinked away a bit of moisture from his eyes. He stood there and stared for several minutes. The baby didn't move, save for the tiny rise and fall of his little chest, but Doug couldn't peel his eyes away.

The nurse came back ten minutes later, and touched his arm to draw him out of his reverie.

"Mrs. Bainbridge is awake, sir. She's asked to see you."

The nurse led him to a room down the corridor, where two beds stood divided by a white curtain. The woman in the bed closest to the door was raven-haired and dark complected, perhaps French or Italian. In the bed by the window, Lucy sat propped up on two pillows, wearing a white hospital gown. She had dark circles under her eyes, but her face lit up when she saw him.

"Doug! Have you seen him? How does he look?"

He grinned, and nodded as he leaned down to kiss her. "Yes, I saw him a few minutes ago. I could only see his head, but he looks beautiful."

She smiled wistfully, a far-off look in her eyes. "I can't wait to see him. They say I'll get to hold him soon, when he needs to be fed."

"Only a few minutes, sir," the nurse said, waiting at the edge of the curtain.

"I called everyone," Doug said, sitting on the side of the bed. "Your mother's downstairs. She's been here all day, of course. Maybe they'll let her come up and see you in a little while." He looked at the nurse with raised eyebrows.

"Yes, Mrs. Bainbridge's mother can be here when she feeds the baby. No fathers allowed, I'm afraid."

"When can I see the baby in person?" Doug asked her.

"When you take him home next week."

Lucy took his hand, gave it a squeeze. "They told me his name is Daniel. Thank you, Doug."

Doug smiled at her. "His middle name's Timothy."

She laughed. "Of course it is. But I like it. Daniel Timothy—I like how that sounds."

"We can call him Danny."

She laughed again. "Of *course* we'll call him Danny, Douglas Bainbridge. No little boy should be called 'Daniel' all the time. Only when he decides to be a brat."

"He'd never," Doug said, grinning.

She gave him a rueful smile. "I'm afraid he's related to you, my darling."

Doug played shocked, and she laughed harder, then laid her head on his shoulder. "I'm so happy."

"Me, too." He brushed aside strands of hair stiff with dried sweat and kissed her forehead.

"It's time for his feeding now," the nurse said, gently inserting herself between Doug and Lucy. "I'm afraid you'll need to leave now, Mr. Bainbridge."

He gave Lucy a quick kiss goodbye, and the nurse shooed him out the door. He looked back down the corridor wistfully, but the nurse made a shooing motion with her hands, and he hurried down the stairs.

**

All of their friends had collected in the waiting room while he'd been upstairs: Kenny and Abbie, Pete and Julia, George and Betty, Fred, and Stuart. Doug could hear their boisterous conversation from the corridor before he pushed through the swinging doors. His mother-in-law stood at the edge of the group, looking dyspeptic.

"Congratulations!" rang out in chorus when they spotted him, and the men rushed toward him, vying to be the first to clap him on the shoulder and shove a cigar in his hand.

"What's his name?" Abbie asked, standing on her toes to look over the men clustered around Doug.

"His name's Daniel Timothy. Danny."

"Well, happy birthday, Danny!" Pete said with a big grin, shoved a cigar in his mouth, and lit it with a match. He held the match out to Doug, who hurried to put one of the four cigars in his hand into his mouth, and puffed it into life.

The acrid smoke burned the inside of his mouth, but he still couldn't help grinning back at his friends.

"How's Lucy?" Abbie asked, looking around Kenny's lanky frame.

"She's just fine," Doug said. "She's awake, and I got to talk with her a little bit before I had to leave because Danny needed fed."

"Mrs. Kinzler!" the young American nurse called from behind them, standing on her toes and stretching her neck to peer over the tall men.

"I'm here," Mrs. Kinzler said, circling around the group.

"Mrs. Bainbridge has asked to see you, ma'am. She's feeding the baby now. Come with me, please." She ushered Mrs. Kinzler through the double doors.

"I don't think this is exactly her scene," Kenny said, nodding toward the swinging doors.

Doug laughed. "Not at all."

"You might think we're overwhelming or something!" George said with a grin. "Wherever would she get that idea?"

"This calls for a proper celebration!" Pete shouted. "Champagne, good food, the works!"

"We should keep our voices down inside the hospital, Peter," Julia said.

"Sorry, dear," Pete said, almost absently, barely glancing at his wife. "What do you say to dinner at Ciro's, Douggie? Steaks and champagne, my treat. Then we can get a suite at the Park, and keep the party going."

"Thanks, Pete, but that's really not necessary."

"Nonsense! We did it for George when Tommy was born. You were away, so you missed it."

Behind George, Betty said, "I heard it was one for the record books." George nodded in agreement.

"You've earned the same celebration," Pete said.

"Alright, alright, you've convinced me. That sounds real swell, fellas. Thanks Pete. But I've got to wait until my mother-in-law is ready to leave, and then make sure she gets home."

"What time do visiting hours end?" Pete asked.

"Eight o'clock, just like at St. Luke's," George said.

"Then I'll reserve a table at eight-thirty," Pete said. "Meet us at Ciro's then, Doug?"

Doug grinned and nodded. "Meet you there."

**

"I'm not sure I should stay alone with that chinaman," Mrs. Kinzler said with a huff an hour later, after Doug told her about his plans for the evening.

"You'll be perfectly safe, Mother Kinzler. Bao is perfectly capable of watching over you."

"Just as long as he knows to keep his hands to himself," she said with a sniff.

Doug stopped himself from laughing out loud with tremendous effort, and had to cover his mouth so she wouldn't see his smile. "I'm sure he will, but I'll talk to him nonetheless." He was amazed he could get the words out with a straight face.

"See that you do, Douglas."

**

At the Park Hotel, in a spacious suite twenty stories above Shanghai, the champagne flowed nonstop. Corks popped every few minutes. People that Doug knew from Pete and Julia's many parties came in and out, all offering their congratulations. Doug lost track of how many cigars he was given. Eventually he lost track of where he'd stashed them all; somewhere he was certain he'd remember, but now his brain was fuzzy and he couldn't.

He was used to cigarette smoke, of course—Lucy smoked, and so did George. But the cigars were something else entirely. He felt lightheaded in a way that was entirely different from the alcohol.

Perhaps the biggest surprise of the night was when Jonesy strode through the door.

"Congratulations, Douglas," he said with a jovial smile. "Kenneth called me with the good news." Then leaning closer, he said more quietly, "Just don't expect me to start calling you daddy." He winked and walked over to the bar before Doug could come up with a decent comeback.

No, he was in too good of a mood this evening to let Jonesy's little jabs get to him. Doug actually laughed.

"I invited him," Kenny said, appearing beside Doug. "I know you've worked pretty closely with him, and I figured you'd want him to know."

Doug put his arm around Kenny's shoulders—a stretch, given that Kenny was four inches taller than him—and patted his other hand on his friend's chest, managing not to spill any champagne. "I'm glad you did. I wouldn't have thought to, and that might've hurt his feelings. Jonesy's a good guy, underneath it all."

Kenny put his own arm around Doug's shoulders, and gave it a brotherly squeeze. "We've got something else in common now, you and I. Fatherhood is wonderful, you'll love it. I mean, it's really hard sometimes; especially at first, when they won't sleep. But then when they fall asleep on your shoulder, and their little face is turned toward you, all peaceful and trusting…" he sighed, and a wistful smile softened his features. "There's nothing better in the whole world."

"It's going to be at least a week until I can experience that," Doug said.

Kenny laughed. "Use that week, old chum. Get all the sleep you can now."

George was standing nearby with a group that Doug recognized, but didn't know well, and he called George's name.

"What's up, buddy?" George asked with a grin, in the deep baritone that resonated like the notes of a symphony.

"How long did it take before Tommy let you sleep all night?"

"Hasn't happened yet," George said. At the sight of Doug's reaction, he laughed out loud, throwing his head back. "He's up to about five or six hours between screaming for milk, which is a vast improvement from where we started."

Doug's heart sank with dread. "How old is he? He's more than three months now, right?"

"Thirteen and a half weeks," George said.

That suddenly sounded like an eternity. Doug's face must have shown it, too, because George started laughing again. He felt Kenny's shoulders shaking with laughter as well.

"Don't worry, old chum," Kenny said through the laughs. "It'll be done before you know it. Then they just keep getting bigger and bigger, and you'll start thinking how wonderful it was when they were little." He took a sip of champagne, and then added, "And if you're completely out of your mind, you'll start thinking how wonderful it would be to have another one, so you can have that little baby in your arms again."

"Run!" George told Kenny, and they all laughed again.

**

Yang Liling had arrived, along with her cousin Yajun—but interestingly, no Pan Yintao—and she was now monopolizing Fred's attention. Stuart approached Doug and bumped shoulders with him.

"Congratulations again, Doug," Stuart said.

"Thanks, buddy. But how are you doing? How are you holding up since..." He didn't know exactly how to put it.

"Since I got arrested and spent a weekend in jail for something I didn't do?" The tone was jocular, but there was genuine pain, and perhaps fear, in Stuart's green eyes.

"Yeah, that," Doug said. "How are you, really?"

Stuart shrugged. "Kenny says there's more than reasonable doubt, now that Mark Chapman confirmed that he saw me leave. But I'm not so sure."

Doug cocked his head. "Why is that?"

Stuart shrugged again. "What if Mark changes his story before Kenny gets him under oath?"

That was interesting. "Why do you think he would?"

"I don't know, just a feeling," Stuart said. Doug stared at him, and after a few seconds he relented and elaborated. "When I saw him arguing with Jimmy Lockhart in the men's room, it looked almost as if he was frightened or something. I don't know, it's hard to describe. I just got a feeling there was something more going on, and Mark was scared of it."

Doug pondered that for a second. "You mean scared enough that someone could pressure him into changing his story?"

"Yeah, maybe."

Doug nodded slowly, rolling that around in his head for a moment. If Mark Chapman was scared of something, and it was obvious to Stuart when Chapman had been talking privately with Jimmy Lockhart—that might mean Mark Chapman knew who killed Lockhart.

Doug needed to talk with him again. And soon.

Stuart was gazing across the room, toward where Fred and Liling were talking with Kenny and Abbie. Doug nodded their direction.

"I think this is the first time I've seen Liling without Pan Yintao trailing behind her."

Stuart made a face. "*She* works on Wednesdays."

"Works...you mean at The Pink Lotus?"

Stuart nodded. "She performs there on weeknights."

Interesting. "But not on Fridays or Saturdays?"

Stuart smirked. "How else could she be Liling's pet lizard when they go out on the town?"

"I thought performers never had weekends off," Doug mused. "I wonder how she worked that out."

Stuart smirked again. "Five bucks says she's got something on her boss."

Doug chuckled. That might fit. Bribery could buy all sorts of favors. Especially in Shanghai. "I wonder who owns the club."

Stuart looked at Doug, head cocked and one eyebrow arched. "Mr. Yang is one of the co-owners, along with his brother, Dr. Yang. That's how Liling got us in there that one time. She bribes the bouncers to not tell her father or uncle; she's not allowed in there, you see. 'It's not a place for ladies.' Ha! But she always gets what she wants, one way or another."

He looked back toward Fred and Liling, and Doug thought he heard a note of bitterness in Stuart's tone.

"Hang in there, buddy," Doug said, patting Stuart's shoulder, and then hurried away. He needed to find Jonesy.

**

"I can't tomorrow night," Jonesy said. "Got plans. How about Friday? That way, we can talk to the other performers when Pan Yintao isn't there. My guess, they line up to spill the beans the minute she's not around."

That made a lot of sense, and Doug wished he'd thought of it that way. "He goes by Liu Fan during the day. Maybe we should talk to him then, when he's not performing his alter ego."

Jonesy seemed to consider that a moment. "Maybe. But let's see what the other 'ladies of the stage' have to say first. Then if we decide to, we can confront Liu Fan with what we learn."

Doug nodded. "Good idea. Thanks Jonesy."

"My pleasure. We've got to get you out of the house now, before you're tied down with baby care." Jonesy chuckled. "I'll meet you at your place at nine o'clock Friday night. Don't over-dress, either. This ain't that kind of club."

179

17

Thursday, April 21

Doug went back to work the next day, but left early to visit Lucy. His mother-in-law was already there, having found her own cab that afternoon. Doug was hoping to have some alone time with Lucy, but Mrs. Kinzler stayed in the room.

First she had to give Doug a blow by blow of every little thing Danny had done the two times when the nurses brought him in to eat that afternoon—every yawn, every stretch, how red his little face got when he cried before a burp came out, and what a cute little sound those burps were.

Doug listened with a polite smile, nodding along, pretending to be grateful. "I feel like I was right there," he said when she'd finally finished.

Lucy gave him a look—one of those looks that said 'I agree with you, but don't push it'—and then said, "Mother, would you go tell the nurse I'd like some fresh water?"

"Of course, dear. I'll put her right on that." Mrs. Kinzler hurried out, no doubt eager for the opportunity to tell the nurse what to do.

"God, she's driving me up the wall," Lucy muttered when her mother had disappeared down the corridor.

Doug chuckled. "That bad?"

"You wouldn't believe it."

"I bet I would."

She laughed. "Yes, I bet you would. For starters, she's been telling me every little thing I'm doing wrong—or at least, *she* thinks I'm doing it wrong—and she even corrected the nurse a couple of times when she gave me advice on nursing him. The poor nurse had to physically insert herself between us so she could get a good look. My mother hovered over me before that."

Doug laughed, too. "I can believe all of it. You know I had to pretend to have a talk with Bao last night, telling him to keep his hands to himself while I was away and he was alone with your mother."

Lucy giggled. "You didn't!"

He laughed again. "No, not really—but she thinks I did. I didn't have the heart to tell her it isn't necessary."

"If you'd tried to explain, she would have banished Bao from the house."

"Don't I know it! I'm not *that* crazy."

Lucy crossed her arms. "She had words for me, about her 'concerns' regarding our moral character here in Shanghai. She did not approve of you going out last night."

Doug's pulse pounded in his ears, though it wasn't surprising that she'd react that way. His own mother wouldn't have waited even that long before sharing her opinion, with righteous indignation fueled by religious certainty.

"What did you tell her?" he asked.

Lucy shook her head. "Not that it will do any good, but I told her a new baby is worth celebrating, and that we're grateful our friends want to celebrate with us. I told her I would have gone if I could, and that scandalized her. 'A woman in your condition? Why, I never *heard* such a thing!'" Lucy put a hand on her cheek, mouth opening in mock shock as she aped her mother's voice.

They shared a laugh. Just at the moment her mother walked back through the door.

"What's so funny, dears?"

Doug and Lucy shared a look.

"Doug was just telling me something our friends said last night. You wouldn't understand the reference, since you don't live here."

Mrs. Kinzler's lips pursed, and her nose raised in the air a little. "I'm certain I wouldn't," she said, the words a little bit clipped. She took a seat, and looked directly at Doug. "Have you written to your parents today, Douglas?"

Doug cringed. "Not yet."

"No? My goodness, you must get right on that. I sent a cable to Herbert this morning, so he'd know the baby is here, and what his name is. And then I wrote him a full letter with the rest of the details, and put that in the mail before I came here. Your mother will be so disappointed if she finds out from someone else."

A shiver of panic ran through Doug's belly. "You didn't write to my mother about Danny yet, did you?"

"Not yet," Mrs. Kinzler said, sounding a little cagey. "I started a letter to her right after I finished Herbert's and Marty's, but I didn't have time to finish it today. I'll try to mail it tomorrow."

So Doug only had tonight to write to his parents. *At least I have that much.* Thank God she prioritized writing to her husband and her son over his parents and ran out of time. It would have been much worse if Mrs. Kinzler had put her letter to his parents in today's mail. But even so, he hated being pressured into doing it right away.

"There was too much going on last night, and I've been at work all day today," Doug said by way of explanation. "I'll be sure to write to them tonight."

Mrs. Kinzler's expression was frosty. "Yes, apparently there were more important things to do last night than to write to your mother about the birth of her grandson."

It was all Doug could do to ignore the comment, so he turned to Lucy and asked her how many times she'd gotten to hold Danny.

"At least a dozen," she said, letting her exhaustion show. "The nurses woke me up every two hours to feed him. I only slept in short bits all night and all morning. Then Mother came right after lunch."

And she'd been awake ever since. He could read between the lines on that one.

"You'll sleep when the baby sleeps for the first two or three months," Mrs. Kinzler said.

Lucy remained sanguine, though Doug wasn't sure how she managed. "Yes, George told me that before Danny was born."

"It bears repeating," Mrs. Kinzler said. "You'll have to let that chinaman do all of the house work for a while. And Douglas, you'll do what you can to make things easier on her, won't you? You'll need to direct your servant so your wife won't have to when she's exhausted."

Doug took a deep breath. "I'm sure Bao and I can manage things while Lucy sleeps."

"And I'll be here to make sure things run smoothly while you're otherwise occupied, dear," Mrs. Kinzler said, patting her daughter's hand. "That's why I came."

Lucy managed a smile. "Thank you, Mother."

Doug didn't miss the tiny note of sarcasm in Lucy's tone, and almost laughed. Mrs. Kinzler seemed oblivious.

"No thanks necessary, my dear. What else is a mother supposed to do when her only daughter has her first baby? I only wish you lived closer to Chicago, but we mothers do what we must regardless."

The nurse came in and announced that Danny was ready for another feeding, "so Mr. Bainbridge will have to leave." Doug gave Lucy a kiss, sorry to leave her. But not sorry to take a break from her mother.

**

While sitting in the waiting room, Doug dashed off a quick letter to his parents on plain stationery. After debating with himself a moment, he opted to forgo tradition and write a single letter addressed to both of them. Given the tone of their last letters, he kept his short and to the point.

April 21, 1938

Dear Mother and Dad,

I'm writing to inform you that your grandson, Daniel Timothy Bainbridge, was born yesterday evening in Shanghai. He weighed 7 lbs. 3 oz and was 20 ½ inches long. Mother and baby are both healthy and well.

Lucy and I are very happy, and I hope you'll be happy for us.

Doug

**

Doug left with his mother-in-law when visiting hours ended at eight o'clock. He told her that Bao had promised something special for dinner, in honor of Danny's birth yesterday.

Mrs. Kinzler didn't look thrilled. "I hope it's not something Chinese," she said. "I don't know how they eat some of the things that they eat."

Doug didn't know how to respond to that, so he just said, "I'm not sure what he's making, Mother Kinzler. Bao is a very good cook, though, so whatever it is I'm sure it will be delicious."

"We'll see, I suppose."

Without Lucy there as a buffer, this could be a long evening. And it could be an especially long week.

**

"Do they have regular radio stations here? Or only Chinese ones?" Mrs. Kinzler asked after dinner. She hadn't complained about the shrimp and cuttlefish with rice noodles, but she had been remarkably quiet. Doug hoped having the radio on would continue that trend.

"There's an American station," Doug said, and turned on the radio. After it warmed up for a couple of seconds, he tuned the dial to XQHA. The static gave way to the music of the band at St. Anna's Ballroom.

"Do they only play swing music?" Mrs. Kinzler asked with a slight frown.

"Mostly that," Doug said. "They do announce the news a few times each evening."

"Do they have a station here that plays Amos and Andy? Or Hollywood Playhouse? Herbert and I like to listen to those. We're not fans of The Shadow, so if that's playing, I'll read one of Lucy's magazines instead."

"They have dozens of radio stations in Shanghai, in several different languages. I'm sure at least one of the English language stations plays American serials." He began adjusting the dial slowly, passing several musical numbers—orchestral, as well as songs sung in several languages—and pausing every time he heard a speaking voice in English.

"Would you mind if we listened to the news before we continue looking for a show?" he asked his mother-in-law when he heard an announcer giving local Shanghai updates in a mid-Atlantic accent that could have been either American or British.

"I have no objection to that," she said. "It's your radio, after all, Douglas."

He had no doubt that she still had opinions, regardless of whose home it was, but he kept quiet and listened to the local news.

"Governors of the Shanghai Electric Company have proposed a rate hike of fourteen percent, to take effect in May. The governors cite the rising cost of coal and urge the Municipal Council to approve the rate change at next week's council meeting to maintain solvency of the utility.

"An unnamed Chinese man was arrested today on Kiukiang Road after firing a gun at an automobile parked in front of the Central Bank of China. Businessman Zheng Yao was wounded in the attack and taken to Lester Hospital in serious condition. Businessman Yang Yanwei was also in the vehicle at the time of the attack and assisted police in identifying the gunman. Police will not comment on possible motive, but unconfirmed reports claim that Zheng and Yang had just concluded an agreement to sell cotton from Yangtzepoo mills to the Japanese military command in Hixi, and the attack was retaliation by the Nationalist resistance."

Doug sat up straighter. Yang Yanwei was Liling's father.

18

Friday, April 22

Mrs. Kinzler's expression when he told her he was going out that night reminded him of his mother's when he was a teenager, home from boarding school for the summer, and had asked if he could borrow the car.

Something about the way her lips pursed for the thousandth time since she'd arrived barely a week ago set him off. He should have kept his mouth shut, but that was God damned impossible.

"Is something wrong, Mother Kinzler?"

She regarded him haughtily for a moment. Then after glancing around to be sure Bao wasn't within earshot, she said, "You probably don't know, Douglas, but many men give in to weakness and initiate adulterous affairs when their wives have a baby. I'm sure your father and mother sheltered you from such things, which is why I'm warning you of it. There will be temptations while Lucy is unable to perform her wifely duties. I know you were raised in a Christian household, so you're equipped with the moral armor to resist painted ladies. But it bears reminding yourself often that those women lead to darkness and moral decay, and happiness lies in waiting for your wife."

Doug hoped to God that was the end of her speech, but she continued after a second's pause.

"When we pray 'Lead us not into temptation,' it is not God's responsibility to keep temptation out of our gaze, but to give us the moral strength to not go where temptation lies. Keep that in mind as you decide whether you would be better off remaining at home."

189

**

Doug was dressed in his off-white linen suit, matching fedora in hand, waiting when the clock on the wall struck nine. Mrs. Kinzler sat on the opposite chair in total silence, studiously avoiding looking at him, flipping through the glossy pages of one of Lucy's magazines.

Bao sat on the couch with a library book in Chinese, occasionally fidgeting with the collar of his shirt beneath his black necktie, still not used to the closeness of it against his throat.

Every time the crinkle of a glossy page turning pierced the awkward silence, Doug glanced at his watch. Where the hell was Jonesy?

It was nine-thirteen when Jonesy knocked. Doug knew, because he'd just glanced at his watch for the thirteenth time.

"Good evening, ma'am," Jonesy said to Mrs. Kinzler, removing his hat.

Doug made the introductions. "Mother Kinzler, this is Mr. Arthur Jones. This is Lucy's mother, Mrs. Kinzler."

"How do you do, Mr. Jones?" Mrs. Kinzler said, flatly, and not rising from the couch. She scrutinized Jonesy for a second. "You're older than my son-in-law's other friends."

Jonesy chuckled. "That's true. Father Time catches up with all of us, doesn't he, ma'am?"

Doug wanted to laugh at the irritation that flitted across his mother-in-law's eyes. "We'll be late, Mother Kinzler. I'll see you in the morning." He put his hand on Jonesy's shoulder and guided him through the door.

**

Jonesy had the cab drop them off on Yu Yuen Road a half-block west of the Paramount. The gate of the International Settlement lay just ahead of them, and Doug supposed they'd stopped here because Jonesy didn't want to force the Chinese driver to endure a Japanese checkpoint only to drive less than two blocks farther. He started walking west down Yu Yuen Road toward the boundary, but Jonesy called his name.

"No, dummy, this way," he hissed.

Doug followed him down a narrow gap—not even worthy of being called an alley—that curved through the triangular point formed by Yu Yuen Road and Bubbling Well Road. It wasn't wide enough for them to walk abreast without brushing against the grimy brick walls and getting filth on the arms of his suit, so Doug kept a few steps behind Jonesy.

Through an even narrower gap between a couple of buildings on his right, he spotted the Settlement gate across Yu Yuen Road, and between here and there at ten-foot intervals were random marker stones that had once divided fields so that Chinese rice farmers knew exactly who was in charge. Looking to the left, the gate across Bubbling Well Road was visible through the tiny gap between those buildings.

A moment later, they emerged from the not-alley onto Yifeng Road in Chinese territory, already behind the Japanese checkpoint.

"A little trick of the trade," Jonesy said with a crooked half-grin, and motioned forward. "This way."

Another block down an alley—a real one this time, with trash cans standing beside back doors, overflowing with smelly refuse—they emerged onto the little back road that Doug had wandered the Sunday morning after Stuart's arrest, at the bend by the end of the old irrigation canal. Unlike that morning, the road now bustled with activity, noise and light spilling out of every open window.

"Last fall, when Japanese shells were falling all across Chapei, and flattening most of the buildings along the Trenches, all the two-bit pimps, dope dealers, and wannabe gangsters there picked up stakes and came out here to the Western Roads, where it was mostly empty fields and hardly any police," Jonesy muttered as he led them down the block. "They threw up these little shacks, and opened gambling dens, opium dens, and cat houses catering to all the refugees fleeing Chapei."

"Isn't this where the Chinese government built all those warehouses to store the unclaimed bodies?" Doug asked, wrinkling his nose at the memory of the stench blowing over the International Settlement from the west all autumn long.

"Yeah, but those were on the main roads. This is what grew in the open space between the roads," Jonesy said. "And eventually the coffins all got tossed into mass graves farther west. With the smell of death and decay gone, this became a decent place to do business if you want to stay out of official oversite. The perfect place for a little club featuring drag performers."

Doug nodded. "But this area is under Japanese occupation. Why haven't the Japanese authorities cleared this all out?"

Jonesy chuckled. "After the Chinese army pulled out in November, the Jap army hardly paid any attention to this area, and sped past on their way to Nanking. The occupation force set up their roadblocks, but otherwise left the area alone. All the warehouses the Chinese built last fall to store bodies emptied slowly, so for a while the stench kept the Japs away, at least until the winter freeze. By then, the rich bastards in their villas out here had hired their own police and struck a deal with the Jap occupation authority. Since most of those taipans are westerners, the Japs were content to let them take care of things out here. They set up a restricted area around their own encampments, but otherwise they let the taipans handle the area."

The easy-to-miss sign for the Pink Lotus Club greeted them above the plain wooden door in the middle of the two-story bamboo building. Jonesy knocked, and a tiny panel in the door opened, revealing the eyes of a Chinese bouncer. It reminded Doug of one of those speak-easies in the States before Prohibition was repealed.

Like that one in Monterrey that Brent Aleshire took him to the night after their graduation from St. James Academy. A hot night in June 1928. Both of them recently turned eighteen years old. A speak full of bohemians from the little artist colony in Carmel, where Brent said "the girls are easy" and they could both pick up someone to take their virginity.

That was the night Doug and Brent had fallen out. Brent sprawled naked on the floor, blood pouring from his nose, red splattering the alabaster skin of his smooth chest, the black eye marring his perfect looks. A naked young woman with bobbed flapper hair knelt beside him, yelling at Doug to stop.

Doug closed his eyes and shook his head to clear all thought of that night.

"We're here to see the ladies," Jonesy said to the bouncer, and held up a dollar bill in the light.

The panel snapped shut, the door lock clicked, and the door opened just enough that they could slip inside. A hand snatched Jonesy's dollar before slamming the door behind them and sliding the lock back into place.

The long and narrow room was pretty full for only being nine-thirty. The tables were all occupied, but there were still a few empty barstools. Most of the patrons were Chinese men, but there were at least two Chinese women seated at different four-top tables, each with a trio of men. A handful of white men in little clusters, plus two Japanese army privates standing awkwardly in a corner rounded out the clientele.

Doug followed Jonesy to the bar; Jonesy took a stool, but Doug remained standing. A handsome young Chinese bartender, young and slender with longish hair, in an open-necked white linen shirt unbuttoned halfway down his chest, approached them with an uncharacteristic grin. "Whatchee want drink?" he asked in cheerful Pidgin.

"Martini," Jonesy said, pointing at himself, then pointed at Doug and said, "gin and tonic."

The bartender bobbed his head and went to mix the drinks.

Most of the room reflected in the mirror behind the bar. Painted pink lotuses of various sizes decorated the wall to his right. But there was something odd about them Doug couldn't put his finger on; something seemed off...

He squinted at the painting closest to them. "Hold on just one minute." He moved his face closer. "Is that a—"

"Yes, it's a butt hole, at the center of the flower." Amusement glinted from Jonesy's green eyes. "Subtle, huh?"

It took Doug a second to remember to close his mouth, then he looked around the room. The collection of men in the audience—and a few women, or at least so he assumed—didn't easily fit a type. A few of them were obvious pansies, but most seemed perfectly normal. "Does everyone here know what this club is?"

Jonesy snorted. "They should, the Pink Lotus doesn't exactly hide it. Not once you're through the door."

Doug frowned. "But Stuart said he didn't realize."

Jonesy gave Doug one of those 'tsk-tsk' kind of looks that always aggravated him. "Your friend Stuart was probably three sheets to the wind by the time they got here. I've seen your friends, you know."

Doug's frown deepened, but he couldn't argue with Jonesy's assumption. He was probably right.

Behind the curtain, someone clanged a gong—a small one, judging by the sound—and then the curtain parted to reveal a Chinese "woman" in a flowing traditional white robe and black sash, an elegant paper fan in one hand hiding half of her face. Tinny Chinese music played behind her, and she began to move languidly. Then she sang, her voice melodic as a bell, and downright, well, *feminine*. Only the square shape of her jaw over an Adam's Apple belied her true sex.

The crowd watched in rapt attention, and after a moment she stepped down from the stage and strolled between the tables, occasionally stopping to sit on the lap of one of the male patrons, or stroking his cheek seductively with her folded fan. Each object of her attention glowed with pleasure. She never stayed with one for long, turning a cheek to have him kiss it and then rising in a rustle of silk and moving on.

She came their direction, the volume of her song increasing with her nearness, and slipped up in front of Jonesy, running her fan languidly under his chin. He grinned like a schoolboy at a high school cheerleader, but she moved on to Doug and stopped in front of him, staring into his eyes and singing with increased emption. Chinese men around the crowd chuckled.

Doug's cheeks heated, and she responded by running her fingers along the side of his face, then under his chin, tugging it gently toward her.

"Kiss her cheek, dummy," Jonesy muttered.

Doug's face burned, but the performer stayed rooted in front of him, her white-painted cheek turned toward him, singing toward the empty stage. He leaned forward quickly, pecking a kiss on the warm cheek and leaning back as fast as he could.

She moved on, and Doug glanced sideways to see Jonesy watching him with an amused grin. "She liked you."

The next performer, to Doug's intense surprise, was a white man—er, white *lady*—in a ruffled lavender evening gown. The crackle of a record player rose behind him—no, *her*—and as the orchestral strains carried across the room her voice rose in a rich contralto singing the title song from *Anything Goes*, the biggest Broadway hit of 1934, in English.

The second she stepped down from the stage, one of the two Japanese privates took a couple of shuffled steps toward her, offering his hand. The goofy grin on his lips highlighted how young he looked— not more than twenty—and the female impersonator 'thanked' him by running both palms along his cheeks, never once breaking song. Her fingers trailed down the front of his army tunic as she turned away with a coy batting of her enormous fake eyelashes.

**

"Hello, hello, hello!" the white drag performer said when she opened the dressing room door and saw Doug on the other side. "Come in, handsome stranger."

The sharp cockney accent surprised Doug. "Thank you. I hope I can ask you ladies a few questions."

"You can do anything you like to any of us here," the white performer said, and a couple of the Chinese performers giggled. "But I hope you don't mind us girls getting out of our lady gear." He tugged the blonde wig off his head, revealing short brown hair slicked back tight against his head, and tape on his forehead pulling up his pencil-thin brows. Plopping down in a cushioned chair in front of a well-lit mirror, he peeled off the enormous fake eyelashes, revealing natural lashes that were plenty long enough on their own, if not particularly dark.

"I'd like to ask you about Pan Yintao," Doug said.

"*Huài dàn*" one of the Chinese performers muttered. *Bad egg.*

"That alley cat don't work on Saturdays," the white one said, wiping off make-up. "Don't waste your time with that one, handsome. She's probably out right now, prowling for some unsuspecting bloke to thwack his marbles."

"*Biàntài,*" the other Chinese one muttered. *Pervert.*

Doug frowned. The image of Ben Trebinski behind a bent-over Pan Yintao came to mind and wouldn't be dismissed.

The white performer turned around, most of his make-up gone now, except for the eye liner. He pulled a pair of pads from the bosom of his dress, and said, "Can I be frank with you, mate?"

Doug wasn't sure he wanted to say yes, but he nodded nonetheless.

"None of the rest of us girls hold with it, you savvy? We gots us a code of ethics, we do. No deceiving gentlemen callers about our, um, true natures, if you know what I mean."

Doug definitely knew what he meant, but just nodded in stony silence.

"My gentlemen friends, they all know I got a dick," he continued, oblivious to Doug's cringe. "They like it, too. Something their wives ain't got for 'em to play with. That's how it is for 'most all of us—we're ladies on stage, but in the bedroom it's all out in the open."

Doug's stomach turned. "But not so with Pan Yintao, you're saying."

The white performer frowned. "She gives the rest of us a bad name, that one. She's a tramp, and a lying one at that."

"She not only tramp here!" one of the Chinese queens said, to laughter from her companions.

The white one swatted a hand their direction. "I got no problem with a girl bein' a tramp. We all gotta find love somewheres, don't we? But I got a beef with *lying* ones who hide the goods."

A chorus of agreement rose from the collection of Chinese drag girls.

He leaned forward, and motioned Doug closer, as if to whisper a secret, but instead continued at full volume. "I heard she always tells the gentlemen she's on the rag, so they don't try to pet her cat, if you know what I mean."

Yes, I know what you mean, for Christ's sake.

He straightened back up and gave Doug a knowing nod. "That tramp don't have a single pair of panties without a big hole in the back, in just the right spot. And if the gentlemen should happen to catch a glimpse of Miss Pan's lump in the front of her panties, they'll assume it's her sanitary napkin."

Doug stood quickly, as much to hide his discomfort as anything. "Thanks for the insights."

"Any time, mate," the half-deconstructed 'lady' said, rising more languidly. Then his hazel eyes slid down Doug's form and back up again.

"And I must say, you ever want to take me for a spin, I'll let you ride this car." He rubbed his backside suggestively.

"I'll let you know," Doug muttered, not making eye contact.

"Me real name's Robert. Robert Cooper." He held out his hand, and after a second's hesitation Doug shook it.

"Douglas Bainbridge," he said, feeling awkward. God, why had he given his real name?

"Pleasure to meet you, Mr. Bainbridge. You come back here and see us anytime you like, gov."

Doug nodded in silence and let himself out.

**

Jonesy still sat at the bar, chatting up the bartender in a way that seemed more friendly than necessary. The young Chinese bartender had his elbows on the bar, leaning awfully close to Jonesy, a smile lighting his face.

Doug's cheeks heated, embarrassed for them, though he didn't know why. Something about witnessing Jonesy flirting, and being flirted with, felt as if it should be embarrassing. To Jonesy, of course, not to Doug; he had nothing to be embarrassed about, damn it.

He sidled up quietly beside Jonesy. The bartender noticed him a few seconds later and straightened his posture. Jonesy seemed startled, though that lasted the barest of seconds. His gruff demeanor returned almost instantly.

"Learn anything useful?" he asked.

"I might ask you the same thing," Doug muttered.

"As a matter of fact, I did. But you first."

Doug relayed what the performers had told him. All except for Robert Cooper making a pass at him. That didn't need to be shared. He could already imagine Jonesy's reaction to that little piece of news, and he didn't want it.

"Interesting," Jonesy said, stroking his chin. "Not sure how relevant it is to your problem, but it's interesting nonetheless."

"It could explain Jimmy Lockhart's contempt for Pan Yintao."

Jonesy shrugged. "Maybe. But that's a big assumption."

Doug crossed his arms, irritated more that Jonesy was right than at his reaction itself. "What about you? Did you learn anything more relevant."

"Sure did," Jonesy said with a cocky grin. "This place opened in late November, not long after the Jap army came through on their way toward Nanking. The Yang brothers didn't waste any time. But even more relevant—Mr. Yang has ties of one type or another to almost every business on this alley. He's got his fingers in so many pots he's had to take off his shoes."

"What a vivid image."

"Don't be an ass," Jonesy said, frowning. "I was kind of proud of that one."

Doug ignored that. "What you're saying is, Mr. Yang pays a lot of bribes to keep a lot of illicit businesses functioning."

"Yes, but you're missing the main angle," Jonesy said, lowering his voice and leaning closer. "He pays those bribes to the Japanese occupation. Specifically, to the Kenpeitai. He and the other rich bastards out here already own their own enforcers, so he only has to worry about the Japs. It seems our Mr. Yang is in bed with the Jap military police out here, and it's a mutually beneficial arrangement."

Doug raised an eyebrow. "How so?" What was in it for the Kenpeitai? Besides money, anyway, which they could get elsewhere.

"He didn't have a whole lot of details," Jonesy said, nodding toward the bartender, who was mixing a cocktail for a middle-aged Chinese man. "But he's heard talk."

"We can hardly rely on rumors."

"No, but they're a great place to start digging deeper." Jonesy's green eyes stared at him knowingly. "And who better than you to go digging into Japanese connections?"

Doug got up from the stool. He wasn't going to comment on that. "Let's go."

Jonesy stayed put. "You go. I'm sticking around."

"Taking in the next show?" Doug didn't relish the idea of sitting through more of this 'entertainment.'

Jonesy made the barest of shrugs, and glanced at the lanky bartender. "I owe someone for the information he gave me."

Doug frowned. "Just pay him the money and let's go." He really needed Jonesy to help guide him back to the secret crossing into the International Settlement.

Jonesy gave him one of those tsk-tsk looks he was so good at, shaking his head. "I'm not paying in *money*, dumb-dumb."

Doug looked over to see the bartender watching them, and giving Doug a mildly hostile stare. As if he were competition.

"I see." Doug put a few dollars on the bar to pay for his drinks. The bartender hurried over and swiped the cash. "He's all yours," Doug said, nodding toward Jonesy. He thrust his hat on top of his head and marched toward the door, where the bouncer opened it just wide enough for him to slip through into the dark night.

19

The cab dropped Doug at the entrance to the Del Monte as the curfew sirens from the Settlement rang across the countryside.

The doorman stepped forward and opened Doug's door. "You made it in the nick of time," he said in an American accent. Doug tipped the Chinese cab driver an extra dollar to compensate him for any trouble he might have getting home now that curfew was in place.

Bright light from the club's open front doors bathed the veranda in gold, and the roar of laughter and conversation echoed off the ceiling as Doug strode inside. There were people he needed to find.

******

Doug scanned the crowd in the second-floor ballroom, until he spotted Mr. and Mrs. Yang on the far side of the room, chatting with another well-dressed middle-aged Chinese couple in Western attire.

In a separate circle in front of theirs were their daughter and niece with Fred, and that troublemaker Pan Yintao. Doug took a deep breath and crossed the dancefloor.

A coy smile crossed Pan Yintao's lips when she saw Doug approaching. Her heavily made-up eyes held his with an amused twinkle.

Fred turned when Yang Liling touched his arm and nodded toward Doug. His eyes widened, but then he grinned and reached out his hand. "Doug! What an unexpected surprise. What brings you to the Del Monte?"

"Last minute decision," Doug said, shaking Fred's hand. "I needed to get out of the house for a night. My mother-in-law, you know." That wasn't untrue.

Fred gave him a sympathetic look and a pat on the shoulder. "I understand. Come, join us, won't you?"

"I'd love to, thanks." Doug turned toward the ladies—and Pan Yintao—and gave them a shallow bow. "Good evening," he said in Mandarin.

"I understood that one!" Fred exclaimed, beaming at Liling. She patted his arm, a slight smile curling the corners of her lips.

Doug laughed. "We'll make a good sinophile of you yet, Fred."

Tong Jian approached, balancing five cocktails in high ball glasses, two in each hand with the fifth wedged precariously between them. Doug was impressed.

"Ah, Mr. Bainbridge, is it not?" he said in English. "I met you at the Metropolitan last week." He handed a glass to Yajun, then one to Liling, then Pan Yintao, and finally to Fred. Yajun slipped her arm through Tong Jian's and sipped her drink demurely.

Pan Yintao took a swallow of her gin cocktail, her eyes never leaving Doug, the blue-shaded eyelids lowered a touch, head back to regard him under those ridiculously long fake eyelashes. Then she sauntered toward him. "It seems I'm the only lady present without an escort," she said in Shanghainese. "But what luck that you appeared to rescue me from solitude." She slipped an arm through Doug's and leaned against him.

Doug swallowed hard, glancing at Fred and blushing. Close physical contact with a female impersonator was not what he'd anticipated. And in front of his friend, no less. "You were hardly alone," he said, also in Shanghainese, inching away from Pan Yintao to create a sliver of space between them.

"I'm not now, am I?" She batted her false eyelashes and took another swallow of her drink., then closed the gap he'd opened.

Fred gave Doug a sympathetic look before turning his attention back to Liling.

"You are taking a night off from your cut sleeve?" Pan Yintao cooed, pressing more firmly against Doug's side.

Doug turned slightly to reduce the contact. "Bao is a friend only. I do not feel that way." He was glad Fred couldn't understand Shanghainese, so he wouldn't have to explain. It crossed his mind that Liling understood Shanghainese, and might tell Fred what Pan had said, should she be eavesdropping.

Of course she's eavesdropping. He almost cringed but managed to keep it from showing.

"What a pity," Pan said, running her eyes up and down Doug's frame. "The position is open, then?"

Doug's mouth dropped open, and he was momentarily at a loss for words. A wicked smile crossed Pan's painted mouth.

"I do not suggest myself for the job, you must understand. I do not desire to be possessed for more than a night." She leaned fully against Doug again. "But tonight is still young."

Doug scowled. "You enjoy playing with men's emotions, don't you?"

Pan regarded him with an enigmatic smile, then snapped open a fan and began waving it. "It is very warm tonight. I want to sit down." She tugged on Doug's arm, making clear that she meant him to escort her. And probably to sit with her.

Doug found an open table along the back wall. He'd be damned if he was going to hold a seat for her—she wasn't a woman, after all—and he took a seat himself.

A flash of anger whipped across Pan Yintao's eyes, but then a triumphant smile replaced it, and she plopped down onto Doug's lap before he could scoot to the table. And wiggled her backside against his groin.

Doug put his hand on her back, about to push her off, but she slapped her fan against his forearm in warning. "You are quite a gentleman."

"I wish I could say the same."

Pan's dark eyes flashed again. But then her smile returned, stiffer now. "Why should I be a gentleman when tonight I am a lady?"

Doug let that go. It was almost like a Jekyll and Hyde split personality, and he was in no mood to argue with Miss Hyde. Instead, he got to the heart of what he wanted to learn.

"How long have you known Yang Liling?"

Pan's smile turned enigmatic again. "You have nerve to talk about another lady when such a beautiful lady is seated upon your lap, Mr. Bainbridge." But then she looked back toward where Yang Liling and Fred stood engrossed in one another to the exclusion of everyone around them. "She and her cousin came to The Pink Lotus the weekend before the festival. Yang Liling loved my performance, and sought me after the show."

The weekend before Chinese New Year. January. "The club must have just opened."

"It was our second week," Pan Yintao said, taking Doug's necktie between her fingers and slowly stroking the silk. Down, then up, then back down. Doug swallowed hard again, and a jolt of nerves swept through his midsection.

"But her father doesn't know she went there, does he?"

Pan shrugged, staring at Doug's tie and not making eye contact.

"But he knows that you are her friend," Doug continued, pausing briefly for her to confirm, but she stayed silent. "You've been out with her at least twice now here at the Del Monte with her parents present in the room. Two times that I've witnessed, but I suspect it had happened before."

She looked up at his face, and he couldn't read her expression. "Yang Liling is a well-bred lady, from a prominent family. She only goes out in the company of her parents." Then she added with a shrug, "Or so they know."

Doug nodded slowly, taking a moment to ponder that. "Does Mr. Yang know you work at his club?"

Pan Yintao's eyes widened in undisguised surprise. But then the corners of her bright red lips curled up. "You are a man of many surprises, Mr. Bainbridge. How did you learn that Mr. Yang is an owner of The Pink Lotus?"

Doug shook his head to indicate he was keeping that information to himself.

"So mysterious," Pan purred, slipping her fingers off his tie and sliding them between the buttons of his shirt. Her fingertips grazed the skin on his chest, her long nails scratching lightly at the fine hairs there.

He took her wrist—careful not to be too rough—and pulled her hand back. "I'm a married man."

Pan laughed, a big hearty laugh with her head thrown back, mouth open. Then she placed her hand flat against his chest, over his shirt and tie, grinning with obvious mirth. "They are all married men, Mr. Bainbridge!"

Doug's cheeks heated. Scott Farnsworth had said much the same thing, in justification of his adultery with Kenny. Not that there could be *any* justification for that...

"You didn't answer my question." He stared hard at her. "Does Mr. Yang know you work at The Pink Lotus?"

A haughty sneer crossed her mouth. "He knows what I am, Mr. Bainbridge. And he knows I am the best performer at his club. He does not want me to go to work for a rival, so he does not interfere with my friendship with his daughter."

That there were rival clubs came as a surprise, but he hid it. "Does my friend Ben Trebinski know what you are?"

Anger flashed across Pan's eyes once again, and was again replaced by an enigmatic half-smile. "He is a sweet boy, that one." She waved a hand in the air, dismissive. "Sweet boys like him don't want to know the truth. The illusion is what they love, and I do not take it from them."

"I don't think Ben would be happy to be deceived."

She frowned. "He is a navy sailor, Mr. Bainbridge. Navy sailors are different from merchant sailors. I have seen their bravado. Haven't you? They brag constantly about female conquests, and they are always together, so they cannot sneak off to see a Cut Sleeve. If they want a boy, they fuck each other in the shadows. Not someone like me—unless they believe the illusion."

For the briefest of seconds, Doug felt sorry for Pan Yintao. But then his indignation on Ben's behalf came roaring back. "You should let Ben decide that for himself."

She cocked her head and regarded him curiously. "You are very intelligent, that is clear—but you do not understand much, Mr. Bainbridge."

Doug stiffened. He understood plenty. "I was at The Pink Lotus tonight, before I came here."

A gleam came to Pan Yintao's eye. "Oh? And how did you find our little club, Mr. Bainbridge? Were the ladies to your liking?"

Doug ignored the implication. "They performed quite well. It was... interesting."

Pan sniffed. "The show is better when I perform."

He'd take her word for it. "I saw a few Japanese soldiers there."

It was her turn to stiffen. "The Japanese go where they want and do what they want."

"Indeed." Doug watched her eyes for a second. "Does Mr. Yang disapprove? Does he have no choice but to allow entry to Japanese soldiers? Or does he perhaps have an arrangement with the occupation forces?"

Pan Yintao rose from his lap. "Please excuse me, I must re-powder my nose. But you may refill my cocktail while I am gone." She sauntered off without another word.

Doug wasn't sure what she was drinking. And the thought of asking Tong Jian—with its implication that he was now Pan's escort—made his stomach sour. So instead, he took his half-drunk gin and tonic and walked over to Mr. and Mrs. Yang.

He gave them a deferential bow. "Good evening, Mr. Yang," he said in Mandarin, and then extended his hand; Yang shook it. "I am Douglas Bainbridge, we met briefly a couple of weeks ago. Here in this ballroom."

"Yes, I remember you, Mr. Bainbridge." A faint smile graced his thin lips. "It is not often we encounter a westerner who speaks our language. And so well."

Doug nodded in acknowledgement. "Thank you for your kind words, sir."

"There is no need to thank me for speaking the truth. When Tolbert Peter told us he has an American friend who can speak 'Chinese,' we assumed his friend knew a few phrases, or maybe a little more. We were surprised to hear you speak Mandarin so fluently, and Shanghainese as well."

Doug almost mentioned that he could also speak Cantonese but remembered his modesty and just bowed his head. "I am pleased to hear that. How often do you meet with Mr. Tolbert?"

"When I am starting a new business, or buying a new asset, I see him often. At other times, not often."

Vague, but not evasive. Mr. Yang was good at this.

"Have you started a new business recently?" Doug hoped his status as a foreigner would earn him some forgiveness for being so direct. They didn't know that he knew better.

"A few months ago. There is much opportunity in the Hixi district."

"Indeed," Doug said. "I rode a bicycle through the area a couple of weeks ago, and I was impressed by the volume of new construction since the last time I visited the Columbia Country Club. Last summer, before the Japanese invasion."

He watched Mr. Yang's face, but the man's expression gave nothing away. "Many Chinese relocated there from Chapei. And others have come from the countryside, peasants displaced by the fighting."

Clearly, he wasn't going to get anything useful from Mr. Yang. He glanced at Mrs. Yang, who listened with a serene, passive expression. Every inch the old-fashioned Chinese lady, seen and not heard.

He spied Pan Yintao standing between Tong Jian and Yang Liling, face freshly shine-free, staring daggers at him. Doug said his goodbyes to the elder Yangs, saying he needed to refill his drink and return to his friend Fred. He downed the last of his gin and tonic on the way to the bar, which was packed with people. He wedged himself between a cluster of men speaking French, and a group of young Americans chattering way too loudly.

They were a mixed group—four men and three women—all in their early twenties, judging as much from their conversation as their looks. Swing music and movie stars. Doug listened in for several minutes while he waited for the bartender to grant him his turn. To his surprise, the group turned out to be native Shanghailanders—born and bred in the Chinese treaty port, the children of expatriate American businessmen who had come here in the early years of the century and stayed for the long-haul.

They were like his own father in Guangdong, or Canton as westerners called it. Except that his father had been sent home to boarding school in California when he was twelve years old. These young taipans had spent their whole lives in China, and yet they thought of themselves only as Americans.

The bartender came down their way, and the seven young Americans ordered Old Fashioneds. Before filling the order, the bartender looked at Doug, assuming he was part of the group. He didn't correct the misconception and ordered a gin and tonic.

For reasons left unspoken, the bartender filled Doug's drink first, to annoyed looks from the young taipans. Doug lifted his glass to them with a satisfied smile as he turned away and headed back toward Fred and the others.

Pan Yintao intercepted him.

"You have been hiding from me," she scolded, slapping his forearm with her fan, though not hard.

"I needed to speak with Mr. Yang," Doug said, not apologizing.

"Yes, I saw." She sounded only mildly irritated, though, and slipped her arm through his and leaned against him again. Apparently, all was forgiven. "You have not asked me to dance."

And I'm not going to. "I'm not much of a dancer."

She glanced at him from the side of her eyes, then lowered her ridiculous fake eye lashes in a display that was probably meant to be demure but seemed garish instead. "You should take a lesson. Then, the next time we meet, you can ask me to dance."

He couldn't help the curiosity. "Do you dance here often?"

A coy smile was her only reply.

He disentangled her arm from his and turned to face her with a slight bow. "Please excuse me, I'm going upstairs to play roulette." Anything to get away from this creature who had latched onto him. He'd seen the way she latched onto Ben a couple of weeks before, and she was relentless; but Ben had also been entirely willing.

Because he didn't know.

20

Doug's discomfort with gambling aside, the third floor was a welcome respite from the clingy female impersonator. And in spite of the chill that ran through him when he looked at the men's room door near the top of the stairs. He shuddered.

Cheers and squeals of laughter rang out from the craps table on the far side of the gambling room as Doug entered. A young woman—English, based on her accent as she shouted—was apparently on a winning streak. The closeness of the space up here made the gambling room stuffy despite the pair of ceiling fans whirring above their heads.

Doug took one of the last two open seats at the roulette table.

"Are you placing a bet, sir?" the attendant asked. He was short and dark-complected, with thick unoiled black hair, and his accent was American.

Doug shook his head.

"The seats are for players, sir," the attendant said, before calling out, "Bets are closed" and spinning the wheel.

Doug nodded in silence and stood, stepping back slowly from the table, eyes on the spinning wheel as it slowed and stopped on number twenty-three. The man he'd been sitting next to dropped his forehead onto his hand while the attendant scooped away twenty dollars' worth of chips.

Doug turned back toward the door—and found house detective Russell standing in front of him. "Not going to try your luck, Mr. Bainbridge?"

Doug faked a rueful half smile. "Afraid I'm not feeling very lucky tonight."

"That's a pity, sir." Russell's eyes bored into him. "Try again later. Perhaps your luck will change."

"Yes, one can hope so. Excuse me." He stepped around Russell.

"I see you found your watch."

Doug glanced at his left wrist, the watch partly visible below the cuff of his shirt. "Yes, I did. Turns out I left it somewhere else. I'd had too much to drink and didn't remember. Good evening."

"It's a long time 'till six o'clock," Russell said, cryptically. "I'm sure I'll see you around."

Something in the house detective's tone sent a wave of dread through Doug's midsection. But then he chastised himself for being silly and nodded at Russell on his way out the door.

Still, the sight of the third-floor men's room door made him shudder again. He hurried down the stairs.

**

Doug found Fred at the bar on the ground floor, talking with Tong Jian. The ladies—and more importantly, Pan Yintao—were nowhere to be seen.

"I wondered where you'd run off to," Fred said with a grin when Doug appeared at his side.

"I went upstairs to check out the roulette table."

Fred's eyes widened. "That's a change! Doug Bainbridge *gambling*?" He laughed at his own joke.

Doug laughed with him. "Don't tell my mother."

"How about your mother-in-law?"

"Don't tell her, either."

Fred laughed again, and slapped Doug on the back. "Poor fella! I feel for you, brother, having your mother-in-law living with you for a whole month. Must be awful."

Doug aped being shocked. "I don't know what you mean. She's a peach."

Fred laughed even harder, clearly several drinks in already. Doug raised his empty glass toward the bartender and asked for a gin and tonic.

"Fred has told me congratulations are in order, for the birth of your son," Tong Jian said to Doug, his English diction crisp and precise.

"Thank you. We're very happy." Doug accepted his drink from the bartender and laid a coin on the bar. "That's right, you met Lucy—my wife—a couple of weeks ago at the Majestic."

Tong Jian nodded. "Yes. It was obvious to me that she was at the end of her pregnancy."

Fred cringed almost imperceptibly. "Sorry for the impolite language, Doug. Tong Jian here is a medical student, so he uses those words out of habit."

Tong Jian looked bemused, so Doug explained. "Some people object to words like 'pregnancy' in mixed company. Seems a little old-fashioned these days, I know, but a lot of people prefer to say, 'with child' instead of 'pregnant.' I'm not sure why—it means the same thing, conjures up the same image, so what's the point?"

Fred shrugged. Tong Jian gave Doug a bow of appreciation. "Thank you for that explanation, Mr. Bainbridge. Foreign manners can be baffling to Chinese people."

"Completely understandable."

"In gratitude for your helpful explanation, I will give you a warning as well," Jian said, and took a step closer. "The young lady you have been spending time with tonight—Pan Yintao—she is not what she seems. Miss Pan is a man in woman's clothing and make-up. This is something the Chinese understand, but foreigners are deceived."

Tong Jian's frankness caught Doug by surprise, and he wasn't sure how to respond, except to mutter "Thank you."

Jian glanced around, and then leaned down close to Doug's face. "If you think to satisfy your needs while your wife is incapable of it following the birth of your child, it could be unpleasant for you to discover Miss Pan's sex when you are undressing."

Doug's cheeks heated. Next to him, Fred cleared his throat loudly, looking off across the room. Tong Jian seemed oblivious. "Thank you for the warning," Doug said, his mouth suddenly dry.

Tong Jian bowed in acknowledgement.

Fred excused himself to go to the men's room, and Doug took the opportunity to break the awkwardness of the moment and find out more about the Yangs.

"Mr. Tong, how well do you know Mr. Yang?" he asked in Shanghainese. "I know you study under his brother, Dr. Yang. But do you know Liling's father well?"

Tong Jian nodded. "Mr. Yang is a very generous man."

Doug cocked his head. "Generous?"

"Yes, very generous. Mr. Yang has introduced me to many important people, including Dr. Ishikawa—apologies, Colonel Ishikawa. He is a first-rate surgeon, only recently drafted into the Japanese army and sent to Shanghai from Tokyo. I have read many of his case studies at St. John Medical School."

Mr. Yang, and not Dr. Yang. That was curious indeed. Doug kept his head cocked to the side. "It was Mr. Yang, and not his brother Dr. Yang, who introduced you to Dr. Ishikawa?"

"Mr. Yang introduced both of us to Dr. Ishikawa. I was honored to be included, along with his brother. I am not family, so he was not obligated to do that."

"But you're dating his niece, are you not?"

Tong Jian nodded, smiling this time. "Yes, I am. Dr. Yang invited me to his home for the festival. That is when I met Yajun, and also when I met his brother. The year of the Tiger has been most fortunate for me, in many ways."

A few more pieces seemed to fall into place, but there were still too many holes in the picture.

It was rare for the Chinese to smile at a stranger or casual acquaintance, so Doug smiled back. "Yes, indeed, that is quite fortunate. But if you'll forgive me, I am curious why Mr. Yang was the brother who knew Dr. Ishikawa, and not Dr. Yang."

Tong Jian's eyes widened in surprise. "Mr. Yang is a brilliant businessman, and he knows many officers in the Japanese command. He dined with General Matsui and met Colonel Dr. Ishikawa there."

Tong Jian clearly saw nothing untoward about any of this. But Doug hid his surprise and raised his glass. "To your continued fortune, Mr. Tong."

Fred returned while Doug and Jian were drinking. "The ladies are out on the portico for air. I told Liling I'd be right out. You fellas wanna join us?"

Doug assumed the 'ladies' included Pan Yintao. One eyebrow rose involuntarily, and Fred laughed. "Yes, she's with them." He leaned close to Doug's ear and whispered, "Don't worry, Douggie, no one's going to judge you because she latched onto you. Stuart didn't know at first, either. She'll get bored and move on soon."

Doug hoped Fred was right. But he somehow doubted it after Liu Fan saw him with Bao at the tailor's. Liu—and his alter-ego Pan Yintao—wouldn't give up his assumption easily.

**

It didn't take long for Doug to learn a night at an all-night club without most of his friends around would start to drag. He glanced at his watch more often than he'd care to admit, and the hands had seemed to slow down.

One bright spot was that Pan Yintao was studiously ignoring him. He supposed she must think that a punishment. Every now and again she would stare at him long enough to make eye contact, and then would raise her nose in the air with an obvious sniff and look away.

215

He almost laughed.

Around half past midnight, he wandered inside and found himself in the middle of the gaggle of young taipans.

"And who are you?" one of the young women asked him, drunk enough to be bold. And loud.

"My name's Doug Bainbridge."

"I thought you might be an American," she said with a satisfied nod. "I was right."

"You're a handsome one," the girl next to her said. She swayed a little, unsteady on her feet. But then she leaned back against the wall for support, and gazed at him with moon eyes.

"Thank you. My wife thinks I'm handsome, too." He couldn't help himself.

"Well! Isn't she a lucky girl?" the first one said. The second one looked disappointed.

"Bainbridge, was it?" one of the young men said. He couldn't be more than twenty-one; twenty-two tops. At Doug's nod, he asked, "Where do you work, Mr. Bainbridge?"

It was a pointed question. Doug picked up right away from the young man's tone that the lot of them were going to judge him based upon the answer. He could tell them he was an officer in the navy, but he didn't think even "officer" would be enough caché to these taipans.

"I work for the United States government." It was the truth, after all.

This revelation was met with a mixture of awe and skepticism. The former from the young women, the latter from the young men.

"A government man, eh? What sort of work do you do for Uncle Sam, old boy?" The look on the young man's face said he couldn't wait to hear what whopper Doug invented.

"I really can't say," Doug said, slow and deliberate, making it obvious he was buttoning up.

"Well, why not?" The young man looked baffled, as if he'd never in his life had anyone decline to answer his questions. Maybe he never had.

"It's classified." Again, it was the truth.

The young man's eyes widened as realization dawned. "I'm dreadfully sorry, old boy. Didn't mean to pry."

Yes, you did. "Quite alright, young man." Doug couldn't help the fatherly tone. He was a father now, after all. He'd have to get used to using that tone soon enough, he might as well practice on these young taipans. The subtle condescension was just a bonus.

"You must be looking into that murder here a couple of weeks ago!" the mooney-eyed young woman said, oblivious. "We missed it. We weren't here that night, we were at the Canidrome." She cast a sideways glance at the other young woman standing haughtily next to her.

"They have the best band in Shanghai," the haughty young woman said, a touch defensive.

"And the best floor show," one of the young men added.

This earned an eye roll from the haughty young woman. "You like the way the girls high-kick."

The mooney-eyed girl ignored all of them. "You know who did it, don't you? You're here to find proof. Oh, how exciting!"

"Helen, he said he can't talk about it," the haughty young woman said.

Helen's mooney eyes turned irritated, but barely glanced at the other girl while batting a hand her direction. "Maggie, don't be a stick in the mud," she said, but looking at Doug.

The young man leaned slightly forward. "Helen, he said it's *classified.*" Then, in a whisper that wasn't quiet enough, he added, "He's probably a spy."

Helen waved that off as well, but still only barely glancing away from Doug while she did so. "Nonsense. Who ever heard of an American spy? You're from the FBI, aren't you? My father said the FBI should send someone to Shanghai to catch the American gangsters smuggling drugs. He said they were all writing to Washington about it."

That was interesting.

All of them were now staring at Doug. He just smiled coyly and shook his head.

Disappointed, the young man closest to Doug looked back at his companions. "He's not going to say, of course. Probably not allowed to." He turned back toward Doug. "Everyone in Shanghai knows Al Israel has ties to the underworld. It's not exactly secret that there's illegal gambling going on upstairs. But I've never heard *anyone* say there are drugs running through the Del Monte. It's a respectable club."

"I appreciate the insights," Doug said, deliberately gruff and impatient. That's how the G-men acted in movies, anyway.

The young man puffed up a little. "*My* money says that man who was thrown from the window was probably working for Jack Riley. They say he's had his eye on the Del Monte for months, trying to get his slot machines out here, but old Al Israel won't have it. I bet Jack Riley sent his man to put some pressure on, and Demon Hyde had him tossed out a window." He turned back toward his companions. "Anyone want to take that bet?"

"You're on!" one of his companions replied with a big grin. He had a thick wave of blond hair swooping over his forehead, and a prominent chin with a handsome cleft down the middle. "Twenty dollars says it has something to do with that flashy dame we saw leaving right before it happened. You know, the one who screamed as if she'd 'found' the body."

That caught Doug's attention. "What makes you think it wasn't accidental that she found the body?"

The blond young man looked triumphant. "I saw her slap him not ten minutes before that."

That was new. Doug knew she'd argued with Jimmy, but no one had ever said she slapped him. "And you think she threw him out a window? Hard enough that he landed on the ground instead of grabbing the gutter?"

The blond young man looked unsure for a second, glancing toward the ceiling in thought. "She was tall enough, and he was a short little fellow."

"Don't be daft!" Maggie said, frowning. "Women *poison*, they don't throw someone out a window."

"Poison or stab," Helen said. "Remember there was that woman a couple of years ago who stabbed her husband and his mistress when she caught them in her bed."

"That's true," Maggie conceded. "But the papers didn't say anything about that little fellow getting stabbed before they tossed him out the window."

"Did they stab him?" Helen asked, breathless, turning back toward Doug with wide, expectant eyes.

"I'm not at liberty to say," Doug said, slowly and deliberately, with the voice of authority one might use if one were actually an FBI special agent.

"No, I suppose you're not," Helen said with a sigh, clearly disappointed.

"We won't hold you up, old boy," the first young man said. "Best of luck."

"I look forward to reading in the papers that you've caught her," the blond one said.

"I'll be happy to take your twenty dollars when it isn't her," the first one replied.

Doug nodded to the ladies and beat a path through the crowd.

**

He found Fred with Yang Liling and her entourage, waiting for a table in the dining room. He pulled Fred aside.

"Have you ever heard of someone called 'Demon Hyde?'"

Fred nodded vigorously. "Of course. That's Al Israel's brother-in-law. They call him 'Demon' because he's Al's heavy."

Interesting. "So, he's got a mean reputation, I take it?"

Fred laughed. "You could say that. I think he's busted plenty of noses, at least. Some say he's broken some legs, too—but that might be exaggerated. I think he likes the reputation, anyway. It makes people afraid to cross him, or Al."

Doug took a few seconds to digest that.

"Why do you ask?"

Fred was staring at him, head cocked, so Doug motioned him close and whispered, "Some young fellas speculated Jimmy Lockhart was working for Jack Riley, trying to get Riley's slot machines into the Del Monte. They think 'Demon' Hyde might have thrown him out the window."

Fred's expression was hard to read. Some skepticism, but also maybe some intrigued contemplation.

"I don't think he would have done it himself," Fred said, slowly, deliberately. "But if his reputation is true, and not just smoke and mirrors, then maybe it's possible he ordered it."

He hesitated, looking like he wanted to say more. Doug nodded encouragement. "Go on."

Fred shrugged. "I dunno, Doug. Seems kind of far-fetched, don't you think? What I mean is, why would they have to kill Jimmy Lockhart even if he *was* working for Jack Riley—which seems a stretch in and of itself, since Riley uses street toughs, not little bitty horse jockeys. But even if he was, *killing* him is such an overreaction. And it would start a gang war, don't you think?"

"The young taipans made it sound like Jack Riley's been putting pressure on Al Israel to let in his slot machines," Doug said. "How much pressure? That's what I'd like to know. Enough pressure that Demon Hyde would feel the need to kill one of Jack's surrogates?"

Fred shrugged. "Good question."

Doug looked off in thought for a moment. "I haven't read anything in the papers that would make me think there's a gang war going on—at least, not any more than usual. But revenge is a dish best served cold. Jack Riley might be biding his time, waiting for the right moment to strike back."

Fred scoffed. "Fat chance! Riley's a hot-headed Irishman. He's got a reputation a mile long, and it ain't one for patiently waiting for an opportunity. He'd hit back hard and fast."

Doug sighed. "If you're right, then it probably wasn't 'Demon' Hyde or any of his men that did it, or else Jack Riley would have taken revenge."

"Glad you came to your senses. You don't want to get mixed up in all that, Doug."

"Thanks, Fred." Still, something about that seemed too pat. Doug filed that away to ask Jonesy about tomorrow.

21

Saturday, April 23

The line rang nine times before Jonesy answered. "Jones." He sounded half asleep still.

"Jonesy, it's Doug. Did I wake you?" He'd waited until noon before calling.

"What do you think?" He sighed, and his voice was calmer when he continued, "I ain't as young as you, Douglas. I don't recover from late nights quite as fast as I used to."

"It's been six hours. Don't you reporters routinely work on less than that?"

"Who says I've been asleep for six hours?"

"Because that's when—" And then the implication set in. Doug's cheeks heated. "Oh, sorry."

"Forget it. Might as well tell me what you're calling about."

"I wanted to tell you what I learned last night. But not over the phone. After I left you, I went to the Del Monte, and I heard some pretty interesting things. Can you meet me for lunch? Somewhere we won't be overheard."

The line was silent for a couple of seconds. "No, not lunch. I'm... busy."

Doug closed his eyes, trying to banish the image of Jonesy in bed with the lanky young Chinese bartender from The Pink Lotus. "Then when?"

"Five o'clock. We can meet at that tavern you and Kenny like over at Honan and Peking roads. I assume he's included."

Doug was a little embarrassed that he hadn't thought to include Kenny. "Yes, I'll invite him. I called you first, though."

"Thoughtful of you." Jonesy didn't sound sincere about that.

"Alright, we'll meet you at the Liberty Tavern at five o'clock."

**

The extra hours gave Doug time to head over to St. Elizabeth's and visit Lucy. He had to wait for a nurse to go in and remove Danny before they would let him down the hall, but he caught a glimpse of the top of his son's head on the nurse's shoulder.

The bed in the front half of the room stood empty, and the curtain between the beds was pulled open. Unsurprisingly, Mrs. Kinzler was in the room. Lucy beamed when she saw him; her mother frowned.

"I see you finally woke up," Mrs. Kinzler said.

Doug forced a smile. "Yes, an hour ago."

"You slept away half the day."

Doug let that go without comment and leaned down to kiss Lucy. He sat on the edge of the bed and took her hand in both of his. "How are you feeling, dear?"

"A little tired, but I'm feeling pretty well, all things considered."

"She has to wake up every two hours to feed the baby. She can't sleep away half the day like you did."

"Leave him alone, Mother."

Mrs. Kinzler scowled. "My dear, you must stand up for yourself." Then to Doug, "You're a father now, Douglas. You have responsibilities at home. You can't stay out all hours of the night."

"Mother, why don't you go ask the nurses to bring me a cup of tea."

"Of course, dear."

Lucy looked at Doug and sighed after her mother left. "I'm sorry about all that."

Doug patted the top of her hand. "I knew she'd tell you I went out last night."

"Yes, it was almost the first thing out of her mouth when she walked through the door." Lucy laughed without humor, shaking her head. "She said you went out with Jonesy. I don't think she approves of him."

"That was my impression as well."

"She said he was 'no gentleman.' I assume you two went out on a mission?" One arched eyebrow told Doug she expected to hear everything.

"We did. We went to The Pink Lotus."

Her eyes widened, and a smile crept up. "Isn't that the drag club where Pan Yintao works?"

"That's the one." He chuckled. "It was an experience, that's for certain."

Lucy leaned forward, eyes aglow. "Was she there?"

Doug shook his head. "She has Fridays and Saturdays off. That's why we went when we did. We wanted to talk with the other performers. About her—him—her."

She was positively glowing with expectation. "Her. Remember? Always 'her' when she's in drag. What did they say? Tell me everything." He opened his mouth, but she hurriedly cut him off. "Close the door though—we don't want Mother interrupting us."

Doug smiled, got up and closed the door. "Too bad it doesn't have a lock." He returned to her side and recounted everything the other female impersonators had told him after the first show—leaving out only the come-on from the English one. He didn't feel any need to get into *that*.

Lucy nodded along. "I could see that about her. I watched her that night at the Majestic, and she does seem that way. She arms herself with it."

Doug cocked his head. "What do you mean?"

"She wears arrogance like an armor. I can only imagine the taunts she's gotten over the years. Or worse. I'm sure she's been beaten up a few times, when someone realized. You men can be brutal, you know."

Doug couldn't help the scowl he gave her. "I didn't realize we were going to launch into an attack against men. While you're at it, do you have any opinions about men who pretend to be women and kiss other men without telling them the truth?"

Lucy's lips pursed. "You don't need to get angry with me, Douglas Bainbridge. You know I believe in honesty—but I also know there are times it's safest to keep certain things quiet until you know how it will be received. And you know as well as I do that men come to blows with each other far more often than women do. Women cut each other down with words—and my impression is Pan Yintao learned that lesson well. Maybe that's why you don't like her."

Doug's scowl deepened. "I don't like *her* because she's an arrogant son of a bitch who puts everyone else down."

Lucy shrugged. "Like I said, it's armor. It deflects any insult you could hurl at her. Or your judgment of her." She patted his hand. "You can be a little judgmental sometimes, of things you don't find 'normal.'"

He stiffened. "You think *I'm* judgmental? You should meet my parents."

Her lips pursed. "I've gathered as much from all the stories you've told me. Seems you've made a lot of progress, given where you started with them. But enough of this—tell me the rest."

Doug took a deep breath through the nose, suppressing irritation over her assessment. She was right of course. She usually was, damn it. "Alright." He hesitated a second, but then mentioned that he left The Pink Lotus without Jonesy. "He wanted to keep talking with someone."

Lucy's eyes lit up. "Oh? Someone handsome?"

Doug shrugged. He supposed the lanky young Chinese bartender was handsome. Probably.

"How exciting!" Lucy beamed. "I'm so happy for him. Maybe he can find someone the way Charlie and Bao found each other."

The reference to Charlie Ford brought a twinge of sadness, a brief tightening around the heart. But he just nodded and continued. "I decided to go back to the Del Monte and have a look around. And hopefully run into certain people."

He gave her the full account of his night at the Del Monte, including his unexpected conversation with the cluster of young taipans, and Fred's thoughts about it afterward. "There you go, that's everything."

"It's quite a lot," she said, sounding impressed.

"What do you think?"

"That there's more to Jimmy Lockhart's presence that night then meets the eye. I agree with Fred about the gang war, and that throws a wrench in the works, doesn't it?" She hesitated, looking up in thought, and Doug allowed her a moment. Then her eyes widened, and she looked back at him intently. "But what if we've got it all backwards? What if Jimmy Lockhart isn't the one working for Jack Riley? Or maybe he is, but someone else at the Del Monte is, too? What if the murder has nothing to do with Al Israel or 'Demon' Hyde? What if it's only meant to look like it does?"

Doug frowned, thinking about that for a moment. "But it doesn't *really* look like it involves Al Israel and his brother-in-law, does it? On the surface, it looked like Mark Chapman was the most likely suspect—after we rule out Stuart, of course—and Dolores Moody is the next most likely. I only got to Al Israel and 'Demon' Hyde after what those kids said." He cringed at calling them 'kids.' They were adults. It had just come out, naturally. Damn it. "They were speculating, and I was only following that thread. It's pretty far-fetched, after all; I don't think very many people would come to that conclusion."

She nodded. "True. But if the murderer is clever enough, he—or she—might have thought through even the most far-fetched possibilities to make sure someone else was always more suspicious than they were."

Doug had to laugh. "Now you sound like one of Agatha Christie's detectives! Where's your mustache, monsieur Poirot?"

She smiled and swatted at his arm. "Don't be an ass. I'm much more like Miss Marple than Inspector Poirot, and you know it."

He put his hand on top of hers. "But far prettier."

She laughed. "Good answer. Now, think about it—the murderer knows he wants to kill Jimmy Lockhart, he's just waiting for the right moment. Jimmy gets into an argument with Mark Chapman in the men's lavatory, and he has his opportunity. But his plans are interrupted when first you, and then Stuart, insist on interrupting the two jockeys' argument."

She leaned forward, eyes intent. "Whoever he is, he saw Stuart running out of the men's room and down the stairs, so maybe he thinks something is happening in there—Chapman and Lockhart have come to blows, perhaps, which would be fortunate for him—but regardless, Stuart running from the scene will be incriminating after Jimmy Lockhart gets thrown out the window, and he knows this. He goes in, finds a handkerchief on the floor, and uses it to muffle Jimmy Lockhart's cries. Maybe he had no idea it was Stuart's and that was just a lucky coincidence for him. Or maybe he'd seen it in Stuart's pocket."

"Still a lucky coincidence," Doug interrupted.

"True—but coincidences can happen. Just not big ones. This is a little one, don't you think? Anyway, the killer stuffs Stuart's handkerchief in Lockhart's mouth, and tosses him out the window. Maybe Mark Chapman was there and saw it all. Our killer threatens him with the same fate—or worse—if he doesn't keep his mouth shut. This is why he was so frightened that day you and Jonesy met with him at the stables.

"Then our killer got lucky again when Stuart was the first one to reach the body. He couldn't have possibly planned that—but it *had* to be a coincidence, because no one could have planned that. We *know* Stuart didn't do it, so a certain amount of coincidence is obligatory. There's no avoiding that."

Doug nodded. "You're right, of course—but getting a court to believe coincidence after coincidence is going to be hard."

Lucy's expression grew sad. "Yes, that's true. But I have confidence in Kenny. And so should you. He'll find a way." She paused for a second, looking up in thought. Then she took Doug's hands and held them tight, staring right into his eyes. "And you're going to get him proof."

Doug shook his head. "How on Earth are we going to prove all that?"

Lucy's stare was so intense, he had to fight not to look away. "You're going to set a trap. Now, who's the best bait?"

22

Kenny was waiting at the bar when Doug arrived at the Liberty Tavern a minute before five o'clock. He was turned sideways on the barstool, watching the door. His smile when Doug walked in was overly big and enthusiastic, obviously nervous.

"Thanks for arranging this, old chum," Kenny said, his voice a touch too loud. His movements were a bit jerky, betraying his nerves.

He's afraid I'm still judging him about Scott. Doug pushed away the thought that he was, in fact, still judging him. Both of them. He'd think about that later. "While we wait for Jonesy, I'll tell you what I learned while I was with him at The Pink Lotus last night."

Doug ordered a beer—he needed to keep his head, and a gin and tonic might be too much this early in the evening—and then recounted again what the other female impersonators had to say about Pan Yintao, and about Mr. Yang.

"Wow, that's pretty unanimous!" Kenny said with a short bark of laughter. "They don't like her at all. I understand why, of course. Can't say I disagree. But I also understand why she does what she does. Sometimes, things are best kept secret, or you'll ruin everything else." His expression grew serious, and his voice quieted. "Things too important to ruin with the truth."

Doug looked away. He didn't want to hear any justifications for what Kenny was justifying away. "Let's wait for Jonesy before I tell you the rest."

Jonesy came through the door at twelve past the hour—better than his usual, Doug mused—and took a seat next to Doug, opposite side from Kenny. "Good afternoon, gents." He got the bartender's attention and ordered a martini. "Douglas, care to enlighten us on these things you didn't want to discuss over the telephone?"

"Let's get a table." Doug took his beer and walked to a table in the back corner. Fortunately, the tavern was only about a quarter full. It was a popular after-work hang-out during the week, but it was still early for a Saturday.

Kenny took the seat next to Doug, so Jonesy pulled out the chair opposite. "We're all ears, Douglas."

Doug leaned forward, over the table, and the others took his cue and leaned in close. Then he related everything from his night at the Del Monte, keeping his voice barely louder than a whisper. He added Lucy's thoughts to the end. When he finished, the table was eerily silent. "Well, what do you think?"

Jonesy stroked his chin. "You know I respect Lucy's insights—she's probably smarter than any of us—but you have to admit there are an awful lot of coincidences that had to line up just so."

Kenny laughed, nervously. "It does sound a bit fantastic."

Jonesy waggled his head from side to side, looking up in thought. "I don't know that I'd go so far as 'fantastic.' I've seen my share of weird coincidences, you know. This might not be as far-fetched as it sounds."

"What we need is for someone to dig into the workings of Jack Riley's gang," Doug said. "Find out if Jimmy Lockhart was connected to him."

Jonesy chuckled, leaned back and shook his head. "You're about as subtle as a Japanese tank, Douglas."

"Who better?"

Jonesy chuckled again, and this time leaned forward, pointing his finger. "Flattery will get you everything—*most* of the time."

Doug arched an eyebrow. "Not this time?"

Jonesy grunted, looking torn. Then he reached into his suit coat and pulled out a folded slip of paper. He plopped it onto the table in front of Doug.

"What's this?"

"Liu Fan's address," Jonesy said. "Courtesy of my new friend, the bartender at The Pink Lotus. You want someone to tell you more about the gangs, this is where you start. Peddle your flattery there, and it probably *will* get you everything." Jonesy waggled his eyebrows in a way that made Doug cringe.

Kenny cleared his throat a little too loudly. "You are the only one of us who knows that person, Doug."

Doug looked down at his hands. "I don't see how this *person* will know the things we want to know."

Jonesy pointed his finger at Doug's face again, stern. "We know something happened between Pan Yintao and Jimmy Lockhart. And exactly what that was might open the door to what we're looking for. You need to get Liu Fan—or Pan Yintao, as the case may be—you need to get them talking."

"I'm really not sure how I can. We all know what kind of person this is. Her arrogance is insurmountable."

Jonesy shook his head, making a faint 'tsk-tsk' sound. "Don't be so obtuse, Douglas. You're already half-way there. Or do I need to remind you how god-damned pretty you are?"

Doug's head snapped up. "Stop it, Jonesy."

Kenny's face was about twenty shades of red.

"Don't pretend you don't know that," Jonesy said with a scowl. "False modesty isn't becoming, you know."

"Neither is indecorous talk."

"Phbt." Jonesy waved that off. "I'm being honest. And direct. I think the situation calls for it. Alright, so maybe you aren't *quite* as pretty as your friend George, but you're better than an average Joe by a mile. Tell him, Kenny."

Kenny choked on his beer.

"The important thing is this—Pan Yintao thinks so. Chew on that, Douglas."

Doug sat and stewed for several seconds, a vein in his neck throbbing. *Damn it, Jonesy!* He knew the reporter was right, but he'd be damned if he was going to say that out loud.

He took the folded slip of paper, opened it, and glanced at the address written there. Not far from here, actually. He folded it up again and slipped it inside his coat pocket. He shot up from his chair and bolted out the door.

23

The neighborhood between Honan Road and Thibet Road was overwhelmingly Chinese, with banners in Chinese script hanging on the facades of brick buildings, or occasionally strung across the street. Doug found the side street he was looking for on Foochow Road a block before reaching Thibet Road, and it occurred to him—quite uncomfortably, to be honest—that this was only a few blocks from his own home on the uptown side of Thibet.

It was a four-story building of grimy bricks, built around the turn of the century like most of this area, and starting to show some age. Most of the paint had chipped away from the window sills, leaving mostly bare wood in its place, open to the elements and showing a bit of wear from the frequent rains in Shanghai.

Not unexpectedly, an older Chinese woman sat in the open window of one of the ground floor apartments, watching the passersby as well as anyone climbing the three steps to the building's front door. "What wantchee?" she demanded of Doug in Pidgin.

"I'm calling on someone in the building," Doug replied in Shanghainese with a shallow bow, averse to mentioning Liu Fan's name. The old woman was probably the wife or mother of the landlord, and he had no doubt she knew Liu Fan often left the building at night as Pan Yintao. He'd rather not have her making false assumptions about the purpose of his visit.

She doesn't know you, for crying out loud. But that didn't quell the uncomfortable shame resting heavily in his belly as he opened the door and mounted the stairs.

The ceiling was lower on the top floor, the hall narrow and cramped. These were the garrets. He found the apartment number on the back side of the building, and knocked on the plain wooden door. No movement came from inside, so after a moment he knocked again. Still getting no response except silence, he turned away, unsure if he felt disappointment or relief.

He was half-way down the last flight of stairs when the building's front door opened and Liu Fan strode in with two shopping bags from Sincere Department Store, one in each hand. He had a pronounced swagger to his gait, but he stopped short at the bottom of the stairs, eyes widening when he caught Doug's gaze.

Then a gleam came to his eyes, and a victorious smile stretched his lips thin. "Good afternoon, Mr. Bainbridge."

"Good afternoon," Doug replied, curt.

Liu Fan didn't react to Doug's tone and walked past him. He turned his head back on the next step. "Are you coming?" He climbed the stairs languidly, his hips swinging in such a way that his backside wagged back and forth in front of Doug's face. A feminine gait. And just how god-damned tight were his slacks? With the short cut of his jacket, it was obvious. No doubt that tailoring was intentional.

The apartment was indeed a one-room garret, cramped and closed off. The lone window looked out onto the wall of the building behind, barely two yards away, and the chatter of conversations in Shanghainese from multiple open windows echoed in the little space.

Liu Fan set his shopping bags next to the dresser, removed his jacket, and hung it on the coat rack standing in the corner. A large and ornately shaped mirror sat atop the dresser, the type an affluent woman might have on a vanity, and a pile of silk scarves to one side completed the look. Opposite the dresser sat a narrow bed, its iron frame speckled with old blue paint that had probably been applied before either of them was born. That and a small table with a single chair were the only furniture; and yet they took up half the floor space.

The shabby feel of the tiny apartment stood in sharp contrast with the expensively tailored clothes worn by its occupant, regardless of which gender he chose to express.

Liu Fan sat on the edge of the bed, crossed his legs, and folded his hands demurely on top of his knees. Almost lady-like. "This is an unexpected visit. I took you for the more reticent type, Mr. Bainbridge."

"This isn't that type of visit."

The amused look on Liu Fan's face annoyed him. "Of course not." The playful tone was even more annoying.

Doug wanted to ask about Jimmy Lockhart right away, but something else nagged at him. "Did you bring my friend Ben here? Or do you have a hotel room for those liaisons?" Just how dishonest was his Pan Yintao persona?

A lecherous grin was the only reply. It turned Doug's stomach, and he looked away. But his eyes landed on a pair of silk stocking tossed onto the floor at the base of the coat rack, and a pair of black ladies' pumps hidden in the shadow of the corner space. His lips pursed involuntarily, and he looked back at Liu Fan, who regarded him with one arched eyebrow.

"Did you come here to talk, Mr. Bainbridge?"

"Yes, as a matter of fact, that's exactly why I came here."

Doug couldn't read Liu Fan's expression. But then the thin young man shrugged and uncrossed his legs. "Very well. What do you want to talk about? Did you come here to hear the lurid details of my encounters with your friend? Yes, I had him twice. Here." He patted the mattress. "Such a gigantic penis, so pleasurable to take, I had to have it again the next night." The lecherous grin had returned.

Doug held his temper with effort. "That's none of my business, and it's not what I came to discuss. I want you to tell me exactly how you know Jimmy Lockhart."

Liu Fan's eyes widened in genuine surprise. "The little horse jockey? I hardly paid him any mind. He was hardly man enough." He held up a pinky finger and wiggled it.

Doug exhaled hard through his nose, fighting the urge to bolt. "It's important that I know what your relationship with him was exactly. It was obvious he knew you, that night he was killed. He called you a freak. I'm sure you remember that."

Anger flashed across Liu Fan's eyes. "Yes, I remember that well," he hissed, every muscle tensed like a coiled snake prepared to strike.

"Clearly he knew what kind of person you are," Doug said, meaning it in more than one way, but leaving that unspoken.

A look of studied indifference settled over Liu Fan's face, and he looked away with a sniff and a silent shrug.

"I need to know how he learned this," Doug said, not at all certain he really *wanted* to know. But it was important. It was for Stuart.

Liu Fan looked back at him, head cocked, a calculating look in his eyes. "How much is this information worth to you, Mr. Bainbridge?"

Doug sighed. "It's important."

"How important?"

"Important." Doug pulled a half-dollar from his pocket and set it down hard on top of the dresser.

Liu Fan eyed the coin with that same look of studied indifference. "Take off your jacket, Mr. Bainbridge. Make yourself comfortable."

Doug hesitated a couple of seconds, but then slipped off his jacket and hung it on the coat rack before taking the seat by the table. "Tell me how you met Jimmy Lockhart. And when was that?"

A hint of smile graced Liu Fan's lips. "It was in December, at the Majestic Café. He asked me for a dance. He was drunk, and he blabbered a lot. But he wasn't a bad dancer. He bought me drinks, so I accepted his attention. He wasn't the handsomest man—you noticed that, didn't you Mr. Bainbridge? But I have had uglier."

"What did he talk about?"

Liu Fan gave him a wicked grin. "Take off your shoes." He himself kicked off his shoes, and then bent forward to pull off his socks.

"I'd rather not."

"Then I'd rather not talk any more. Good day, Mr. Bainbridge." But he made no move from his seat on the side of the bed.

Doug exhaled hard, and then reluctantly bent over to untie and slip off his shoes. "There. Now tell me what Jimmy Lockhart talked about that night you met him."

"I am barefoot, and you are not."

"That wasn't the bargain."

Liu shrugged. "He talked a lot about his silly horse races. I pretended to be interested, of course, and he kept talking about them. He bragged about his wins, and always had an excuse for his losses." Another shrug. "In hindsight, he was not much of a man. But he insisted he would do much better next year. Bragged about it incessantly."

Doug cocked his head in curiosity. "Oh? How could he be sure?"

"Something about a guarantee, and lots of money?" Liu Fan waved a hand dismissively. "Men brag about money so much that I barely listen. And you should take off your socks now if you want to keep asking questions."

Doug didn't like the direction this was going one bit. "I'm not comfortable being barefoot in someone else's home."

Liu Fan just smiled. "Then take off your shirt and tie, if you must keep your socks on. I will take off mine." He tugged his tie loose and pulled it from his collar, then started unbuttoning.

So, this *was* going that direction, damn it. *Not a chance.* But he had to keep Liu talking at least a little bit longer. Doug leaned forward and yanked off his socks, angrily tossing them on top of his shoes.

Liu made a sort of 'tsk-tsk' noise, but continued unbuttoning his shirt, and then slipped it off his shoulders. He was slender, almost skinny, but with a bit of definition in his shoulders. His torso and arms were as smooth as a child's. Or a woman's. Perhaps that was thanks to Dr. Yang's pills.

Doug looked at the ground and took a few seconds to ponder what Liu had said thus far. Jimmy Lockhart thought a winning streak was 'guaranteed' for some reason. Fixing races? But how could he do that? Liu Fan was unlikely to know, so Doug filed that away for later.

"Can I assume his hostility toward you was because you brought him back here, and he discovered your little secret?"

Liu's eyes flashed for a brief second, but then his expression turned coy again. "He took me to his apartment, other side of Thibet Road, close to the racetrack. He was very drunk and could barely climb the steps without my help. He couldn't get the key into the lock, I had to help him with that. It was obvious I would have to do all the work, but I've done that before." He waved a dismissive hand again. "Once we got inside his apartment, he was all over me. His hand almost found my secret, so I dropped to my knees and took him in my mouth."

Doug scowled. "I don't need those kinds of details."

Liu shrugged. "He enjoyed himself. You would, too." His eyes fell to Doug's lap before riding back up to his face. "But he insisted on going down on me. I said no, and tried to stop him, but he was stronger than he looked. He held my arms down and yanked off my panties—then he jumped back, cursing. I reached for my panties, but he punched me across the face. Then he punched me again." Liu's face contorted with rage. "I'm glad someone killed him! He deserved to die. But I was not the one."

Doug regarded Liu with sympathy, and what he hoped was kindness. "I know you weren't the one who killed him. But you might know something that would help us find out who did. It wasn't my friend, but we have to prove someone else was the killer, so he doesn't hang for it."

Liu Fan stood, slowly, languidly. "Then it is important to you, isn't it?"

The ship's warning bell seemed to go off in Doug's head. "I just want to help my friend."

"He was not nice to me, either," Liu Fan said, lips pursing. "He did not beat me the way the horse jockey did, but he shoved me onto the floor in front of everyone at The Pink Lotus."

Doug's sympathy vanished. "That was because you weren't honest with him."

Contempt washed across Liu Fan's face. "I was hiding nothing! It is not my fault he was too stupid to know what kind of club he was in."

Doug didn't have an argument for that, and he closed his mouth.

"I don't have to pretend there. And we don't have to pretend here, Mr. Bainbridge." He slipped his suspenders off his shoulders, letting them dangle. Then he started unbuttoning the fly of his slacks.

Doug shot up from his chair and grabbed his jacket off the coat rack.

"Now you are not being honest, Mr. Bainbridge."

Liu Fan's words stopped him in his tracks. "I don't know what you're talking about."

One side of Liu's mouth twerked. "I can see what kind of man you are. I am not blind. I know what you want. And I will not tell anyone."

Doug's mouth had gone dry. "You're wrong," he croaked.

Liu shook his head. "I am not wrong." His pants slid off his hips and fell to the ground.

Doug's gaze stayed on the young man's naked form for several seconds. Then he snapped out of whatever inertia had gripped him and looked down at his shoes and socks. He stooped to snatch them up, flung open the door, and marched down the hall.

He didn't stop until he was at the next floor down. Then he plopped onto a stair and put his socks and shoes back on as quickly as he could, face burning. He tugged on his suit jacket and stormed down the rest of the stairs.

24

Dolores Moody looked startled when she saw Doug at her door. Then she smiled and exhaled hard. "Oh! Mr. Bainbridge, isn't it? I thought you were my neighbor, coming to yell at me for playing my record too loud."

She was wearing a floor-length evening gown of gold silk with a sequined bodice, and her blond hair was curled and pulled tight into a pile on top of her head. Her lipstick was bright scarlet.

"Did I come at a bad time?"

She looked back at the little clock on her wall, which showed twelve minutes to seven o'clock. "I can spare you two minutes, then I have to go." She stepped aside and let Doug in.

"You're working tonight?"

Something in his tone made her lips tighten into a thin line. "I'm meeting a gentleman *for dinner*. A nice old fella. His wife died of the typhoid fever in November, and he's lonely. I've been his dinner companion several times now." She wagged a finger at Doug's face. "He's not lookin' for nothin' but companionship, so don't go telling your friend Scott that I'm stepping out on him, 'cuz I'm not. I told you before, I don't do that for money. Understand?"

Doug held out both hands in front of him. "I understand. Promise." He glanced at her clock; eleven minutes to seven. "I came to ask you some questions, but it might take more than one minute. Mind if I escort you to where ever you're meeting your gentleman dinner partner?"

Her expression relaxed, and she nodded. "Let me get my wrap. It still gets chilly at night sometimes." She returned from the other room a moment later with a long silk scarf wrapped around her shoulders, the ends dangling beside her bosoms.

"You know I've been looking into Jimmy Lockhart's murder, trying to prove my friend Stuart wasn't his killer," Doug said while she locked her apartment door. Then she took his arm and they started down the stairs.

"Yeah, I remember. Had much luck?"

"Some." Doug let that linger in the air for a couple of seconds. "Some witnesses told me they saw you slap Lockhart that night. Others said they saw you pull your arm from his grip only ten minutes before he took his fall out the window. You didn't tell me any of that when I was here before."

She stiffened. "Look, Mr. Bainbridge—I may not be the classiest or most well-bred girl you'll meet, but I was raised with manners. You don't speak ill of the dead. Jimmy Lockhart had his faults, like anyone— and maybe he and I didn't get along so good, truth be told—but he wasn't a bad fella, and I'd rather not say anything that might imply he was."

"I understand that. And I commend you for it, I really do. But a man's life might be at stake over this. I need for you to be completely honest about what happened that night. Everything you know."

They stepped through the building door onto the narrow street, alive with Chinese and Russian children playing in the street, old men sitting on stoops playing mah jong, and women leaning out windows gossiping with their neighbors. Dolores looked all around, tense.

"Alright, I'll tell you everything," she said quietly, leaning her face close to his. "This way—I'm meeting the gentleman at the Metropole Hotel. The *lobby*."

"I understand," Doug said, and steered them north toward Foochow Road.

"First thing you gotta understand—Jimmy weren't the type of fella to take no for an answer. Not once he got a mind that he wanted something."

"And he wanted you."

She stiffened again. "Only when he felt like it. But when he felt like it, he really did."

Doug knew the type. "Go on."

"The first time he took me out, last year… well, he assumed something he shouldn't have. When I wouldn't go to bed with him, he got real sore and asked if he weren't good enough for me. The implication being I shouldn't be so picky. You get the picture. I almost didn't go out with him the next time he wanted to hire me—but twenty bucks is a lot of money, so I took it and reminded him it was just for a night out, nothing more. And that time he was a perfect gentleman.

"But then that night at Del Monte's, he was all worked up for some reason. Got real handsy. And I mean *handsy*—puttin' 'em places he shouldn't be puttin' 'em if you know what I mean. That's why I slapped him. He called me a two-bit whore, which is wrong on both counts. I told him I'd do more than slap him next time he tried something, and he left me alone after that."

Doug stopped and turned toward her, staring hard into her eyes. He tightened his grip on her arm. "What did you mean by 'more than slap him?'"

A touch of fear crossed Dolores's eyes, but she raised her chin and squared her shoulders. "I didn't' mean I was gonna kill him! You gotta believe that. What I meant was I'd introduce his balls to my right knee."

The image of Jimmy Lockhart in a fetal position on the floor, grabbing at the front of his pants and crying like a baby made him smile.

Dolores exhaled in relief and grinned back at him. "I can handle men like him."

"I bet you can," Doug said, and they resumed walking. "Was Jimmy working for Jack Riley?" He needed to get to the point fast, as the curved façade of the Metropole Hotel loomed a block ahead.

"Jack Riley? The 'Slots King?' I—I don't know. I've heard Riley's got his fingers in the dog races, but I've never heard nothin' about him getting into horse racing."

"Maybe that's his next move," Doug suggested. "Maybe Jimmy was his entrée. Or Riley thought he was."

"I don't know…" Dolores sounded genuinely doubtful. "Don't get me wrong, Jimmy was no angel. I know I didn't paint him in the best light just now—and it was all true, mind—but I don't think Jimmy would get involved with fixing horse races."

"Why do you say that?"

"Well, I mean, it was obvious he loved racing. Everyone knew that about him. I just can't imagine anything or anyone making him turn crooked on something he loved as much as racing. He wouldn't do that."

They stopped in front of the marquis of the Metropol, and Doug took a few seconds to ponder what she'd said. Something wasn't right— it was like a jigsaw puzzle piece that looked like it ought to fit, but you couldn't get it to fall into place no matter how hard you pushed it with your thumb.

"Listen, Mr. Bainbridge…"

He'd been staring at the sidewalk, and he snapped his gaze back to her. "Yes?"

"I know Scott's got shore leave again in another week, and he said he was going to call me…" her voice trailed off into hesitation.

"I'm sure he will." He hoped that was true, actually.

"If you see him, would you mind saying I asked after him? I know it's not polite for a gal to chase a fella like that, but you see, it ain't so easy finding a nice fella to settle down with when you're… past a certain age." She made a face, but then squared her shoulders. "I didn't want a husband when I was young enough to get one—I wanted to be a dancer, have a career in show biz. But you reach thirty and your high kicks don't come so easy no more. A girl starts thinking about a nice home with a nice fella. But trouble is, they ain't linin' up no more. So when a girl gets lucky and comes across a nice fella who's a handsome devil like Scott, and he gives her a call—well, she's gotta do everything she can to nail him down. And that's all I'm doin' now. So just do me a favor, for all I told you tonight—tell Scott I asked after him, and hope he's doin' alright. Will ya?"

Doug took her arm from his and patted her hand. "I will. I promise."

Her bright blue eyes might have been a little damp when she smiled at him and turned toward the doorman, striding into the Metropol with her head high.

25

"Oh, hello Douglas. I was beginning to wonder if you'd be home for dinner." Mrs. Kinzler's disapproval was writ large on her face. "I'll go tell Bao to set you a place."

"Thank you," Doug said. He wasn't *that* late. Hell, it wasn't even seven-thirty yet.

"Mr. Bainbridge is joining us for dinner, Bao," Mrs. Kinzler said at the entrance to the kitchen, overly loudly. "Please set a place for him right away. And don't dawdle and let the food get cold."

"Yes, Missy Kinzler," Bao said, hurrying out of the kitchen as best he could in his coat and tie and dress shoes, a plate and silverware in his hand.

"And be sure that glass is spotless," she added, her volume still almost a shout.

"He can hear you, Mother Kinzler. He's not hard of hearing."

Mrs. Kinzler's lips tightened into a thin line. "You must speak forcefully to Chinamen, or they won't respect you."

"That's not true." Doug shook his head and folded his arms across his chest. He'd had about enough of this. "You can speak to Bao the same way you would any other human being."

Mrs. Kinzler looked off across the room, lips pursed. "The younger generation is too bold. In my day, we were taught to *respect* our elders, and not to criticize them."

"And I'm sure you were also taught that when you're a guest in someone's home, you respect your host and follow their house rules."

Her face snapped toward him, her mouth open.

"And one of our house rules is to treat everyone in the house as a regular human being, not as a servant. I expect you to speak to Bao as respectfully as Lucy and I do. Is that clear?"

Mrs. Kinzler looked across the room and kept her mouth firmly shut.

"Dinner is ready, mista Doug." A hint of smile graced Bao's lips as he said it.

Doug had to smile at him. "Thank you, Bao. Have a seat." He enjoyed the look of irritation on his mother-in-law's face as she took her seat across from Bao.

Doug sat at the head of the table and grabbed the bowl of vegetables to dish onto his plate. "Why don't you tell me all about your day, Bao."

**

Sunday, April 24

Doug was still half-asleep when Bao knocked on the bedroom door. "Yes?" he called sleepily.

"A letter come for you, Mista Doug."

"Just a moment." Doug stretched and yawned, and it took a few seconds for his brain to grasp that it was Sunday, and there was no mail today. He tugged on his bathrobe and went out to the living room.

"I put it on the table for you." Bao said.

Mrs. Kinzler was sitting at the table, fully dressed as always, sipping a cup of Oolong tea and eating a piece of buttered toast. The newspaper was open in front of her. To the Society page, he couldn't help noticing.

His name was scrawled across an otherwise blank envelope. No return address or sender, no postage.

"Who brought this, Bao?"

Bao shrugged, setting a cup and saucer in front of Doug, along with a little pot of tea. "It was taped to the front door when I got the newspaper."

Curious. Doug broke the seal and pulled out a single slip of paper, folded into thirds.

Stop asking about things you don't need to dig into. We're watching you.

If you don't listen, you'll pay. That's a guarantee.

I hope your wife is comfortable in Room 28 at St. Elizabeth's.

A cold dread dropped like a stone into the pit of Doug's stomach, and then chills ran up his spine and down his arms. He shivered.

It was typed, and unsigned.

"Douglas, you're as white as a sheet." Mrs. Kinzler stared at him with concerned eyes.

He didn't want to worry her. But he also needed to act. Fast.

He marched to the telephone on the side table next to the couch and rang the operator. "Shanghai Municipal Police, West Precinct station, please, Gordon Road."

A working-class English voice answered, first in English, then with the single Shanghainese word for "Police."

"Good morning. I need to speak with Detective Inspector Wallace, please. It's an urgent matter."

"The detective inspector's not in yet, sir. I can take a message for him, but he don't always come in on Sundays."

"It truly is urgent that I speak with him. Could you have him rung at home and tell him to call Douglas Bainbridge? As soon as he can."

There was silence on the line for a second. "I'll have to get the sergeant's permission to ring the detective inspector at home, sir. What's this about?"

Doug took a breath, trying to calm his nerves. "It's in reference to a murder investigation. I've received a threat, directed at both me and my wife. It's anonymous, but it's likely from the murderer."

"What's anonymous, sir?"

"The letter I received this morning, threatening me and my wife."

"The detective inspector might just want to know about that. I'm sure the sergeant will let us ring him up. In the meantime, we'll send a constable round, sir. What's the address?"

Doug gave him the address and hung up.

Mrs. Kinzler was standing at her seat by the table, staring at him open mouthed. "What's that about threats? What kind of threats? What's going on, Douglas?"

Doug held up his hands to reassure her. He hardly wanted to get into the whole thing with her, though. "I'm sure it's nothing to worry about. I called the police as a precaution, and because it might be evidence in a murder investigation." He left out that the Shanghai Municipal Police weren't involved since the murder had been outside of the International Settlement's boundaries. "A friend of ours was accused of murder—a murder he didn't commit—and I've been helping our friend Kenny to find evidence to clear Stuart's name. This letter is threatening me if I don't stop."

"Let me see the letter." Mrs. Kinzler extended her hand.

Doug had to think of an excuse fast. "That's probably not wise. The police will probably dust it for fingerprints."

Fortunately, she accepted that, dropping her hand back to her side and mumbling, "Of course."

**

The police constable who arrived a few minutes later was a few years older than Doug, probably mid-thirties, with a thick brown mustache and a heavy English accent. He introduced himself as DC Hendricks. He held the letter in his gloved hand, reading it with furrowed brows.

"Well indeed, sir, this is a nasty business. I'm dreadfully sorry for the fright, sir. Seems they probably mean to scare you. Happens all the time. Don't necessarily mean they aim to follow through with it. Still, best be cautious as you go about your business the next few days, sir."

I always am. "I will. As a precaution, I'd like a constable posted outside my wife's hospital room until you catch this person."

"Oh, I don't know about that, sir," Hendricks said. "I don't count it likely this miscreant would go after your wife, sir. If he's serious about doin' you harm, he'll follow you and watch for an opportunity to ambush you. He ain't goin' to attack your wife in a crowded hospital ward."

Doug didn't agree, but he nodded and thanked Hendricks. "Please ask Detective Inspector Wallace to call me."

"I will indeed, sir. Good day."

After closing the door, Doug marched toward the telephone and dialed the operator. "United States Fourth Marines, please."

**

A marine lance corporal was standing in the lobby of St. Elizabeth's hospital when Doug and his mother-in-law arrived thirty minutes later.

"You must be waiting for me, corporal. I'm Commander Bainbridge."

"Pleased to meet you, sir," the corporal said. He was stiff-backed but didn't come to attention or salute since Doug was out of uniform.

"This is my mother-in-law, Mrs. Kinzler. Come with us, I'll show you where to stand guard."

"Yes, sir."

Mrs. Kinzler had been silent the entire way to the hospital and remained so as they walked to Lucy's room.

"You can stand guard here, corporal," Doug instructed. "Don't allow anyone into the room except me and Mrs. Kinzler; and the nurses, of course."

"Yes, sir."

They found Lucy asleep, and her mother marched right to her side and took the only chair beside the bed. She removed a book from her purse and started reading, not looking at Doug. Doug sighed, and crept to his wife's side, carefully leaning down to brush a kiss on her forehead.

She stirred, and he cringed. He'd been so careful. Her eyes fluttered open. "How long have you been here?" she asked sleepily, and then yawned and stretched.

"Only a few minutes. I'm sorry I woke you."

"Don't be sorry. I look forward to seeing you every day."

Mrs. Kinzler scooted her chair closer, the wooden legs scraping loudly across the tile floor. She took Lucy's hand. "There a marine corporal standing guard outside your room. Someone's threatening to hurt you if Douglas doesn't stop asking questions about a murder."

It was all Doug could do not to order his mother-in-law out of the room. He could feel the veins throbbing at his temples.

Lucy's eyes grew so wide the whites outshined the blue irises. "Doug? What's going on?"

He knelt beside the bed and took her other hand. "Don't worry, darling. The police think it's an idle threat. I called in a favor and got a marine guard as an extra precaution, that's all."

"I know you, Doug. You wouldn't have asked for that if you thought it was just an idle threat."

He should have known she'd see through that. "Like I said, it's just an extra precaution. I think the threat to you is low."

She breathed a little easier, but then her eyes narrowed. "The threat to *me* is low—but what about you? Are they after you, Doug? What's going on?"

"I'm fine, don't worry."

She sat up bolt straight. "Don't worry? Of *course* I'll worry! We've got a baby, Doug! What will I do if something happens to you?" Her eyes teared up.

"There, there, dear," Mrs. Kinzler murmured, patting her daughter's hand.

Lucy snatched her hand away, not even looking at her mother. Mrs. Kinzler looked stunned, then stiffened and looked away.

"Nothing's going to happen to me," he assured her.

"Maybe you should stop asking questions now."

This stunned him. "What? I can't let Stuart down. He and Kenny are depending on me."

She shook her head emphatically. "You've got what they need. Someone threatened you if you don't stop asking questions—that right there proves there's someone else out there that doesn't want you to prove Stuart didn't do it. If that's not reasonable doubt, I don't know what is."

She had a point. But it was still a risk. Juries were unpredictable things. He had to see this through.

But he also had to tell her something. She was staring at him with her arms crossed over her chest.

"I'll talk it over with Kenny, and if he thinks we have enough, I'll stop." In truth, he should have called Kenny right after he'd arranged the marine guard, before leaving home.

That seemed to mollify her.

They talked for the next forty minutes about Danny, and when her mother left for a visit to the ladies' room Doug filled her in on what he'd learned from Liu Fan and Dolores Moody—but leaving out Liu Fan's stripping. He wasn't comfortable telling her about *that*.

"It definitely sounds like you're picking close to the vein," she said. "Mark Chapman said they were dangerous people, and he was frightened; now they've made threats directly to you. I'm sure Kenny will agree you have enough, once you tell him all of this."

"Hopefully."

The nurse came in, frowning at the marine corporal standing beside the door. "It's time to leave, Mr. Bainbridge. Baby needs feeding."

He kissed Lucy and walked toward the door. The nurse followed him out. Doug stopped to talk to the corporal, but the nurse wagged a finger at them.

"You men will have to take your conversation outside the ward. I'm bringing the baby down the hall in a moment, and you can't be nearby. We must protect baby from germs."

"We'll move a few steps away," Doug said, and nodded for the corporal to move a few feet.

"I'm afraid you'll have to leave the ward entirely. No men allowed near the baby its first week."

Doug turned to face her directly and looked down at her stern expression with his own. "The corporal here has been assigned to guard Mrs. Bainbridge's door for her security, and he can't do that from outside the ward. He must remain within sight until another marine comes to relieve his shift."

"I'm afraid we can't allow that," the nurse said, jutting out her chin. "You must both leave the ward before I bring the baby. If you don't comply, I'll have to call the doctor."

"Be my guest," Doug said, crossing his arms. "I'll be happy to remind the doctor of International Settlement Regulation forty-seven bee two, concerning penalties for interfering with a security operation within the Settlement." He'd made that up, but she seemed to buy it. Her eyes widened briefly, but then she scowled with a quiet "humph" and stormed off.

Doug and the corporal moved a few feet farther from the door. "We didn't have an opportunity to speak privately before," Doug said, keeping his voice quiet. "The threat I've received against me and my family is from a criminal gang, but we don't know which one. That's why I've asked you to not let anyone into the room except the nurses, me, and my mother-in-law."

"You can count on us, sir."

"Thank you, corporal. I wish I knew more, so I could tell you more specifically what to guard against. We have friends who might like to visit my wife—but for now, we'll have to keep out any visitors."

"We might be able to help you, sir," the corporal said.

"Oh?"

"I know a lot of fellas in the Friends of Riley," he said. "They're good guys, all of 'em. Every American marine in Shanghai would jump to help 'em with anything. Except baseball, of course—we gotta beat 'em in baseball. But otherwise, we'd do anything for Jack Riley and his boys."

Doug almost cringed but stopped himself in time. It was well-known that Jack Riley indulged the Fourth Marines with cheap booze and plenty of girls, and in exchange they gave him all of their business at his 'Blood Alley' dive bars. He'd even installed his slot machines in the Marines' officer's club, which was clearly against regulations.

"How might that help me, corporal?" Doug was pretty sure the marine didn't mean to find the thug who'd threatened him and Lucy among the 'Friends of Riley.'

"Jack Riley knows all the gang leaders in the Shanghai underworld, sir. If anyone can find out which gang is threatening you, it's Jack Riley and his lieutenants."

That was the *last* thing Doug needed. But getting this marine corporal to understand that would be a pointless endeavor. "I appreciate the offer, corporal. I have my own connections that are working to identify the thugs, but I'll be sure to let you know if I could use your help."

"Yes, sir," the corporal said with a firm nod. "Just ask, and we'll do it for you."

**

Doug went down to the lobby and located a pay phone. He deposited a nickel and asked the operator for Kenny and Abbie's residence. Abbie answered, and he told her he needed to speak with Kenny about Stuart's case.

"Hi there, Doug. Have you learned something?" Kenny's voice said over the line a moment later.

"In a manner of speaking." Doug filled him in on what Dolores Moody had said the night before, and the threat letter he'd received this morning.

"Good lord, Doug!" Kenny sounded genuinely alarmed. "What are you going to do?"

"I called the police right away. They sent a constable around, and he's supposed to have Detective Inspector Wallace call me. I've worked with the inspector before, a couple of times. He'll remember me. They wouldn't post a guard at Lucy's hospital room, though, so I called in a favor with the colonel over at the Fourth Marines. He sent a guard over, and they're going to rotate duty until the threat's eliminated."

The line was silent for a second. "How do you think you're going to eliminate that threat, Doug? What are you going to do?"

He wasn't entirely certain. "I'm thinking that over. Can't be too careful."

"Anything I can do to help? It seems they're following you, but no one's following me. If there's something you need done, let me and your friend Jonesy take care of it for you."

That wasn't a half bad idea, but Doug hated the thought of putting Kenny in danger. Jonesy, on the other hand, would relish it.

"Let me think about it. I'll call you later."

He slid another nickel in the slot and asked the operator to call Arthur Jones. He wasn't sure Jonesy would answer—he didn't most of the time—but luck was with him today.

"Jonesy, I need your help with something. Can you come right away?"

"Sounds serious," Jonesy said, a note of concern in his voice. "Are you ok?"

"I'd rather not talk about it over the phone. Meet me in the lobby at St. Elizabeth's hospital. Can you be here in ten minutes?"

"I'll head right over."

**

For once, Jonesy was right on time. "What's this all about?" A look of concern came to his green eyes. "You sure you're ok? You're not one to pace the floor."

Several people sat or stood in clusters around the lobby. Doug nodded toward the men's room, and Jonesy followed him. After checking below the stall doors to be sure the room was empty, Doug got Jonesy up to speed on the situation. "So, I need your help figuring out how to get around this threat."

Jonesy nodded slowly. "You've got to get better at this fast if you want to make a good spy."

"I'm not a spy, Jonesy."

"Yeah, yeah, yeah."

"I'm not, damn it! I'm an Intelligence Officer. That's not the same."

"Semantics," Jonesy muttered.

Doug let that go. "Do you have any ideas for me?"

Jonesy was silent for several seconds. "Yeah, maybe." He took a step back and looked Doug up and down. "What size are you?"

"Forty-two regular. Why?"

"Pants?"

"Thirty-two waist, thirty-four length. What do you have in mind?"

Jonesy nodded slowly. "Yeah, you've got the right build. I think it'll work."

"*What* will work?" This was getting annoying.

"Is there a back way out of here?"

"The hospital? I'm sure there is."

"Let's go find it."

26

Doug followed Jonesy into a narrow side street behind the Foochow Market, a couple of blocks east of Thibet Road and the Recreation Ground in the heavily Chinese section of West Foochow Road.

The little street—not much more than an alley, being so narrow Doug could almost stretch his arms out and touch the buildings on either side—only ran for a block, and Jonesy opened a olive green door under an awning of the same color. Doug followed him into a dimly-lit store, air thick with dust and the musty odor of old cloth.

The white man behind the counter, slender and tall, about forty-five years old with thinning hair and a high forehead, nodded at them. "Jonesy."

"How are you, Frank? I need to outfit my friend here like an off-duty marine. Got anything his size?"

Frank looked Doug up and down. "Let's see, forty-two shoulder, I think. Thirty-two or thirty-three waist—"

"Thirty-two," Doug said.

Frank shrugged. "You're a tall one—probably thirty-four leg, am I right?"

Doug nodded.

Jonesy chuckled. "You're good, Frank."

"Been doin' this a long time, Jonesy." Frank looked back at Doug. "What size shoe?"

"Eleven."

Frank grunted with a single nod. "Be right back."

After he disappeared through a narrow door, Jonesy turned to Doug. "Frank Martin was in the Fourth Marines during the Great War. The Germans were mostly washed up in Asia by the time we got in, so the Yang Pat was a cushy assignment even during the war. He mustered out in '20 but stayed in Shanghai and opened this joint. A military goods store. He's got connections in Manilla and Guam who send him surplus of just about anything, navy and marines. He's got contacts with the British navy, the Italian navy, and probably others. You wanna look like one of those, Frank can set you up. Keep that in mind for future reference."

"Not a spy, Jonesy." But Doug couldn't help a tiny smile of amusement. This felt a bit like being in one of those cloak and dagger dime novels. Kind of exciting, actually.

Jonesy chuckled and shook his head. "Whatever you say."

Frank emerged from the back a moment later with a stack of khaki clothing and a pair of scuffed boots. "Try these on." He motioned his head to a curtain dangling from a rusty rod in the corner and thrust the stack at Doug.

Doug took the clothes to the corner, set them on the little chair there, and pulled the curtain. He frowned when it left big gaps on either side. He crammed himself as far into the corner as he could as he stripped down to his underwear, hoping Jonesy wasn't standing somewhere that would give him a peek.

A couple minutes later, he laced up the boots and stood, looking down at himself. He supposed he looked like a marine on shore leave, but would it be enough to fool anyone?

"You done yet? Let's see," Jonesy said.

Doug pulled back the curtain and took a step out into the small store.

Jonesy's smile confused him—was it mocking? Admiring? Amused? He couldn't tell.

"Not bad! Not bad at all. I think you can pull it off." He looked at Frank Martin. "He'll take it."

"That'll be two dollars and twenty-five cents," Frank said to Doug.

Doug couldn't help his surprise. For surplus clothes and used boots? "Why so much?"

A look of impatience flashed across Frank's face. "Inflation. Do you want the duds or not, mister? Ain't no skin off my nose if you don't."

"I'll take them," Doug said, and stepped back into the corner and pulled his wallet and change from his pants pocket. He paid the ex-marine two dollars and a quarter and accepted a brown paper sack with his own clothes and shoes shoved unceremoniously inside.

Jonesy put a half-dollar on the counter. "For your discretion."

Frank's hand swept the coin away in a blink. "As always."

Jonesy took the paper sack from Doug as they stepped back out onto the cobblestones of the narrow alley. "I'll take charge of these. I know the concierge at the Metropol Hotel, and he'll hide this away for us and not say a word to anyone."

"He's not going to think we're..." Doug couldn't force himself to put words to the thought.

Jonesy smirked. "You're not coming with me. You don't want to be seen going into a fancy hotel dressed like a common marine, do you? No one would buy that you're staying there, and I sure as hell don't want anyone thinking I'm your sugar daddy. That's the last thing I want, to get banned from the Metropol for 'gross indecency.' Especially when I haven't been indecent."

He added that last part with a wink, and Doug had to suppress the urge to smack him.

"So what am I supposed to do while you go to the Metropol with my things?"

Jonesy shook his head at him with a tsk-tsk sort of expression. "You really do need to get better at this." He held up his hands. "I know, I know—you're not a spy. So what? Someday you might need to be, seeing as we're behind the Japanese lines, and they aren't likely to get any friendlier to American interests in the coming years. So get yourself into the mindset of an American marine on shore leave in the fabulous city of Shanghai—what do you think they think about? Girls, booze, and good times. Start thinking like a marine grunt, and go to it. Act like one of them, and blend in. I'll catch up with you."

"But how will you find me?"

Jonesy gave him one of those looks as if to ask why he'd asked such a dumb question. Then he turned without answering and strode back toward Foochow Road. "Blood Alley's that way!" he called over his shoulder, pointing back the opposite direction. Then he disappeared around the corner in front of the market.

**

It wasn't as hard to find as Doug feared. Once he reached Avenue Edward VII—the boundary between the International Settlement and the French Concession—it was easy to spot groups of American marines crossing into "Frenchtown." The thoroughfare was packed with cars and rickshaws, and the sidewalks were equally packed with pedestrians of every conceivable nationality. Car horns and shouts in multiple languages blended into a cacophony of sound.

Following the marines as all of the groups meandered in more or less the same direction, Doug crossed into the French Concession, and then wound through the streets for a couple of blocks until he reached Rue Chu Pao San, the infamous stretch of narrow road lined with dive bars. American marines mingled with merchant sailors of countless origins, and the requisite Chinese and Russian women with heavily painted faces and short dresses.

A fight broke out between a pair of marines over a Russian woman who stood aside with a look of indifference. Their companions and throngs of strangers formed a circle around them, shouting encouragement. He was in the right place. *Welcome to Blood Alley.*

The Manhattan Bar stood at the eastern end of the street, not far from the French Bund and the riverfront. A steady stream of American marines entering the front door made Doug wonder if there was any room left inside.

The clank of pull handles, the rattle of spinning wheels, and the dinging of bells from the line of slot machines in the back carried over the constant din of shouted conversations, reaching him at the front door of the long narrow tavern.

"Never seen you around, private," shouted a tall buzz-haired redhead in the corner with sergeant stripes on his shoulders. "What unit are you with?"

Doug swallowed hard, thinking fast. "I just arrived. Never been to Shanghai before. I was in San Francisco before, but got transferred to the *Valparaiso* in January. Major Cartwright's my CO."

"January? Hell's bells, private! Where ya been since then?"

"Manilla for three months. We got to Shanghai three weeks ago, and I just got shore leave."

"Whatcha doin' here by yourself?" the corporal standing next to the sergeant asked. "Where's your pals?"

This was a dangerous question, and Doug had to navigate the answer carefully. "I'm looking for 'em. I hear 'em talk about this place all the time, thought I might find 'em here."

The looks on the groups face were somewhere between pity and mocking.

"I think they ditched ya, private," the sergeant said with an amused grin.

"You said it's your first time on shore in Shanghai?" the corporal added with a laugh. "Hell, I think they just hazed your ass."

The whole lot of them hooted with laughter. Doug joined in with an 'aww shucks, they got me' kind of sheepish smile.

"You can hang out with us, private," the sergeant said, beckoning him over. "Walkin' around by yourself out there, you'll be a target for every pickpocket and con artist in Frenchtown."

"Thanks, sarge," Doug said, exaggerating the real gratitude he felt at being included.

"Thanks nothin', you're buying the next round of drinks, private!"

All five of them ordered a beer and a shot of whiskey, and the corporal shoved Doug toward the bar. He knew better than to request a gin and tonic in a place like this, so he made it six orders. He carried the shots back in one trip, went back for four of the beers, and one final trip with the last two—his and the sergeant's.

"To your first shore leave in Shanghai, private," the sergeant said, and everyone downed their whiskey. It burned the back of Doug's throat, and it was all he could do not to cough. He wasn't a fan of the flavor of whiskey, either, and had to fight not to make a face at the nasty aftertaste.

Then a familiar face caught his attention coming out of a back room. He had to look twice to be sure, and then wedged himself between the bar and the cluster of five marines, so his own face was hidden.

'House Detective' Russell from the Del Monte strode by a moment later, a big lump in his coat pocket the shape of a thick stack of bills. Doug watched him over the top of his beer glass—the beer here was watered down and barely drinkable—and he didn't interact with any of the patrons, just marched out the door and disappeared.

Doug glanced at his wrist, forgetting that he wasn't wearing his watch.

The sergeant noticed. There was a calculating look in his gray eyes. "It's quarter to eight, private," he said, and then nodded toward the clock behind the bar. Doug had his back to it, but looked over his shoulder now that it had been pointed out specifically. "Got somewhere to be?"

Doug shook his head. "Naw, just wondering where my buddies took off to, that's all."

A moment later, a shorter figure emerged from the back through the same door Russell had taken a moment before, and the bar erupted in applause and shouts of "Jack!"

He raised a hand to acknowledge the applause, and the bartender handed him a tumbler with at least three fingers of whiskey, neat. "Lucky Jack" Riley downed half of it in one gulp.

"You don't know who that is, do ya, private?" the sergeant goaded, knocking on Doug's elbow. Doug pretended ignorance.

"That's ol' Jack Riley. 'Lucky Jack,' the Slots King of Shanghai, and friend to the United States Marines. He owns this joint, and a bunch of others, too. Half his friends and business associates are former marines. He's as close as they come to one of us." The sergeant put an arm around Doug and gripped his shoulder, giving it a shake like half a bear hug.

"Sounds like a swell fella," Doug said, and somehow managed to not choke on the words.

"The best."

Doug really wanted to sneak out of The Manhattan Bar and follow 'Detective' Russell back to the Del Monte—or anywhere else he might stop in between—but there was no graceful way to disentangle himself from this group who had adopted him.

"Another round!" the sergeant shouted, setting his empty beer mug loudly on the bar. "This one's on you, Smitty."

Doug inwardly groaned at the thought of another shot of whiskey and another mug of tasteless beer.

**

By the time the curfew sirens rang out from the International Settlement at ten o'clock, Doug could barely stand up without holding onto the bar for support. The ring of conversation inside The Manhattan

Bar died down, and then everyone shouted in unison, "Fuck the curfew, this is Frenchtown!"

Doug laughed, a bit of a guffaw followed by a giggle that wouldn't seem to stop, and the sergeant smacked him hard on the back.

"The coppers catch you out on the street after ten in the International Settlement, they'll lock you up 'til morning." He was swaying on his feet—or was that Doug's head swimming?—and his speech was a little slurred. "That's why we marines party in Frenchtown. No fucking curfew."

"Smart." Doug's voice sounded a mile away in his own ears.

"Damn right!"

Sometime later—time no longer having any meaning—they stumbled out onto Blood Alley, the sergeant shouting into the night about needing some pussy, some god-damn pussy. "You too, private. We gonna get you a china girl."

Doug shook his head—too hard, but he didn't care—and said, "Can't, sarge." Then he grinned and motioned the sergeant to lean down closer. "I'm married," he said in a stage whisper.

"Married, huh? What the hell you go and do that for? Then you *really* need some china girl pussy." The sergeant stood straight—but weaving—finger in the air and announced, "We'll find you some. But first I gotta piss."

Doug couldn't remember later where they went or how that got there, only that it was a dark and narrow alley between some buildings, with trash strewn everywhere. Then the sergeant shouted, "What the fuck is goin' on here?"

An American seaman stood behind a bent over Chinese man, both with their pants around their ankles, while the Chinese man's face was buried in the naked groin of an American marine, his pants bunched underneath a muscular white ass. All three sprang up instantly, the marine tugging up his pants in a hurry and running off into the night. The seaman bent down to grab his pants but got tangled up and fell.

So many figures rushed around Doug it was all a blur. But then he saw the marines he'd been drinking with kicking and punching at the seaman, who curled up in a ball, arms over his face. Others held the naked Chinese man's arms while still others punched him in the gut, over and over.

"Stop it! Stop it!" Doug shouted, but no one seemed to hear. "Stop!" he yelled louder, so loud that his throat hurt. "They weren't hurting you!"

"They're fuckin' faeries, man!" one of his companions said. "C'mon, you can kick this chink in the balls and teach him a lesson he won't never forget."

Doug stood frozen for a second, and then his stomach wrenched, and he bent over and vomited all over the brick pavement. Wave after wave came out, a toxic mix of whiskey and beer and stomach acid.

Echoing somewhere he could hear laughter, and someone saying, "New fella can't hold his liquor!" He didn't look at any of them, just turned and ran away as fast as he could without stumbling. He weaved so much his shoulders slammed into the sides of the buildings a few times before he found the end of the lane and emerged onto a wider street with sailors and marines milling around.

Blood Alley again. He stumbled off in the direction he thought would take him back toward Avenue Edward VII and the International Settlement, winding through unfamiliar streets, startling a middle-aged Russian man with a long beard walking his poodle. The poodle barked at Doug, who barely avoided walking right over it, and its owner cursed at it—or him—in Russian until they had rounded a corner out of sight.

After what must have been a few wrong turns, Doug emerged onto the brightly lit Avenue Edward VII. It was eerily silent, no cars or rickshaws rushing past, no pedestrians, the streetcar tracks empty in both directions. Only an SMP constable patrolling on the opposite side of the street made any sound, the heels of his boots clicking on the pavement. He eyed Doug with suspicion as he strolled past but made no move to approach. He legally couldn't, of course; this side of the avenue was in the French Concession.

Doug leaned against the corner of a building for stability and waited until the constable disappeared so he could cross the street into the International Settlement. His brain was slow, but he formed the thought that it would be almost impossible to reach home without getting caught; but then he thought of Dolores Moody's apartment, just a block and a half from here. She would put him up for the night.

The damned constable across the avenue had slowed down, though, keeping his eye on Doug. Then he stopped, peered into a store window for a moment, and strolled back the way he had come.

Keeping a watch on Doug.

"I need to look like I've gone away," Doug mumbled to himself, out loud. He stumbled back down the side street he'd most recently been on. But then hands grabbed him from behind. His heart leapt into his throat, and he thrashed out wildly.

"Knock it off, it's me," a gruff voice whispered. Doug stared into the mustachioed face for a moment before recognition dawned.

"Jonesy?"

"Shhh! Keep it down."

"Where ya been?"

"Keep your voice down! I've been keeping an eye on things from the shadows, getting the lowdown from the ladies of the night. They're all terrified of saying anything about Jack Riley or his more nefarious activities—kind of like Mark Chapman, huh? They *will* say he's keen to get his slot machines into swankier joints, but so far only the Canidrome has bitten. They already had betting on the greyhounds, so it wasn't a stretch. But here's where it gets interesting—seems he's absolutely desperate to get his slots into the Del Monte, since Al Israel has gambling there already, but old Al keeps turning him down. Seems Demon Hyde even threatened Jack's life if he ever shows his face there again."

Doug struggled to keep up, but the mention of the Del Monte snapped his brain to attention.

"I saw someone from the Del Monte!" he said, and Jonesy put his finger to his lips again. Doug continued in more of a whisper. "That house detective who talked to me after Jimmy Lockhart got killed—his name was Russell, a southern fella—he was there tonight. At the Manhattan Bar. I saw him come out from the back, from the office, I think, and he had something in his coat pocket like a big stack of money."

Jonesy patted him on the chest. "Seems we're onto something. Now let's get you off the street, pronto."

"OK," Doug said with a goofy grin, weaving. "Where are we goin', buddy?" He leaned against Jonesy, throwing an arm around his shoulder.

"Little place I know of. We'll be safe there 'til morning."

27

Monday, April 25

He walked through fog, dense and swirling, following the sounds of shouts and grunts. Trepidation tingled in his midsection, but he kept putting one foot in front of another, reaching his hands out in front of him to wave away the fog. Figures emerged, slowly, as if they'd materialized before his eyes. A young Chinese man, naked, with two ridiculously big marines holding each of his arms while the red-haired sergeant punched him in the gut, over and over. He only paused to throw a kick at the curled-up seaman on the ground, whose face was a blur.

Doug crept closer and leaned down to get a better look. The pantless seaman turned his face toward Doug, and it was Scott Farnsworth, with blood flowing from a crack in his full red lips.

He looked back at the marines to shout at them to stop, and the naked figured being held by the arms and punched in the gut was Kenny. Where had the young Chinese man gone?

A booted foot kicked Scott again, and he cried out. Then he looked at Doug and said in a croaking voice, "Help me. Please, Doug, help."

Doug looked back at the marines. "Stop! These are my friends! They're good men. They don't deserve this."

But Liu Fan strutted behind them, naked except for the garter strapped to each calf; the way he'd appeared when Doug had fled his garret. He pointed at Doug. "He's one, too."

"No, I'm not!" Doug yelled. But Liu only laughed, a devilish cackle that echoed far too loudly in the mist.

273

"He *is* a faerie!" The sergeant said, pointing at Doug. "Look at him!"

Doug looked down then, and he was as naked as the day he was born. How did that happen? He was wearing something a minute ago, he swore...

"Get him!" the sergeant yelled, and the marines who had been punching Kenny and kicking Scott—where had those two disappeared to?—came running, but in slow motion.

Doug turned to run, but his legs felt like cement pillars, and all he could do was scoot them across the ground. His leg muscles ached as if he'd run a marathon, the pain tingling up from his calves and radiating through his thighs.

Liu Fan was in front of him now—no, it was Pan Yintao in a dress, except that it was torn to shreds and revealed his body and his genitals. Doug reached out to ask for help, but when Liu raised his head, his face was swollen, black and blue, blood caked around his mouth and nose.

*

Doug awoke with a splitting headache. He cracked his eyes open, and the daylight slipping around the sides of the drawn shade made it hurt worse. He put his hand to his forehead and clamped his eyes shut.

"Good morning," Jonesy said from the other side of the room.

Doug peeked with one eye to see the stocky reporter sitting on a chair a few feet away, fully dressed, his bowler hat in his hands. Doug glanced down; he was still wearing the marine shore uniform, lying on top of the bed covers. Only his shoes had been removed. "Where are we?"

"A safe place," Jonesy said. Then with a little shrug he added, "An unofficial inn, shall we say, known only to those of a certain inclination who need somewhere safe to, um, socialize."

Doug didn't like the sound of that. "So, they think I..." he couldn't get himself to form the words.

Jonesy chuckled. "I'm sure, but that's a compliment here. Personally, I haven't been here since my earliest days in Shanghai. But they remembered me. Janice took one look at you and told me I'd moved up in the world."

"Great," Doug muttered, and sat up slowly, trying to minimize the pain that jolted from the base of his skull to his forehead.

"I brought your regular clothes back from the Metropole." Jonesy scooted the brown paper bag toward the bed with his foot.

Doug leaned down—God, that hurt his head—and pulled his clothes and shoes out of the bag, setting them onto the bed beside him. He looked back at Jonesy. "Do you mind?"

"Not at all," Jonesy said with a devilish grin, leaned back in his chair, and folded his hands across his lap.

Doug closed his eyes and signed. *Damn it, Jonesy!* "I meant would you mind giving me a little privacy?"

"After rescuing you from certain arrest last night?" Jonesy shook his head and made a tsk-tsk sound. "Killjoy." He stood and took two strides to the door. "I'll be right outside. Come on out when you're decent again, and we'll go get some breakfast."

**

The coffee was good at the little French bistro around the corner, and Doug devoured a croissant with orange marmalade.

On their way out of the nondescript house that served as an 'underground hostel for sexual deviants'—Jonesy's words—Doug had been greeted with big knowing grins from the two women sitting together on the couch—a black American woman in her late thirties named Janice, and her half-French half-Chinese girlfriend Antoinette. "Fun night?" Janice asked. Doug had looked away, hurrying toward the door.

"He's shy," Jonesy said to laughter as Doug bolted out the door. "First time."

"Feeling better?" Jonesy asked him now with a sardonic half-smile.

"A bit."

"Good. Let's go over what we've learned." Jonesy leaned over the table so he could talk quietly. "That 'house detective' Russell shoots to the top of our suspect list, I think. He can only be up to no good taking money from Jack Riley while working for Al Israel out at the Del Monte. The only question is, what was his connection with Jimmy Lockhart? And why did Lockhart have to die?"

"Any idea how we can find out?" Doug had none himself, but Jonesy was used to digging around in everyone's metaphorical closets.

"Yeah, but you're not gonna like it."

Doug braced himself. "Go on."

"We need to talk to Liu Fan again."

**

They walked through the revolving front door of Sincere Department Store on East Nanking Road the moment the store opened and made a beeline for the Men's department.

Doug spotted Liu Fan brushing invisible lint from a stack of perfectly pressed and folded slacks. "We need to talk to you," he said quietly.

A plump white man of about forty came over, dressed impeccably in a dark pinstriped suit, scarlet red silk tie, and matching scarlet pocket square. Mother of pearl inlaid gold cufflinks completed the look of a man who knew how to dress. "May I help you, sir?" he asked Doug in that posh British accent usually only heard on the BBC.

Jonesy stepped in. "I'm looking for a new shirt to go with this suit."

The man's nose wrinkled involuntarily when he gazed at Jonesy's well-worn light gray suit. "I'm sure we can find you something that will improve on what you have. Come with me, sir."

Jonesy gave Doug a sly wink as he turned and followed the pompous head salesman toward a shirt rack.

Liu Fan regarded Doug with a look somewhere between amusement and arrogant self-assurance, like he knew all along Doug would come back sometime. "How may I help you, sir?" he asked. It occurred to Doug that this was the first time he'd heard Liu Fan—or Pan Yintao—speaking English.

"I think you know more than you've said."

"About?" Liu Fan's flawlessly trimmed eyebrows arched in mock curiosity.

"About the Jimmy Lockhart affair. You know things you haven't told me."

Liu Fan's mouth stretched into a Cheshire Cat grin. "I might have told you if you had stayed. You would know now. But you did not want to play along." He added this with a shrug and returned to brushing off stacks of slacks.

"I didn't like the rules of the game."

Liu Fan glanced sideways at him. "If you want to play on my board, you must play the game of my choosing. My rules."

Doug exhaled hard in exasperation. What the hell was he supposed to do? "I'm not going to give you what you want. That's not negotiable."

Liu Fan spun to face him, eyes narrowed. "How you know what I want? You never ask." His anger had made his English devolve toward Pidgin. "Maybe all I want is 'lookie no touchie.' You not play along, you not get answers."

The Pidgin phrase 'lookie no touchie' was common enough in Shanghai, from grocers who wouldn't allow shoppers to touch the fruit unless they bought it, to street pimps who wouldn't let a customer touch the prostitute until he handed over his cash; and everything in between.

Liu Fan's use of the phrase didn't make Doug any more comfortable with the rules of the game.

The store was filling up with customers, and a few white men had begun browsing the neckties along the aisle. Doug leaned a little closer to Liu, pretending to look at something Liu was showing him. "I don't know how you think we're going to do that here. And this needs to end here. I need you to tell me everything you know before I leave, or I'll make up some complaint to your boss."

"Excellent choice, sir," Liu said loudly, holding up a pair of gray checked slacks in front of Doug's waist, letting the legs unfold and drape toward the ground. "Come with me, I will measure you."

Doug had the feeling he'd just been coerced into buying a suit of clothes he didn't need. But that was a much smaller price to pay than what Liu had asked of him the first time, in his garret. He followed the young Chinese salesman toward a tall mirror, where Liu pulled a tape measure from his pocket, knelt, and unrolled the tape from Doug's ankle up his leg.

All the way up his leg. Into the crevice at the top of his inner thigh. Doug cleared his throat. "I think you measured too far."

Liu Fan's knuckles pressed against Doug's genitals, the thin fabric of his pants and boxer shorts the barest of distance between them and direct contact. "No, not too far. You want the latest cut, sir. Very stylish." He proceeded to do the exact same thing on the other leg. "We always make sure they are the same."

Doug doubted that, but he endured the interminable moment of uncomfortable contact with red-faced stoicism.

Liu stood, tape in hand. "Raise your arms, sir." Doug raised his arms, and Liu slipped the tape under them and around his back, bringing the ends together snuggly across his chest.

And his thumbs brushed Doug's nipples. Both thumbs, both nipples, no accident. Doug exhaled hard through the nose in impatience.

"Forty and one sixteenth." Liu announced, writing it down on a notepad. Then he murmured. "Very nice."

"Is this necessary? You haven't told me a thing yet."

"Arms down, sir." Liu took the tape measure and wrapped it around Doug's shoulders. "Forty-two and two sixteenths. Very nice, indeed." He jotted it down.

Next, he measured from Doug's shoulder to his wrist, his fingers trailing slowly down Doug's arm. "Thirty-five, and it must have extra room for these muscles." He briefly squeezed Doug's bicep. And then for reasons unspoken, he repeated the process on the other arm. And of course he got the exact same measurement, at the cost of an extra feel.

"Be patient, sir. I will let you try it on in a moment." Liu said, apropos of nothing. He scurried away, leaving Doug to stand in bemusement beside the tall mirror.

He reappeared a moment later carrying a charcoal checked suit coat and a white herringbone shirt, and he motioned for Doug to join him. "Bring the pants, please, sir." He led Doug toward a door, and whisked him inside, closing it behind them. "Try these on, sir," he said far too loudly, but then leaned closer and whispered, "You change, and I'll talk."

Doug nodded, and dutifully took off his jacket, tugged off his necktie, unbuttoned and removed his shirt, and then after a second's hesitation he unfastened his belt and stepped out of his pants. He stood in front of Liu in his garter, socks and boxer shorts. "Satisfied?" he muttered through clenched teeth.

Liu's gaze ran up and down, slowly. "Hmmm…" Then he held up a finger and slipped out the door. Doug wasn't sure what to do, so he pulled on the new pants Liu had picked out, the ends dangling low enough that his heels caught them on the floor. He'd have to endure Liu making tailors marks on them, and perhaps 'double-checking' the inseam, God help him.

The door cracked open, and Liu slipped in again. As he closed the door, Doug looked at the white bundle of fabric in his hand. Liu unfolded it then and held it up. A pair of underwear briefs, the new style often called 'jockey shorts.'

How ironic.

"A stylish young gentleman like you, sir, should be wearing the latest style of everything. Those boxer shorts are for men older than thirty." The look in Liu's dark eyes said he wouldn't hear any argument.

Doug's mouth had gone dry, and he stood rooted in place. With an impatient roll of his eyes, Liu grabbed the waist of Doug's boxers, tugging them down.

Doug grabbed Liu's wrist, too hard, and the young man winced. "Stop this now." It was too late, of course; his boxer shorts already lay around his feet, and once he released his grip on Liu's waist the young men's gaze went exactly where Doug didn't want it to.

Liu took a step back, holding the new briefs out of reach. "You have played the game well, Mr. Bainbridge. I commend you, on everything." His gaze ran up, down, and back up again, lingering. "Now that you have shown me everything, I will tell you everything. I said 'lookie no touchie,' didn't I?"

"You did," Doug said through clenched teeth, his jaw aching at how hard he clenched it.

Liu handed him the briefs and took another step back to watch Doug putting them on. Then the pants, which were the light woolen fabric of a suit one might wear in the summertime in San Francisco or Washington, D.C. But here in Shanghai, such lightweight wool was reserved for spring and fall, and abandoned in favor of linen in the summer. It was almost too late for it now. Liu knelt in front of Doug to make a chalk mark on the pants below Doug's ankle.

"Start talking," Doug said.

"I was going to when I finished my mark," Liu hissed. "You are too impatient."

Doug refused to apologize, and kept his mouth clamped shut.

"I heard Jimmy Lockhart talking to the other tiny man that night," Liu said, rising slowly, his gaze trailing up Doug's leg and groin. Doug became painfully aware that the new briefs created a bit of bulge where his boxer shorts had not. "I needed to powder my nose, and I left your friend Ben to get me another drink. On my way, I passed Jimmy Lockhart talking to the other tiny little man, the one everyone had cheered when he came in."

"Mark Chapman."

Liu shrugged. "I never heard his name. I only knew he rode racehorses, same as Jimmy. But he was better looking than Jimmy. And I'm sure he wasn't as tiny everywhere." He again held out his pinky finger and wiggled it, the same as he had in his garret.

"I get it," Doug muttered, but then consciously moderated his tone. "Go on. What were they talking about?"

"Money, I think. I don't know, but Jimmy said, 'You have to hear me out, this deal is worth thousands.' That is all I heard then, but later when your friend Ben and I left the gambling room—Ben had lost his money at roulette and had no more—I saw Jimmy taking the other one by the arm and say 'I have to talk to you, *now*.'"

Doug's breath came faster. "Outside the gambling room? Then this was on the third floor, wasn't it? Did they go toward the men's room there?"

Liu shrugged. "Maybe. I didn't see where they went. But it was that direction."

"Did you hear anything else? Anything about 'the deal' Jimmy wanted to tell Mark about?"

Liu shook his head. Then his eyes went to Doug's chest, and a grin spread across his lips. Doug realized he'd stopped dressing, and in irritation he reached for the white herringbone shirt hanging on a hook beside them.

Once he'd buttoned it up, Liu stepped close and tugged at various places, checking the fit, presumably. But when he tugged at the front, his fingers slipped inside the fabric a little farther than necessary, and the fingertips ran across Doug's skin and through the chest hairs.

Doug pulled away. "I thought you'd already gotten everything you wanted."

Liu grinned as he stepped back. He spoke in Shanghainese then. "You are as beautiful undressed as your friend Ben is, everywhere but one place. You should not be ashamed of that, because he is extraordinary there. But you are a much better dresser, Mr. Bainbridge."

Doug closed his eyes, willing himself not to shove Liu out of the way and bolt. The thought of running right to the head salesman and telling him that Liu had made indecent advances was tempting, but...

He opened his eyes. "Did you ever see Jimmy talking with any of the Del Monte's men? Perhaps one who was keeping a watch over the gambling?"

There was a flicker in Liu Fan's eyes. He said nothing.

"You did, didn't you?"

"They are dangerous," Liu said, shuffling backward until his back was against the door.

"Tell me."

"Why should I? Those men are dangerous."

"Because that was our deal. I played your game, by your rules, and now you have to pay out."

Liu Fan shook his head emphatically. "How can I know you won't do something stupid that puts me in danger? That tells them I was the one who told you?"

Doug stepped toward him and gripped both of his wrists. "Because I'm not stupid, and I won't do that. And we had a deal." He tightened his grip to the point that Liu winced a little, and didn't let up.

"I will tell you," Liu said at last, only after tears had started forming in the corners of his eyes.

Doug loosened his grip but didn't let go.

"Not long before that, when your friend Ben was placing one of his bets at the roulette table, I saw Jimmy go by from the craps table, and he stopped to light a cigarette. One of the Del Monte's men was standing next to where he stopped, and I saw him talk to Jimmy."

Doug's pulse quickened. He leaned his head closer and said as sternly as he could manage, "What did he say?"

Liu hesitated, and Doug tightened his grip again, eliciting another wince. "I could not hear them over the spin of the roulette wheel—but I can read lips when it is obvious, even in English. I have worked here since I was eighteen, I can understand English well. And this Del Monte man was obvious, the way he moved his mouth. He talks slower than most, I think."

Like a southerner? The thought popped into Doug's head effortlessly. "Then tell me what he said."

"I think he said, 'You better make the deal, they are losing patience.'" He switched from Shanghainese to English for the quote.

Doug's mind raced with possibilities. "And this was right before you left the gambling hall, when you spotted Jimmy Lockhart forcing Mark Chapman toward the third-floor men's room?"

"Not long before."

Bingo. He released Liu's wrists. "Thank you, Liu Fan." He took a step back and bowed.

Liu looked started at the polite gesture, but after a second's hesitation he returned the bow. "And I thank you for playing my game, Mr. Bainbridge," he said, returning to Shanghainese. "I enjoyed our game very much. Perhaps someday you will have me join you and your cut sleave. That I would also enjoy."

Doug shook his head. "You misunderstand. Bao is like a member of my family. We do not have the relationship you assume."

Liu's expression was doubtful, but he didn't argue this time. "Then perhaps I could have him myself? He is very attractive."

Doug doubted it, given that Bao had mentioned Liu Fan's reputation for arrogant pomposity. "You will have to ask him yourself, Liu Fan."

A devilish grin came to Liu's lips. "I will, Mr. Bainbridge. And perhaps you would like to watch us. I know I would like that, and I think you would, too."

Uncomfortable memories flooded back, and Doug forced them from his mind. But he had tensed, and his back ached between his shoulder blades and the base of his neck. "I am not that way."

Liu's doubtful look intensified, and this time he argued. "I can read you, Mr. Bainbridge. Others cannot see it, but I can. You need not feel ashamed—many men enjoy both men and women. It is natural. Before westerners came to China, our grandfathers did not have to choose. Some still don't."

"You're wrong," Doug said, but Liu Fan had already slipped out the door in a flash and closed it again.

**

"You got roped into buying a suit, huh?" Jonesy said with an amused smirk when Doug carried the items to the pompous head salesman.

"Did Liu Fan serve you well, sir?" the head salesman asked in that crisp and affected BBC accent.

"Yes, thank you. I am afraid he forgot to mark the jacket alterations, though."

The head salesman frowned. "I will see that he is disciplined for that oversight. My deepest apologies, sir."

"No, that won't be necessary. It was my fault, you see. It seems Mr. Liu and I have mutual acquaintances, and I distracted him with talk about that."

The head salesman was unmollified. "It is inappropriate for Sincere Department Store staff to engage in *personal* conversation with customers. I will remind Mr. Liu of this."

Doug faked a chagrined smile. "That explains why he was so reluctant to respond at first. I'm afraid I was quite insistent. I should have dropped the subject sooner, it seems. I'll know better next time."

The head salesman looked down his nose at Doug. "Very well, sir. I shall make a note of your inappropriate behavior toward staff, and I must warn you that if it is repeated you will be asked not to return to Sincere Department Store."

It was all Doug could do not to slap the haughty look off the man's face. "I'll bear that in mind," he said stiffly.

The next two minutes were terribly awkward while the salesman checked the fit of the suit jacket and made chalk marks on the shoulders and back seam. Jonesy stood by and watched with undisguised amusement.

"I don't give you enough credit, Douglas," he said when they left the department a few minutes later. "That was an admirable performance."

Doug kept silent while they made their way to the front door onto Nanking Road. But once they'd reached the corner away from most of the crowd, he spun on Jonesy and laid into him.

"I have had *enough* of inappropriate advances from your type, Jonesy. I don't understand your preferences, but I'd let it be if you and your type would. But you all have to keep making disgusting advances, and I've had it!"

"Whoa, whoa, whoa! You need to take a step back and cool it."

Doug clenched his teeth. "Don't tell me what to do, damn it. *I'm* not in the wrong here."

Jonesy glared at him. "Before you lump us all together, let's be crystal clear that I have *never* made advances on you, Douglas Bainbridge. And neither has your friend Kenneth, no matter how head over heels in love with you he is. He would never. And I'd eat my hat if you said Bao or Charlie had ever made advances on you." He took a step closer, menacing. "I take it Liu Fan misbehaved back there, probably using his information as leverage. That's rotten, and you have every right to be upset by that, so I'm willing to forgive and forget just now— but don't you *dare* lump the rest of us in with him."

"Damn it, don't get self-righteous with me!" Doug said with enough force that spittle flow from his mouth onto Jonesy's lapel. Momentary panic swept through him that the stocky reporter might slug him for that, but it passed. "You are *constantly* making suggestive comments at me, Jonesy."

"Oh, for Christ' sake! That's what you're equating to an advance? Don't flatter yourself. I tease you because I thought you were my friend. I've been around a long time, and I know men routinely make much more suggestive jokes to women than I've made to you. You need to get over yourself."

Doug seethed in silence. But as the seconds passed, with Jonesy glaring unrelentingly at him, reason slowly sank in amid his outrage. Jonesy was right, about all of it. Neither he, nor Kenny, nor Bao or Charlie had ever made inappropriate advances; and Jonesy's jests were no worse than what most men made to women on the regular.

The image of Scott's face closing in for a kiss in the dark in Manilla sprang to mind—but Doug had to admit he might have given Scott a false impression by not explaining how he knew about the *nán jì*, the young male prostitutes loitering behind sailors' bars in Yangtzepoo and Nintao.

And maybe also from the way Doug had looked at Scott's bare thighs on the beach that day...

He put that thought away in an instant.

"I'm sorry, Jonesy," he said, but looked down and didn't meet his eye.

Several seconds of silence passed, until Doug hazarded a glace up. Jonesy was looking at him with concern in his green eyes.

"Want to talk about it?" his tone was surprisingly gentle.

Doug shook his head and looked away.

"Then let's get you home. You can tell me what you learned when we get off the street."

28

"Sounds like we're close," Jonesy said when Doug finished recounting what Liu Fan had told him. He'd left out the humiliating parts, what he'd had to endure to get Liu's information. And Jonesy had been kind enough not to ask.

They were sitting around Doug and Lucy's kitchen table, cups of tea in front of them—a splash of gin in Jonesy's—with the teapot in the center of the table.

"I think so, too. It's pretty obvious Jimmy Lockhart was approached by Jack Riley—or someone in his gang, the 'Friends of Riley'—to either fix horse races the way Riley fixes dog races, or to convince Al Israel to let Riley put slot machines in the gambling hall at the Del Monte."

Jonesy shook his head. "Lockhart wouldn't have any pull with Al Israel. I think his job was to convince Mark Chapman to join a race fixing scheme, since Chapman seems to be on a big winning streak. When Chapman didn't agree, Lockhart got physical with him. And then somebody threw him out a window."

Doug looked at him doubtfully. "So, you think it was Mark Chapman? I thought we'd decided we believed him."

Jonesy leaned back, crossed his arms. "I still think I believe him. Probably. But maybe we're looking at this all wrong. Maybe the reason Lockhart was killed was because he failed to close the deal with Mark Chapman. Couldn't cajole him into participating. So one of Riley's other agents threw Lockhart out the window. He was useless to them if he couldn't get Chapman on board, you see." He sat forward again, pointing his cigar in Doug's direction, a gleam coming to his eyes.

"Maybe Chapman witnessed something, and then the killer threatened him if he didn't keep his mouth shut. That would explain why he was so frightened that day we talked to him at the stables."

Doug had to admit that made sense. "Then it would seem 'house detective' Russell is our top suspect. He's clearly working for Riley, his inside man at the Del Monte; and Liu Fan heard him tell Lockhart he had to 'close the deal,' just moments before Lockhart was killed."

"You got it," Jonesy said, grinning.

Doug sobered. "But how do we prove any of that?"

"Let's go talk to Kenny," Jonesy said, rising and reaching for his hat. When Doug didn't immediately rise, he looked at him with impatience and asked, "What's the matter?"

Doug dismissed the unpleasant image of Kenny lying naked on his back atop his desk, a naked Scott Farnsworth between his legs, hips thrusting, his fingers buried in Kenny's mouth. He thrust his chair back and stood. "Let's go."

**

Kenny answered the knock on his office door, to Doug's relief. He smiled when he saw them. "Doug, Jonesy, to what do I owe the pleasure?"

"We have a lot to tell you," Doug said.

Kenny's eyebrows shot up. "Oh? Good news, I hope."

"We may have cracked the case," Jonesy said, closing the door. He took a cigar from inside his jacket. "Mind if I light this?"

"Not at all." Kenny struck a match.

"But we don't have any real proof," Doug hurried to explain, after Jonesy's boast about cracking the case. "It's a good theory, based on some witness testimony I got today. Let me fill you in, and you can decide if it's sufficient to move forward."

He recounted what Liu Fan told him at Sincere Department Store, again leaving out the tawdry parts. There was an uncharacteristic softness to Jonesy's eyes while he repeated the story, and he hoped

Kenny wouldn't notice. Unless he was imagining that. He concentrated on retelling the facts. He concluded by summarizing their theory that Jimmy Lockhart had been sent to convince Mark Chapman to help fix races, and was killed by someone else when he failed.

Kenny's eyes kept getting wider. When Doug finished, the tension seemed to evaporate from his face and shoulders. "Wow! That's a lot to take in."

"You said it," Jonesy agreed, and puffed at his cigar. He tapped the end against an ashtray on Kenny's desk.

That ashtray sat right where Scott had stood the day Doug spied them from the fire escape…

"Doug?"

He looked up to see Kenny staring at him, concerned. "You've gone white as a sheet. What's the matter?"

He and Kenny had already been over this, and though Doug still had lots to say about the subject, he'd be damned if he was going to rehash it in front of Jonesy. The stocky reporter was bound to take Kenny's side, anyway. Another voice rationalizing it away, that was the last thing Doug wanted to hear.

"Liu Fan is terrified of anyone finding out he was my source for this information," he said instead. "You'll never get him to testify under oath."

Kenny frowned. "I'm sure you're right. I could subpoena him, but he would disappear into the masses."

"And issuing a subpoena would identify him, anyway," Doug said.

Kenny sighed. "True. I guess I'll have to defer to you two—given what we now know, how can we prove it?"

Doug was afraid Kenny would ask something like that.

"You're not going to like this, either of you," Jonesy said.

Doug closed his eyes, praying Jonesy didn't mean to go back to Liu Fan again. He wasn't sure he could handle that. He sighed and opened his eyes. "You might as well tell us what you have in mind."

"First, we have to find a way to talk with Al Israel—and that ain't gonna be easy. We'll have to convince Demon Hyde first. But we need to tell him we have credible reasons to believe one of his lieutenants at the Del Monte is secretly working for Jack Riley, so we can get his cooperation."

Doug's eyes narrowed. "His cooperation for what?"

"We have to set a trap."

29

How Jonesy got them the meeting, he wouldn't say.

The atmosphere at the Del Monte at five PM was strange—quiet without any patrons, and yet awash with activity from bartenders, waiters, and bouncers setting chairs on the floor or carrying trays of clean dishes to the kitchen and bars.

Al Israel's office was on the ground floor, down a narrow back corridor in the corner of the villa. Al himself sat behind his desk, drumming his fingers. "You got five minutes," he said after his brother-in-law 'Demon' Hyde shut the door.

"One of your enforcers up on the gambling floor is working for 'Lucky Jack' Riley," Jonesy said without preamble. "We're convinced he's the one who threw Jimmy Lockhart out the window a couple weeks ago. Lockhart was also working for Riley, but not so good at it."

"You got proof?" Demon Hyde said, standing beside the window and cracking his knuckles.

"That's why we're here," Jonesy said. He nodded toward Doug. "My friend here is a private investigator, hired by the attorney for the poor slob who's been blamed for Lockhart's murder."

"We have to prove this man is the real killer, and to do that we have to set a trap for him," Doug said. Did the nerves make his voice waver? He hoped no one noticed. A private eye wouldn't be nervous. He pictured Sam Spade in his seat.

"How?" Al Israel asked, his stare boring into Doug.

"He knows who I am. He saw me come in here just now. My bet is he's keeping close by, watching how long I'm in here with you. In a minute, I'm gonna raise my voice, like we're arguing. You play along, see?"

Al looked at Demon Hyde, who barely shrugged.

"What do you mean I got a spy on my staff? You got proof of that?" Al shouted.

Doug froze. Was he being serious? Was he outraged that they'd accuse one of his men?

Thank God Jonesy read him right and played into it. "Why else do you think we're here?" he shouted back.

"Then show me the proof!" Al slammed his palms on his desk. The whack echoed in the small room.

"I ain't got it with me!" Doug yelled. Had that been too loud?

"I'm not gonna accuse one of my own men without proof, wise guys." Al's reply, though not shouted, was loud enough anyone in the corridor would hear it.

"Where you keepin' your proof?" Demon Hyde asked, equally loudly.

Doug glanced at Jonesy. They hadn't scripted this out, and now he wished they had.

But Jonesy took up the mantle without missing a beat. "A lady who frequents this establishment says she has proof. She's a performer at a little dive in the Badlands called The Pink Lotus. Says she and someone else there have proof this fella's workin' for Riley, feedin' him info on everything you do."

Doug had to admire how convincing Jonesy sounded. And how loud.

"I can get it from her, tonight," Doug said, consciously keeping his voice too loud for the little room. "I'm meeting her near Soochow Creek, uptown. Once I have it, I'll take it to the cops at Sinza station. It ain't far from there."

"You get proof one of my men's workin' for Riley, you bring it straight to me." Al Israel's finger jabbed onto the desk, and Doug had to wonder if he wasn't acting right now.

"Why not let the cops do your dirty work?" Jonesy said. "Besides, if the cops don't nab him, I've got no story." The glint in his green eyes said he was enjoying this performance.

"Get outta here!" Al Israel shouted. But his dark brown eyes held a hint of amusement.

Doug and Jonesy grabbed their hats and hurried out the door.

A shadow disappeared at the end of the corridor.

**

Doug left his building at quarter to eight, as darkness was settling over the city. He glanced both directions down the sidewalk; they were there somewhere, unseen.

Instead of walking toward one of the major thoroughfares—Thibet Road a couple blocks to the east or Bubbling Well Road a couple of blocks to the south—he struck off westward down his own little street, deeper into the neighborhoods of Shanghai uptown. It was quiet here this time of evening, few pedestrians and few streetlights.

He listened for their footsteps, butterflies flitting around his stomach. They had to be following, sticking to the shadows. But no sound reached his ears. He began to doubt himself. Perhaps they hadn't taken the bait. Or had he and Jonesy been wrong entirely?

No, he was certain they were right. And he needed to trust that these men couldn't resist the bait. He kept his ears peeled for the slightest out of place noise.

At last—the crunch of a newspaper under foot, the telltale sound of someone taking great effort to creep soundlessly, but unable to see the wadded-up newspaper that had been thrown out some door or window and had lain unseen on the sidewalk until a foot found it in the dark.

Doug's pulse quickened, and the butterflies tumbled in his stomach. Even though he'd known they would be there, the confirmation of it still triggered a fear response.

A small glow briefly lit a darkened doorway on the opposite corner at Park Road, and then disappeared. Jonesy taking a puff on his cigar to let Doug know he had seen him. A second glow two seconds later would mean he'd seen a second person behind Doug. Doug held his breath and was relieved when none came. Just the one pursuer, then.

They'd been right.

He turned right onto Park Road. He'd have gone left if he were taking the back way to St. Elizabeth's hospital, but right if he were going to the nearest police station. Or going toward Soochow Creek.

At the Avenue Road intersection, he hesitated, looking both left and straight ahead, acting torn. Left would go to the Sinza police station a block away, but continuing straight ahead would reach Soochow Creek in three blocks.

After a moment of pretend deliberation, he crossed Avenue Road, continuing northward up Park, and picking up his pace just enough to give the impression of a purposeful, urgent stride without seeming that he was onto his tail.

As the glow of the streetlight at the corner of Avenue Road faded away, he heard the footsteps behind him clearly for the first time. His pursuer had sped up, less concerned now about being heard and more concerned with catching Doug in the dark before he reached the next intersection one long block away.

Inside his coat pocket, Doug gripped the handle of his Colt .45 service revolver.

Light spilled onto the street as a door opened twenty yards ahead. The footsteps behind Doug fell silent. Pan Yintao stepped out the door on the arm of the lanky bartender from The Pink Lotus. She was wearing a scarlet red cocktail dress and matching gloves, while he was dressed in an open-collared white shirt and dark slacks, no hat. They were laughing as if he'd just told her a joke.

Doug hurried forward to intercept them at the bottom of the building's stoop.

They acted startled to see him. A touch over-the-top on Pan Yintao's part, but Doug hoped it wasn't too obvious.

"They're behind me, but don't look," he muttered. "Now we pretend to have a really intense conversation. No need to say anything sensical, as long as we all keep our voices quiet like this. Now you." He looked at the lanky young man.

"I got a new record today," the bartender said, almost stumbling over the words, his eyes wide from the nerves.

"That's good." Doug nodded encouragement, with the side benefit of appearing to prod the fellow. He looked at Pan Yintao. "Now you say something, anything, but act like you're frightened, and then shake your head at the end."

"The girls at the club say this one has a nice cock, but he never showed it to *me*." Then she aped a frightened look, touching the collar of her cocktail dress. "Can you imagine the nerve? He has a beautiful cock that he shares with the others and *not with me*?" She started shaking her head. "We've worked there for months, and not even a peek!"

"Dial it down a little bit," Doug said, while taking a step even closer than he already was and pointing a finger right at Pan Yintao's throat. "Act frightened, but not like you're about to fake die on stage at the Shinza Theater, ok? Now, shake your head again. Good. Now one more time, and now start looking around like you're afraid to be seen with me. Very good."

"Should I say something again?" the bartender asked, seemingly oblivious to the fact that he just had.

"You're not as afraid of me as she is, but still worried. You're doing fine, but now look at her as if you're concerned about what she's going to do. Maybe say something to her and shake your head, like you're telling her not to do it."

"Don't do it," he said, shaking his head.

Doug closed his eyes briefly. Bless his amateur heart. "No, say something a little longer than that, but shake your head like you just did."

"I can't dance well but I dance by myself in my room when I play my records," he said, and then remembered almost too late to shake his head.

Good enough. Doug leaned closer to Pan Yintao and put his hand on her shoulder. "And now I want you to look like you're thinking it over. Not that much, just listen to me like you're keeping an open mind about what I'm saying. That's good. Now glance at him—good—now back at me. And now look down at my shoes and nod. That's very good. Now nod one more time, still looking at my shoes. Excellent."

He took a step back from them and looked at the bartender. "Now say one more thing to her while shaking your head, and she'll say something angry in response."

"I don't think you're the best performer at the club, just the best dressed one."

Genuine anger flashed across Pan Yintao's face, and she hissed, "You wouldn't know a good performer if she stood on your dick and ground her heel in until it came out the other side."

Doug almost laughed despite the tension. He took Pan Yintao's arm and steered her down the street in the direction from which he'd come.

Where they were certain to pass his hidden pursuer.

If only Doug knew for certain where he was hiding. He stayed on the left of the trio to be a barrier between his pursuer and the other two. He kept his palm around the handle of his service revolver in his pocket, but that arm was the one Pan Yintao was holding onto as she walked between the two of them.

The movement, when it came, was right beside them, mere feet from Doug.

Doug dove forward in the nick of time. The sound of ripping fabric filled his ear, and then he spun to face his attacker, pulling his revolver from his pocket and cocking it.

A knife glinted in the faint light from the streetlamp half a block away. Pan Yintao screamed, a haunting sound somewhere in between a woman's scream and a man's yell. The knife jabbed into the bartender's side. The young man's eyes went wide, and his mouth hung open in shock.

Everything went slow motion. The bartender looking down at his side and seeing a wet red stain spreading, then his knees buckling. Doug bringing his gun arm around toward the attacker, whose face was still hidden under the rim of his hat. The attacker spinning around behind Pan Yintao and bringing his knife to her throat. The sound of running feet.

"Drop your gun or I'll cut her throat!" The southern accent was unmistakable, even before the outline of 'house detective' Russell's face confirmed his identity.

"Police! You're surrounded," Detective Inspector Wallace's voice rang over a bullhorn, echoing between the brick buildings. A bright electric spotlight flashed on, bathing the whole street in blue-white glare.

The bartender moaned and rolled onto his back, both hands clamped against his bleeding side. Jonesy rushed into the light, the gun in his right hand pointed at Russell, but he stopped and knelt beside the fallen bartender, shaking open his handkerchief. He moved the young man's hands and put his handkerchief in their place, pushing down until the fellow cried out. Even with his left hand working the wound, his right gun-hand never wavered from Russell.

"You had better drop that knife, Mr. Russell, before they shoot you," Doug said.

"If they shoot, they might hit the lady instead," Russell said in his southern drawl, giving Pan Yintao's shoulders a shake for emphasis. A terrified gurgle escaped her lips.

Doug shook his head. "The police have Sikh marksmen who won't miss, and their bullets won't hit Miss Pan, either."

"He's speakin' the truth, sir," Detective Inspector Wallace said over the bullhorn in his peculiar accent somewhere between Scottish and working-class English. "You'd best drop the knife in the next three seconds...Two...One..."

"Alright!" Russell said, and dropped the knife, cursing under his breath. The knife clattered on the pavement and bounced away.

Several bearded constables in red turbans rushed forward, surrounding him with batons aloft. Russell raised his hands in the air. Pan Yintao squealed and scurried away, her high heels clacking on the pavement as she ran toward Doug and threw her arms around him.

"My rescuer!" she said breathlessly into his ear. Doug almost laughed. It was very Hollywood.

"We need a medic!" Jonesy shouted. Beside him, the bartender writhed back and forth, moaning softly. Jonesy's left hand stayed clamped in place over his side. "You're gonna be ok, you hear me?" Jonesy said to him, softly.

Doug slipped out of Pan Yintao's embrace and walked up beside Jonesy. He put his hand on his friend's shoulder and left it there until an ambulance arrived.

30

Tuesday, April 26

Doug slammed the phone receiver onto the cradle the fourth time he got no answer at Kenny's office. Where had he been all morning? He knew Doug would need to talk with him, after 'house detective' Russell's arrest.

The thought of where Kenny might be—and with whom—wouldn't quit niggling him. With a huff, he picked up the receiver again, asked for an outside line, and told the operator to connect him with the Foreign YMCA on Bubbling Well Road.

"YMCA," a young American voice answered.

"I'm looking for Scott Farnsworth. Did he check in yesterday?"

After a few seconds of silence, the young man said, "No Farnsworth here, sir."

"Are you sure? He always stays there."

Another couple seconds of silence. "Nope. Just double-checked, and we got no Farnsworth right now."

Doug vacillated between relief and consternation. "What about Kenneth Traywick? Do you have a guest by that name, perchance?"

"No, sir. I'm sorry."

Doug hung up without thanking him and marched to the radio room. Officers on shore leave had to provide the location where they were staying. He'd find Scott; he just hoped he didn't find Kenny with him. "Get me the bridge on the *Valparaiso*."

**

It had been a long time since Doug had driven a car—not since he'd left Washington almost three years ago—and he ground the gears a few times when driving away from the rental lot beside the J.M. & Co. Motorworks in Pudong, before he finally got into a rhythm.

Sitting on the point of land across the Huang Po River from downtown Shanghai, the one-time farming village of Pudong now housed numerous warehouses along the wharfs, as well as the J.M. Motorworks, the Nikka Cotton mill, and several buildings of the British Cigarette Company. But a third of a mile east of the Huang Po, the tin-roofed shacks fell away and the landscape was still dominated by marshy rice fields crisscrossed by drainage ditches. Peasant workers in dark tunics and conical hats stooped in the shallow water.

The Pootung Highway ran down a raised roadbed several feet above the surrounding countryside for fifteen miles, eastward toward a collection of buildings on the coast, along the edge of the wide mouth of the Yangtze River estuary. One of the many British Cigarette Company factories belched smoke from a tall brick smokestack, and to the south of it Doug parked in a gravel lot beside a bowling alley. In front of him the three-story Pootung Hotel and its colonnaded balconies faced onto a sandy beach, wet from the morning tide.

Inside the lobby, a short middle-aged Chinese man greeted him in Pidgin. "Wantchee room, mista?"

Doug shook his head and removed the photograph from inside his jacket. "I'm looking for this man," he said in Shanghainese, setting a silver coin on the desk.

The man eyed him suspiciously. "Are you here to cause trouble?" he asked in Shanghainese.

Doug shook his head, never breaking eye contact. "Just to talk."

The man slipped his hand over the coin and pocketed it. "Upstairs, third door on the left."

Doug thanked him, climbed the stairs, and knocked on the door he'd indicated. Heavy footsteps approached, and the door flew open.

"You're early!" Scott Farnsworth said through a wide grin, which quickly faltered when he saw Doug in the hall. His white shirt was unbuttoned all the way, the shirttails waving in the breeze from the open French doors onto the balcony, and he held a small book in his right hand, one finger holding a spot.

"You were expecting someone else, I presume?" Doug asked.

A flush came to Scott's cheeks. Then a look of uncertainty crossed his face. "Why are you here, Doug?"

Not for the reason your expected guest is coming, I'm sure. "The ship said you were staying here, instead of the Y as usual. Can we talk?"

"Of course." Scott stood aside and let Doug in.

"Before we get to the reason for my visit, I have to know—were you expecting Kenny?"

Scott looked at the floor. The only sound was the door creaking as it closed.

"What about Dolores Moody?" Doug asked, quieter.

"I did what you asked of me, Doug," Scott said quietly, but with a strong note of bitterness piercing Doug's midsection. "I went out with her again last night, ok? I made sure people saw us together. That should quell the rumors for a while. Isn't that what you wanted? What I do behind closed doors is nobody's business."

"Dolores might have something different to say about that." Doug instantly regretted that when he saw the pained look on Scott's face.

"Don't you think I know that? But this is what you asked me to do."

"Not *this*," Doug said, motioning around the room. "Not secret rendezvous with married men."

Scott looked up, glared at him. "How else do you think it's done? Why do you think I came all the way out here? This is as discreet as I can be." He took a step closer, pointing his finger. "You can't have your cake and eat it too, Doug."

Doug's cheeks burned. Scott was right, but he wasn't about to admit that out loud. He changed the subject and nodded toward Scott's hand at his side. "What book are you reading?"

Scott brought it up, surprised. "This? Uh, it's called 'Better Angel.'"

Doug forced a friendly smile. "I haven't heard of that one. What's it about?"

"Uh..." Scott opened the book to where his finger held the place, glancing at the pages there as if searching for a life ring. "It's about this fella named Kurt Gray..." his voice trailed off.

"Go on."

Scott swallowed hard. "In college, he discovers he prefers men to women. Then he falls in love with this fella named Derry, and after a while the two of them fall in love with this other fella named Tony..." his voice trailed off again, and his face and neck turned crimson. "That's as far as I've gotten."

Doug's mouth hung open for a second; then he clamped it shut and looked away. "Where on Earth did you find a book like *that*?" He couldn't believe anyone was allowed to publish such a story.

Scott cleared his throat. "Your wife gave it to me."

*

After Doug recovered from his shock at that revelation, which took a moment, he walked to the French doors and stood on the threshold to the balcony, looking out over the flat, wet sand stretching toward the East China Sea. He didn't know what surprised him more—that Lucy knew of books like *that*, or that she'd gone out of her way to give one to Scott.

He turned back toward the room slowly. "What have you taken from your reading?"

Scott's cheeks were still as red as apples, but at least his neck and forehead had returned to normal color. "That it's normal. That I'm not a freak just because I want..." his voice trailed off, and he looked down.

Doug took a few breaths. "It's not uncommon, wanting what you want," he said, slowly, measuring his words before they left his mouth. "I've learned that. But you have to know you'll have no future in the navy. You've already taken too many risks. Didn't you learn from Nick Bonadio finding out?"

Scott's face snapped up. "We're more careful than ever, the others and me. Someone always stands guard, and we take turns..." He clamped his mouth shut, and his entire face turned as red as a beet again. Then he looked away. "I've said too much again, I'm sorry."

Doug took a deep breath, suppressing his initial reaction. "I'm glad you're taking precautions. But you know that can only do so much. Sooner or later, everyone in the hierarchy is going to wonder about you." *The ones who don't already.*

Scott swallowed hard, and nodded in silence, still looking away.

"Think long and hard about what path you want to choose." Conflicting emotions raged in Doug's gut. His advice was for Scott's own good; but the pain in his friend's eyes broke his heart. It would be a hard road, no matter which fork Scott took.

Footsteps approaching in the hall grabbed his attention, and Doug realized with a start that he hadn't latched the door. He took a step that direction, but then a hand pushed it open, and Kenny burst through with a grin as big as Canada and a bouquet of flowers in his right hand.

"Fresh lotus blossoms for you—" His expression dropped the moment his eyes met Doug's, and his face turned white as a sheet. "Oh." He sounded almost frightened.

"You told me this was over." Doug hated that he sounded like a father scolding an errant teenager. *Better get used to that...*

Kenny looked down, the shame on his face radiating like a cold draft.

"Doug's right," Scott's voice said behind him. "We have to end it."

Doug turned his head in surprise. The sadness in Scott's eyes was matched with a certain resoluteness.

Kenny continued to stare at the floor.

"Let's go for a walk, Kenny." Doug put his hand on his friend's shoulder and guided him toward the door. Kenny set the flowers on the little table and walked out with him.

Doug ignored the suspicious look the proprietor gave them as they crossed the lobby. He waited until they were outside, on the beach, before he spoke.

"It's not good for either of you, Kenny. Scott has to move on for the sake of his future, his career with the navy. That's important to him, you know. He comes from a navy family. He worked hard to get where he is. And you have a beautiful family that you don't want to jeopardize."

"I won't let it jeopardize my family. Abbie doesn't have to know."

"That's not right, and you know it, Kenny."

His eyes turned pleading. "I can be discreet. I've always been discreet. You know what I mean, Doug—I told you before that Abbie and I used to, you know, enjoy ourselves with other couples. We were always very discreet about it, no one ever found out."

"This is different, and you know it. I don't know how you did it before—and I don't want to—but even if you rented a hotel suite with another couple, that would only look like a private party; no one would ever assume that you were... you know." His cheeks heated at the thought. "Renting a hotel room with another man looks entirely different. Did you see the look the proprietor gave us when we walked through the lobby a little while ago?"

Kenny shook his head, looking down at the sand. "I wasn't looking at him." He sighed. "But I know what you mean."

"It's dangerous, for both of you. He could call the police. Or worse." He shook his head to clear the image of the navy seaman and the naked Chinese man being beaten by the marines in that alley the other night.

Kenny sniffed beside him, and Doug glanced over to see tears flowing.

"I'm sorry I lied to you," he whispered.

Kenny's voice was barely audible over the sound of the waves. Doug put his hand on his friend's shoulder. "You know I forgive you, Kenny. But you've lied to your wife, too."

Kenny stopped walking, turned to Doug with wide, frightened eyes. "I can't tell her, Doug. I can't! It would ruin everything. I'll stop it. I promise I will, as long as you don't make me tell her. Clean slate going forward, ok?"

Doug took a deep breath, let it out slowly. "I would never make you tell her. It would break her heart. I guess you promising not to continue it, that's good enough. But you have to swear this is it, no more."

"I swear. Honest, I do."

"I believe you." He stopped walked and faced Kenny. "You go on home now. Don't go back in there, understand? I'll talk to Scott."

"Thank you," Kenny said, almost a whisper. He stood there for a second, then gave Doug an awkward handshake and hurried toward the parking lot.

31

Wednesday, April 27

Doug sat in the back of the courtroom while Kenny presented their evidence to Judge Helmick. The American judge listened soberly—he was the epitome of the expression—and then looked at the prosecutor.

"What say you, Mr. Prosecutor?"

The prosecutor stood, buttoning his jacket. "Wade Russell has not confessed to the murder of James Lockhart, Judge. The evidence presented today by the defense is suggestive at best."

"*Highly* suggestive, I would say," Judge Helmick replied. "More suggestive, I would submit to you, than the evidence you have presented thus far against Mr. Vandermeer. Does the prosecution still believe that it could convince a jury of Mr. Vandermeer's peers beyond a reasonable doubt that he was the one who killed Mr. Lockhart?"

Doug had to smile. The judge was all but telling the prosecutor to drop the charges.

"I'd like to request a ten-minute recess, Judge," the prosecutor said after several seconds of silence.

"We'll take a ten-minute recess," the judge intoned, banging his gavel one time and walking from the room.

Kenny patted Stuart on the back, and then turned toward Doug with a jubilant look. He hurried toward him. "I think we've done it!" he said, beaming.

Doug returned his grin. "I think so, too. How's Stuart feeling?"

"Expectant. And relieved, I think. So am I." His expression changed, and he looked down at Doug's feet. "Listen, Doug, about yesterday—"

Doug held up his hands. "You don't have to say anything more, Kenny. It's all settled."

"No, I do have something else to say before we forget it ever happened."

Doug nodded slowly. "Alright, go ahead and say what you need to."

"I just—I know I apologized yesterday, but I want you to know I meant it. But also...I want to thank you. For caring. For caring enough to confront me when I was being stupid and endangering my marriage. And you did it with compassion, and didn't condemn me or cut me off, for which I'll always be grateful."

Doug's chest constricted. "You're welcome, Kenny. I'm glad to help." He motioned toward the door. "I've got to go. Lucy and Danny are coming home this afternoon."

"Can't you stay a little longer? We'll be back in session in a few minutes, and we'll know for certain if Stuart's free."

"Sure, I'll wait."

Kenny looked down. "I love you, Douggie," he whispered, and his eyes glistened. He cleared his throat. "I don't know what Abbie and I would do without you."

Doug nodded without a word, afraid his voice would crack if he tried. Kenny patted his shoulder awkwardly and hurried back toward the defense table.

**

"Doug, wait!"

Doug turned at the sound of Stuart's voice. He was emerging from the court room doors, and hurried to catch up to Doug in the hall.

"Congratulations!" Doug said when Stuart reached him. The prosecutor had come back from the recess to say he was dropping the charges. Not a surprise, but still a relief.

"Thanks, Doug. I owe you a steak dinner for this."

Doug laughed. "I was glad to be able to help."

"Kenny told me the danger you were in. I—I can't believe you did that for me."

"You're my friend, Stu. I'd do it again if I had to."

Stuart nodded, silent for a few seconds. Then he cleared his throat. "Well, thanks again. I mean it about that steak dinner." He grinned, and hurried back toward the courtroom, presumably to talk with Kenny. Doug watched him for a moment, and then silently prayed he'd never have to solve another murder as long as he lived.

**

Thursday, April 28

"Danny and I are going to take advantage of this beautiful spring day and walk to the Recreation Grounds," Mrs. Kinzler announced, taking the sleepy-eyed little bundle from Doug and cradling him in her right elbow. "You dears take a well-earned rest. We'll be back in half an hour."

Doug had just finished burping the baby—a task that mystified him, no matter how much 'encouragement'—that is, instruction—his mother-in-law had provided. The sound that had come out of his tiny son's mouth had shocked him by its volume, and the acidic waft of spit-up that came out on his blanket over Doug's shoulder made him curl his nose.

He and Lucy had taken Danny for his first walk in the baby carriage yesterday, not long after mother and son had arrived home. Since then, the child had slept, cried, eaten, cried, burped and spit up, and now seemed on the verge of sleep again.

Once her mother had disappeared out the door with her baby, Lucy fell backward onto the couch with a heavy sigh. "Good lord, I don't know how we're going to do it, Doug."

"We'll be great at it in no time," he said with more enthusiasm than he felt, taking her hand in his. "You'll see. We've got Bao to help. And also your mother for the next couple of weeks." He'd added that last part uncertain how much they'd ultimately appreciate the help.

"Let's talk about something else. *Anything* besides babies and what to do with them."

After spending weeks talking about the murder of Jimmy Lockhart, Doug would have found talk about the baby a refreshing change of pace. But he kept that to himself and used the case as a change of subject for his wife.

"I think some good has come out of this whole ordeal with the Jimmy Lockhart murder," he said.

Her face brightened. "Really? Do tell."

"I'm pretty sure Scott is going to ask out Dolores Moody again. I wouldn't be surprised if he asked her to be his steady girl. And we would have never gotten to know her if she hadn't been involved in the case somehow."

A strange look clouded Lucy's blue eyes, and she scrutinized him for several seconds. The intensity of her gaze made him uncomfortable.

"What?"

"Should I presume you encouraged this?"

Doug tensed at the pointedness of her tone. "It solves a problem for both of them. It makes perfect sense."

She cocked her head, but still with that scrutinizing gaze that almost made him squirm. He held perfectly still, to the point of stiffness. "What 'problem' does this solve for her? I know what 'problem' you think Scott has that Dolores will solve for him, so don't even try justifying *that* to me. I want you to tell me how this could possibly benefit her?"

He scowled. "She's told me herself, it's difficult being a single woman of a certain age—*her* words, not mine, don't get in a huff about that—and Scott fixes that problem."

Lucy sat up straight, crossing her arms and frowning. "By shackling her with a man who doesn't really want her? Do you think she needs a *charity* boyfriend, Doug?"

He exhaled hard. "How else do you think it's done?"

"Oh, I know how it's done, Douglas Bainbridge. I just expected you'd be smart enough to know better."

Now he crossed his arms. "What is that supposed to mean?"

"That nothing changes if we don't change, Doug. You can see that, can't you? If Scott just goes along to get along, then nothing changes, and this same problem will keep facing men like him. Over and over and over. And everyone pays the price for that, including women like Dolores Moody."

He frowned. "So, what am I supposed to advise him to do? Ignore the fact that rumors are holding back his career? Forget about ever getting promoted? That's ridiculous, and you know it."

He immediately regretted his tone, seeing the flash of anger cross her eyes. But it disappeared in an instant, and she looked suddenly exhausted. "I understand. Really, I do. You can't ask him to sacrifice his future when that's important to him. The tragic thing is, though—he *is* sacrificing his future in another way. And hers with it."

She was right, but he couldn't see any way around it. "That's just the way things are."

"Because everyone lets that be the way it is."

He sighed and leaned back against the couch. He put a hand on his head and sighed a second time. "I don't understand why I keep getting involved with people like that. With deviant tendencies."

"Preferences, not tendencies."

"Not much different, is it?" he snapped. Then he shook his head. "I'm sorry."

She took his hand. "You know I'm not a very religious person overall, but I *do* believe in God and Jesus and all that. When I was a girl, my grandmother Gustafsson used to say that God places the same obstacles in your path until you learn the way around them or through them." She turned to face him directly, looking deep into his eyes. "Maybe God wants you to learn something, and he keeps sending these men into your life until you do."

Doug frowned. "What could I possibly learn from them?"

She shook her head, a rueful smile gracing her lips.

"What?"

"I love you more than words can say, and yet you are the most obtuse man sometimes, Douglas Bainbridge."

It had been a while since someone had called him 'obtuse,' but it still stung. He had always resented that label. "How on Earth am I being obtuse now?"

"By being exactly what you resent. I hear you complain regularly about how judgmental your parents are, and how miserable that made you. *Still* makes you. And yet, sometimes you can be very judgmental of people you think are 'deviant.' But what you call deviant is perfectly natural to them, do you understand?"

He stared at her hand on his, his mind rushing with all manner of conflicting thoughts.

"So, the next time you get angry about some judgmental thing your parents wrote in their letters, think about how you've reacted to Jonesy, Kenny and Abbie, Scott, and even Pan Yintao." She put a finger on his chin to turn his face toward hers; he resisted for a second, but then relented when she kept the pressure on his chin. "Will you do that for me? For Danny?"

That struck like a thunderclap.

But she was right, of course. She usually was. "I'll do my best."

**

"I'll burp him, you go get some sleep," Doug said that night, reaching for the infant fidgeting in his wife's arms.

She reluctantly handed over the tiny bundle, hanging on until Doug had the boy pressed against his chest. "Let him rest his head on your shoulder," she said, though he knew that already. His mother-in-law had drilled *that* home many times in the last twenty-four hours.

He patted the tiny warm back as he'd been taught. Then he bounced his knees like he'd seen Lucy and her mother do, feeling silly at first. But then something magical happened, and the baby's gurgles drew him into a contented state, where the bouncing seemed the most natural thing in the world.

Lucy was watching him, and he briefly removed his patting hand from Danny's back to quietly shoo her toward the bedroom. Her tired eyes looked grateful, and she disappeared down the hall.

The gurgles faded into silence, and then the rising and falling of Danny's chest against Doug's shoulder was all he felt.

Doug carefully took the now sleeping infant off his shoulder and nestled his head in the crook of his elbow. His eyes remained closed, but a murmur and sigh escaped the boy's mouth, and his tongue worked for a few seconds before he went still again, save for the rising and falling of his little chest.

"I'm going to be different from them," Doug said, thinking of his mother and father. "I'll hug you, and I'll hold your hand, and I'll let you play as loudly as you like. You'll know I love you. And I do love you, Danny. You and your mommy are the most important people in the world, you remember that, OK?"

32

Friday, April 29

Doug found Jonesy lunching at the bar in the Cathay Hotel the next day, as usual.

"Douglas, always a pleasure to see you," Jonesy said with a twinkle in his green eyes, looking over the top of his martini glass as he took a sip. "I heard they dropped the charges against Stuart."

Doug nodded. "You must have talked with Kenny already?"

"Of course. He's my named source. I turned in the story yesterday. Didn't you see it in the morning papers?"

Doug's cheeks heated. "Sorry, I forgot. I'm a little tired, you see."

"Oh yeah, you've got that baby at home now, don't you? Keeping you up at night?"

Doug groaned. "He wakes up crying every two hours. Lucy goes out to feed him, but at least once each night she comes back into the room to make me burp him so she can go back to sleep."

"Seems fair to me."

Doug arched an eyebrow. "That's awfully modern thinking, Jonesy. Especially for a man who was never in that position himself."

"Touché."

"How's your, um, friend? Is he going to recover?"

"He's going to be fine, thank God. Just a flesh wound, the knife didn't hit anything vital. The only trouble is, he doesn't want to see me." He sighed. "I suppose it serves me right. He's mad at me for putting him in danger. And he's right to be mad. I shouldn't have done that to him."

Doug shook his head. "We needed someone escorting Pan Yintao who would be believable in that role, and not connected to me in any known way. He fit that bill. You did the right thing, Jonesy."

"Cold comfort." Jonesy took a bigger swig of his martini.

Doug couldn't help the regret over his role, even though it had absolutely been the right thing to do. "I'm sorry I had to ask you to do that."

"Don't give it another thought," Jonesy said, his jovial smile seeming a bit for show. "We do what we have to do to get by, and that's what we did. And we'd do it again. The kid will be fine. And there are plenty of other fish in the sea."

He bumped Doug's knee with his own. The twinkle of amusement in Jonesy's eye said he was needling him, but Doug wasn't going to let that get to him anymore. He'd promised Lucy. And Danny.

"I wish you all the luck in the world," he said, eliciting a look of wide-eyed surprise from Jonesy. Then his mischievous gleam returned.

"You know I always cast a wide net."

Doug laughed.

Jonesy looked like he didn't know how to take that, and returned his focus to his half-eaten club sandwich.

"I saw your friend Ben at the Rec grounds yesterday," he said, and wiped a crumb from his mouth with the cloth napkin in his lap. "Poor fellow's lovelorn and confused."

Now it was Doug's turn to look surprised. "Don't tell me Pan Yintao actually told him who she—who he really is?"

"She did indeed. She was dressed as Pan Yintao, of course, and Ben was about to pick her up for a date, but she invited him in to talk. He expected she was going to break up with him, but never dreamed what the real truth was."

"How'd he react?" Doug asked. "He didn't hit her, did he?"

"I don't think so. He didn't say one way or the other, but he strikes me as the gentle type at heart. He only said he stormed out."

Doug grunted. "You can hardly blame him for that, can you?"

"No, not one bit. While I understand Liu Fan's motive for keeping Pan Yintao's true identity secret from the men *she* seduces, it's still shady business. Ben was right to be angry. He'd been deceived. And he was also right to be a little repulsed—though he's probably not as repulsed as he lets on." He didn't elaborate.

Doug was certain he'd never said a word to anyone but Lucy about Ben getting blowjobs from Patrick Callahan or Scott Farnsworth. And Lucy wouldn't repeat that. Sometimes it was as though Jonesy could read people's minds.

The thought made him uncomfortable, and he looked away. "He'll find someone more appropriate soon enough. But maybe I should go talk to him, try to cheer him up. I don't suppose he happened to tell you where he's staying?"

"As a matter of fact, he did."

Doug could only shake his head in amazement. "How do you get people to tell you these things?"

"Tricks of the trade. You gotta know how to ask. People want to talk, you just gotta know how to get them started." He popped the last of his sandwich in his mouth. "Anyway," he said between chews. "You wanna talk to him, you can find him staying at the YMCA. The one for foreigners, over on Bubbling Well Road. I think your friend Scott is staying there, too."

"I know it."

Jonesy got up from his barstool, downed the last of his martini, and grabbed his hat off the bar. "A pleasure as always, Douglas. Don't be a stranger." He winked as he turned away.

******

A crowd was gathering in front of the Customs House, a block down the Bund from the building where the navy had its office. Arriving ships rarely had big crowds these days. Not since the battle for Shanghai began last August. But this ship, pulled up to the wharf in front of the

Customs House, was packed with white faces gathered at the rails, inching down the gang walk, and collecting on the shore.

Doug decided to take a stroll down the bund for a while instead of going directly back to the office. He crossed the wide avenue and walked down the riverfront side. The din of conversations reached him when he was still half a block away—some excited, some apprehensive, and all in German.

"What's happening?" Doug asked a mustachioed police constable standing watch with his hands clasped behind his back.

"Jewish emigrés, sir," the man said in a thick Irish brogue. "Viennese, I heard tell."

Fleeing the Nazi takeover of their country two months before. Doug hardly blamed them. They'd been stripped of their citizenship. And stories had been trickling out of Germany for years about the way Nazi brownshirts blatantly abused Jewish people in public. Things could only get worse for them now that Herr Hitler was emboldened by his takeover of his home country.

Still, a ship full of hundreds of permanent arrivals was a far cry from the former days when steamship liners routinely arrived with hundreds of short-term tourists and businessmen. The many hotels could accommodate those easily enough. But where were all these people going to live?

He mused that aloud, rhetorically to himself, but the constable heard him and answered.

"The Japanese military authorities in Hongkou are arranging all that. They're putting 'em up in tenements they've confiscated from the Chinese inhabitants, east of Japantown." He shook his head. "I wouldn't want to be none of these Jews wandering around Hongkou after dark, I'll tell you that, sir. Chinese gangs will be right hostile to 'em."

Doug nodded. There was a Russian community over in Hongkou east of Japantown, mingled amongst the Chinese majority. In fact, the city's synagogue was located in that neighborhood, founded thirty-some years ago by Russian Jews fleeing the Cossacks. And now several hundreds of German-Austrian Jews would be joining them. He could only imagine the overcrowding. And the squalor.

Then it struck him; these emigrés were going to be near Japantown, and near the wharfs where Japanese naval vessels moored. Japanese seamen, marines, and most importantly weapons, would pass by that neighborhood regularly. And these Jewish emigrés—refugees, really—might be more open to working for him than the Chinese he'd approached these last several weeks.

He turned around and headed back to the navy office.

EPILOGUE

Wednesday, July 20, 1938

The intercom on Doug's desk buzzed. "Ensign Farnsworth to see you, Commander."

Doug pressed the button. "Send him in."

"He has a civilian with him, sir. A lady."

That was surprising, to say the least. "I'll be right out."

Dolores Moody stood next to Scott Farnsworth in the waiting area, her left arm through his right. She wore in a navy-blue dress with little white polka dots, a matching hat with veil, and white gloves. Scott wore an off-white linen suit. He held a card in his left hand.

"Hello Scott. Miss Moody," Doug said. "To what do I owe this pleasure?"

"We came to let you know that we're getting married on Friday," Scott said, a little louder than was necessary. No doubt the extra volume was so the staff officers would overhear the news. After a second's awkwardness, he held out the card in his left hand.

Doug beamed at him. "That's wonderful news." He glanced at the card as he took it; it was an invitation to their wedding, Friday at five o'clock in the afternoon, at the American Court for China. *No church wedding.*

"You're one of the first people we've told," Dolores said. "After all, you were the reason we met in the first place."

"At your birthday party," Scott hastened to add. As if he felt the need to subtly clarify that it wasn't because Doug had told him to date women.

"Yes, I remember that night well."

"There'll be a small reception after," Dolores said. "We don't need nothing fancy, neither of us. Just a light supper."

"That sounds lovely." Doug said looked up at Scott. "Are you two planning a honeymoon getaway anywhere?"

A flush came to Scott's cheekbones.

"Just a couple of nights," Dolores said. "At a beach hotel somewhere in Pootung."

Uncomfortable images came to Doug's mind, of Scott with Kenny in that breezy room. He wondered if those same images were what Scott was hoping to conjure up to get through his wedding night…

"I believe I know the place," Doug said, glancing at Scott.

**

Wednesday, August 3, 1938

The Shanghai Times arrived late that morning. Bao usually had it waiting at Doug's place when he sat down to breakfast, but its spot was empty. "Where's the Times?" he asked Bao when he brought out his scrambled eggs and bacon.

"Not here yet," Bao said with a shrug.

There was a single knock on the door a half-hour later, when Doug was about to leave for work, dressed in his white Navy uniform. He opened the door to find the Times sitting there. The teenaged Chinese delivery boy was starting down the stairs, but Doug stopped him. "Why is this newspaper late today?" he asked in Shanghainese, a touch sternly.

The delivery boy looked unperturbed. "They stopped the presses. Had to reprint with a new front-page story." Then he sprinted down the stairs.

Doug unfolded the paper. The headline blared in big, bold type:

NIGHTCLUB OWNER KILLED IN CLUB
AL ISRAEL, OWNER OF DEL MONTE, FOUND SHOT IN OFFICE

Doug went back inside and sat in his armchair. He called to Lucy, "Come see this."

"What is it?" she asked, and he pointed at the headline. They read it together, silently, she reading over his shoulder.

Al Israel had been found at five AM in his office, slumped over his desk in his Chinese dressing gown. The office was ransacked, and police reported signs of a struggle. The lockbox was open and empty, so robbery was the probable motive.

But one detail buried midway down the article caught Doug's attention, belying the robbery angle. Al Israel had been shot in the back of the head. Not in the front, as if he'd been shot during his struggle with a robber. No, he'd been killed execution-style.

They'd come to eliminate him. They'd only made it look like a robbery.

Doug immediately thought of Jack Riley and his slot machines.

******

Monday, August 22, 1938

The steamship's horn bellowed over the sultry afternoon. The pavement of the Bund was still wet from this morning's monsoon downpour, and whisps of steam rose from the blacktop, which was now bathed in midday sunlight. Haze blanketed the Huang Po River, leaving the warehouses of Pudong blurry in the humid air.

"We're going to miss all of you," Betty said, eyes glistening. "Each and every one of you." And then she started crying for real. Abbie embraced her, and Betty held her tightly.

"We'll write, of course," George said, clasping Pete's hand. "We've gotten a lot of practice, writing letters to family these last many years in Shanghai. Same practice, just changing the addressees."

"I have to tell you, buddy, I'm a little bit envious," Pete said, and then brought George into a manly hug—the kind where only chests touch and arms slap each other's backs two or three times before releasing. "If the financial sector ever gets back to normal, we'll be following you. But after all these years of Depression, who knows when the hell that might be?"

"Doug, it's been a pleasure," George said, taking Doug's outstretched hand and gripping it tightly. He clapped his other hand on Doug's shoulder.

"We'll miss you, buddy," Doug said. "That hospital is lucky to get you."

"Back home again in Indiana," George said with a sardonic grin. "It's a three-hour train ride to see family, so at least our parents won't pop in every day. But it's close enough they'll get to be part of Tommy's life." He and Betty were from Fort Wayne, and in three weeks' time he would begin a new position at The Methodist Hospital in Indianapolis.

"Good luck!" Doug said with a laugh. George chuckled and shook his head in doubt. He moved on to Kenny.

Lucy was hugging Betty now. All of the women were crying, but Betty was almost sobbing. Even Julia dabbed at her eye with her handkerchief.

"it's the right time to go," Betty said resolutely, reassuring herself as much as anyone else. "We've been thinking about it ever since Tommy was born; you know, being around family again. We want to have more kids, and we want them to know their grandparents. And with the rise in crime lately..." her voice trailed off, and she resumed crying in earnest.

"We'd been talking about it for a while," George said to the men almost under his breath. "I got the offer from Methodist a couple of months ago, but I kept putting them off. It wasn't until Al Israel got shot in his own office at the Del Monte that I realized we couldn't raise Tommy here, not with the way Shanghai is spiraling downward. Where will it stop?"

"That's why they call these 'Evacuation ships' nowadays," Kenny said.

It was true. Shanghailanders had started leaving in droves that summer, and steamships now carried away more Americans and other foreigners than arrived—with the conspicuous exception of German Jews, who continued to arrive by the thousands. But that was another kind of evacuation, Doug mused. And of course, the Russians and Japanese in Shanghai weren't going anywhere.

The ship's horn gave another long blast. "Time to get going," George said. Betty took Tommy from their *amah* and kissed everyone's cheeks again. George gave each of them another quick handshake, and then took Betty's arm and guided her toward the gang walk. She looked back and waved, but George kept his gaze forward.

They all stayed to watch the ship pull away from the wharf, passengers at the rails waving handkerchiefs, and then steam downriver toward the Yangtze and the sea. It disappeared around the bend in front of the Japanese heavy cruiser Izumo parked in front of Japantown.

The eight remaining friends—Doug and Lucy, Kenny and Abbie, Pete and Julia, Fred, and Stuart—turned back toward the Shanghai skyline in silence.

END

Thank you for reading The Pink Lotus. If you enjoyed this book, please tell a friend, update your social media, and/or write a review on Amazon, Goodreads, or other forum.

Questions or comments? Feel free to contact me at www.garretthutson.com.
Want to know when my next book comes out? Go to my website and sign up for my newsletter.

Also by Garrett Hutson:

In A Safe Town

The Jade Dragon

Assassin's Hood

No Accidental Death

Hidden Among Us

Spy Tango

The Swiss Conspiracy

Gray Paree

Each Hidden Passage

About the Author

Garrett Hutson writes upmarket historical mysteries and spy fiction. He lives in Indianapolis with his husband, their three adorable dogs, and one odd-ball cat. He has one grown daughter. You may contact him at his website, www.garretthutson.com.

Afterword

This is a work of fiction, and the characters and events portrayed are fictitious, although I have alluded to some real historical events and persons.

When I have alluded to historical figures in the story, most are **not** portrayed as characters, and are, to the best of my ability, discussed by the characters in their correct historical context. Examples include President Franklin Roosevelt, Chiang Kai-shek, Du Yuesheng, "Lucky Jack" Riley, Joe Farren, and General Matsui of the Japanese occupation force. On occasion it has been necessary to have a real historical person appear (*briefly*) in the story; these include Al Israel (owner of the Del Monte), Admiral Harry E. Yarnell, and Judge Milton J. Helmick of the United States Court for China.

The USS Valparaiso in this story is fictional. While there was a USS Valparaiso in the United States Navy in the 1850s and 1860s, that name has not since been reused by the navy. The U.S. Navy has a penchant for reusing ship names multiple times, so I feel comfortable using that name here in a fictional context. I have endeavored to portray an Omaha-class cruiser as authentically as possible for that time period, including ship layout, number and size of guns, crew size, and number of officers.

The incidents and interactions onboard the USS Valparaiso are all fictional, inventions of my imagination. However, I believe them to be realistic based upon the later first-hand accounts of countless seamen during World War 2.

The other ships mentioned by name for the Asiatic Fleet were real ships, and I have made every attempt to describe them accurately.

The Sikorsky prototype helicopter was real, and I have taken only minimal liberties with its development timeline. The first recorded flight was in 1939, but I'm certain there were top-secret test flights before then. It seems reasonable to me that an early demonstration may have been given to fleet Intelligence Officers, and so I feel comfortable depicting such a demonstration in the opening chapter.

As always, I have done my best to be as historically accurate as possible, except where noted above. Any errors are mine alone.

Acknowledgments

This book required the input of many people who contributed to its development in ways big and small. First, many thanks to my awesome partners in the IndyScribes critique group—Laura VanArendonk Baugh, Stephanie Cain, Stephanie Ferguson, Peggy Larkin, Jim Meeks-Johnson, Jim Thompson, and Chelsea Sanders—who patiently read and critiqued many sections of the first and second drafts, and provided excellent feedback. You all really are the best!

My deepest thanks to Patti Horwood, Jan Cain, Roxx Tarantini, and Jennifer Maher, who took the time to read the entire manuscript and provide valuable insights and feedback. Your insights were amazing, and you helped bring out the best in this story. It is definitely better for your comments.

Thanks to Steven Novak for another amazing cover that really captures the essence of the story.

Thank you always to my long-time close friends, who have taught me the meaning of "found family" for twenty-plus years. You know who you are. I've said it before, but the notion of "found family" is so important in my life and my writing, and I hope I've done justice to it in this story of Doug Bainbridge and his friends.

And lastly, most importantly of all, my constant gratitude and devotion to my husband David Lee, for ceaselessly letting me live the crazy, frustrating, exhilarating, depressing, yet wonderful life of a fiction writer without complaint, and for always being supportive through its myriad ups and downs. I love you always and forever, far more than you can ever know.

-Garrett B. Hutson, January 2023

9 781953 846037